Advance Praise for *Fractured Justice*

"This authentic, intelligent and gripping novel of courtroom suspense dares to profoundly examine the elusiveness of truth—legally, psychologically, morally—in order to explore the meaning of justice for terrifying crimes. The reader is kept off-balance to the last pages and ruminating far beyond that."
—Joseph Wambaugh, bestselling author of *The New Centurions*, *The Blue Knight*, the *Hollywood Station* series, and numerous other crime novels

Praise for James A. Ardaiz's Previous Book *Hands Through Stone*

"*Hands Through Stone* tells a frightening story with all the tension and color of a first-class mystery novel . . . a revealing insider's view of the [Clarence Ray Allen] investigation."
—Denise Noe, CrimeMagazine.com

"Ardaiz's writing about police work is in depth . . . The final chapter was thought provoking and put a different perspective on the death penalty for me . . . had me thinking about the book long after I had finished it."
—TrueCrimeReader.com

"Goes inside the room at Fran's Market and gives not only the events on the infamous night but the feelings of the horror of the seasoned investigators. A must read for readers and writers of mystery books. Highly recommended!"
—Terell Byrd, *The Poison Pen*

"A fascinating and engrossing book. Ardaiz handles the story sensitively and with a gentleness one doesn't expect from a hard-nosed prosecutor. I highly recommend reading it."
—Diana Bulls, *Kings River Life*

Fractured Justice

A Matt Jamison Novel

James A. Ardaiz

Pace Press
Fresno, California

Fractured Justice

Cover image: Shutterstock

Published by Pace Press,
an imprint of Linden Publishing
2006 South Mary Street, Fresno, California 93721
(559) 233-6633 / (800) 345-4447
PacePress.com

ISBN 978-1-61035-298-7

135798642

Printed in the United States of America
on acid-free paper.

Library of Congress Cataloging-in-Publication Data on file.

This book is dedicated to the law enforcement officers and prosecutors who spend their days and nights protecting us. And, as always, to my wife Pam, who has been supportive of my endeavors since the day she agreed to go out with me. To my friends who gave their time reading the manuscript and offering their thoughts: Lisa, Betty, Nancy, Patty, and Barbara most of all. Thank you. And to my friend Bud, who has always been there to support me and will now be there in spirit. I will miss you my friend.

Prologue

November, 2005
Tenaya County, California

The great Central Valley of California depresses the broad plain of the Golden State. Walled on the west by the mountains of the Coast Range that drop down into the Pacific and on the east by the ripping upward thrust of the granite blocks of the Sierras, for thousands of years the hills of the great Valley swayed with tall grass that once stretched like a rustling ocean as far as the eye could see. But now the once limitless grassy expanse only hugs the Valley rim.

Today State Highway 99 bisects the Valley, and along the concrete ribbon cities cluster, each drawing its measure large or small from the passing parade of cars and trucks making their way through the searing heat of summer and the cold damp of winter. At night the city lights that blur the dark sky of the Valley quickly give way to country road blackness, illuminated only by the stars or the moon. The nights of the valley seldom conceal predators the way the side streets of the great cities that shroud them in darkness do. It is expected to be a quiet place, and most of the time it is, so that when violence breaks the quiet, it is explosive and shocks the senses.

The man whispered quietly, his words soundless to the object of his attention. He paused briefly to ensure there was no one watching, then struggled slightly with the weight of the bundle he carried across the road next to the canal bank. The cold November moonlight caught the shimmering water of the canal, one of many that still crisscrossed the community. The coursing streams of water were open arteries drawing through them the lifeblood of a city making its inexorable transition from rural farm town to metropolitan mass.

A thin mist rose off the water's surface, the liquid black and shiny against the canal bank, flickering like the scales of a snake. He had chosen this location precisely because of its isolation, a vestige of the past as yet not encroached by the city's relentless need to remake itself.

The only sounds were those of a city sleeping in the embrace of night, waiting for dawn. The movement of the zipper broke the silence as he opened the heavy plastic bag and gently slipped it down around the body of a motionless young woman. There was nothing to disturb the two of them, only the softly lapping water enhancing the moment. He felt a flicker of tenderness that caused him to caress her hair as he laid her down on the bank and knelt beside her. The moonlight framed her face. She was very nearly perfect to his eye, an alabaster statue for only him to admire, created at his hands. Soon he would have to share her but not now. For these few moments she still belonged to him alone.

He gently drew back strands of hair from her face and looked into her eyes. He knew it wasn't so, but he could feel her looking back at him, only at him. It was almost enough—to be all that a woman would ever have and to feel her final submission to him.

He slipped his hand inside her blouse, sliding the edges open, drawing his gloved fingertips slowly down the cleft between her breasts. He placed his face close to hers, cradling her neck, her lips parting slightly at the movement. Suddenly he drew back; he would not allow himself to succumb to this temptation. He reached into his pocket, his fingers gripping tightly around the shaft that concealed a razor-edged blade. He felt the metallic hardness through his thin latex gloves as he pulled it out, the steel catching the glint of moonlight on the blade as he flicked it open. He drew his arm back. With one last stroke his creation would be complete. He let his anger build, drawn from deep within the dark place that was his alone, and then focused all of it in one violent downward slash.

Part One

Chapter 1

Matt Jamison hadn't been able to get to bed until well after midnight. Yet even in sleep his churning brain held him in restlessness from weeks of frustration and days filled with one adrenaline surge after another, leads cresting and then sinking into an abyss of tangled conjecture and dead ends. With the discovery of a second sexually tinged murder, the siege of violence was creating dread in the community. As a prosecutor specializing in violent crimes, sexual assault, and murder, he knew he had a predator on the loose who had the stealth and cunning of a jungle cat, walking the streets without arousing terror until he struck.

The sound of the phone shattered the early morning silence, pulling Jamison from the rest he so desperately needed. His eyes still closed, Jamison's hand reached automatically toward the nightstand by the bed, his mind lifting its thinning veil of morning grogginess.

"Yeah." He didn't bother to say hello. He saved hello for the daytime and the early evening when it might be a friend or a woman or both. Lately he hadn't had time for friends and regrettably there were no women who would call him at this hour.

It was the rumbling voice of his investigator, Bill O'Hara, uttering the word "Boss." He knew who it was from the first word. Only O'Hara called him "Boss."

Jamison held the phone, waiting for O'Hara to continue. There was no point interrupting the silence with a demand for information. O'Hara would speak when he was ready to speak.

"I just got off the phone with the sheriff's dispatcher. Detectives have asked for us to roll. We have another girl—maybe connected to the two other cases."

Jamison stopped him right there. "What does that mean, 'maybe connected?'" He had no patience for ambiguity. All he could think of was that now they had a third woman probably dead, and so far nothing solid or even circumstantial to a build a case on any suspect.

Jamison sat up in bed and reached for the light switch. No point in trying to keep the light from waking him. He was awake, his mind beginning to race.

O'Hara's voice took on the deferential tone that for him passed as respect. "Well, Boss, all I know is the on-scene detective said to tell us it looks like another one. Maybe it's connected, maybe not. You want me to go or you want to send Ernie?" Jamison's other investigator was Ernie Garcia. He had been working the murder case of the second young woman.

"No, don't wake Ernie. Pick me up in fifteen. I'll be outside waiting." Jamison hung up the phone without saying good-bye. O'Hara wouldn't hear the good-bye anyway. He didn't consider good-byes important and if Jamison had stayed on the line all he would have heard was a dial tone.

As Jamison rolled out of bed and began dressing, he recalled his first day as a prosecutor when the district attorney, William Gage, sent him down the hall to meet the investigator. He had knocked on W. J. O'Hara's door expecting to see some florid-complexioned stereotype of an Irish cop. What he saw was a chocolate-skinned black man staring back at him with an irritated expression. Jamison had stood there for an instant too long before speaking. "You're O'Hara?"

Anticipating Jamison's question from his expression, all O'Hara said was, "What, don't I look Irish? Who the hell are you and what the hell do you want?"

That was his introduction to Willie Jefferson O'Hara. Known as Bill to most people and Willie to a select few, O'Hara had fifteen years of detective experience with ten in the sheriff's crimes against persons and homicide units before, as he put it, he decided to ease things up and work for the DA. He explained that this was the only way he could keep "stick-up-their-ass suits" from screwing up his cases.

After Jamison had introduced himself, the investigator's eyes narrowed slightly before he nodded his head. "You're the new deputy DA?" The tone of O'Hara's voice sounded like he was talking about something left on his lawn by a dog in the neighborhood; then he told him to shut the door on the way out.

After that, O'Hara would hold his hand out when Jamison had an investigation request and let him watch carefully while he slowly lifted the pile in his inbox and put the young prosecutor's request at the bottom. Slowly though the two men built a relationship as Jamison's cases got bigger.

Finally over a year later, the day arrived when O'Hara took Jamison's investigation request, looked him in the eye for a moment, and then placed it on the top of the pile. O'Hara never said a word.

Jamison had grown used to O'Hara's personality. When he was put in charge of the violent crimes unit, he requested O'Hara as his investigator. That was the day O'Hara started calling him "Boss." For most people, when O'Hara called you "Boss" it slid off his tongue like the last vestige of a deep cough. The first time he said it in their new relationship he smiled, or at least what seemed to pass for a smile with him. Jamison couldn't remember what O'Hara called him before that because he didn't recall O'Hara actually ever using his given name.

After hanging up the phone with Jamison, O'Hara sat on the edge of his bed and stretched his full six-foot frame, feeling every one of the aches he had so carefully acquired day by day over the years. He looked down at the growing bulge of his once flat stomach. Now it only flattened out when he stood and even that last defiance of age was disappearing.

He stood up and put on his pants, which he had draped over a chair the night before to preserve some semblance of a crease, then slipped on the shoes by the side of the bed. He reached into the nightstand drawer and removed a leather holster with lamb wool on one side and strapped it around his right ankle. Then he reached for the Walther PPK sitting on the nightstand and slid the Walther into it, adjusting the ankle holster until it fit comfortably.

He moved his ankle around to check the balance of the Walther on his right leg; it took a minute to adjust to the extra weight. O'Hara always carried a backup gun when he went into the field. As he explained, "That's what cops do who want to come home at night."

He opened the briefcase by the side of his bed, looking inside to see the dull blue-black nine-millimeter automatic that was his authorized duty weapon. He slid the heavy automatic back into its belt clip on his right hip. He checked the briefcase for cuffs and extra ammo clips, then flicked it closed, grabbed a jacket, and headed for the door.

When he was working on a case his social life ground to a halt; relationships were an obligation he didn't make time for. His second wife had found that out and said good-bye long ago. His first wife walked out with their daughter for much the same reason. The more time passed, the more he regretted the empty space in his life. It seemed to him that the passage of time should do just the opposite, but he realized that while time dimmed some regrets there were others it burnished to a hard edge. The investigator now accepted that if his future held a long-term relationship, it would probably be with his work partner rather than with a woman. Not that he didn't like women. In fact, he loved women. Women would say the same thing about him except that they would also say he loved his job a lot more and that he had a tendency to love too many women at the same time, a fact that O'Hara had not yet seen as a character flaw, but rather as he put it, "Something like a vine reaching out for new ground; it's just part of its nature."

Still, while it didn't appear that many women were amenable to his hours or his flexibility when it came to emotional attachment, he often pointed out, "It only took one—or two—or . . ." then he would laugh. He believed that eventually he would find someone and that would be it. But for now, the right one, wherever she was, would have to wait.

Chapter 2

Watching the bank of the canal safely from the veil of darkness, the man reached into his pocket and felt the smooth handle of the knife that within the last hours had once again found its purpose. Touching it made it feel alive, made him feel alive because of what he could do with it and what he had just done with it. Now he had watched the first officer arrive at the edge of the canal, just as he had watched the punctual early morning jogger who stumbled on the dirt path when the man's eyes caught the pale figure lying bathed in the moonlight exactly as he had displayed her. She was, after all, his creation, and while he craved admiration for his handiwork, of necessity he had to accept it from a distance. The reaction of the first person who stumbled across his creation was his substitute for open adulation.

He had waited patiently for the investigators to arrive and for his stage to be lit by the fluorescent footlights of criminal investigation. He enjoyed watching, just as an artist or a filmmaker enjoys the reaction of people admiring their artistic accomplishment. Then he would slip away knowing that tomorrow he would read his reviews carried on the terse explanations of detectives and reporters breathlessly describing his triumph.

The investigation lights blazed with the sound of field generators rumbling in the background. He smiled once more. His stage was illuminated. Like a night predator watching other animals approach his kill, he lingered for a final few moments before slipping noiselessly away into the night. There was nothing left to see. Already he knew the play by heart and this was not the last line.

~

At the same moment across town, Jamison waited at the curb for O'Hara. He pulled his leather jacket tighter around him, trying to warm himself in the chill air, and began to pace. Six feet and almost an inch, he had carefully combed dark brown hair and deep-set greenish-blue eyes that at moments like this darted edgily around. Patience was not one of his virtues.

He looked over at the briefcase sitting at the curb nearby, mentally inventorying its contents: two legal tablets, several pens, a candy bar, and a month-old package of beef jerky for "just in case." It also held a nine-millimeter automatic nested in a leather belt holster, also for "just in case." Jamison didn't like to carry a gun but it was there. Other than the firing range he had only pulled it out once before. He remembered the way he had forced his hand to remain steady, the surging adrenaline pulsing through his entire body. Carrying a gun or going into dark places with arrest teams didn't fit in with what they taught him in law school about being a lawyer, and it still didn't.

O'Hara pulled up in his Ford, which was supposed to be an undercover car, but even kids recognized it as a cop car because of its glaring blue paint. Except on official business, O'Hara would not set foot in this car. He preferred his maroon Cadillac, which he drove with considerably more respect than he drove his assigned county vehicle.

Jamison threw his briefcase in the back and settled against the seat, welcoming the warmth of the heater.

O'Hara reached toward the ashtray where a slightly smoked cigar sat tilted against the rim. Jamison knew it was a habit O'Hara had picked up working homicide scenes, especially where the bodies had been in the sun for a while. He preferred the cigar smell to the various odors he had worked around over the years.

Jamison turned up his nose. "Bill, you aren't going to smoke that damn thing, are you?"

In a small gesture of grudging accommodation O'Hara rolled his window down part-way and blew out a stream of fetid smoke. He made sure to let a little of it drift toward the passenger side before he spoke. "Okay, the watch commander at the sheriff's department called to say that Puccinelli, the night detective, wanted us out in the field as soon as possible. They got a young woman at the edge of a canal. He didn't have much detail, but enough to say that it looked like the same MO as the others, Ventana and Johnson." The mention of Maria Ventana and Mary Ann Johnson immediately replayed those crime scenes in Jamison's mind. Even now he could close his eyes and see every detail. He hoped what was ahead of them wasn't going to be as grisly as the others.

His investigator drove well over the speed limit, probably pushing sixty down the empty city streets. Jamison had learned right away that cops didn't pay much attention to speed limits except when it suited them. When he first started riding with O'Hara, Jamison would feel his feet involuntarily reaching for a nonexistent brake pedal. Now he hardly looked up.

O'Hara turned onto the service road that bordered an irrigation canal. The early morning sky was just beginning to lighten, showing slight streaks of rose in the distance, the moon a silver disk against a still dark sky. O'Hara drove toward the bright-as-daylight outdoor beams used to illuminate nighttime crime scenes. The sound of the generator sitting in the back of the sheriff's department crime scene truck resonated in the morning quiet.

The water ran slow and dark through the canal, just a shallow stream in the winter months, becoming a swiftly flowing current in the spring and summer. A heavy fog hung low over the area, rising up from the dirt roadway along the side of the canal. Yellow tape cordoned the perimeter. The light brown earth glowed white under the glare of the big crime scene lights, a spill of illumination along the darkened roadway. In the center of the light was a body spotlighted in death like a single actor on a darkened stage.

Jamison and O'Hara stood a short distance outside the yellow plastic tape that kept people away while drawing the attention of everyone within sight. Even from fifty feet, Jamison could tell the victim was a young woman and immediately knew that whoever did this to her would leave a scar on even the most jaded homicide investigator's memory, a distinctive calling card of obscenity.

Everything about this girl's body seemed to Jamison to raise the specter of a sex murder, a half-naked woman stripped of her dignity and modesty, her terror still frozen on her face. The young woman's bared breasts were exposed to the lights focused on her by strangers, the dark patch of hair between her legs in sharp contrast with the whiteness of her thighs. Jamison's reaction to what he saw had not changed over time. Since the first time he had been to a murder scene he was struck by the lack of dignity in violent death. The personal privacy of victims set aside, and all their secret parts a matter of clinical evaluation, becoming evidence to be examined.

The two men walked up to the edge of the yellow crime scene tape draped around the perimeter, carefully looking over the area, watching the on-scene investigators search for anything that struck them as unusual. An experienced investigator would almost immediately seize on something that didn't look right and begin to look for whatever else may not fit.

Jamison had learned long ago that while time was of the essence in a murder investigation, the body was the one thing that would wait. For the deceased, time was no longer an issue. Homicide investigators would stand and look at a murder scene, taking it all in like the tableau of a monumental painting splashed with the reds and browns of violence. In time, the individuality of most murders began to blur, lost in the numbing repetitiveness of violent acts, looking so much the same that investigators no longer really saw the faces of the victims. But not this time; not this one.

Something stood out immediately to Jamison. The body lay near the edge of the canal but he knew it hadn't been simply thrown down like discarded trash. It almost took his breath away to see her lying there, her bright red top vivid against the bluish-white color of the skin. Her breasts were exposed but the top was pulled to the sides, as if she herself pulled the shirt apart, draping it suggestively. Her unclothed legs spread neatly apart instead of at the grotesque angles that bodies fold themselves into when they are simply thrown down. She had been carefully laid down by her killer. It had been his only gentle act. That her murderer had taken the time to do so was the first thing that struck Jamison.

He could tell from O'Hara's expression that he was thinking the same thing. They had both been to many crime scenes. So many that it wasn't blood or trauma that transfixed them now as they walked toward what was someone's child, sister, friend. The killer had ripped the victim open from the chest to the pubic area, allowing her insides to spill out, the pinkish strands of intestine protruding above her belly, no longer restrained.

The cold ground bore very little stain; there was not enough blood soaked into it for what had been done to defile her. No sign of a struggle. What blood there was had simply spilled from the gaping open wound as the body rocked with the violence of the deep slashing motion. It hadn't been pumped out by a still beating heart. And the small puddle was only beginning to tinge dark brown from the edges. The blood hadn't been there long enough to turn the brownish-black color that would have indicated the body had been there for hours.

They reached the same conclusion simultaneously. This girl was probably dead when her killer had carefully placed her where she was found. Then he opened her up in one ripping motion, taking away her last vestige of dignity in a deliberate act of desecration. No violent struggle took place where they stood. The eviscerating slice was clean.

Other than the runner who had seen her lying there in the shallow light of early morning darkness, nobody else had approached her. In some respects the fact that she was obviously dead was a relief, not because of the gaping slash wound, but because if emergency technicians had been called to the scene, they would be focused on saving a victim, not on preserving evidence.

Jamison and O'Hara waited until photographers and other crime scene technicians carefully examined and photographed the area for footprints and tire tracks. For some vague, uneasy reason, Jamison didn't think they would find footprints worth anything. This scene was too well constructed by whoever created it. This murderer wasn't likely to have left evidence behind. He was too meticulous. If there was anything to be found, chances were it was going to be because he wanted it to be found.

O'Hara took his eyes off the body and turned toward Jamison. His rumbling voice was low and discreet. "She wasn't killed here. She would have struggled if she could. And"—O'Hara's eyes met Jamison's—"she just wasn't dumped either, Boss. The whole thing doesn't look right."

Moving as close as he could without stepping into the immediate crime scene or in the circle of glaring lights, Jamison said, "This guy wants us to see."

Without taking his eyes off the body, O'Hara responded, "Wants us to see what?"

"He wants us to see what he can do." O'Hara's right eyebrow lifted up slightly while he rubbed his upper lip, unconsciously smoothing his mustache, seeming to think about what Jamison's comment would mean if it was true.

O'Hara felt a pulse of anger at being taunted by a predator. He caught the attention of Art Puccinelli, the senior sheriff's homicide detective sent to the crime scene. He had known "Pooch" since he was a rookie cop and O'Hara a senior homicide investigator. Now that Pooch was in homicide and O'Hara had moved to the DA's major crimes unit, their paths continued to cross often.

"Pooch, are the forensic boys finished?"

The detective turned and gave a slightly crooked smile of greeting. “I think they’re done. This ground’s like concrete. We’re not going to find any footprints.” O’Hara nodded his understanding. Tenaya County was in the middle of an alluvial valley and was spotted with patches of clay-like dirt that had pressed and baked itself into adobe hardness. People walking over it left no more of a track than anyone would leave stepping on a sidewalk.

Pooch waited until the technician gave him a nod, the signal that he was done and confirmation that there were no tracks.

O’Hara took out a notepad, waved his hand toward Puccinelli, and moved just inside the yellow crime scene tape perimeter. He had one more question before they all became involved in the minutia of the next few hours. “Pooch, do we have any idea who she is?”

“No ID yet by the family but I’m sure.” Pooch didn’t turn his head before answering. “The first officer responding called in a general description. She fits the description and photograph of a young woman whose mother reported her missing a little over a day ago, but right now that’s just a maybe until we have a positive from the family.”

O’Hara was quietly persistent. “Her name?”

“Terry—” Puccinelli flipped through his notes. “Symes. Twenty-four years old. We don’t have much. Just that her mother reported her missing from her apartment. The incident report said there were no signs of a struggle. No signs of forced entry. So we don’t know if whoever did this came into her apartment or grabbed her someplace else or,” he added with a frown, pushing his notebook into his jacket pocket, “why she would be at this location.” Puccinelli shrugged. It was going to be a long morning.

O’Hara scribbled the name in his notebook. He knew the routine. First they would ID the victim and then try to find out who she was last seen with or who might have had a motive to hurt her. Cases like this were extremely difficult even under the best of circumstances if the killer was a stranger.

Now all they had was a dead girl and somewhere out there were grief-stricken parents to whom they could only make hollow assurances.

With a growing fear that this crime was related to the other murders they had been investigating, O’Hara doubted that they would find much useful evidence with this one either. He carefully followed a route to the body through small flags stuck in the ground that indicated some kind of impression in the rock-hard dirt.

Jamison watched from outside the perimeter tape, waiting until O'Hara called him in. He rubbed his face, feeling the growing stubble. His eyes burned from lack of sleep and stress as a thought reverberated in his head. *A third murder and we haven't got a damn thing.* The same thought had been keeping him up each night for the last month as he tried to wrap his brain around the other two murders. With the Maria Ventana homicide and the Mary Ann Johnson murder there were stark similarities that nobody outside of the investigative circle knew. In the drug screen of blood from Ventana and Johnson the lab had found toxic levels of heroin and barbiturates that the pathologists said were the cause of death, almost instantaneously stopping their hearts. Each woman had been missing for approximately twenty-four hours and had been dead for approximately five or six hours before they were found. The mutilating wounds were simply gratuitous desecrations of the bodies after the women were already dead.

But Ventana and Johnson weren't junkies—at least there was nothing to indicate they were. Jamison had learned a long time ago that junkies might share needles but they didn't share their drugs and they wouldn't waste them to kill somebody else. This guy moved in a circle where junk was accessible; that was something but so far it only meant that this guy swam in the same muck with a lot of other bottom-feeders.

As he waited to learn if the other similarities were present with this third young woman, Jamison looked over at O'Hara while thinking, "Why do these damn things always happen in the middle of the night?"

Snapping on a pair of latex gloves, O'Hara stepped in from the side and knelt near the slowly darkening puddle staining the dirt. She was lying flat on her back, unclothed except for the red blouse. Pooch had already called to have a liver temperature taken to ascertain an approximate time of death.

He searched for any small thing in the area around the body that might give them a lead. The sightless blue eyes of the young woman stared up at him, drained of life like the dead leaves of autumn, a sight that always unnerved him. O'Hara resisted the urge to close her eyes. As much as possible the body would be left in the condition it was found for the final examination by the pathologist at the autopsy.

O'Hara carefully moved her arm. No full rigor yet. It was fortunate that they had found her fairly quickly. After thirty-six hours other things start to happen as the body begins its inexorable return to nature; things morticians can't easily repair. Nothing like that had shown up yet.

He gently moved her head. The resistance was noticeable. Usually rigor mortis first began with the eyelids, neck, and jaw within two to six hours of death. O'Hara moved his hand down to the reddish-purple coloration around her buttocks and pushed gently against the skin. A whitish color appeared where the pressure had forced back the pooled blood in the tissue. Slowly the blanched area caused by the pressure began to resume the color of the surrounding tissue. He knew that after four or five hours the lividity from pooling blood would have set and the skin wouldn't have blanched when he pressed. He concluded chances were she had been dead somewhere between three and four hours, certainly no more than six.

He studied every inch of the girl's body, memorizing each feature and contour. His own daughter was only slightly younger. He had allowed her, like her mother, to slip out of his life. Another regret that her face was only a memory for him, lost to the passage of his own neglectful years after the divorce and his ex-wife's bitterness. But he couldn't help thinking of her when he looked down at the young woman stretched out in the dirt. O'Hara talked to the still body in a low voice, "Sweetheart, I'll do my best for you. Whoever did this to you, I'll get him."

It was a promise he had made too many times before to too many victims, but he had almost always been able to keep it. And for those whom he hadn't, the cold cases and unanswered questions rebuked him in his quiet moments, never seeming to fade away. The job and the memories aged him, just as they aged everyone who did what he did.

She had a small slicing wound near her throat from the flick of a knife. O'Hara was certain that the wound was the result of the killer's attempt to control a struggling victim, to terrify her into submission. The eviscerating wound as well as his own instinct told him the murderer used a knife from the beginning as a threat to force compliance. A similar cut had been on Johnson's body. Ventana had almost been decapitated so the pathologist hadn't been able to determine if she initially had the same slicing wound on her neck.

Experience had taught O'Hara that it was far easier to kill a person with a gun than it was with a knife. A knife was a close-in weapon and, except in the hands of an expert, it was always an impetuous choice. Most people have an incredible fear of being cut and just the appearance of a knife could paralyze people who weren't accustomed to violence. In this case he was certain that the man who used the knife to abduct her had a sadistic streak and enjoyed the scent of fear.

There were faint red marks around the wrists. Looking down at her ankles, O'Hara saw identical marks. Bindings would bruise the skin if they were tight or the person pulled against them.

The strands of her hair were damp and limp, framing her face like the long fringe of a scarf. Her hair was too moist to be wet simply from the morning fog. It had the look of being washed and left to dry in the air. O'Hara ran his gloved hand lightly over her shoulders and legs. They were dry. No morning dew on the body. Based on the location he found nothing to explain the wet hair except the conclusion that he didn't want to reach.

He looked over at Puccinelli. "Ligature marks. She was tied in some way." O'Hara leaned in close to the body, the unmistakable smell of slowly thickening blood and exposed organs penetrated the air—and something else. His head snapped back, another familiar odor piercing his senses.

Jamison waited with growing impatience until O'Hara waved him over. He carefully walked to the body and squatted down. It no longer unnerved the young DA to see people staring up with eyes that had lost the shimmer of life and become dry, opaque lenses into nothingness. O'Hara pointed at the hair. "This guy washed her off before he left her here."

It wasn't a question. It was a statement. Same as the others.

Jamison's face squeezed into a grimace. "He wanted to make sure that nothing was on her for us to find." O'Hara eyed him with a furrowed brow. Jamison had grown used to O'Hara's expression of disdain when somebody restated the obvious implications of his conclusion. Murder normally happened in a rush of emotion or anger or after deliberation with cold intent. But the killer frequently looked down at the victim to see if they were really dead, or to think for a moment about what they had done, and maybe, in rare cases, to admire their work. Killers often unintentionally marked their presence at crime scenes with individual hair strands that fell without notice, small threads of fabric, sometimes saliva or semen or a piece of skin—the flotsam of their bodies. Trained detectives would pick at the minutia for the detritus that would tie the scene to the killer.

"It's more than that," O'Hara said as he leaned closer to the body. "You smell it?"

Jamison put his face closer to the body and recoiled as the thick odor struck him full in the face. The acrid smell was unmistakable. Jamison quickly realized what O'Hara had already surmised. The killer knew what they would be looking for and he had gone to great lengths to ensure they would not find it.

O'Hara carefully stepped back and muttered with undisguised disgust, "Bleach. She's been doused with bleach. Just like the others. We aren't going to find anything."

His eyes questioning, O'Hara turned his head slightly toward Puccinelli, who answered his question before he said anything. "Yeah, I smelled it too. The body's clean, I know. But there were loose hairs on her breast. Not hers. I could tell that just from a visual exam. We haven't combed the pubic area yet. Maybe there's something, but this guy didn't leave much that I can see, except the hairs." Puccinelli hesitated. "Same as the others."

O'Hara nodded. "Yeah, same as the others." He stood up. "Pooch, you have an address for this Terry Symes?" Puccinelli glanced sideways at him, hesitating before answering. Jamison understood the hesitation. Pooch was the lead investigator and it was important to interagency cooperation that his control be respected. O'Hara added, "If you don't mind we'd like to go over there and take a look."

Quickly scribbling the address, Puccinelli handed O'Hara a slip of paper. "Wait for me, okay? I'll be over in a little bit. I got a patrol unit sitting on the place to make sure nobody screws with it by accident." He was looking at Jamison. It was a warning that went with the permission but it was primarily aimed at the lawyer. Jamison was used to it. Cops never forgave you for being a lawyer. The only reason district attorneys got a pass was because they were necessary to the process. But Jamison knew that to cops "necessary to the process" also included going to the can after they drank their morning coffee. Jamison recognized he was only being given permission because he was with O'Hara.

As O'Hara walked away Jamison hesitated a moment, intently concentrating on the face of the young woman on the ground, the features losing definition in the whitish pallor that marked the slow drawing away of the blush of life. He thought, *What had her life been like?* It troubled him each time he thought about what a killer took away. Everything a person had and everything they might experience in the future—gone in an instant.

These were questions that he could only ask himself. Jamison sighed deeply. *Wherever she was now, what was she thinking or was she thinking at all?* He had asked himself the same question eight years before when cancer took his father. He hadn't died a violent death but it had not been easy. Jamison felt a twinge of guilt remembering how little emotion he felt as he had looked down at his father, all of their past finally behind. But he hadn't wished him suffering. At least the last thing his father had seen had been the faces of people who cared about him and not the face of a murderer. He pushed thoughts of his father to the back of his mind. He would do his best for her. It was all he could do. He turned slowly and walked away.

As he slid back into the front passenger seat of O'Hara's car, Jamison said nothing. O'Hara started the car and only after they had been driving for a few minutes did O'Hara say anything. It wasn't dramatic or profound. Jamison turned at the sound of the sharp expletive. "Shit." O'Hara didn't say anything else for an almost interminable thirty seconds. "Shee-it," he repeated, turning the word into two syllables.

There was nothing to add. Both men knew that when people killed someone, except where they acted with scrupulously planned premeditation, they almost always left something. O'Hara always said that killing somebody and getting away with it was a lot easier than people thought. But the reality was that it was lucky for the cops that most murders were impetuous acts caused by any of the usual motives: anger, jealousy, lust, or revenge, with the killer more likely than not fortified with generous amounts of booze or drugs, sometimes both.

Except for those acting with deliberate intent, the other thing O'Hara had taught Jamison was that most killers panic—they don't think clearly and they make mistakes. That didn't mean they wouldn't try to hide what they did, but it did mean that most of the time killers were acting quickly and without careful thought to how well they were covering their tracks.

Both of them understood that what applied to most people didn't apply to this crime scene. This was an act done in cold blood, an act considered beforehand, weighed, evaluated, and then performed ruthlessly—the worst kind of murder, a passionless infliction of death. The kind of people who did that were rare but they were out there, and Jamison and O'Hara knew one was out there now, waiting and likely watching.

While they were driving to Terry Symes's apartment a call came over the radio from Puccinelli. He didn't say much because news organizations monitored police broadcasts. All he said was that he had a positive identification consistent with their discussion. He didn't say how or why.

O'Hara didn't ask any questions. If news people became aware of who the victim was they would stumble over themselves trying to be the first one to reach the parents and catch their reaction for the six o'clock news. Puccinelli was just making sure when the victim's mother and father were confronted with the fact that their worst fears had been realized it would be in private. It was a small accommodation to their dignity, but it was all he could do for them at the moment.

Chapter 3

The white sheriff's cruiser with gold-and-green stripes down the side was parked in front of Terry Symes's apartment complex on a street lined with sycamores. The empty branches cut into the gray morning sky that blanketed the Central Valley of California almost daily during the winter and the thin winter skeletons of wood cast no shadow.

The apartment house was fairly typical for a woman Terry Symes's age, nothing fancy but a step up from the places where many college students lived. There was substantial lighting around the building complex and there was also a single light outside each door. The victim's apartment, now guarded by a sheriff's deputy, had the only light that was still on.

Across the apartment complex courtyard were several clusters of young women and men encircling an older woman and man and silently watching the deputy.

The sheriff's deputy met them half-way. He kept his voice low. "Just a warning. That's the girl's parents over there." He pointed across the courtyard to the older couple and lowered his voice even more. "Is she the one they found by the canal?"

The deputy stepped back as O'Hara nodded circumspectly. "Too bad. I'll stay here as long as you need me. I had the manager unlock the door so it's open. I looked around the apartment. Not much to report. The keys were in an ashtray on a shelf by the door, so when she left she didn't take them. Either she forgot them and walked out thinking she was coming back or whoever took her didn't plan on her coming back. But somebody hit the lock button on the doorknob." He stopped talking as the two older people walked across the apartment's center lawn toward them.

The woman's face had a pasty pallor. The only color was in the puffiness around her red-rimmed eyes from crying. She was going gray at the temples and her hair was lank and uncombed but her eyes were wide open, expectant. Jamison was relieved when O'Hara brushed past him as the couple approached. Neither of them wanted to be the one to turn her terror-filled apprehension into hopeless grief. Her husband following closely behind her had a look of profound sadness. "Are you police? Do you know what happened to Terry?" she asked O'Hara, instinctively picking the older man.

The investigator's voice took on a gentle quality, "Ma'am, we're with the district attorney's office and we're doing some follow-up to the missing person report I believe you filed."

The question came back with more insistence, "Do you know what happened to my daughter?" Her eyes were pleading. Jamison could tell that O'Hara didn't want to keep her waiting, although he knew the older detective more than anything hated being the one who took away the hope. But it was Puccinelli's case.

"There's a detective assigned and he should be here any minute. Meanwhile maybe you could answer some questions for us?"

The mother grabbed at O'Hara, pulling at his jacket with quick bird-like motions. "Our daughter called us every day. She didn't call Saturday or Sunday. I thought maybe she was out somewhere," she said, turning to Jamison. "You know, on a date or with friends? When she didn't call Sunday I drove over and the manager let me in. Her car is still parked in the back. I knew she wouldn't just not call, so I called the police. The policeman—he said to give it another day, that this often happens. He looked around inside but there wasn't anything. Nothing was gone—except her." She waited for some kind of response.

"Was the porch light on when you got here or did you turn it on for some reason?"

"It was on. Terry turned it on at night and she turned it off in the morning. She always did that. She was . . . she was always afraid of the dark, from the time she was little." The mother gave a wan smile as if she was divulging a little family secret.

Jamison took a closer look at the door. There was a peephole and no sign of forced entry.

As if intuiting Jamison's thoughts, Mrs. Symes offered, "My daughter always kept the door locked and the chain attached on the inside." Jamison nodded. That answered one of his questions: Why would Terry Symes let anyone in?

Just at that moment Puccinelli arrived. Jamison sensed O'Hara's relief. He felt it himself. O'Hara stepped back to make room for Pooch. "Mr. and Mrs. Symes, this is Detective Art Puccinelli."

Acknowledging the two men from the DA's office, Pooch reached out with his hand and put it on Mrs. Symes's shoulder. "Ah, Mr. and Mrs. Symes, is there a place with some privacy where we can talk?"

When Puccinelli and the parents were far enough away Jamison asked, "Bill, if he took her from here, then either she let him in because she knew who he was or she wasn't worried about who he was. Either way, she had some reason not to fear him."

"Or she did the one thing young women are told not to do—open the door to a stranger." O'Hara's fingers slowly stroked his upper lip. Jamison could hear the hiss of air escaping through O'Hara's teeth. "We're not going to find anything here. I can tell you that right now."

They kept their eyes on the door while the wailing moan of Terry Symes's mother echoed throughout the courtyard, the wrenching cry of grief that sounds the same in every language. Once you hear it, you never forget it.

Chapter 4

The bright lights in the University Hospital morgue always seemed to make the place feel even colder to Jamison, leaching the color out of everything in the room, including the institutional green tile and linoleum covering the walls and floor. It didn't help that the temperature was kept down or, as Jamison wryly commented, they certainly weren't trying to keep any of the "guests" warm. And then there was the smell, the ever-present faint miasma of death that ventilation could not seem to erase.

Dr. Sam Gupta had already begun his examination of the body of Terry Symes when Puccinelli, Jamison, and O'Hara arrived. Gupta, a short, very dark middle-aged man of Indian descent whose accent bore the lilt of his native India smiled as they walked in. A brush of gray hair circled the middle of his head, sticking out of the surgical cap he usually wore to cover the baldness. He had been doing autopsies for over twenty years and everyone appreciated his medical expertise, if not his efforts at humor. "So I am guessing a knife was used?" He then laughed at his own morbid observation of the obvious. O'Hara gritted his teeth. Puccinelli simply shook his head. Jamison understood the dark humor of the autopsy room and gave Gupta the benefit of a strained grin.

No matter how many times Jamison saw bodies stretched out on stainless steel tables, it jolted him. Perhaps it was the sterility of it or, as he once told O'Hara, the personal violation involved as a bunch of strangers photograph and poke the corpse, and then open the body with the same deference that you would give to a can of tuna. By the time the pathologist was ready to do a post-mortem examination, a "post" they called it, the body had been picked over by technicians removing anything that might be worth looking at. Hairs were removed along with any fibers or debris. Then the deceased was washed down so the pathologist could see what he or she was looking at or for.

Terry Symes's body reflected starkly against the polished stainless steel of the autopsy table. The pronounced lividity on her body had finally darkened to a purplish hue, painted down her side in the bruised tone of pooled blood that death settled on everyone allowed to lie for long periods. Jamison stared at the ugly red slash that opened half her body. He couldn't help thinking how cold she looked lying there, her lips almost colorless, her eyes now shut, and her body still.

Puccinelli directed the sheriff's identification bureau technician to begin taking pictures from different angles around the autopsy table, the tableau a still life of cold flesh and glinting stainless steel.

A man dressed in hospital greens came through the swinging door while Gupta was pointing out various areas he thought should be photographed. The man stood watching for a moment with detached clinical interest before Gupta said, "Ah, Dr. St. Claire, there you are." Gupta turned to the investigative team. "This is one of the anesthesiologists who does lab work down the hall. He occasionally likes to scrub in."

St. Claire glanced in Jamison's direction. "I was here when Dr. Gupta did the autopsy on the slit throat."

Realizing he meant Maria Ventana, the first of this killer's victims, Jamison was rankled. He remembered that another doctor had come in, but he had been wearing a surgical mask and Jamison hadn't focused on him at the time. And while it wasn't uncommon for medical staff to appear and observe autopsies it disturbed him when doctors didn't describe people by their name, only by their disease or by the wound that had taken a person's life. Ventana was a slit throat so maybe that made Symes an evisceration. But Jamison understood that was how the staff on this unit maintained their detachment while they performed what always unfairly struck him as butcher's work.

In some respects Jamison realized he wasn't much different. Frequently he forgot victim's names, the images of the crimes becoming the identity of the victim in his mind. As for his initial revulsion at detectives and medical observers eating pizza during an autopsy, he had now learned that in his business, you ate when you could because you might not get another opportunity for hours.

Gupta's voice jolted Jamison back to the present when he asked Dr. St. Claire to reach under Symes's body, turning her slightly as Gupta ran his gloved fingers down her spine. St. Claire glanced at Jamison briefly and then spoke while he pushed against Symes's back. "I do some work down here with dogs, anesthetic reactions, and that sort of thing. The synergistic effects of the heroin and barbiturate interest me." Then he added, as if he had perhaps made an inappropriate assumption, "If that's what killed her like the others. Guess we don't know yet?" St. Claire looked up at Dr. Gupta who acknowledged that the body was properly positioned, and then he held out his hand in Jamison's direction. "Alex St. Claire," he added with a trace of a British accent.

St. Claire must have picked up on the hesitation as Jamison looked at the outstretched hand. "Sorry." He peeled a glove off. "You a detective? Don't worry, I washed. It's Dr. Gupta you have to worry about, not me." Gupta's laugh was a clear sign that he didn't take offense. Jamison finally took St. Claire's hand. He was surprised at the firmness of the grip.

Gupta explained, "Mr. Jamison is with the district attorney's office. He's a prosecutor." He nodded toward O'Hara and Puccinelli. "These two are policemen."

Keeping his eyes on Gupta as the pathologist made a deep incision allowing further opening of the chest cavity, St. Claire asked Jamison, "A prosecutor? You handle cases like this?"

"Yeah, I handle major-crimes-against-person cases, take them to trial."

Gupta interrupted. "Dr. St. Claire, would you mind doing the blood draw? I need three vials."

Smiling as he looked at Jamison, St. Claire said, "Excuse me." He turned back toward Gupta and slipped his glove back on. "Of course. Let me get some tubes." Jamison started to say something about preserving the chain of custody but Gupta was right there, and he nodded, and waved his gloved hand at Jamison. Normally each person who handled evidence was considered "in the chain of custody." Their names would be recorded on the tag attached to the bagged evidence or in some way so that questions couldn't be raised about mishandling or contamination—legitimate questions, anyway. Defense attorneys never seemed to run out of things to question and implications to cast.

Jamison had never been a defense attorney and he had no inclination to be one. But that was what his father had been, and through the years growing up he had heard all the justifications for what his father did. Jamison just couldn't see himself sitting next to a child molester or drug dealer and rationalizing that he was upholding the Constitution. But he also knew that he couldn't separate what his father did from what his father was in his eyes, so he knew he couldn't be objective and he couldn't tar all defense attorneys with the same brush.

He watched as St. Claire performed the blood draw and carefully placed the vials in a shallow stainless steel tray. Gupta would initial them to document the chain of custody.

Gupta's initial conclusion was no surprise. Symes was already dead when the slashing wound was delivered, just as Ventana and Johnson. The mutilating wound on each victim, including Symes, was simply a vicious act done to horrify. Without more tests he said he couldn't be sure, but Gupta suspected that they would find the same toxic stew of heroin and barbiturates in her system that was in the bodies of the other two victims. He also found a small injection site in the cut on Symes's throat and concluded that was the likely site of injection of the heroin-and-barbiturate mixture. There was bruising at the base of Symes's head indicating that she had been forcibly grabbed. It was identical to the type of bruising that had been found on the back of the necks of the other two women. Other than that, Gupta had nothing.

Disappointed because they had made so little progress, Jamison was filled with frustration and feelings of impotence. Every hour they failed to find this murderer was another hour that some other young woman walked in the shadow of her own death.

Chapter 5

November, 2005
One week later
Tenaya County, California

The headlights of the car moved with measured familiarity down the pitch-black road, the asphalt a washed-out white in the bright beams, dissolving to silver in the distance. The radio carried a news clip from a press conference. The driver reached over to find music, brushing back the cascade of light brown hair that fell across her face as she turned her head. She didn't want to hear news. Politics was for her father. She was still young. She wanted to hear the sounds of voices singing about life and the anticipation of the next moment. Life was what she was all about.

On this clear night, moonlight bathed the old headstone markers near the iron fence edging the roadway and the faces of aging monuments of lives long forgotten were briefly illuminated as the car's headlights followed the turn. Even now as an adult, Elizabeth Anne Garrett still felt a slight shudder as she turned to the roadway cutting through the two cemeteries that had cradled the dead for more than one hundred years. She knew there was nothing to be frightened of, but that didn't change the feeling of being watched. That feeling had never gone away.

She shivered involuntarily just as the corner of her eye caught the flash of light in her rearview mirror, headlights flickering in a sequenced dance with a brief flash of red. Her first thought was reflexive. *I didn't do anything wrong.* She looked at the rearview mirror more closely to make sure. The glare of the headlights made it difficult to see anything except the outline of the vehicle behind her. She pulled over into a dirt parking area near the cemetery gate and pressed a button, lowering the window, the damp cold fall air seeping into the warmth of her car as she released her seat belt and started to look behind her, shutting off the engine.

He was at her car before she was aware of his presence. The gloved hand lightly rested on the sill of the open window. Elizabeth looked straight into an expanse of black leather that almost filled the window. He was standing so close to the door it startled her. "Oh—" It was all that came out of her mouth, the words choked off as her throat closed involuntarily, her eyes focusing on the other gloved hand and the dully glinting silver shaft that rose from the leathered fist.

The moonlight slid over the knife as it turned slightly and moved in a fluid motion through the window and near her face. There was something almost reptilian about the blade as it swayed in his hand. The silver light made the razor edge flash and then disappear as the unsheathed steel turned straight, lightly touched her throat, and then raised itself before her face. She couldn't see the face of the man holding the glistening sliver of steel. He said nothing. He didn't have to.

Elizabeth's blue-gray eyes widened, flicking back and forth with the minuet of the blade as it swung lightly side to side, inches from her eyes. A tremor rose from her abdomen, sliding up through her chest like a fog, her mouth trembling as her lips parted, the breath going in and out in short bursts, puffing clouds of soundless mist in the chill air.

His face was still in the shadow of the unlit roadway as he opened the door. Reaching in with liquid movement, his hand grazed across her leg, lightly drawing his leather-tipped fingers down the inside of her thigh. Elizabeth felt her body move closer to the center console, pushing against it. There was no place to move.

He pulled the blade back, twisting it again toward her face and then resting the tip against her throat, pressing just lightly against the skin as his hand moved up her leg. She could feel the pulse of her heart moving against the needlelike point. He didn't push any harder, allowing the tip to slide down like a slowly moving teardrop.

She closed her eyes and waited. She could not will herself to move, the touch of steel a paralyzing carapace holding her body still as it moved down her neck with the whisper touch of a caress. The blade slid away leaving the sensation of a rivulet of trickling dampness moving down her flesh. She didn't need to open her eyes to realize the blade was again in front of her face. She could sense it, like someone standing near her bed in the darkness while she slept. It was there. He was there.

She forced her eyes open just as moonlight caught the stain of crimson on the point of the blade. She saw him stare at the blade for a moment, his eyes widening as if it was unexpected, then turn his gaze to her face, letting the stiletto tip linger for a moment in front of her, allowing the scarlet drop to glaze the steel. He drew the flat of the blade across the leather driver's seat in an almost delicate feline motion, cleansing the tip.

His face lowered to her level, the nighttime shadows distorting his features as he used his teeth to pull the glove from his left hand. He raised his finger to his lips, a soundless gesture, and then his ungloved hand slid again slowly up the inside of her thigh.

He drew his head back just enough for the silver light to cross his face as the heat of his hand floated up her leg. The deep-set eyes glowed black. She felt a shudder wrap her body as his face moved toward her. His words came out in a whisper. "Remember me?"

Chapter 6

The call from O'Hara pulled Jamison from another night of fitful sleep. The Symes case, like the other murder cases, had run into nothing but a wall of questions leaving Jamison desperately searching for answers. When the phone rang, O'Hara's voice ground through his sleep-fogged brain. A young woman's car had been found and she was missing. Jamison's mind began to clear. Even with his crime-calloused mind he recoiled at the thought there might be another one.

O'Hara continued. "We don't have a body. We have a car with the door unlocked, what looks like a blood smear on the seat, and some indications that a knife was used. So far there is no reason why the driver would have left the car at the location where it was found."

Jamison heard the click as soon as he said, "Pick me up."

As O'Hara sped through the darkened streets Jamison tried to block out the muffled crackle of the sheriff's dispatch radio while he attempted to collect his thoughts. Three homicides in the last month, each about ten days apart. Jamison pulled the scenes of the three murders to the front of his mind, searching again for anything that might help him find a link between the crimes when they arrived at the scene. He already knew the similarities. It had played out so many times in his mind that he could even hear the sounds.

He could feel in his gut the growing dread that now there was a fourth. And Jamison couldn't see anything clearly except that he hadn't been able to prevent it.

Outside the lightly fogged car window the dark landscape rushed by them as O'Hara headed toward the new crime scene. Jamison rubbed his face, stress seeping through his pores at the thought that they had another murder and they still had no suspect.

The words of his old friend Dr. Aaron Levy kept ringing in his mind. After the Ventana and Johnson murders, Jamison felt he was missing some obvious link. He went to see the middle-aged psychologist for insight. Unlike many psychologists who testified, Levy didn't look for excuses for criminal behavior. He looked for explanations that made sense, which he delivered with the accent of his native Brooklyn.

Jamison had known Levy for a considerable portion of his life. The psychologist and his father had been friends and, at various times of his life, Levy had counseled Jamison when he needed to talk to somebody. Indeed, the older man had somehow sensed a void in the younger man and whenever Jamison felt that void, Levy had been there to fill it. Their conversations helped Jamison understand how the past had shaped him and that once he understood, it was best to leave it buried.

Levy had taken the time to educate him about the type of person he was likely chasing and Jamison had been an eager student. "Most people think," Levy had said, "that because someone commits a monstrous act that they are monsters, look like monsters, act like monsters. But the reality is that psychopaths look just like the rest of us. Every malignant thought they carry in the dark recesses of their minds, and what we see is the aftermath, the result of their twisted fantasies. We are shocked when we see their faces on the news because they look just like us."

Two days after the Symes murder, Jamison paid another visit to Levy. Leaning back in his office chair, the bearded psychologist had softly offered that even though the information released had been minimal, the pictures of the three victims had told him that Jamison was looking for someone who had very *special* characteristics. That was, their prey embodied all the aspects of a classic sexual sadist serial killer.

Jamison had nodded and then placed a number of crime-scene photographs on the table. Methodically, he had gone over the details of each murder and the victims' backgrounds with Levy, hoping he might offer some insight that would bring him closer to a more refined focus. It had puzzled Jamison that none of the victims had been sexually assaulted even though the crimes appeared overtly sexual in nature.

They had carefully examined the pictures of the crime scenes spread out on Levy's desk in striking slashes of red and pallid skin tones. Levy had separated the pictures that focused on the faces of the victims and said, "What gives sexual pleasure is not necessarily the sexual act itself. He may be impotent. He may take his pleasure in private as he fantasizes about what he has done. What they think, how they think, and why they do what they do is only limited by their own dark thoughts."

Levy's hand had moved the photographs across his desk like tarot cards shuffled by a soothsayer. But as Jamison had watched, he knew that Levy was drawing upon years of experience rather than some mystical insight. After a thoughtful silence, he had said, "These murders appear extraordinarily cruel and yet, what you tell me is that when the horrible wounds were inflicted on the victims they were already dead. They were all missing approximately twenty-four hours and then killed several hours before they were found. So the killer spared them the pain of his desecration and yet he kept them alive for hours before he killed them." He had murmured the last statement as if asking himself "What did he do in that time?"

As his implied question hung in the air, Levy had continued. "My guess is that he fed on the sight and smell of their fear. All of these young women look very similar, correct?"

Jamison had acknowledged that his investigator, Bill O'Hara, had noticed this early in the investigation; each of the victims were similar in age, hair color, complexion, and build. Even their facial features were similar.

"These victims are selected in advance, I think. We know that suffering is the most important thing to the serial killer. They are without conscience, moral restraint, or a sense of society's boundaries. Their entire focus is on themselves and their own desires. Many are in fact highly intelligent."

As Jamison rose to leave, Levy had put his hand on his young friend's arm. "Matt, these are not crimes of impulse. There is a ritualistic pattern. Each woman has been displayed as an example of his power and his control of the situation. The grotesque wounds that were inflicted are about power. They aren't about pain. He has done that to show *you* what he can do because he intended for these women to be found. He wants *you* to feel fear. That is part of his pleasure."

Now as Jamison rushed to this new crime scene, Levy's words were planted in his mind. "That he will do it again is inevitable. There is a reason all his victims look alike and we most likely will not know that reason until you find this man."

Jamison sat back in the seat as O'Hara sped through the darkened streets, wondering what the young woman looked like whose abandoned car they were rushing to.

Chapter 7

Jamison's mental replay of the psychologist's analysis snapped off when he saw the emergency lights breaking the darkness ahead. Even from a block away, the flashing lights of two sheriff's cruisers threw off flickering red-and-blue patterns that caught the tips of the rows of stone markers bordering the road. The criminal identification bureau van was there, its bright generator-driven lights turning night into high noon. All the lights surrounded one small vehicle sitting in a dirt-and-gravel parking area near the cemetery gate.

As he got out of the car, the cold night air hit Jamison in the face. He looked around. The roadway cut directly between two cemeteries that had been there since the turn of the century. Once carefully tended stone markers were now blackened by neglect as families moved on. A twinge of guilt nibbled at Jamison. His father was out there in the darkness resting under a flat bronze marker indicating the newer generations of the deceased. He hadn't visited in the years since the funeral. Tonight would be no exception; there were others who demanded his attention.

He followed O'Hara down the pitted roadway, picking his path carefully and regretting his choice of loafers instead of heavy shoes. Puccinelli was standing twenty feet from the vehicle, observing the identification bureau technicians. Jamison joined O'Hara near the detective. The silver hair of Detective Puccinelli reflected the generator-driven lights. Jamison heard O'Hara's voice over the steady rumble of the gas engines. "Hey, Pooch. What've we got?"

Taking a cigarette from his mouth, Puccinelli looked up from his notebook and shook his head, the dense cloud of exhaled smoke hanging in the damp air. "Don't know much. The car belongs to an Elizabeth Garrett. Her parents live a few miles just north of here. Apparently she was still living at home. The report I have is that she was supposed to be spending the night with a girlfriend and was going to go to work from there, but evidently Garrett changed her mind and decided to head home."

Pooch looked down at his notepad and added, "A neighbor of Garrett's parents saw the car as he drove by and called her father. He came over right away. That was about ten thirty. He said the car was unlocked and the keys were gone. At this point all we know is that this would not have been her normal route home and if it hadn't been for the neighbor coming this way we wouldn't have known anything until this morning when she didn't report for work.

"We've got a lot of footprints but the dad's been here; the neighbor's been here. The first deputy on the scene has been here. God knows who else has walked around. We got multiple tire tracks too. Could be the father's, could be the neighbors. Who the hell knows? Between the gravel and the dirt it's going to be damn near impossible to make a clear tire track."

O'Hara acknowledged the difficulties. It would be a break if they found a tire track they could match with a tire of a suspect vehicle, but that was the starting point.

Puccinelli nodded to Jamison. "Matt, got you out too?"

Pushing his mouth up to somewhere between a grimace and a smile, Jamison said, "Yeah, Pooch, had nothing else to do at four a.m. so still with it. Anything in the car?"

The detective's weathered face reacted subtly to the use of his nickname by the young prosecutor. "The driver's seat has a blood smear right down the side," he answered. "You can see the imprint of what looks to me like a knife blade at the top of the smear. You can take a look."

Puccinelli hesitated and then stepped closer. "I hate to say it, but I think we got another one like the others. The only break we may have is we know from her girlfriend that she's only been missing for five or six hours. If this is another one, then if he follows the pattern she's still alive out there somewhere." Pooch paused before adding, "At least for now."

Jamison followed O'Hara as he made his way to the open driver's door of Garrett's car. O'Hara thumbed the switch on his flashlight and carefully swept the small circle of light over the interior. Next to the left side of the driver's seat there was a dark reddish smudge, as if something had been wiped off against the upholstery. At the top of the stain the partial outline of what looked like a thin knife blade could be seen. The first case had also involved a car and a bloodstained slice had been left in a similar spot. A day and a half later the driver, Maria Ventana, had been found dead on a blind access road several miles from where her car had been left.

Dr. Levy's words still echoing in Jamison's mind, his stomach began to churn when he considered the possibility the killer was watching them at that very moment. Levy had said this type of killer frequently waited in hiding to watch the reaction to his handiwork. Jamison peered into the darkness that bordered the crime scene like a black curtain. He saw nothing except the night-shaded monuments to the dead.

Jamison stared at the bloodstain on the car's seat. If they were lucky and it was the same killer as the other victims, they had slightly less than twenty-four hours left to find this Elizabeth Garrett alive—after that they would find her dead. It was like the countdown to an execution. But that was twenty-four hours from the time she was taken and they had already lost at least five or six trying to discover if she was gone and what might have happened.

Puccinelli, watching with detached interest, told them, "The sheriff wants a meeting with the rest of the detectives working the case. We're meeting in two hours. Maybe you two can sit in?" He was asking. It was evident to O'Hara and Jamison that Pooch needed some backup of his own and he had decided they were it.

"Okay." Jamison nodded. "I need to call the district attorney and let him know because the press is going to be all over this."

He heard O'Hara muttering, "As soon as they crawl out of their holes when the sun comes up." Jamison didn't disagree and besides, O'Hara wouldn't care if he did.

Chapter 8

After another hour at the crime scene, it was clear nothing more would be gained from them standing around. O'Hara drove Jamison home so he could clean up before their meeting with the sheriff.

On the way back Jamison called Ernie Garcia, his other investigator. It was still early and the eastern sky was just beginning to crack from its overnight slumber. He filled Ernie in on the new crime scene and asked him to go straight to the sheriff's office and hold it together until he and O'Hara could get there.

Jamison preferred sending Ernie out when a political relationship needed to be maintained. He generally wouldn't say anything until he had digested all the facts and merged them with his observations. Ernie said that it was his Mexican heritage that allowed him to project an easy que será manner, including an accent that he hauled out when it suited him. But there was a big difference between the easy manner Ernie projected and the steel hidden behind it.

Ernie was unlike O'Hara, who could scare the hell out of people when he got his back up, his eyes drawing into narrow slits that could burn a hole through someone. Jamison had come to trust both of them completely and long ago decided that he would bet his life on either man.

Three years earlier, Ernie decided to make the switch from working in the sheriff's homicide unit to the DA's office in order to try and maintain some type of family life. He had admitted to Jamison his wife had given him an ultimatum about his hours as a homicide detective, and he hadn't regretted it. She prepared a dark green vegetable juice concoction every morning for Ernie and put it in a thermos, insisting that he drink three glasses of it daily to keep up his energy and to try to stay as slim as his stocky body would allow, a challenge when the rest of his colleagues' diets consisted primarily of burgers and sodas. Privately, after agreeing to taste it, O'Hara had said if drinking green slime was what it took to keep a wife happy, it would be easier to stay single.

When Jamison entered his apartment, the sun was just beginning to warm the horizon. He looked at his watch: less than an hour before the meeting. Every hour that ticked by was one less hour for Elizabeth Garrett to be found alive. At this moment it was seventeen hours, maybe less. Racing the clock to save her life was all he could think about.

His apartment looked no different than it had when he left over three hours earlier. In fact, Jamison ruefully had to admit it probably looked better when he left because it was still dark. There wasn't much, a couch and a beanbag chair that survived both college and law school and a battered outdoor umbrella table in the kitchen with a plastic tablecloth and four folding chairs purchased at a yard sale. The only items of value were the stereo and his expensive coffee, both probably worth more than the small television balanced on a TV tray.

He pushed aside the week-old milk that was sitting toward the front of the refrigerator and reached for the orange juice; the color still looked right. He had already had three cups of coffee. There would be more down at the sheriff's office. The problem for Jamison was that cops would drink coffee that tasted like used crankcase oil. He would buy a cup and take it into the meeting. He would need it.

Jamison ran his hand over his face and hair. Everything he touched had an oily film. He walked into the bathroom and turned on the shower. He would be in the office by seven o'clock to update the district attorney before heading over to the sheriff's meeting. Jamison reached for a towel in the laundry basket—he had given up folding them a long time ago—and settled his mind again on Elizabeth Garrett, whose face he had seen on the fax of her driver's license. She could have been a sister of the other three victims. The resemblance to them was that striking. In an instant he knew that where there had once been three, there were now four.

At that moment Elizabeth Garrett began to stir. She felt like her eyes were weighted with lead and struggled to open them even slightly. She also felt the sapping exhaustion of the emotion of the last hours. Opening her eyes did not increase her awareness of where she was, it only disoriented her more, the blackness of the room, the sensation of waking, realizing she was in a different place and nothing was where it was supposed to be. The only feeling, other than the pounding in her head, was a slowly emerging awareness of her body.

A fog of muddy sensations broke through her efforts to see. Since she was a little girl she had been terrified of the dark. She still kept a night light glowing in her bedroom. Slowly her mind regained the context of the last few hours. She lifted her arm toward her face. Something held her, not hard, not soft, just there. She could feel her body pulling against something but all she could focus on was that she could not move more than slightly. Her mouth was dry; her tongue searched for moisture but there was none.

The fear of the darkness and the grip of disorientation rose up from her stomach like a cold wave, pushing out an unrecognizable animallike sound. She had never before heard a primal shriek of pure terror and now it rushed out of her, filling the darkness, falling into nothingness. Her throat closed in a guttural rasp. She closed her eyes against the blackness, the only control she had. The noise was faint, soft against a hard surface, quickly growing louder. Elizabeth could hear it moving toward her, muffled, but she knew the sound—running footsteps.

The light slipped through the opening door, cutting across the blackness of the room, a sharp swath that lit walls bleached by the piercing beam. Elizabeth turned her head toward the light but her eyes could not adjust. All she could see was a black outline backlit. The voice was soft, almost soothing.

"You're awake." It was not a question. It was a statement. "I wasn't ready for you yet. I thought you were still asleep." He paused, running his hand across her leg. "I'm sorry. I forgot, you don't like the dark." Elizabeth stared at him, memories of the past and the reality of her present creating a jarring kaleidoscope of emotions. "We don't need these anymore, do we?" He tugged at the restraints. Elizabeth's mind was clear now. She watched as he released the restraints and ran his hand down her body, the warmth of his hand and the familiarity of his touch oriented her mind. She knew what would happen next.

Twenty minutes after meeting with the district attorney, Jamison walked down the hall toward O'Hara's office. Here and there silver duct tape across the carpet held down a fraying tribute to county frugality, and in some places even the duct tape had curled into a shabby fringe.

A small circle of light from a lamp illuminated the desk in O'Hara's office. A curl of blue smoke from a lit cigar in an ashtray rose up toward a growing haze near the ceiling. Jamison shook his head. *Wasn't it supposed to be illegal to smoke in a public building?* O'Hara looked up and gave him a half-smile that might have also stifled a yawn. "Good morning, Boss."

"Morning, Bill. You ready?"

"Yeah." O'Hara pulled his long legs down from the desk and slowly lowered his feet to the floor. He paused, taking in the dark circles under Jamison's eyes. "Guess we both need more sleep. The big guy work you over?"

"The usual," Jamison replied. "Gage knows we're doing as much as we can. He just wants to have something he can throw out to the newspeople so it looks like progress is being made. I think he'll say it would be detrimental to the investigation to reveal what we know."

O'Hara snorted. "We don't know shit. Just as long as he keeps the news people off our asses I'm okay with it."

Jamison sucked in the sides of his cheeks to tamp down his frustration. "Well that's just fine, but it wasn't your ass that had to sit in front of his desk and tell him we got nothing on three victims and now maybe on four. C'mon, let's go."

It was seven thirty when O'Hara and Jamison headed for the meeting. With no breaks in the case yet they would have to make their own. The pressure was beginning to crawl up the back of Jamison's neck and twist into a knot. They needed to do something besides wait for a body to turn up. He just didn't know what it was.

The conference room at the sheriff's department was definitely Jack Bekin's turf. Bekin was sometimes referred to as "Mover." It was a nickname that most people would think came naturally from sharing the same name of a moving company. That was part of it, but the actual reason was that Bekin made things happen. When he spoke, people moved, local politicians moved, and sometimes so did the governor. It didn't hurt that the sheriff was also built like a Freightliner truck, massive and square, with no neck and no hair, just a huge slick head sitting on an enormous body. People just didn't argue with Mover Bekin, and Jamison knew that today would be no different.

Jamison scanned the faces of the men around the table, eager to spot Ernie, who merely shifted his eyes in Jamison's direction and shook his head discretely. He had nothing either, so there was no point in Jamison trying to stall until Ernie gave him the background.

Bekin raised his eyes when Jamison and O'Hara entered the room. He didn't raise his head. Bekin had a way of turning his whole body when he looked from side to side, as if his head and his body were all one piece, something like the turret of a tank swinging that big cannon in the direction it wanted to fire. It was a habit that Jamison believed was used for intimidation and it generally succeeded.

Today was no different. As the two took their seats alongside the other half-dozen men around the table, Jamison noticed that Bekin's gaze moved past him as if he were a piece of furniture in the corner. Bekin's gaze finally came to rest on O'Hara, who had just taken a seat.

"Willie, you handling this clusterfuck for the suits in the DA's office?"

O'Hara smiled. After making himself comfortable at the long conference table, he responded, "It's sure not the same as riding patrol with you back in the old days, Mover. Sheriff, how you doin'? Matt Jamison and I are working these cases along with Ernie. We don't want to get in the way. We're just here to help out where we can."

Mover's eyes slid down the table to gaze at Jamison, who knew what the sheriff was thinking. Mover didn't trust lawyers and didn't like their presence in murder investigations. To him they were all the same; they took up room that would be better used for open-air space. And while Jamison was a prosecutor, he recognized that to Bekin he was just a lawyer who was working in the DA's office to camouflage his true character. But the sheriff was sophisticated enough to know how to take the credit when prosecutors helped his people crack a case, or to spread the blame when they didn't—in his eyes a win-win proposition politically. Jamison understood Bekin's rules. The most important thing was not to let Bekin think he was intimidated.

O'Hara waited a moment, then shifted to a business-like tone. "Mover, the district attorney sent us to assure you that any arrest or search warrants could be prepared as quickly as possible."

O'Hara nudged his knee against Jamison's leg, a signal it was time for him to say something. It hadn't gone unnoticed by anyone in the room that O'Hara was the first person Bekin spoke to, not Jamison.

Jamison pushed his pen across the yellow legal tablet that he had dropped in front of him on the table, an old courtroom habit that gave him an additional second or two to think. "Sheriff Bekin, the district attorney wants you to know that we'll help you in any way we can, but Mr. Gage made it clear that this is *your* investigation and we are merely to assist as you request."

He swallowed the sour taste from groveling but this was the role he was expected to play if he and the investigators from the DA's office were going to be allowed in at this stage of the case. Everyone knew the district attorney's office would eventually have to take responsibility, win or lose, once the case moved to a courtroom. But cops didn't look at it like that. They figured the guy was guilty when they made the arrest, and if there wasn't enough evidence they wouldn't have made the arrest in the first place. From their perspective every case they had handed to the DA was a winner. If the DA lost, it wasn't their fault.

However, both the sheriff and the DA had a history from three years before with the loss of a major gang murder prosecution because the sheriff had refused to allow prosecutors to be involved in the decision to conduct a search of a gang headquarters. The search was held to be illegal and they lost murder weapons that would have linked gang leaders directly to three murders. That was why District Attorney Gage had begun involving his top lawyers and investigators in major cases to make sure that everything was done before the case was handed over. Mover had been unable to argue that he hadn't made a mistake excluding prosecutors from the investigation. The result was that for now there was an uneasy truce.

Jamison realized that Bekin didn't care about him or anything he had to say as long as he stayed out of the way. Jamison knew the drill. O'Hara would be given the deference of a professional and Jamison would be listened to only when he was spoken to.

The sheriff fixed his gaze on O'Hara and then slid his eyes around the long, scarred wooden conference table. Finally his body turned enough for his gaze to rest on his own man, Puccinelli. "So, Pooch, what you got?"

Puccinelli's face showed every line of fatigue from the preceding weeks. Jamison noted Pooch could barely keep the frustration out of his voice or his words as he began. "We have the worst of all possible situations. We have a player that nobody's seen before and he's started out at the top of the crime chain. So far we have three dead women—same general age, same MO. This morning we have a new victim who's missing, and we have every reason to believe, based on the pattern, that it's the same guy. But we won't know until we find her, and based on his MO we don't have long to find her before he kills her."

He flipped open his file, pulling out several packets of large color photographs of the different crime scenes. He laid the photographs out on the table in four separate groups. A projector tray was set up with a screen pulled down from the ceiling. Puccinelli apologized. “Sorry I don’t have a Powerpoint. No time, so we go with old-school.” He stood and put a picture up on the screen of the three women who had been murdered.

“We don’t have much. There’s no physical evidence at any crime scene that will give us a break on the identity of the killer. We’ve looked statewide at sex offenders who are out. We’ve looked at modus operandi files, no hits. But what you can see from the photographs of these three victims is that they are remarkably similar in appearance.”

Clearing his throat, Puccinelli looked around at the men sitting at the table. A few were taking notes, but most of them were sitting quietly with their hands folded over their chests, their eyes drifting across the crime scene photographs clustered on the table, waiting for the new case—the one that had a victim who might still be alive, Jamison thought.

Pooch placed a photograph of Elizabeth Garrett on the projector tray so that her face showed up on the screen over the photograph of the other three. “Here’s the new one that we think may be connected—Elizabeth Garrett. We found her car last night. You can see how much she resembles the others.”

He shuffled through another pile of crime scene photographs before putting a new one on the projector tray. “This is what we found last night inside Garrett’s car. You can see the outline of a knife or what looks like a knife at the top of a blood smear on the car’s seat, so it’s pretty clear he cut her but not badly enough to cause much blood loss. Tests so far are consistent with her blood type, so we have a pretty good idea what he’ll do to her if we don’t find her first.” He switched back the picture of Garrett.

“Where Garrett’s car was stopped we found nothing. We got tracks all over but there were so many people out there you can’t tell which track is which, and the scene was pretty scuffed up by the time our forensic boys got there. Even if they find something, I don’t think we’re going to get it today. Her father told me that she wouldn’t have taken that route to get home. Why she took that route, and why she stopped the car, we haven’t a clue.

“Garrett’s an elementary school teacher. She had dinner with a girlfriend last night. She was supposed to spend the night at her house but the girlfriend says she changed her mind. Said she wasn't feeling well and would sleep better in her own bed. I talked to the girlfriend. Nothing there so far, but all my interviews have either been on the phone or just short face-to-face. We will be following up with everyone this morning. They didn't talk to anybody at the restaurant, no guys, nothing strange. Her parents are obviously terrified.

"Here's what we do know. Every one of these women was found dead within a day and a half after they were last seen and they each had been dead around four to eight or nine hours when they were found." He cleared his throat again. "Bottom line, the clock's our enemy. I think if this same guy took this Elizabeth Garrett, we got until maybe ten tonight to find her alive. No more. After that we'll just be picking up the pieces."

Pooch put the composite photograph of the previous victims back on the screen. "Of the three dead women, one was taken from her car and the other two were taken from their homes. No sign of forced entry. Each of the murder victims was cut viciously, slashed on different parts of their bodies with an extremely sharp knife, but the wounds were post-mortem. Dr. Gupta says he thinks all three murder victims were actually killed by a toxic injection of a heroin-barbiturate combination. Basically the killer injected them with that shit and it stopped their hearts. Each victim had several human hairs and some dog hairs on their bodies. The human hair came from an African American, but there's no hair bulb on any of the pieces. They were all clippings. We're working to see if we can get any mitochondrial DNA from the hair, but I don't think it will take us anywhere. My guess is that the perp is placing the hair there intentionally, so I'm going to speculate that he's just screwing with us.

"We know they aren't random killings because all the victims so closely resemble one another, but other than that we have no common link. Their jobs were all different. There's no semen or bodily fluids, nothing that looks like rape or sodomy or anything in their throats—nothing. Whoever this asshole is, he knows something about crime scene investigation because he's covered his tracks."

He put a photograph up of a crime scene showing a woman whose head lolled back at an unnatural angle, the slash across her throat a vivid mélange of torn flesh and bone.

"The first victim—Maria Ventana. A teenage couple discovered the body lying on the side of an isolated road several miles from her car."

Puccinelli put up a photograph of the car and continued. "There was a smear of blood on the seat just like with Garrett."

He shook his head with disgust. "She'd been washed down with bleach, but she bled out more at the scene . . ." Puccinelli's voice trailed off while he picked up another file, moved one of the photograph packets to the center of the table, and spread it out.

"The second victim was Mary Ann Johnson. Since both Maria and Mary Ann start with 'M' we thought maybe there was some weird link but after the third, Terry Symes, and now Elizabeth, we don't think that has any legs. As for Johnson, she either let the guy in her house or left with him. Some joggers found her in the park, laid out in the grass. Body was washed beforehand just like the first one. Her wrists were cut to the bone. She was loaded with the same shit that killed Ventana and had a slicing wound near her throat where Gupta found a puncture mark. Gupta thinks that's where the drugs were injected. He couldn't find it on Ventana, probably because of the way her throat was cut. Same kind of hairs left on her body as Ventana."

Puccinelli put up a photograph of a young woman lying on dirt, her chest slit open from her throat to the top of her pubic area. "Terry Symes was the last one. Like Johnson, she either met this guy somewhere or she was taken out of her house. Best guess is she left the house with this guy because her keys were still inside. Why she let this guy in we have no idea. There was no sign of forced entry.

"Same kind of cut on her throat as Johnson and in the cut Gupta found a small puncture left by a syringe. She was also washed down with bleach like the others."

He paused to look around the room. "Again we found several hairs on her breast, which looks like his calling card. If she was sexually assaulted we can't find any indication of it so a so motive is unclear, but her clothing was off—why, we just don't know. There's one more thing. These women weren't just dumped where we found them. They were displayed—carefully laid out—so the killer wasn't in a hurry.

"The rest of the bad news—there's no DNA, maybe because he washed every one of the victims down with bleach. My guess is he was wearing gloves the whole time but he definitely made sure there was nothing for us to find."

Puccinelli placed his pointer on the table. "Sheriff, every one of the men here has been working day and night on these cases along with all the other detectives who got pulled off of burglary and anywhere else we could find them. What I just told you—that's all we know. We have three women dead, all between the ages of twenty-four and twenty-eight, and a fourth case that we think is related but we haven't found the victim—yet. He's obviously kept each victim in a location where he doesn't expect to be seen or he's keeping them in a vehicle, but we have nothing—nobody saw them leave or saw a vehicle. Nothing. All we know for sure is that somewhere toward the end of the twenty-four-hour period after they disappear, they show up dead and they've been dead for four or five hours. He must expect them to be found, so we can speculate that he picks the location where he leaves them because he expects activity. Based on the pattern, if he has our new victim we've got until tonight to find her alive."

Puccinelli paused, leaving an opening for questions or observations from the assembled detectives. All he received were stony faces. They all understood what they were facing.

Detective Bennie Washington broke the silence. A former college running back, Detective Washington weighed every bit of 235 and even the growing roll around his middle looked hard. He had a leathery dark brown complexion with gray hair peeking through a tight buzz cut. He was a man other men deferred to in part because of his bulk but also because his voice betrayed an edge of controlled menace.

"Sheriff, all of us been working day and night on this case along with all the other detectives who got pulled from anywhere we could find 'em. We looked at the background of each of these women." He threw his pen down on the notepad in front of him. "So far, the only thing we can come up with for certain is that each of them either opened the door for this guy, or they stopped for this guy, or he met them someplace. The obvious thing is that the two women who were at home either knew this guy or they had no reason to be afraid of him. Now that don't make a lot of sense that they had no reason to be afraid of him unless for one thing."

Washington looked around the room before adding what they had already whispered to one another. "Another thing, Mover, we can't figure out why that other gal, Ventana, and now this Elizabeth Garrett, would have stopped for somebody at night unless they recognized his car or—well, if they thought he was a cop. Same with the women who opened their apartment doors."

Sheriff Bekin closed his eyes. Washington added, "Sheriff, something about how this guy talked or how he looked made those women feel safe. We're thinking maybe this guy is either dressed like a cop or maybe he even *is* a cop."

The other sheriff's detective at the table, Thomas "T. J." Longworthy, wasn't known as somebody who talked a lot. An Oklahoma boy, he wasn't an intimidating man to look at, but whenever he worked on a case, he was known to be like a dog with a bone. He wouldn't let go and he didn't give up. Now he spoke up in a slow drawl. "Sheriff, this Maria Ventana, she gets described the same way by everyone who knew her. She was bright and well-liked, and cautious. Sounds just like Garrett.

"But one thing that stands out. Both Johnson and Symes lived alone. Ventana had a live-in boyfriend and Garrett still lived with her parents so it makes sense that this clown wouldn't have gone to their homes because there might have been somebody there. That means he must have known enough about them to be aware of that, and second, he was either waiting for them to drive by or he followed them, so it just isn't likely he picked any of them at random. The best guess is that for some reason they all had to have come across him in some way. But what it is that links each of them to him, that's the key and that's what we haven't been able to figure out."

Mover's body slowly turned until his eyes focused on Ernie Garcia. The voluble Mexican American had developed a reputation as a careful investigator who traveled easily between the Mexican-American community and the non-Hispanic community. As usual Ernie had remained silent, listening intently before forming an opinion. "Ernie?" Mover recognized from experience that Ernie's perceptions were always worth hearing.

Ernie slid back his chair and crossed his arms against his chest. "Well, we know that all three women were injected with the same kind of drug combination. We know that combination is on the street because it's been seized from a number of drug dealers and a few junkies. So one question is where did the drugs come from?"

Picking up the thread, Puccinelli added, "Find the source and maybe we find the buyer?"

Ernie nodded. "Maybe there's something specific about the drug mix. Maybe somebody's been buying this stuff who is isn't your usual junkie." He scanned the men around the table, then continued. "Next, I don't think a black man did this. The pattern doesn't fit for me, and the African-

American hair on the bodies is too obvious. The hairs were right there where we couldn't miss them and the rest of the bodies were clean, so I agree the hair is just to screw with us." He looked around the table. All heads were nodding.

"Third, if it's a cop, then he could be shaking down junkies. You know, he makes a stop and takes their drugs. Maybe tells them he's going to let them go this time but they owe him a tip or something."

Washington put the period on Ernie's methodical analysis. "Fucking junkies would wet their pants thinking he did them a favor even when they'd want to spit on him for taking their dope. But then, he doesn't dump the drugs or turn them in. I don't think a cop would be making buys around here, but I guess it's possible, and no junkie's going to use his drugs to kill some woman. Our guy isn't an addict. Whoever did this maybe isn't a bottom-feeder, but he knows where they swim. We need to find out real quiet whether a cop's been seizing drugs without making an arrest. Some of these guys might know."

Mover shrugged and shook his head. His voice came out in a growl. "I don't think this is a cop but if it is . . ."

The sheriff's voice trailed off before he took a long look at the men seated around the table. "If this asshole is a cop then we need to take him down, and I don't care what you have to do. Just do it." His voice raised, he continued, "Ask our people which dealers they think may be putting this shit on the street and maybe we can narrow down where the perp got it. Then we go to those dealers and tell them we just want to know if they've heard of anybody unusual buying this drug or if they've heard any rumors about somebody shaking people down for drugs. Have them ask around. Pull in all the markers on our snitches, anything we can get."

Mover hesitated, weighing the possibilities. "We need to check the evidence locker for drugs that've been booked in. Make sure it's all there. Maybe somebody's taking this shit out of evidence bags and using it. If this is a cop . . ." He shook his body from side to side. "Fuck." He spit the expletive out of his mouth like a gunshot.

Mover slowly inhaled before he spoke again, making a sound like a sucking vacuum. "When you squeeze the dealers, don't be gentle. I don't give a shit whether they admit what they do and we can't use it. Tell them we already know what they do or we wouldn't be talking to them in the first place. No Miranda rights, no nothing. Just get it out of them, and make them know that if we find out they knew something and they didn't give it to us we'll fuck them over every time they walk out their door from now until they got six feet of dirt over their faces."

Everyone around the table remained silent. Jamison was aware that each of them knew the gravity of the situation and understood what the rules were—there were no rules.

Swiveling his chair, Mover turned back to Ernie. "Any other thoughts?"

"Well, if this guy's a cop," Ernie replied, "he either showed up in a uniform or flashed a badge. If he stopped the cars, then he had to have a red light or something that made them think he was a cop. But that assumes they thought he was a cop. Doesn't have to be a cop. Maybe they all knew him and either let him in because he was familiar to them or they recognized his car?" Ernie paused, his hand absently sliding the photographs around.

"We need to check all the sheriff's logs to see if any patrol units were in the vicinity at the time these women got snatched."

O'Hara interrupted. "Enough with the speculation." His voice was rough with frustration. "We're down to hours if we want to find Garrett alive. Tomorrow we could be tripping over another body. Why don't we go over our background check again on every one of these women, where they went to school, to church, work, gym, all of it? Maybe there's something we missed, some crossover between them. Matt Jamison and I will work the Garrett case with Pooch."

O'Hara was giving Jamison a rope to pull himself into the case if that's what he wanted, but Jamison realized that if the Garrett case was blown, he could wrap that rope around his neck. At the press conference when the tough questions were asked, everybody would be looking at him.

But O'Hara was right. Jamison nodded. He was in.

The sheriff shoved his chair back, slowly raised his bulk up, and placed his hands on the table. "Pooch, you divide these cases up, get the background checks on the three dead women we got and look to see if there's anything that may be a common factor. Hell, maybe they all had traffic tickets from the same cop. Maybe they shop at the same damn store. Whatever. Get any other detectives you need to help."

Mover gave a forced smile that looked more like a grimace from acid indigestion. He couldn't keep the smirk off his face. Jamison could feel the temperature drop as he realized that Mover was setting him up.

Mover raised his voice, and pushed a thick finger in Puccinelli's direction. "I want you to handle the Garrett background personally and take O'Hara and the DA over there with you. I don't need to tell you what's going to happen if we don't find that girl before midnight."

Mover then snapped his finger in Jamison's direction. "And *you* tell *your* boss that if this all turns to shit and that girl turns up dead, then one of you better be standing next to me at the press conference after we find that body."

Chapter 9

As they walked slowly back to the district attorney's office, Jamison waited for either O'Hara or Garcia to say something, but neither of them said a word. Finally he blurted out, "Was there some reason you decided that it would be a good idea for us to help do the background on Garrett? I mean, she's the only one who may still be alive and now if something happens to her Bekin's going to punt and say the DA's men were on that case."

"*Boss*"—Jamison rolled his eyes because of the inflection—"we figure out what happened to Garrett and we'll have proven that we belong right next to the sheriff's people when there's a major investigation."

Jamison snorted derisively. "Yeah, and if we don't find her, then who's going to take the fall?"

Ernie stopped walking. "Garrett—Garrett's going to take the fall."

That stopped Jamison and O'Hara in their tracks. He was right. Credit or blame weren't an issue here. O'Hara simply nodded. Jamison felt his face redden. As usual, Ernie had little to say but when he did his words resonated.

Minutes later Pooch joined them and they sat in Jamison's office, sifting through a stack of sheriff's reports. They had been through them before, but looked again knowing sometimes your eyes missed something. Not this time; they discovered nothing new that caught anybody's attention. O'Hara read from one of the reports that two of the victims had received traffic tickets in the last year, but they were from different cops. The others had no traffic records, so he continued, "They all went to different high schools. Symes and Ventana graduated the same year as Garrett. Johnson was a year behind them. All of them went to Tenaya State University at the same time. Maybe they met one another there?"

Jamison bit down on his pen before pulling it out of his mouth. They didn't have time to waste on unlikely possibilities. The minutes on Elizabeth Garrett's life could be literally ticking down. They had to pick something with real potential. He laid the pen down on his legal pad. They had to start somewhere.

As he listened to the seasoned detectives, Jamison felt some reassurance. At least his instincts were in sync with theirs. "The girlfriend. What do we know about her?" Flipping his notebook open, Pooch ruffled through several pages before stopping. "She didn't have much to give me when I talked to her. She said they had dinner at the Packing Shed Restaurant. Apparently Garrett suddenly changed her mind about spending the night with Ewing and she was going home to get some sleep."

Jamison was familiar with the restaurant. "Where her car was found seems out of the way if she was driving home from the Packing Shed."

"Maybe she got lost, missed her turn after a few drinks in her," O'Hara suggested. "Who knows? She didn't call her parents and tell them her plans had changed and that she was coming home but it was late and maybe she didn't want to wake them. Anyway, let's get Ewing where we can talk to her again. Women share things with girlfriends that they don't share with parents. Maybe she knows something that we haven't heard. We'll talk to her parents after we talk to her."

They glanced discretely at their watches, the metronome cadence of the mental countdown ticking inside their heads.

Elizabeth Garrett was staring at the man sitting at the edge of the bed. The throbbing, dull headache reverberated inside her head, bouncing back and forth across her skull like a thudding tennis ball. Her throat burned from last night when she woke up to blackness and screamed. He reached for her hand as she pulled back, sitting up straighter on the bed. She could feel her entire body convulse as he leaned over her. The only sounds she heard were her rapid breathing and inside her head the sound of her own heartbeat.

Cheryl Ewing sat in the district attorney's office. She seemed nervous to Jamison, as she looked around at the beige walls of the room used to talk to witnesses. It wasn't set up like an interrogation room; the chairs were more comfortable and the atmosphere wasn't designed to intimidate. Pooch had gone to the Packing Shed Restaurant in hopes of picking up some information while the other three questioned Ewing. He had called O'Hara to report that he was still digging but while the bartender remembered the women, nobody had seen anything unusual. He would head back as soon as he talked to one more waitress.

They tried not to do anything to make Ewing any more nervous. Before they had even started she was twisting her hands back and forth, rubbing them and looking at the floor, then the table, anywhere but directly at them. An attractive brunette with dark brown eyes, Ewing worked as a personal shopper for Macy's. Based on conversations with Pooch, they quickly established that she had been Elizabeth Garrett's senior year roommate. It was likely that she would know more about Elizabeth's private life than either of her parents.

Jamison chose to watch while O'Hara led the questioning. He didn't have a feel for Ewing yet. Besides, he wasn't that much older than her and age often added a little more authority, especially when an older person was talking to a younger person.

O'Hara quickly moved through the preliminaries, keeping the tape recorder to the side where it would be as unobtrusive as possible. Not only did a tape recorder make people nervous, it distracted them and O'Hara had no time to waste.

"Cheryl? May I call you Cheryl?" O'Hara kept his voice low and smooth. Talking to women required special skills. O'Hara had explained to Jamison that with women you needed to be a bit more oblique in your approach than with men. Over the years he had found that with a man you could move right to the point, but with women they only got to the point when they were ready; pressing them only made it more difficult to get where you wanted to go. "Just like in marriage," O'Hara always laughed.

"Cheryl is fine," she replied. "So like I told Detective Puccinelli, we were going to spend the night at my place. Beth said she didn't have to be at school at eight in the morning that day. They had, you know, like some kind of teacher meeting or training thing and she said she had a substitute. So we thought it would be okay to maybe do more than we usually would on a work night, you know? But then she said she was fighting a cold and decided to go home. That's it. Believe me, I wish I could tell you more." Her eyes began to fill up with tears.

O'Hara kept his voice soft, sympathetic. "I understand, but maybe there's something that you don't realize is important. What's Beth like personally? Parents often have one view of their children even when they're adults, and when kids get away from their parents they sometimes behave entirely differently. Did Elizabeth have a lot of boyfriends? What kind of men was she attracted to?"

Cheryl reddened slightly. "Are you like asking me if Beth had a wild side? I mean, sure we went to a lot of college parties together, but she was pretty careful about guys."

"Careful in what way?" Ernie asked.

Cheryl's discomfort was noticeable. "I mean she could be pretty reserved and it took a long time before she ever talked about really personal things."

O'Hara caught her hesitation. "Personal things? You mean about relationships or more than that?"

"There are things Beth told me I don't know if she shared with anyone else, including her parents, you know? But they happened years ago . . ." Her voice trailed off.

Leaning in closer, O'Hara tried to create a sense of a private conversation. "Look, Cheryl. I—we appreciate your loyalty and your respect for Beth's privacy but we need to know everything we can about her, and we don't know what may turn out to be important. Do you understand? We need to find her."

Ewing became more emotional as the reality of the situation overwhelmed her. "Something happened to Beth a long time ago, before we met. I think she was maybe only fifteen or sixteen." Cheryl looked around at the room and the investigators.

O'Hara's voice took on a soothing tone, almost like a therapist trying to create deep trust before drawing out some buried secret. "What did Beth tell you?"

"All I know is about maybe a month ago she seemed very agitated all day. Eventually she said she had seen some guy that day who she thought was out of her life. She wouldn't tell me his name, but she told me that when she was sixteen or seventeen she started to meet him secretly. I think he was a little older. Apparently it lasted about a year, maybe more."

Ewing paused, taking a sip from the glass of water Ernie had brought to the table. Her voice had begun to tremble.

"She wouldn't say very much, just that the whole relationship was a mistake and she had tried to get out of it. But he kept showing up wherever she was, leaving her notes, that kind of thing, and I think she ran off with him or something? I don't know. She wasn't very clear and after a few minutes, she just shut down. Wouldn't talk about it. I don't think her parents knew about it—that he had shown up again."

O'Hara leaned back in his chair. "This guy that she saw the day you two talked, do you know if she started seeing him again or anything like that or was he possibly stalking her?"

"No, at least that wasn't my impression. Like I said, she said that they just kind of ran into one another. I guess he just showed up behind her and said hello, but I'm not sure. She was really emotional. I didn't want to ask too much. But whatever else happened, I don't think she wanted to see him ever again. For a while after that she just wanted to stay home or go out with me. It was kind of creepy, but we're friends and I tried to help. But she really didn't want to talk any more about it, and I didn't want to pry. Do you think maybe this guy did something?"

O'Hara seethed. This is what happened in investigations. Jamison knew it well. There were always disconnected bits and pieces, people who held back information, and here it was. This was as close as they had gotten all day to a potential suspect.

Jamison moved his chair closer to Ewing. "Ms. Ewing, as I told you when we were introduced, I'm Matt Jamison. I'm a lawyer, a prosecutor with the district attorney's office, and I handle cases like this. Are you certain Beth didn't give a name, not even a first name when she talked about him?"

"No, all she said was that she hadn't seen him for ten years and then one day, a couple of weeks ago, he just showed up out of nowhere while she was at the mall."

"Did she ever say she saw him again?"

"Not that I know of."

"And last night at dinner at the Packing Shed? Could he have been there?"

"It's a place where we go whenever we get together. There are a lot of people our age there. It would be hard to know—busy place. You understand."

Jamison smiled. "I've been there a few times. Anything else? Anything at all?"

Cheryl looked around the room and shook her head. "I'm really sorry. I should have tried to pull more out of her. And I should have insisted she come back with me last night." The young woman's eyes rimmed with fresh tears.

Jamison understood there wasn't much more to be gained from Ewing, and gestured toward Ernie. "Okay, I'm going to ask you to sit down with Mr. Garcia and give him the names of any guys you can remember that went out with Beth or she may have mentioned, including college. Don't worry about whether you're sure or not. Let us handle that. Okay?"

Ernie moved over with his notebook open as O'Hara and Jamison left the room and walked to Jamison's office.

O'Hara's face was a black cloud, darker than usual. "Boss, whatever happened between Garrett and this guy was a long time ago, but even so, you never know. Some of these guys . . ." O'Hara's mouth drew into a firm line.

"All right, Bill, I know there's a possibility that this guy might be back, even if it doesn't seem likely."

Jamison had handled enough sex offender cases to know that some of these men lurked around for years, obsessing about women or, worse, kids. Whatever made them tick was buried inside a twisted mind, keeping track of a woman from some shadowy netherworld, stalking her furtively for months or years. Coming after her again wasn't outside the realm of possibility. In any event, they couldn't ignore it. Anything could slink into consciousness from the dark recesses of sexual obsession.

"Bill, I say we go back to the parents and just get right to the point. We haven't got anything else. We just need to close that door. If the guy's still around we'll find him."

A sharp burst of air popped through O'Hara's tightly closed mouth. "If this woman has some asshole from her past following her, then that might mean . . . that maybe the other cases aren't connected, even though there's a similarity in the MO—I don't know. But we can work on the relationship between the cases later. Right now, we need to find this girl before we find her on the side of a road somewhere. Let's go talk to the parents."

O'Hara slid behind the wheel after walking ahead of the others to the county car, leaving Ernie and Pooch to catch up with them at the parents' house. While O'Hara drove, Jamison buried himself in the reports, not sure what he was searching for.

Maybe all four victims attending the same school had dated the same guy, but Jamison realized that since three of them were dead, it would be almost impossible in the time they had to find one person who each of them had known. But it had to be someone that Garrett knew also and they needed to concentrate on her. There was nothing they could do for the others now.

Jamison reread Puccinelli's report on his interview with Garrett's father while O'Hara turned on the country road to the Garrett home. The insistent drumbeat of reality filled Jamison's head. Elizabeth Garrett's life was balanced on their assumptions—*assuming* she was still alive and *assuming* the man who had killed Symes, Ventana, and Johnson had not decided to change his pattern. And that *assumed* whoever had taken her was the same person responsible for the other kidnaps. There was only one thing he knew for sure: there was no doubt what was going to happen if they didn't come up with something and fast.

O'Hara turned down a side street. Both Pooch and Ernie were following closely behind them. The house was at least twenty-five or thirty years old. Ranch style on two and a half acres, it was a long and single-story house, beige-colored adobe brick decorating the front, the cedar shake roof showing the edges of wear from the brutal heat of summer and the dampness of Valley winters. The yard was well maintained, grass closely clipped, bushes trimmed. The rest of it was fenced-in pasture.

A man who appeared to be in his early fifties opened the door. His eyes visibly fatigued, he looked at them warily. The gray sweater he was wearing seemed to fold seamlessly into the ashen pallor of his face.

O'Hara spoke first. "Mr. Garrett?"

His eyes fixed on the badge O'Hara held out, the man quickly replied, "I'm Ben Garrett. You want my brother, Mike." He said nothing more, simply motioned for them to follow him and led them down a short entry hall.

O'Hara knew what was coming. He had been here before too many times. The worst part was that it was never different. He already knew how Elizabeth's parents would look, just as he could envision the faces of the parents of the other victims too. Regardless of how much they had steeled themselves for the worst, there was always a flicker of hope in the parents' eyes when they saw him or another detective walk through the door. O'Hara knew that he had to keep that glimmer of hope alive until the moment when he'd walk through that door again, either with their loved one alive or with the image of death still fresh in his mind. It never got easier.

In some ways O'Hara envied Jamison. He was still a believer. When he held out hope, it was because he believed it. But O'Hara had reached that point in his life that he had to pump himself up in order to give the Garretts of the world what they needed instead of what he really felt. He didn't consider himself a cynic or a pessimist. He was, he thought, a realist. Unfortunately reality had taught him to expect the worst. O'Hara turned the corner of the hallway and put on his comfort smile.

Detective Puccinelli arrived and joined the others in a large room overlooking the backyard. The furniture was comfortable and without pretense. Two couches cornered a large coffee table scattered with partially empty mugs of coffee and the remains of pastry on two dishes. In the far end of the room were two reclining chairs facing a television that sat against a wall dotted with the photographic memories of the center of a small family. The wall held every highlight of Elizabeth Garrett's life, the small child growing through the moments that marked the passage of adolescence and signaled the woman who represented the future, the collage of the family dream.

There were several clusters of people standing or sitting in different areas and sounds of someone in a kitchen filled the room, blending with the low murmur of conversation. O'Hara led the way with the others close behind him, and a hush came over the room followed by utter silence. Ben Garrett extended his arm toward a middle-aged couple seated together on a couch. "Mike, these men are here about Elizabeth."

Mike Garrett stood up slowly. Younger than his brother, his face was roughened and creased by years in the sun, consistent with the farmer they understood him to be. His eyes were dry from lack of sleep and now they were glaring at strangers who had come crashing through the sanctity of his life. He had the set of jaw that said he preferred control, but the way his mouth twitched told O'Hara that he knew he couldn't control this. When Garrett failed as a farmer, he could accept the consequences of nature—the droughts and winds and storms. But now hard work and determination meant nothing.

Garrett stared at the tall black man walking toward him. Garrett looked at O'Hara's hands. He thought he could tell a lot by a man's hands. In O'Hara's hands there was strength. These were the hands that held his daughter's safety. He waited for a detective to speak.

Pooch had spoken to Mike Garrett earlier. He moved to the front and extended his hand. "Mr. Garrett, I'm Detective Puccinelli from the sheriff's department. We spoke early this morning?" said Puccinelli, jogging the man's memory. People receiving emotionally charged news often did not really see faces or hear much of anything after that.

There was a flicker of recognition as Elizabeth Garrett's father nodded. "Yes, we spoke." Puccinelli waited for the question, and they always asked. Garrett was no different. "Do you know anything more?"

Ann Garrett, who had remained seated, looked at him. Her eyes widened, waiting for his response to her husband's question. Pooch deflected the direct question.

"We're still investigating every lead. Right now these men would like to talk to you. This is Investigator O'Hara and Investigator Garcia from the district attorney's office and Mr. Jamison, the prosecutor in charge of—" Pooch hesitated. He didn't want to say "homicide" or "major crimes"—"The prosecutor assigned to help us with your daughter's case."

O'Hara took a deep breath as he prepared to speak.

~

Jamison remained silent and waited for O'Hara to take the lead. He had less experience dealing with families in these circumstances to know the best way, if there was one, to probe such an open emotional wound.

O'Hara took the father's hand while placing his left hand on Mike Garrett's arm. Jamison noted how this subtle gesture conveyed very real sympathy and allowed O'Hara to move inside the emotional defenses that were almost certainly present. "Mr. Garrett, perhaps we could speak to you and Mrs. Garrett privately?"

Garrett spoke softly to his wife. "Ann, let's go in the living room."

Rising slowly from the couch, she reached for her husband's extended hand. She still hadn't spoken. Only her eyes gave away that vacant stare that came with profound emotional trauma. Jamison could see the resemblance to the photographs of her daughter that lined the walls. With one major difference—in the photographs the face of her daughter radiated with the optimism of youth.

Mr. Garrett led the detectives and Jamison to the next room and then, with the uncertainty that came from using something that he had been told to be careful with, sat down next to his wife in a matching chair separated by a small table that displayed more photographs of their daughter bordered by small ornate frames.

Exhausted faces stared at Jamison, who decided the best thing to do was to edge his way slowly into the conversation.

"Mr. and Mrs. Garrett, my name is Matt Jamison. The district attorney, Mr. Gage, has assigned me, Mr. O'Hara, and Mr. Garcia to the investigation of your daughter's disappearance. As you know, " He hesitated, searching for the right words.

Jamison desperately needed to find the common connection that tied Elizabeth Garrett to the other women, but it would terrify these people if he abruptly tied their daughter's disappearance to the other victims and what had happened to them. The wail of grief from Terry Symes's mother was still ringing in his ears.

The Garrett's daughter was their only key and there was very little time to dance around feelings, but he couldn't bring himself to ignore their emotions. In these cases there was a fine line between efficiency and cruelty.

"Mr. and Mrs. Garrett, first of all I want to tell you how sorry all of us are that you and your family are going through this. We want to do everything we can to help but we don't have much time"—Jamison caught himself. "We need to get information out to all the other officers who are working on this case." The last thing he wanted to do was frighten these people by implying that he thought their daughter had only hours to live.

"Does Elizabeth have a boyfriend, anybody that she dates regularly?" O'Hara interjected, drawing their attention away from Jamison.

Mike Garrett shook his head. "Our daughter is a beautiful girl, Mr. O'Hara. She's dated a lot of young men but nobody steady. She's a teacher and lives with us. Elizabeth is trying to save up a down payment for a house. I would've helped her, but she wanted to do it herself. That's her way, always has been. If there was a young man she was seeing now, I think we'd know."

Jamison picked up the thread. "Maybe she was meeting somebody?"

Elizabeth's father shook his head. "She would have called, let us know."

The quiet voice of Ann Garrett injected itself. "She was with her friend, Cheryl—Cheryl Ewing. She said she's talked to you this morning. They had dinner together, and we didn't expect Elizabeth last night. She was going to stay at Cheryl's. She wasn't going to teach the next day—today, I guess. That's all I know."

Puccinelli cut in. "Your daughter's friend, Cheryl"—he glanced down at his notepad—"we just finished talking to her again. She said that Elizabeth left the restaurant around nine and said she was going straight home. She didn't talk about meeting anybody."

Jamison reflected to himself that sometimes young women didn't share everything with parents or even cops. But they needed to probe further and gently. The detectives began to work. O'Hara asked, "Has she had any bad breakups recently, young men who were angry about the relationship? Anything like that?"

Mrs. Garrett shook her head. "Nothing that we're aware of."

Jamison caught O'Hara looking down at his notebook. He knew O'Hara had nothing written in it. The notebook was just a prop that he used to make people feel as if he had something. People watched too many television shows about cops these days. He had learned from watching investigators that if they didn't do something people had seen on television, people would possibly think they didn't know what they were doing because they had seen an actor do it differently. Slowly Jamison had come to the same conclusion as O'Hara. Now he never watched cop shows on television; he found them infuriating.

Mrs. Garrett sat quietly. Her husband had responded to most of the questions.

O'Hara concentrated on her, addressing her directly. "Mrs. Garrett, sometimes daughters tell their mothers things that aren't shared with fathers or anyone else." He glanced at the father, who nodded with an expression of understanding.

"Is there anything that you can recall? Did Elizabeth mention anybody she was interested in that she might be seeing? I'm sure you understand that any contacts Elizabeth might have had could be important. Is there anything in Elizabeth's past—maybe when she was younger?"

Jamison caught the subtle sideways glance between the two parents. He interposed himself slowly, softly saying, "Mr. and Mrs. Garrett, sometimes you never know what's important and people often don't talk to us about things they may think won't be helpful." Jamison glanced over at O'Hara to see if he was taking the right lead. O'Hara nodded almost imperceptibly, acknowledging that they needed to give these people an opening that would minimize any hesitation on their part. Although it never made any sense to Jamison, he had learned early on that people often didn't disclose facts, either because they didn't think they were important or they were afraid of what the investigator might think. "We spoke to Cheryl and she said that when Elizabeth was about sixteen something happened. She didn't know much but she said that a young man was involved with your daughter—that she left with him for a brief period of time. We were unsure of the circumstances."

Jamison said nothing about the possibility that this man had reappeared in Elizabeth's life. There was no point in terrifying them. He would see what he got from them first.

Mike Garrett straightened in the chair; his words snapped with rising emotion. "Elizabeth was young. He was older, a man already, and we would never have allowed her to see him. He took her and thank God we found her, but after that she wouldn't talk about it. He claimed she went willingly with him. But she wouldn't have done that. I pressed charges—she was underage—but she just would not talk about it. The police treated it like the two of them ran off together. I tried to explain that she wouldn't have done that but nobody paid any attention. That was a long time ago."

Jamison kept his expression neutral as he realized the implications that whatever happened had involved the police and therefore left some record. He said nothing, certain that the detectives caught the same thing.

Ann Garrett's eyes were locked in a vacant stare as her husband's anger rose. Jamison could see the tears track across her cheeks as she silently listened.

Garrett raised his voice, and folded his arms against his chest. "I don't want anybody to think Elizabeth would just take off. She wouldn't. This isn't the same. Not the same at all . . . it was ten years ago. We don't want you to think . . ."

Jamison held up his hand, trying to slow the rush of words and emotion. "Mr. Garrett, we aren't saying it's the same situation. But what we need to know now is who this man is. We need to look at everything. Sometimes—well, like I said, you never know what might be important. You said, 'he took her'?"

Ann Garrett remained quiet as she seemed to regain her composure. Leaning forward, she turned her eyes away from her husband. Jamison sensed that she was about to say something she had never intended to disclose.

She looked over at Jamison. "Mr. Jamison? What my husband is trying to say is that when Elizabeth was fifteen she became involved with a young man who was a few years older. But at that age a few years make a big difference. It went on for at least two years before we found out. Of course we were deeply upset and wouldn't allow the relationship to continue. She told me that she had broken it off with him, told him that she couldn't see him anymore."

She reached over, taking her husband's hand. "I'm sorry, Mike." Her hands twisting the hem of her dress, her pale complexion suddenly flushed. She inhaled deeply before speaking. "Elizabeth was in her senior year in high school. We thought it was over between them, at least that's what she said. But she didn't tell us that he was still coming around, trying to restart the relationship. Then he showed up after school one day. He carried on—how much he loved her, missed her, and to please meet with him one last time.

"And so she got in his car with him and let him talk while he drove. But he just kept driving and eventually they were someplace in Los Angeles. He took her to a motel. She would only tell me that she was frightened."

Mrs. Garrett paused, her trembling hand reached for a glass of water. Her husband looked away as she continued speaking.

"Elizabeth has never told us exactly what happened except that the next day when he stopped the car at a red light, she jumped out. She ran to a house and told a woman who answered the door that she had been kidnapped. She called the Los Angeles police and we came and got her.

"After she came home she just withdrew. She wouldn't talk to us about it. She refused to see a therapist, and would not help the police either. When they arrested him, he told the police that she had gone with him willingly. They told us that without her they had no case. The charges were dropped and we haven't seen him since."

The words had come out in a rush, like a long-awaited unburdening, Jamison thought. Mike Garrett sat in stony silence, his face still turned away.

O'Hara gently addressed Ann Garrett. "What was this man's name?"

Mike Garrett spit it out. "Alex St. Claire." Suddenly he jerked his head around to face them, anger boiling over. "That was his name, the bastard. And if I ever see him again, you better get to him before I do. He ruined our daughter. She was never the same after that."

Exhausted, Mike Garrett slumped in his chair, his hands so tightly clasped together that Jamison could see the whites of his knuckles straining against the gnarled fingers.

"Alex St. Claire?" Jamison's head snapped up. He repeated the name with evident surprise in his voice that betrayed some measure of familiarity. Jamison immediately regretted his lapse.

Mike Garrett's eyes opened wide and then narrowed as his face darkened with the memory. "Do you know that name?" It was an accusation, as if Jamison had revealed some secret that betrayed his trustworthiness.

Jamison caught the slight movement of O'Hara's head, his eyes cautioning the young prosecutor, the expression on his face trying to conceal that he didn't know why Jamison abruptly reacted to the mention of the name.

For a moment, Jamison held his breath, and then he spoke, measuring his words. "I might know who that is, but I need to be sure we're talking about the same person."

He turned toward Ann Garrett, certain that she would be more likely to know the details. "Mrs. Garrett, would you happen to know anything about what happened to this St. Claire? I mean, do you know what he was studying and might be doing now or where he went to school—anything that might help us locate him?"

Ann Garrett looked up at the ceiling and then lowered her head to stare at her hands in her lap. "At the time all of that happened I remember Elizabeth said that he planned to become a doctor, that he was going to go to medical school. Elizabeth said he had taken his medical entrance exams and that he had very high scores. He was supposed to be brilliant." A rueful, bitter expression crossed her face like a shadow. "But he wasn't smart enough to stay away from a high school girl."

Her voice broke. She was on the edge of tears, her breath coming in shallow gulps of air. "I only met him once before all that happened. Mike told him to stay away from Elizabeth and we never saw him again except after what happened. We saw him at court."

Interrupting, Mike Garrett blurted out, "I remember that son of a bitch standing there with his lawyer. He looked back at me and smiled. I should have just killed him right there." Again, Ann laid her hand on her husband's arm. Mike Garrett lowered his voice. "He enjoyed seeing our pain. That's what I remember about him—he enjoyed seeing our pain."

Jamison kept his eyes fixed on the Garretts, listening carefully, looking for any sign of concealment, but he had seen none. He and the investigators needed to rush back to the office, but he wanted to get the last detail he could squeeze from them. "Mrs. Garrett, is there anything else?

Ann Garrett's eyes revealed her bitterness. "She told me he forced her. Other than that she wouldn't talk about it. She never would have gone voluntarily. She told me later that she had been seeing him without telling us, but no, there's no way she would ever have run off with him. I know my daughter. She wouldn't have done that."

Jamison nodded, thinking maybe she would and maybe she wouldn't. People were always shocked at things their children did and would insist that they would never do such a thing, until they were forced to confront reality, and even then they would rationalize. Right now he was less concerned with whether Elizabeth had a teenage wild streak that got her involved with Alex St. Claire than he was with the confluence of the man who had been present at the autopsies of the murder victims as well as a key figure in the life of a woman who was now missing under similar circumstances.

Jamison turned to the investigators to see if they had any more questions. O'Hara, Ernie, and Pooch shook their heads. "Thank you both. As soon as we know anything, we'll be in touch," he told the Garretts as he got up from his seat. "The district attorney, Mr. Gage, has said that we're to give your daughter's case the highest priority. We can find our way out."

As the four men rushed to their cars, Pooch, O'Hara, and Ernie simultaneously asked, "Alex St. who?"

"Alex St. Claire," Jamison answered. "At the start of the Ventana autopsy a doctor named Alex St. Claire walked in while it was going on and gave Dr. Gupta a little help. I didn't remember him until he introduced himself to me at the Symes autopsy. Remember, Bill? You were there. He's an anesthesiologist who also does work with the effects of anesthesia on animals. I remember that he said he was interested in the effects of heroin and barbiturates on the victims. It's too big a coincidence, St. Claire and Elizabeth Garrett! And then he shows up at the autopsies, just looking around? We need to find this guy and I mean *now*."

O'Hara sucked his mustache into his mouth, and then he suddenly cried out, "Son of a bitch," recalling St. Claire at the autopsy. "Son of a bitch! Okay, we go to the hospital and see if St. Claire's there," he continued, not waiting for Jamison to reply. "It sounds like he's our boy but we have no basis for an arrest, and if he has her we need to find out where she is before he lawyers up. Look, I don't want to tell the hospital operator that we're looking for St. Claire if he's there. They'll just tell him we're looking for him."

He turned to Pooch and Ernie. “Can you go see what records there are on this guy? We’ll head to the hospital. If St. Claire’s at the hospital we can control the situation and size him up. If he’s our man and we show up with a bunch of people he may run, and then we’ll never know where she is.” O’Hara paused before stating the alternative. “If he’s not there, then we’re going to have to find out where his snake hole is for the night and move as fast as we can if we want to find this girl alive.”

O’Hara slapped the steering wheel as he rapidly pulled out of the driveway. The car was moving well past seventy when he expressed his thoughts about St. Claire out loud. “Once an asshole, always an asshole.”

Chapter 10

Ernie and Pooch were checking for any file or arrest report on St. Claire and running a Department of Motor Vehicles check for an address. Both men had been told to keep their information to themselves because of the possibility of press leaks. The sheriff's office was like a sieve of information for reporters. For the moment they would assume that Garrett's St. Claire and Dr. Alex St. Claire were one and the same but they had to be cautious about making an accusation when they had virtually no hard evidence to back it up, and if St. Claire had taken Garrett they needed to get the location out of him. In that regard their suspect held the cards and they didn't have any read on him as to how he would react to questioning. But the circumstances had sent O'Hara's instincts into overdrive. If St. Claire was their man, then he knew the type and it wasn't going to be easy.

Dr. Gupta was in his office going over autopsy reports and dictating when Jamison and O'Hara knocked on his door. "Ah, Detective O'Hara, Mr. Jamison, what may I do for you?" Gupta smiled as he looked up at the sound of the knock on the door. "Do you have a question?"

Jamison tried to conceal his sense of urgency. "Dr. Gupta, during the Symes autopsy, I recall there was another doctor who came by, a Dr. St. Claire as I recall? Do you remember?"

Gupta put down his dictation microphone and looked up at him with a quizzical expression. "Of course. Dr. St. Claire comes by often during autopsies. I do not recall if he was there during that particular one, but I have notes. Why do you ask?"

During the drive to the hospital, Jamison had arrived at a plausible explanation least likely to arouse suspicion as to why they were asking about St. Claire. "We—I have a question about the handling of the blood samples in the Symes case and I remember he helped take them, and also I thought I might ask him a question about the effects of heroin and barbiturates."

The pathologist pursed his lips, and frowned at the slightest inference that there might be a problem with the way he handled the blood samples. "I myself signed all the blood tubes."

The challenge in Gupta's voice prompted Jamison to quickly try to avoid any kind of insult. "There isn't any problem, Dr. Gupta. We just need to make sure that everyone who was at the autopsy or handled any evidence is accounted for. You know how defense attorneys challenge everything."

Gupta nodded thoughtfully, accepting the explanation. "I have not seen Dr. St. Claire today but perhaps he is in his office. It is down the hall near the animal lab. Just turn right out my door and go down to the next hall and turn right again. You should see it."

O'Hara pressed, "And if he isn't there, would you happen to know how to find him, an address maybe or a phone number?" Jamison could see that his partner was becoming increasingly edgy. They needed to speed things along.

"I have a phone number that I have used once before, but it goes to a pager service. He called me right back, but I know it was not a home phone. So no, I have never had a reason to call his home. I do not know his home address if that is what you are asking. You should be able to get that from the main office. I do know that he does some work at his home because he has mentioned it. Is there some hurry? He should be in tomorrow."

"No hurry." Jamison shook his head. "I just like to get my questions answered as soon as they come up. Otherwise it drives me crazy. Thank you, we'll fill you in." As they were about to leave Jamison asked, "Dr. Gupta, does Dr. St. Claire have any family locally that you are aware of?"

"Dr. St. Claire does not speak about his personal life. He seems totally dedicated to his work. I know he went to medical school in England. He mentioned a fatal accident involving his parents, but it was evident that he did not wish to talk about it. As for his family, I have no knowledge about any details."

They didn't expect St. Claire to be in his office so Jamison and O'Hara weren't surprised to find it locked. Even after showing their badges to the manager of the hospital personnel office they were unable to get more than an offer to call Dr. St. Claire to get his permission to give out his personal information, unless they were willing to say it was an emergency. If Dr. St. Claire wanted his phone number and address given out, then he would have to make that decision, and not her.

The last thing O'Hara and Jamison wanted was for anyone to call St. Claire and warn him they were coming. So O'Hara nonchalantly waved his hand and said they would return the next day and see him in his lab, assuring the manager there was no urgency. As they left the hospital O'Hara called Puccinelli.

O'Hara accelerated roughly out of the parking lot, heading toward the address Pooch gave them. Pooch didn't explain how he got it except to explain that the Department of Motor Vehicles address wasn't a home address. He would meet them there. Jamison called Ernie and asked him to coordinate information and assistance if they needed it.

As he sat back in the seat, Jamison tried to put together a strategy to handle the situation from a legal perspective. He wasn't a cop and he wasn't planning to crash any doors. That kind of thing he left to the uniforms and to his investigators, O'Hara and Ernie. They had to get inside St. Claire's home and they had to do it in a way that wouldn't be messy and possibly create a hostage situation if Garrett was in there.

The possibility of St. Claire's involvement was their only real lead so they couldn't afford to make any missteps that might compromise their investigation or a future case. Jamison knew what O'Hara's reaction would be, but he asked anyway. "What about a search warrant? We go into St. Claire's house and take it apart. If Garrett isn't there at least we have him under control so he can't do anything if he has Garrett someplace else."

O'Hara chewed on his unlit cigar. "We haven't got time to get a search warrant." He looked at Jamison for a moment to make sure he was being clear. "There's no time. If we're wrong let's know it now, and if we're right, then you and the rest of the lawyers can justify it later."

Jamison didn't respond. He knew what O'Hara was getting at, that they would have to do what they had to do to get in. The girl's life was in danger and they would push the envelope to get into the house any way they could. O'Hara would do his job, and Jamison would do his, including cleaning up any legal mess.

Whether he stated it or not, he was aware that he was climbing the ladder of legal ambiguity, or maybe descending it, depending on one's perspective. He had learned that sometimes choices had to be made instantly under pressure and they weren't made with a law book in one hand and a gun in the other. They were made based on the circumstances and the potential consequences to human lives. The logic of reality and the logic of the law were not always synchronized.

The streets rushed by as O'Hara sped across town. "What about a phone number?" Jamison asked. "Was Pooch able to find anything?"

"There's a phone number to this address. I don't know how Pooch got it because he said that it wasn't listed. Probably somebody he knew at the phone company. I didn't ask."

Right. Better sometimes not to ask, Jamison thought. Law enforcement was something of a subculture of barter and exchange that traded in information and favors. Everybody kept a mental list and was expected to collect at some time and to reciprocate when needed. The only rule was that you didn't take advantage and you didn't burn your source. If there was heat, then you took it yourself.

The house was in an upper-income residential area, with large, mature trees on spacious lots. Jamison looked around to see if anybody was outside the home. This was the kind of neighborhood where their cars would attract attention very quickly. O'Hara parked down the street away from the home, right behind Puccinelli, who was waiting for them.

"What we got?" Pooch asked as he climbed in the back seat of O'Hara's car.

"Here's what," O'Hara replied. "We know there's a history between St. Claire and Garrett and we also know that according to her parents he's done something like this before. We haven't got time for a warrant so either we get in by bullshitting St. Claire or get in the hard way, straight through the door, and let the result be the justification."

Jamison's expression was impassive as O'Hara continued outlining the rest of the plan to Puccinelli. "My thinking is that I go to the door and see if he answers. I'll try to get him to talk and get some sense of his reaction." O'Hara's directions to Pooch were specific. "You go look around the side of the house and see what there is. If he has her in there maybe you can see something."

Pooch nodded, accepting the plan. But he stated his reservations. "If St. Claire's got that girl in there, I don't know how he could do it without somebody seeing something or hearing something, especially in this neighborhood. I'll look around the back, but I'm betting he isn't there."

"Understood," said O'Hara. "But we got nothing else so we go with this."

"You think we should try the phone?" Pooch asked.

There was a split-second pause. "No phone," O'Hara replied. "Unless he doesn't answer the door, then I think we try the phone."

Jamison experienced a sinking feeling that all this was taking too much time. A furtive peek at his watch told him it was already past 2 p.m. They were going around in circles that they couldn't seem to close. "You guys do what you have to do. I'll wait in the car." Jamison knew that was the best place for him to be.

As O'Hara walked up to the house, he instinctively reached behind his back to adjust the automatic he had pulled from his briefcase and pushed inside his belt at the small of his back. He wasn't overly worried about a physical confrontation but neither was he certain how this situation would develop. Because St. Claire was a doctor, unless he panicked, there was a strong chance he would use his brain first. But if St. Claire opened the door to a gun-holding O'Hara, everything could quickly go to hell.

Nobody answered his knock on the heavy front door. O'Hara waited and knocked again. The drapes and windows were closed and there was nothing to indicate anybody was home. Out of the corner of his eye he caught Puccinelli slipping down the side of the house. He knocked again. No answer. O'Hara walked across the yard and saw Puccinelli heading back to the driveway. "Anything?"

"The whole place is closed up tight. All the drapes are closed. I couldn't see anything. It doesn't look like anybody's in there, Bill."

O'Hara hurried back to his car and shook his head in response to Jamison's questioning expression. After he spoke with the dispatcher, he told Jamison, "The thing that's giving me an itch is this doesn't make any sense. This guy's a doctor but nobody really knows where he lives, and nobody seems to be able to reach him except through a medical exchange. That tells me this SOB doesn't want anybody to know where to find him. Everything's now telling me for sure that when we find him, we find her."

"Bill?" Jamison's expression showed his question before the words came out.

O'Hara knew the younger man was thinking about how much time they had left. His voice softened slightly. "Matt, in this business you do the best you can. You use your gut and your sense of smell and whatever else tells you to react; then you hang on to your ass and go. We go with what we got. Everything else will happen or not happen in a matter of minutes or seconds when the shit hits the fan."

He had been there before, and O'Hara just didn't want to be there again like those other times when he had been too late. In his gut he could feel that the too late hour might already have passed.

Pooch's car pulled next to theirs within a minute. "What now?"

They needed to put somebody on the house to watch it in case St. Claire showed up, or in case he was actually in there and tried to leave. But O'Hara didn't think either one was going to happen. Nothing about the house told him that it was used on a regular basis. They could insist that St. Claire be called through the medical exchange but that wouldn't assure a response, and then St. Claire would know that police wanted to talk to him.

"Put somebody on the house to watch it, Pooch." O'Hara pulled out, with Pooch right behind him.

They drove to the nearest convenience store two blocks away to confer on what to do next. Before leaving the car O'Hara called Ernie, filling him in and asking him to make a call to somebody whose name Jamison didn't recognize. Then O'Hara removed his little book from his coat pocket, quickly scanning through phone numbers, addresses, and notations crammed on the sides and tops of each page. When he found what he wanted he got out of the car and made another call on his cell phone. Jamison could see him speaking rapidly and gesturing while talking. Whatever he was asking it was clear by his body language that he wasn't getting it easily. Then he visibly relaxed and returned to the car.

"This is going to take a minute," he told Jamison.

As soon as his cell phone rang, O'Hara was out of the car again. Jamison could see him writing furiously in his little book while he kept the phone jammed between his ear and his shoulder. He then made another quick call and stashed the phone back in his pocket. Puccinelli was standing next to the open passenger window talking to Jamison when O'Hara returned waving a piece of paper.

"Ernie called in a marker at the power company. I just talked to his contact. We got an address for our boy and it's out in the country. He may not have to tell anybody where he is, but if you want electric lights you got to tell the power company where to put the plug."

Obviously, Ernie and O'Hara had gone through a back channel and gotten billing information that was usually confidential. Every cop knew other cops who had retired and took specialized security jobs. But contacts were maintained and information was traded freely by the underground blue fraternity that surreptitiously bypassed legal impediments they considered irritating. Jamison had a momentary flush of guilt that he was so easily willing to overlook how the information was obtained.

O'Hara slid back into the driver's seat. "Okay, we got a house and I'm betting it's going to have a lot of room around it. Ernie will meet us."

Puccinelli was right behind them as O'Hara pushed his way into traffic, popped on his blue flashing lights in the back, and turned the side red light on. It didn't mean people would pull over but most of them would get out of the way of two cars with flashing lights.

Jamison tightened his seat belt as O'Hara began taking hard corners, slowing down only enough to check for oncoming traffic. He was waiting for O'Hara to say something about backup but O'Hara stayed off the radio. He was confident of O'Hara's judgment but still felt compelled to ask, "Bill, are we going to call for backup officers?"

"Look, Boss"—O'Hara didn't take his eyes off the road, but Jamison could feel them boring through him anyway—"we don't know if that girl is with him or even if he's the guy we want. We call for backup and the press is going to be right behind them. You ramp up an assault on the house and you ramp up the possibility of somebody getting hurt, and that includes the Garrett girl. So we aren't going to do that. We can't prove he has Garrett without finding her, and we can't do that without finessing this asshole doctor out."

He stole a quick glance at Jamison and went on. "We can wait an hour for a bunch of SWAT boys to dress up in their little black ninja suits so they look good going in, which gives us one less hour if somebody else has that girl, or we try to control one man before he can turn it into a hostage situation and everything turns into a shitstorm."

Jamison was aware of O'Hara's notorious contempt for people who had to dress up before they did their job, which meant that SWAT was constantly fodder for his jibes. O'Hara was old-school. "You go in and you kick ass, period. You don't need a special uniform to do any of that." With that, O'Hara reached for another cigar.

Truth was, what O'Hara said made sense to Jamison. If Elizabeth Garrett was in there, St. Claire would keep the girl to trade, and that would allow them to regroup if indeed they had a hostage situation. With Ernie Garcia on the way that would give them three investigators with guns to handle the situation until backup arrived, but it wouldn't look like an army.

He was only window dressing, and that was fine with Jamison if it helped to lend credibility to their story that they needed information about drug interaction and Gupta had recommended St. Claire as the source.

They hadn't figured out the explanation for how they got his address, but they were counting on their appearance putting St. Claire enough off-balance that he wouldn't ask that question until after they had gotten the situation under control. Still, Jamison worried. "Bill, what happens if it turns into a shitstorm?"

O'Hara turned his face from the road momentarily to look straight at Jamison. "Then we call for backup if we have time, and if we don't have time, then we do what we have to do to make sure that girl doesn't die."

"And if we're wrong?"

"Matt, sometimes there's no right or wrong, there's just now. You make a decision and nobody's going to care about why until it's all over. They're only going to care about the consequences. There's always somebody who thinks they would have done it differently, but they never seem to be somebody who has ever actually done it at all."

O'Hara paused. "The moment you pull a trigger it's always when you have the least amount of time to think. After you pull the trigger, everybody has a lot of time to think. The difference is that you're the guy that has to pull the trigger. You'll never know if it might have turned out differently if you had only waited another second. The people who think you should have waited longer are almost always people who don't have to do the waiting."

Neither man said anything else the rest of the way.

⁂

The man turned back toward Elizabeth when her body movement rustled the bed she was lying on. He stared at the nude woman stretched on the bed before him, his eyes flat pebbles of obsidian as he took in the cream-washed smoothness of her skin and the frame of long hair he had so carefully arranged en tableau. He held a camera in his hand that he seemed to be adjusting. An empty camera tripod was standing several feet from the foot of the bed. He smiled tenderly.

"Would you like some water? You must be thirsty." He fastened the camera to the tripod. "I'll get you some water, and then we can begin. I'm almost ready now."

He reached out and slowly ran his hand up her naked thigh, the touch so light that she could only feel the transfer of heat from the tips of his finger on her cool flesh. It was the caress of a lover. He leaned down near her, sensing the tension as she stared at him. His voice a whisper. "Life is enough of a solitary journey for people like us, Elizabeth. We should be grateful our paths have crossed again."

Chapter 11

O'Hara drove past the house belonging to St. Claire according to the power company records. They needed to get a sense of what they were up against. The small wooden farmhouse had seen better years, the wooden siding in need of paint, the Valley sun having relentlessly bleached the color into a dry memory of what it had once been. It had very little around it except high grass in an unused pasture. A dark blue Lexus O'Hara recognized as registered to St. Claire stood parked near the front entry. There was a garage attached to the two-story structure. The long access driveway made it difficult to approach the house without being heard and seen. It couldn't be helped.

They regrouped a quarter mile away to decide on a plan. Ernie Garcia rolled up behind Puccinelli and joined them. Ernie pulled his stocky frame from his unmarked car, giving a quick nod to the waiting men.

Quickly formulating a strategy to approach the house, O'Hara understood it was a bad situation because they were facing so many unknowns. It could be nothing or it could be a mess. They could end up with a dead victim and everything they did would be questioned. But if they did nothing *and* ended up with a dead victim, everything they didn't do would also be questioned.

He began giving directions. Puccinelli would wait at the front of the gravel driveway where he could keep an eye on the house and block any attempt at escape as well as act as backup. Ernie would come across the pasture area from the side while O'Hara and Jamison approached from the front. O'Hara would distract St. Claire while Ernie tried to look in through a window. There was no time for a more sophisticated approach. If Garrett was alive inside this house every minute was critical.

O'Hara counted on years of experience and his gut sense to tell him what was going on with St. Claire. He could smell fear and nervousness on a man as it seeped soundlessly from his body. Watching the eyes of a man, the way he talked or moved his hands or sweated, O'Hara would know if there was something there, and in the end, O'Hara would always go with his gut.

It was risky and they all knew it. O'Hara paused and let what was unsaid sink in. He was willing to lay it on the line using all his instincts, and he was willing to accept the consequences. He wanted to see it in their faces that they were willing to go with his judgment.

His voice became very quiet as he said, "Matt, you can stay out here with Pooch or you can go with me. If you go with me, then I think you better take that gun out of your briefcase. Don't shoot yourself, and you better not shoot me in the ass if you come in behind me. And take that badge you've got next to your driver's license and put it out where it can be seen."

While Jamison was thinking that he had never learned about this kind of thing in law school, the other men were looking at him, waiting to see how he would respond.

He looked straight at O'Hara. "I'm with you, Bill."

Despite the words he had just uttered, an alarm went off in Jamison's mind like a church bell. *What part of this seems like a good idea?*

He reached in the back seat of the car and opened his briefcase; the blue-black nine-millimeter automatic gleamed dully as the opened lid let in a flash of sunlight. He pulled the weapon out, checked the safety, and pushed in the slightly ejected clip before pulling back the slide and chambering a round. He could sense the others watching him.

It had always been enough to know that he had a loaded clip but no round was chambered so he couldn't accidentally shoot himself. Now the only thing between shooting himself or somebody else was the safety on the automatic, which he again fingered to make sure it was on.

Jamison was scared, but he also knew what he was most afraid of was failing in the eyes of the three men who were with him. He sensed a sour taste rising from the back of his mouth and swallowed several times to force the bile down. The automatic felt heavy as he held it, and then he pushed it into the back of his pants. As the others walked to their cars, Jamison asked O'Hara, "Okay, Bill. What're we going to say?"

"*I'm* going to say that we need to ask him some questions about the effects of heroin and barbiturates on people and that Gupta recommended him. *You* stay in the car, in front of the house, so he can see you. He wouldn't expect a lawyer to come out here if we were going to arrest him, so you just smile when he looks out. And keep the window rolled down while I'm at the door. I'll scratch my head and you'll know I think he's got her. I'll keep talking and you wait. If all hell breaks loose, then you get on that radio."

The adrenaline was pumping through his system and Jamison could feel his heart racing. He was trying to listen to O'Hara and at the same time he felt the bulge of the automatic at the back of his pants. This wasn't at all the same as at the gun range. He had to ask. "Why do I keep the window down?"

The response was clipped. "So you won't get glass in your face if somebody shoots at you and you won't have to shoot through glass if you do need to use that gun you've kept stuck in your lawyer's briefcase." The older man softened his voice. "Matt, you're going to be just fine but remember, you *don't* have to do this. You can go with Pooch."

Trying to sound more confident than he felt, Jamison said, "I'll stay with you."

O'Hara gave a nod of acknowledgment. "Just keep your eyes on me and remember Pooch is back there and Ernie's on the side. Make sure before you do anything that you know who it is that's in front of you, and *remember*, you shoot me with that thing and you're really going to be sorry." He wasn't smiling.

~

The tires made a crunching sound on the scattered gravel covering the driveway. Neither man said a word as they rolled to a stop. As O'Hara got out he glanced back directly at Jamison. "Remember to roll down the window."

O'Hara walked rapidly to the front door, looked to see if there was a doorbell, and then knocked, quickly stepping back and to the side. He waited and then stepped up and knocked again, calling out St. Claire's name. "Dr. St. Claire? This is Bill O'Hara from the district attorney's office. Dr. Gupta said you could answer some questions we have. You here?" He started pounding again on the door. After a moment O'Hara glanced back at Jamison and made a slight head gesture to indicate that somebody was coming to the front of the house.

As he heard approaching footsteps, O'Hara stepped back from the door. His badge was hanging from the breast pocket of his coat. There was a pause as the footsteps stopped on the other side of the door. He wasn't familiar with St. Claire's voice but it was definitely a man's voice that broke the silence. "Who did you say you were?"

"Bill O'Hara from the district attorney's office. Is that you, Dr. St. Claire? Could you open the door, please? I have a deputy DA here with me and we want to ask you a few questions about the effects of certain drugs for a case we're preparing for trial. Dr. Gupta said that we should ask you because you're an expert."

There was a long silence before the person inside said anything. "See me at my office tomorrow, please. I'm busy now and I don't like to be bothered when I'm working."

O'Hara moved closer to the door. "It will only take a minute. Just a few questions." O'Hara didn't like the situation. He couldn't see St. Claire and he couldn't see what St. Claire was doing on the other side of the door. Most of all he didn't like the fact that St. Claire wouldn't open the door to talk. This was how cops got killed. O'Hara made an instinctive step to the side.

All his senses began to tingle. There was something about the tone of voice, something that sounded like a man trying to keep himself calm but barely succeeding. O'Hara had seen and heard enough men in situations where they were cornered. There was an edge to their voices that told him they were about to do something stupid.

All of O'Hara's senses told him that the stupid meter of the man on the other side of the door had gone into overdrive. He stepped away and moved his hand behind his back for his gun.

Moving quietly down the side of the house, Ernie could hear O'Hara's voice and another voice, a man's voice, but he couldn't make out what the man was saying. The curtains were drawn. He couldn't see much through the narrow gap where the curtains didn't quite close. He moved as close as he could, stepping into the remains of a forgotten flower bed, the sun-dried remnants of plants making a cracking sound that he couldn't avoid as he peered into the window.

A woman lay spread-eagle on the bed. She was completely naked. Ernie saw a camera mounted on a tripod at the foot of the bed. The woman's bare legs and the upper part of her body were just visible through the gap in the curtains. Ernie wasn't sure if it was Garrett, but he could see that her feet were tied to the corners of the bed. A thought flashed through his mind: *Who else could it be?*

He didn't hesitate. Ernie stepped back and took a running leap at the window, hoping his shoulder and the gun would smash as much glass out of the way as possible before the rest of his body came through.

In the front of the house, O'Hara's instincts were sending him electric jolts of warning. He raised his voice and edged his hand farther toward the small of his back. "Dr. St. Claire? I really need to talk to you. Open the door, please." This time he put a little more authority into his voice, hoping that perhaps St. Claire, if it *was* St. Claire, would open the door at least enough so he could see him.

Ernie went through the window headfirst, smashing the glass with his gun and forearm. He didn't feel the shards of glass left in the window frame as they cut into his back and the front of his legs and arms. He didn't hear the cracking of glass exploding inward. The momentum of his jump took him straight into the room, the crashing glass and the screaming woman all joining in a burst of noise as he hit the wood floor.

Suddenly the noise of crashing glass, and the unmistakable sound of a screaming woman reverberated throughout the house. O'Hara snapped his head to the right, and when he heard the sound of running footsteps inside the house, he hit the front door full force with his shoulder, pushing the aging wood off its hinges along with what was left of the casing around the doorframe.

Jamison opened the car door when he saw O'Hara break through the front door. He could hear the crash of glass on the side of the house and now a shrieking woman. He didn't know where O'Hara or Ernie were. He turned and grabbed at the radio mic, pushed the side switch on, and began yelling who he was. The tenor of his voice rose as he kept shouting. He had never paid attention to O'Hara before when he used the radio and now he didn't know whether he was sending or receiving. The dispatcher asked him to identify himself. Jamison kept yelling that he was District Attorney Jamison and they needed help. Whether the press overheard or not was the last thing on his mind.

He dropped the mic when he saw Puccinelli's car slide into the driveway. Pooch jumped out and moved toward the house before the car finished rocking. His gun was drawn and raised slightly in the air as he raced past Jamison still sitting in the car. The dispatcher's disembodied voice was demanding to know who was on the radio and trying to get specifics of the situation, but the mic now dangled by its cord. Jamison was out the door and running toward the house too.

Elizabeth Garrett heard the sound of glass crashing but nothing made any sense. There was yelling and the sound of people running. For an instant she thought there was a man with a gun. *He's going to kill me!* She thrashed at the restraints, trying to pull herself free but the man was pulling at her. She couldn't understand him. She could only see a gun and the blood running down his arms.

Ernie fought the momentary disorientation and scrambled to gain a sense of the room. The screams from the bed drew his attention to his right. He felt shards of glass bite into his hand as he pushed himself up from the floor. The door was open. He couldn't see anybody else, but he could hear the heavy pounding footsteps of someone running, the sound growing closer. O'Hara was yelling but Garrett's screaming mixed all the sounds into mindless noise.

Ernie quickly regained his sense of the situation. Garrett was lying on the bed, her eyes wide, screaming hysterically. He struggled to untie her feet and then reached into his pants for a pocket knife and sliced at the bindings. As soon as he cut through one of the bindings, she began kicking at him like a drowning person pulling down her rescuer. He kept telling her he was a cop and to calm down, but the more he talked the more she resisted. Finally he threw his body on top of her to hold her down while he cut her wrists free and pulled her off the bed.

He looked back at the broken window and then at the open door to the bedroom before deciding to hold her down below the bed while he adjusted his focus on the door. He yelled to O'Hara that he had her. But he didn't know if O'Hara could hear him. He also didn't know if the person running toward them from the front of the house was O'Hara or St. Claire.

~

When he heard the sound of shattering glass and screaming, St. Claire ran for the back of the house. At almost the same moment, the front door crashed behind him. He ran toward the bedroom, yelling Elizabeth's name. St. Claire looked over his shoulder and caught a glimpse of a large black man holding a gun pointed in his direction, shouting at him to stop. He was almost to the bedroom doorway when he felt a crushing blow against his back as O'Hara tackled him, and then the air went out of his lungs as he hit the floor.

While he had his knee in St. Claire's back, O'Hara pulled one arm behind St. Claire and shoved it up until he heard him scream in pain. O'Hara's voice sounded like the snarl of a rampaging animal. "Shut the fuck up or I'll break your arm."

Seeing no weapon in St. Claire's hands, O'Hara shoved the gun back in his pants and pulled at his belt, feeling for his cuffs, but nothing was there. He had either forgotten to slip them in his belt or they had dropped out in the chase. "Just lie still or you're going to hurt even worse." O'Hara pushed St. Claire's arm up a little more to make his point, noting with satisfaction that he screamed again.

"I'm a doctor. You're making a mistake! What the hell are you doing?"

O'Hara leaned down next to St. Claire's ear. "You may be a doctor, but *you're the one* who made the mistake, asshole. Now lie still." He pushed his knee harder into St. Claire's back.

~

Jamison followed Pooch through the broken front door, fumbling for the gun that was starting to fall out of his pants. He pulled it out and held it in the air, keeping his eye on Puccinelli. He heard O'Hara roaring for St. Claire to stop. Then he heard a crash and the sound of a man being hit so hard that the air coming out of him made a whooshing sound. O'Hara's voice sounded different than anything he had ever heard. There was a knife-edge to it that even scared him. He moved warily toward O'Hara. The adrenaline coursed through his body like an electric current.

When Jamison found O'Hara, he had one knee in St. Claire's back with the doctor's arm pulled behind him. Suddenly all the noises that had been almost unintelligible a moment before, began to separate. The woman was still screaming and Ernie was shouting that he had her. St. Claire was yelling to leave Garrett alone, that they didn't understand, while O'Hara kept barking at St. Claire, "Shut the fuck up or I'll break your arm."

There was a flash of chrome steel as Puccinelli grabbed St. Claire's other arm and ratcheted the handcuff. O'Hara pulled the arm down that he had pinned to St. Claire's back so that Pooch could cuff that hand, allowing O'Hara to stand up while Pooch took control.

Even a seasoned cop like O'Hara couldn't help but look startled at what he saw in the bedroom. Ernie was on the other side of the bed, his gun hand extended across the mattress and blood soaking through the shredded sleeve of his shirt, while with his other arm he struggled to hold down a thrashing, naked woman, kicking and hitting him.

Jamison's heart was racing and all at once he realized the gun was in his hand. O'Hara turned and saw him, then glanced at the gun. Jamison realized he had the gun pointed up at the ceiling with his thumb on the safety. Somehow he had hit the clip release and the clip was sticking slightly out of the butt of the automatic, which meant he wouldn't have been able to fire if he wanted to.

He brought the gun down to his side and tapped the end of the clip to push it back in, hoping that nobody noticed his gaffe. Jamison caught O'Hara shaking his head as he observed him shove the gun back inside his belt. O'Hara nodded toward the bedroom. "Maybe you can help Ernie?"

As he stepped sideways past St. Claire both Jamison's and St. Claire's eyes locked. What Jamison saw for a brief instant wasn't fear; it was a glacial disdain he would never forget. Jamison turned away and looked inside the bedroom.

Ernie was tearing the sheet off the bed to cover someone on the floor, pieces of glass scattering as he shook the spread. Jamison stepped around the bed, his footsteps grinding glass shards into the wooden floor.

Elizabeth Garrett looked up at him, her eyes focusing. She seemed to realize the men around her were there to help. Then she began to cry, a low keening sound that came from deep down inside her. Jamison knelt down to reassure her, pulling out his handkerchief and wiping at the smears of blood on her face and arms. There were other voices in the hallway. Moments later men in sheriff's uniforms filled the house.

Jamison wanted to ask her what happened, but it was evident that she was in shock. Ernie talked quietly to her while Jamison went to the bedroom doorway to keep any unnecessary people out. He looked outside the door to see what O'Hara and Pooch had done with St. Claire. He saw no one but milling sheriffs officers until emergency medical people came rushing down the hallway. O'Hara, St. Claire, and Puccinelli weren't in sight.

Twenty minutes later, Jamison stood outside the house with O'Hara and Garcia nearby. Ernie's arms were a crisscross of sliced flesh painted with antiseptic, gauze patches administered by the ambulance crew covering the deeper cuts. The forensic crew crawled over the interior and the garage like ants gleaning the last small crumbs from an abandoned picnic table. Inside the garage there was a gurney with a stainless tray top just like the one in the morgue.

The walls of the garage were covered with soundproofing. There was a bench on the side with bottles of various chemicals with names Jamison didn't recognize, but he spotted several gallons of bleach sitting on a shelf. A small refrigerator quietly purred in the corner, containing more chemicals and vials. There was nothing in St. Claire's Lexus.

With a uniformed deputy standing nearby, St. Claire sat in the back seat of Puccinelli's car, shifting slightly at the discomfort of the handcuffs that bound his wrists behind him. He stared in the direction of the knot of men who were gathered in a tight circle away from the rest of the deputies, the men who would control what would happen next to him.

As if on cue, the four men separated themselves from the commotion, gathering as men often do who have been through an adrenalin-charged moment together. Pooch pointed at the suspect in the car. "I got on the phone to the sheriff." He looked a little apologetic when he said it. "I had to call my boss." He shrugged. "So what now?"

O'Hara answered without hesitation. "We take this asshole downtown for interrogation. You put him in a room by himself first. Don't take him near any telephones or through booking. Run him straight to the interrogation room and let him sit there. Leave the cuffs on. We'll follow you."

The first rule was to get a suspect off-balance. Let him feel helpless and not in control. Let him begin to debate with himself, ebbing and flowing between bravado and fear. That took time. They would let him sit and stew while they decided who would ask the questions.

Another deputy would sit in the back seat, guarding St. Claire while Puccinelli drove straight to the sheriff's office. He pulled out just as the first television crew pulled up.

Jamison, O'Hara, and Garcia were the last to leave the house. Ernie was in the back seat. His car was being driven back to the garage by a young deputy sheriff eager to create a role for himself in the action. O'Hara drove while Jamison, coming down from the adrenaline rush, struggled to organize his mind, trying to figure out what he would tell the DA. Gage took his call right away. Jamison didn't waste any time. "We have Elizabeth Garrett and we have a suspect in custody." He kept it short but he was still having trouble controlling the rapidity of his breathing. His body hadn't flushed out the last rush of adrenaline and he could feel the nausea rising up as he began to come down from his body's natural stimulant.

Gage let the words sink in before responding. "Yeah, I got the call from the sheriff himself. Bekin let me know that his office had taken down some doctor. Is that right? You got a doctor in custody? The girl? Is she okay?"

"Yes, sir, he's a doctor and we have him in custody and yes, the girl's okay. She's pretty shaken up. But it was O'Hara and Ernie Garcia who took him down." Jamison looked at O'Hara and shrugged. "Ernie went through a window and he grabbed Garrett. She was tied to a bed. O'Hara tackled the doctor, a guy named St. Claire. Detective Puccinelli was right behind and they both cuffed him up. We've got him on the way to the sheriff's office now for interrogation, but I wanted to call you so you can call the girl's parents. I'm on my way downtown now."

"Bekin told me a little differently." Gage's voice didn't conceal his cynicism about Bekin's version.

"Yes, sir, but I'm telling you that's what happened. I'm not making any public statements. The press was starting to show up at the scene so O'Hara and I left with Ernie. Detective Puccinelli has the suspect and is transporting him to the sheriff's office. We're only minutes behind him, but I wanted to talk to you first and let you know what was going on."

Gage knew the politics of the situation. Bekin wouldn't like the district attorney's office taking credit for the bust, but it pleased Gage to know that

Bekin would have to share the credit; he would have to play ball. Any way Gage looked at it, Bekin was going to have to come up with a consolidated version. The truth would be saved for police reports and the courtroom. The sound bite was for news at six. Whoever made the first press statement would control the version that would move across the city.

The district attorney turned his attention back to Jamison. "Matt? Good job. You tell O'Hara and Garcia I said the same about them. I'll talk to you when you get to the office. There'll be a press conference but . . ." Gage paused, measuring his words carefully. "You don't have to be there for that. You have the interrogation. Call me when you get downtown."

Before he finished hanging up the phone, Gage asked his secretary to get the Garretts on the phone, and after that to call his favorite crime reporter from the paper, and maybe one or two of his favorites at the local television stations. He looked at his reflection in the broad expanse of glass that opened up the city to him and slid the knot of his tie to his throat. There was no point in worrying about how much weight television cameras added to his face. He was long past being able to hide it. Gage heard his secretary's voice as she stuck her head inside his door. "Mr. Gage, Sheriff Bekin is on the line and Mr. Garrett is holding."

"Tell Bekin I'll be with him in a moment. I'm on another call."

Jamison rode quietly for the first few miles after they left the area. He needed to pull back emotionally from the event and regain some legal detachment. Intellectually he knew he'd lost that when he rushed into the house with a gun drawn, but now it was time to be a lawyer.

There was something nagging at him that he couldn't identify until it finally dawned on him. He sucked in his breath so sharply that O'Hara's eyes were drawn off the road, sliding to the right, his eyebrow raised like a question mark. O'Hara shook his head. "Okay, Matt, what is it?"

"St. Claire kept yelling we were making a mistake."

O'Hara turned so suddenly that the car swerved. "You want to tell me what that's supposed to mean? Every asshole we arrest says we're making a mistake."

"It means I want to know exactly what we have."

O'Hara slid a fleck of wet cigar tobacco wrapper to the front of his mouth, popping his tongue against his lips, ejecting the soggy particle. He shook his head and gave Jamison a long withering look as Ernie shrugged slightly and rolled his eyes. "Do they actually teach you that shit in law school or does it just seep into you and rot your brain from the inside?"

"All I'm saying is that maybe there's something here that we aren't seeing, Bill. You think about it. These two have a history and we don't know what that history really is until we talk to her. That's all I'm saying."

Ernie was muttering under his breath that he was sure this asshole was connected to the deaths of the other women. Sensing that O'Hara was looking at him from the corner of his eye, Jamison said, "I'm just saying that we need to be sure we have all the pieces. It might be true that he did those other women, but if he did, then everything we do is going to come back at us if we don't do this right." Jamison didn't feel the need to explain that a bad search or a bad interrogation would taint any evidence they got from it, including being able to use it in those other murder cases.

His words seemed to mollify O'Hara and Ernie but he could tell they didn't share his concerns. It was best to move on.

"Ernie, when we get in, I want you to go to the hospital and keep an eye on Garrett. I need you to talk to her as soon as she calms down. Nobody else talks to her first. Understand? You get in there before any press. I need to know what happened here. Then you call me or Bill and fill us in. I've got to hear from her about what happened with St. Claire when she was younger. And I want the police reports from *that* case."

"I need to change my shirt."

Jamison shook his head. "Forget your shirt. Nobody's going to stop a cop walking into that hospital with a bloody shirt. Straight to the hospital."

Jamison turned back toward O'Hara, catching the needle on the speedometer hovering around seventy-five. "Bill, why are you driving so slowly?"

Chapter 12

Jamison and O'Hara stood in a darkened area adjacent to the interrogation room, watching St. Claire through the one-way glass. St. Claire hadn't asked for a lawyer and Jamison wasn't going to ask him if he had one. That would come soon enough but hopefully later—after they had a chance to get something out of him.

After he briefed the sheriff for the joint press conference that was now underway in front of the courthouse, Puccinelli walked in, gesturing to be filled in.

Jamison didn't care about press conferences. They were for Gage and Bekin. Right now the man he was watching was more important to him than answering reporters' questions because sooner or later he and St. Claire were going to cross paths in the most direct way possible, a courtroom.

St. Claire sat on a hard metal chair, his eyes riveted on the mirrored window behind which Jamison was standing. His face showed no fear; his body was as quiet as stone. Jamison felt rising anger as he detected on St. Claire's otherwise impassive face a slight curling of his mouth at the edges, like an observer, detached, emotionless, as if he was engaged in something about which he had absolutely no personal feeling.

Jamison wanted a piece of this man's flesh, to turn his arrogance into submission, but he knew his role was to wait. He told O'Hara and Pooch, "I'm just going to watch. You two work out how to do the questioning."

They understood what Jamison meant. One man would take the lead and the other one would follow, like a dance where anticipation and reaction dictated the ebb and flow of movement. They had done this more times than they could recall. Jamison knew they remembered the moments when they caught the whiff of a suspect's fear and resignation, when they saw the defiance begin to seep out of a man and puddle on the floor like the release of a bladder when panic took over.

Puccinelli entered the interrogation room first and silently removed the cuffs on St. Claire. It was an orchestrated entrance. A minute or two later, O'Hara followed. He was the man who had taken St. Claire down, and St. Claire would remember that it was O'Hara who hit him in the back and held him down, dominating him physically.

The session would start with O'Hara observing as Puccinelli sought to establish a rapport with St. Claire, and then O'Hara would step in like a razor slash. Good cop, bad cop. Although he could play either role, O'Hara preferred to be the hammer.

O'Hara watched St. Claire, sizing up how he was going to approach him, taking into account that smart people were almost always easier to break than stupid people. A smart person would try to think of an explanation that was exculpatory. All their lives their brains had given them an advantage but most didn't realize that not talking was the smartest thing they could do.

That was the key for O'Hara; St. Claire was definitely a smart person. Keep him talking and lying and lying and talking, and then draw the inconsistency out of him piece by piece, like an artful seduction.

But there were times when the hard steel chair held soulless suspects with twisted minds—sociopaths and psychotics—who felt no guilt or remorse. These were the people who stripped interrogators of their most effective weapon, which, with most people, was a sense of guilt. But guilt only worked if you had a conscience. Sociopaths had no conscience and psychopaths had no reality except their own.

O'Hara wasn't sure what kind of man he was looking at. He could feel his gut twisting as he watched, and the worst part about the sickening feeling in his stomach was his suspicion that St. Claire was enjoying the moment.

St. Claire shifted easily in the gray metal chair. Unlike most of the men and women who had previously sat in that same seat, he didn't look down when the detectives entered. He didn't blink rapidly. He didn't initiate any words of protest or admission. He just waited, his face a dry mask.

"Mr. St. Claire?" Puccinelli began, keeping his voice neutral.

"*Doctor* St. Claire. *I* am a physician. I take it *you* are a detective?" The words were uttered with a precision of enunciation, each syllable clipped and clear.

St. Claire had deftly put Puccinelli on the defensive. Lines were being drawn and Pooch found himself answering a question instead of being the one asking it.

"Right—I'm Detective Puccinelli and this is Investigator O'Hara."

St. Claire's mouth drew up into a subtly bemused expression. "Yes, Mr. O'Hara and I have already met. Am I under arrest?" The passive voice and the detached tone of intellectual curiosity, clinical and removed, was unmistakable, as was the contempt it carried.

"Not exactly."

St. Claire turned abruptly to O'Hara. He had quickly decided who was in charge. "Then am I free to leave?"

Puccinelli kept his voice low. "Not exactly."

"Then what—*exactly*? If I'm not under arrest, then why crash through my door and put me in handcuffs? Why am I sitting here while your colleagues stare at me through that ridiculous mirrored glass over there?"

Puccinelli picked up his notebook, flicking open his pen. "We heard a woman screaming." As soon as he said it, he realized how foolish it sounded.

"Ah, I see. You gentlemen were just driving by and you heard a woman screaming? Could it be that she was screaming because someone was crashing through the window?

"I do watch television, occasionally. Aren't you gentlemen supposed to read me my rights? I do have rights, don't I?" St. Claire leaned back and casually crossed his legs. "By the way, thank you for removing the handcuffs. I never realized how uncomfortable they were, but then I don't have the experience with them that you gentlemen have."

Sensing a brief moment of vulnerability O'Hara said, "My understanding is that you do have *some* experience." He was rewarded with a small twitch at the side of St. Claire's mouth and a flicker of irritation.

O'Hara moved closer and tried to reframe the questioning. "Dr. St. Claire? Your name is Alex?"

"My name is Alex. Are we friends now, Investigator O'Hara? What may I call you?"

O'Hara didn't rise to the bait. "Perhaps it would be better if I simply called you Doctor. Let me explain a few things here. Elizabeth Garrett disappeared sometime late yesterday evening or early this morning. She never came home. Her parents were understandably worried."

St. Claire's head tilted back against the chair, a bemused expression still planted on his face. "And I immediately came to mind?"

O'Hara managed to fight off his impulse to grab St. Claire by the throat and snapped. "You came to the mind of her parents."

"I don't think her parents ever liked me. We didn't get off to a good start. I was hoping to work on that. But, Investigator O'Hara, you didn't ask me in here to discuss old relationships or new ones, did you? Pleasant as this discussion is, if you have a question perhaps you should simply ask it?"

O'Hara responded evenly. "Before I ask any questions I think it's only fair that you get an explanation for why you're here."

St. Claire's eyes narrowed before answering. "I would prefer that you simply get to your questions and I will decide what I want to answer—if anything." One corner of his mouth curved upward in unconcealed contempt.

There was no choice. O'Hara had to bring out his Miranda card. He stared at the words he knew by heart and began to read the liturgy of the law written by men who had never smelled the sweat of an interrogation room or seen slowly drying blood framing the outline of where a victim had lain.

When O'Hara was finished, he asked St. Claire if he understood his rights. St. Claire responded, "Do I understand? It seems simple enough. Yes, I understand."

O'Hara paused before he uttered the key phrase, "Having these rights in mind, do you wish to speak to us now?"

It was like watching the inner works of a complicated timepiece as it manipulated the second hand tick by tick. "Well, perhaps an attorney would be best. What do you think, Investigator O'Hara? Do I need a lawyer?" St. Claire's head cocked slightly to the side.

"Do you?" O'Hara replied. "That's up to you. I can't give that advice but I can tell you that without you speaking to us we will never know your side, and so our conclusions will not have the benefit of any explanation you might have. We will simply have to decide what to do without knowing whether there is another side."

They were now even. St. Claire would have to decide whether to say anything more in an attempt to create ambiguity, or to accept the fact that silence might very well let the detectives draw an adverse conclusion from what they thought they knew.

St. Claire's eyes moved from O'Hara to Puccinelli before focusing again on O'Hara. "Perhaps, Investigator O'Hara, I should consider consulting with an attorney. I think you've drawn a wrong conclusion, but I don't believe anything I say will actually influence you, will it?"

"I won't know until I hear what you've got to say." O'Hara was under no obligation to repeat the question. He decided he would wait those few interminable seconds to see if he could squeeze anything further from St. Claire. It was a matter of waiting him out, and letting the silence create uncertainty.

Hundreds of men, and some women as well, had sat in that steel chair, and as amazing as it always seemed to O'Hara, most held out hope that if they said just the right thing, the detective might raise his hands, admit he had been mistaken, and throw open the door.

His face expressionless, St. Claire's head again tilted back slightly. "Elizabeth and I have what some might call a complicated relationship," he began. "She is not all that she might appear to others and certainly not to her parents. We share what might be called unusual interests. But I think that such things might not be easily understood except between the two of us."

St. Claire allowed a slight smile. "I sense, Mr. O'Hara, that when you came to my home and said you wanted to ask about the effects of certain drugs, that you were simply engaging in pretense. You believe I took Elizabeth against her will, don't you?" The blackness of St. Claire's pupils glittered like obsidian.

With the hope of getting something useful, O'Hara decided to slightly shift the conversation. "We did want to ask you about the results of our toxicology tests on the three women that have been killed over the last several weeks. You participated in the autopsy of two of them with Dr. Gupta."

"And what is it you wanted to know? Actually I was present for all three autopsies. Perhaps Dr. Gupta does not clearly recall, but it should be easily confirmed by his records. Do you really want to know what I think? Or is it that you're trying, rather obviously I might add, to learn if I had something to do with those dreadful crimes?" St. Claire's mouth locked into a thin line, slowly parting before uttering words. "Yes, Investigator O'Hara, I do know the effects of the drugs found in those women. I *am* an anesthesiologist. But I assure you there are many easier ways to kill people. If I were really inclined to do something like that, *Investigator* O'Hara, I know how to do that without anyone finding out—*if* I were so inclined."

He glanced at the mirrored glass and then settled again on O'Hara. "I think, Investigator O'Hara, that you do not have my best interests at heart. I believe I would like to speak to an attorney before saying anything further. Do you have a recommendation?"

"I don't make recommendations like that." O'Hara shot him a long level look, and then he reached behind his back for the handcuffs, grabbed St. Claire by the arm, none too gently, and pulled him up. Sliding the doctor's right arm behind his back, O'Hara snapped the cuff on the right wrist and then on the left, giving it an extra squeeze to get the last possible click of the ratchet. "Have a seat. We may be a while. Make yourself comfortable."

Chapter 13

As he squeezed the last ratcheted click out of the handcuffs on St. Claire, O'Hara's expression almost cut through the glass window of the interrogation room. Jamison knew that O'Hara didn't like to lose, and he had just lost the first round. The hunted had mocked the hunter.

The ringing of his cell phone diverted Jamison's attention.

While Jamison listened, Ernie explained that he was having problems controlling the situation at the hospital. "Her father's mad as hell, Matt. He's demanding to know if St. Claire had something to do with this, and every time St. Claire's name gets mentioned the nurses turn around. It's only a matter of time before the whispering starts and we won't be able to keep a lid on who we have in custody. Did you get anything from St. Claire?"

"Bill didn't get much. St. Claire decided he wanted a lawyer. He just screwed with us but he did say that there was a relationship between him and Garrett. What'd Garrett tell you?"

"She said that St. Claire kidnapped her at knifepoint but that she doesn't remember much. She said she thinks she was drugged. I had them draw blood but the toxicology screens are going to take a while so we aren't going to know right away. If he raped her, then she didn't know it, but I had them do a rape kit anyway. She says she woke up on the bed where I found her."

"Anything else? Anything that will tell us how he moved her?"

"She doesn't know anything more except that she thought she was being stopped by a cop, and then St. Claire showed up at her car window. It's hard to get much out of her right now with her parents hovering over her. The nurses have given her meds to calm her down, and a sedative."

"Anything about what happened between the two of them in the past?"

"I asked about that, but she started to cry. I backed off." Ernie hesitated. "Amigo, she's pretty shaken up. This wasn't the right time to ask questions about what happened between them in the past. I could be wrong but I don't give a damn whether this guy's a doctor. I think St. Claire's a sadistic son of a bitch and we need to start looking at him for those three other murders. Doctors may be smart people, but that doesn't mean they don't have a crazy switch somewhere in their brain."

As Jamison hung up, the back door to the interrogation viewing room slammed open, hitting the wall as O'Hara stormed through the doorway. Puccinelli followed closely behind. From the tight-lipped expression on Pooch's face he had already had the benefit of a tirade from O'Hara and the gist of it was still being uttered as O'Hara stormed in. "Fucking asshole. I will take him down if it's the last thing I do on earth."

It wasn't often that somebody caused O'Hara to lose control, but St. Claire had succeeded. Jamison said nothing while O'Hara vented. St. Claire may have enjoyed his game with O'Hara but he wouldn't enjoy what happened when Willie Jefferson O'Hara got pissed. Unfortunately neither would anybody else until O'Hara finished with St. Claire.

He waited for a lull in O'Hara's verbal eruption before speaking. "Bill, I got a call from Ernie. Garrett made a statement. Book St. Claire for kidnap and assault with a deadly weapon."

O'Hara calmed down enough to consider what Jamison said. "Anything else?"

"I'm not ready to go for anything else."

"He's going to make bail."

"Then he makes bail. Right now we've got to think this through."

O'Hara glared at him. "And if he runs?"

"If he runs, then we can use it against him. That may be the best thing that could happen. Book him for kidnap and assault." Jamison could feel the heat from the scowl on O'Hara's face. "We'll sort it out in the morning."

"Look, Matt, this case is beginning to smell like those three murders."

Jamison shook his head. "Maybe. After talking to Ernie, I think we need to be careful."

"What did Ernie say?"

"Garrett said St. Claire kidnapped her."

"But something's bothering you. Is that it?" The scowl on O'Hara's face deepened.

"I don't know. There's something, a feeling. I don't know. This guy isn't your run-of-the mill perp. We need to be careful. I'm sensing that he did the other murders, but maybe we're missing something. Until we know, we play it out the way it looks."

"So you're going to make a charging decision based on a feeling?"

"Why not? I make decisions all the time based on *your* feelings. This guy has a history with Garrett but she hasn't given it up yet, particularly with her parents hanging all over her. We're going to have to know what that history exactly is because we're going to hear it when I try this case. As for the other cases, we're going to need some breaks before we can up the charges."

O'Hara sucked in enough air to make his chest noticeably expand. "Okay, Boss. Your call. *You're* the lawyer."

Jamison understood there was a big difference between the investigators' job and his. His investigators were untroubled by uncertainty. To arrest, they just needed a suspicion. To charge, he needed proof. It was the difference between the sound of ratcheting handcuffs and the sound of a judge's gavel hitting the bench.

"We'll sort it out in the morning. We'll let her rest, and then tomorrow we talk to Elizabeth Garrett."

Chapter 14

It had been a long night, first going over every scrap of what they had, and then writing reports. They had to get something to eat and stopped at a local hofbrau to grab a sandwich and a beer. One beer turned into several and it was after midnight by the time O'Hara dropped Jamison off at his apartment. He was drained. The exhilaration of the entry into the house had given way to the exhaustion of his adrenaline-soaked body crashing.

In the morning when Jamison arrived at the office, the front desk receptionist told him that the district attorney wanted to see him. As he walked down the hall other deputy DA's walked out of their offices. Some shook his hand. Others applauded as he passed by, others commenting on his picture in the paper. He hadn't seen the newspapers, but obviously they had.

He stopped by his office to see what had piled up. A copy of the newspaper was lying on his desk with pictures of the house and a photo of him from a previous case. Unnamed sources had described the rescue of Elizabeth Garrett and included him as one of the men who had crashed into the house with guns drawn. He didn't feel heroic. Ernie and O'Hara were the heroes as he told everyone. But he had been there, and he accepted the acknowledgment from his peers and the respect that showed in their eyes.

District Attorney Gage congratulated him on the rescue and quickly moved to the issue of the investigation of the murders.

Jamison told him they were still digging and they still had problems tying all four cases together with St. Claire, but only a few on the inside were aware of this. Gage understood the difficulties, but reminded Jamison the cases were front-page news.

He left Gage's office with the district attorney's words hanging in the air. They needed to charge St. Claire and they needed to resolve the murders. Another clock had started ticking. Gage needed an answer for the press and Bekin was pushing for murder charges.

The rest of Gage's words were just noise. The district attorney would handle the press conference to announce the charges, but later if the charges had to be dropped or modified, Jamison knew he'd be the one facing the cameras and the questions all alone.

Jamison was feeling the bind he was in. He had to file formal charges within twenty-four hours and those charges would determine whether he could justify the million-dollar bail he had demanded or if he could ask for a no-bail order. But the only way to get that would be to charge St. Claire with capital murder.

He rubbed his eyes as he stared at the rough draft of the charging papers. He knew what everyone was thinking, O'Hara, Ernie, Gage, and Bekin. He was thinking it too. There were striking similarities between the other three murders, but the evidence wasn't there yet. All they had was a whiff, but suspicion wasn't proof.

After he finished his report, Ernie stopped by Jamison's office. Jamison could see that he wasn't moving quickly. Crashing through a window was for young men, and Ernie was well past being able to simply stretch out the soreness of hard physical action. Jamison accepted the stapled report that Ernie had handwritten for a secretary to transcribe—the typed version would come later. It was clear from Ernie's face something was irritating him.

Ernie got right to the point. "Okay, so I think St. Claire did those three women. *Do you?*"

From the intensity of Ernie's voice Jamison knew that he needed to come up with an answer that would satisfy him. "If you're asking me whether I think he did those women, then my answer is that I strongly suspect he did. If you're asking me whether we can prove he did them, then my answer at this point is no."

Ernie nodded, as Jamison continued. "Bring me something. Proving St. Claire killed those three girls will require that we prove that he kidnapped Garrett. We need this case in order to make those cases." Jamison stabbed his pencil into his tablet to emphasize the point. "Yesterday you said you thought maybe she was holding back. You still think that?"

Ernie rubbed the back of his neck. "I don't know. Maybe it's the way she talks about this guy. It's . . . it's hard to put my finger on it, but you know how some women who know their attacker will say 'he did this and he did that'? She kept calling him Alex."

"That's it? She kept calling him Alex?"

"That's not everything." Ernie shrugged. "Yesterday you said we needed to have the whole story and I know I chewed on your ass about it, but there *is something* more there. I just know it. I believe that he kidnapped her. And I think St. Claire would have killed her, just like he killed those three women." He looked expectantly at Jamison, waiting for some kind of affirmation.

Jamison chewed on his pencil. A woman's demeanor when talking to the police wasn't necessarily indicative of what happened. Not all women were hysterical. Some were very calm while others could hardly talk. But very quickly in his career he had learned to trust the hunches and instincts of experienced cops. Even if they had only an undefinable sense that something was troubling them, he had learned to respect it.

O'Hara lumbered into the office, sat in the chair next to Ernie, and slid his long legs out in front of him. "Okay, Boss, Pooch is walking the paperwork over from the sheriff's office and rumor has it that the sheriff told him to ask for murder charges. So what're you going to do?"

Jamison shifted uneasily in his chair, pulling a legal tablet directly in front of him and unconsciously putting a number one at the top. "We have enough to charge assault with a deadly weapon and kidnap. Maybe we can add attempted rape, but right now we don't have anything but suspicion about murder. We could charge it but a lot is going to have to come together before we can make murder charges stick. Ernie says he thinks she's holding something back about St. Claire but he isn't sure what. Just a feeling . . ."

Finishing the sentence for him, O'Hara interjected, "Either way it leaves a hole in her story that McGuiness is going to drive a truck through." O'Hara watched for Jamison's reaction. He didn't have to wait long.

"Tom McGuiness?" The lead on Jamison's pencil broke as he pushed it down into the tablet.

McGuiness won a lot of criminal cases and every prosecutor knew that if a defendant had money and was guilty, he hired McGuiness, although McGuiness would say all his clients were innocent. At least that's what he would maintain after he got his retainer—in cash of course. And that was what he would say when the cameras were rolling.

But it was the expression on his face when he turned away from the cameras that irritated Jamison the most, that sly smile—like someone bet his rent check in a poker game, and then McGuiness watched the person fold when he couldn't make the raise.

O'Hara watched the play of emotion on Jamison's face. "My friend Frankie Lara at the jail called to tell me that St. Claire had a visit from McGuiness and that McGuiness told the jail sergeant there would be no further questioning of his client without his being notified. So what's the plan?"

Jamison looked down at his legal tablet with only the number one written on it and nothing more. "We have to talk to Garrett, and we have to know about her relationship with St. Claire—all of it, from day one. As for murder charges, it's way too soon for that, and if the sheriff's office pushes for that, I'll tell Bekin to come up with the evidence. We haven't even found the link between St. Claire and these other women and, well, there's something about this guy—I was watching him. He's like a block of ice."

From the expression on his investigators' faces Jamison could tell that he was pulling on a scab. It couldn't be helped. "First we make the Garrett case."

O'Hara leaned forward. "This asshole is our guy. I can feel it."

"Bill, maybe you can feel it, but I have to prove it. Right now the Garrett case is full of cracks and even a third-rate defense attorney could find them, let alone a shark like Tom McGuiness."

O'Hara leaned forward and waved his hand slowly in the air for emphasis like a karate chop. "Listen to me, Boss. I *will* get the evidence."

Jamison squirmed at O'Hara's promise to get the evidence as O'Hara pressed ahead. "Charge him with the murders, Matt. Puccinelli is bringing over those charges and I can tell you right now Sheriff Bekin is on Pooch's ass to force our hand on this. Either we charge St. Claire or Mover Bekin is going to be holding a press conference and the district attorney down the hall is going to be looking for you. You and I both know if you want to make a pig squeal you have to pull on his tail first."

Jamison knew O'Hara had a point. Even a defense attorney who thought he had a good case was smart enough to know there's always a chance he could lose. And at this point, McGuiness had the advantage of knowing what they didn't know about his client. If they raised the stakes, even a little, they might draw a reaction from McGuiness that would tell them he knew something about his client that concerned him. That might make the defense attorney want to make a deal before the prosecution figured out what they hadn't yet found.

He thought about it. He could add attempted rape to the charges but not murder. There was enough evidence from the circumstances to imply rape as a motive and it was the kind of charge that would make McGuiness squirm when they turned on the cameras. It was difficult to claim consent when the woman was found tied to a bed. But Jamison calculated that when the press asked him the inevitable question if there was any link to the other murders, he would simply say that he was not prepared to comment. It was a perfectly ethical response but the unspoken inference would send out big ripples when it hit.

So that was the game. The law trumped feelings, common sense, and even the most experienced gut. Jamison's emphatic tone didn't leave any room for misinterpretation. "I'll NCF any request for murder charges if Puccinelli brings them over. You might let him know that before he walks in my door." NCF meant no charges filed and it would be stamped in big red letters across the charging request.

O'Hara kept his eyes level on the younger man. "As long as I know you think he killed those three women and you're only holding back on the murder charges at this point because of some lawyer bullshit, then you and I are on the same page."

"Yeah, well that lawyer bullshit is called proof. You get that for me, Bill, you and Ernie, and I'll take a murder charge to the wall. You know that." Jamison noted both investigators were waiting expectantly for him to decide how to proceed. "Okay. Let's go talk to Garrett, and then we come back and meet with the rest of the team and see what we got."

Jamison blew out a long sigh.

Chapter 15

It was still early in the morning, hours before visitors were allowed. The halls were strangely quiet except for the hum of a machine a janitor was using to wax the floors. The three men walked toward the nursing station and saw that somebody had ordered a uniformed officer to be seated outside the door to room 412.

Jamison stood at the nursing station desk and held out his badge. The nurse on duty studied it carefully before saying, "We let her family come in before visiting hours, and her mother's in with her. The father's down in the cafeteria." Jamison thanked her and led the way.

Ann Garrett was seated by the side of the bed, holding her daughter's hand. As they drew closer, she looked up and offered a weak smile of recognition.

Jamison cleared his throat. "Mrs. Garrett, do you remember me, Matt Jamison from the district attorney's office? I think you know Ernie here and remember Bill O'Hara."

He calculated that her family would be most cooperative with the man who had crashed through a window to save their daughter. He could tell that he was right by Ann Garrett's grateful smile when Ernie extended his hand in greeting.

Jamison then directed his gaze to the young woman sitting up in bed, pillows piled behind her. A small gauze covering was taped to the left side of Elizabeth Garrett's neck, more bandages and blood-flecked nicks covered parts of her left arm. The thing that struck him immediately was how much she resembled Ventana, Johnson, and Symes, something that hadn't been as clear in the frantic minutes of the day before. Her hair framed her face, long light brown strands falling in waves. Something about the way she looked at him immediately distracted him, and instinctively he filled the unsettling moment with a rush of words. "Ms. Garrett, my name is Matt Jamison. I'm a deputy district attorney. You know Ernie and perhaps remember Bill O'Hara. They're both investigators working with me."

Both investigators nodded their heads and smiled.

"I'm sure you must be tired but I need to talk to you if I can. I'd like to go over a few things." He turned to Mrs. Garrett. "We should do that in private if you don't mind. I'm sorry, Mrs. Garrett, but we really need to talk to your daughter alone for a few minutes."

Ann Garrett bent over to kiss her daughter's cheek before rising to leave the room. Her eyes never left Elizabeth's.

Elizabeth grabbed at her mother's hand. "It will be all right, Mom. Don't worry about me."

Jamison paused a moment before speaking. "Ms. Garrett, we realize you've been through an unimaginable ordeal but I have some important decisions to make. Sometimes it's easier to talk about what happened with us than it is to talk with your family and friends present."

She said nothing at first, slowly smoothing the blanket in front of her while fixing her eyes steadily on Jamison. "I understand," she began softly. "I've told Detective Garcia what I remember. I haven't talked to anyone else. My dad wanted to know what happened, and I even told him that I wasn't ready to talk about it."

Jamison kept silent, trying to decide where to begin. "We found your car near the cemetery. Why was it there?"

Her eyes filled with tears. She began breathing more rapidly and Jamison assumed she was reliving the moment in her mind. He needed to be careful to keep her from breaking down. After a violent encounter, some women did, but either way, the retelling of their story was always emotional and painful.

Elizabeth continued slowly, with deliberation, explaining that she had been adjusting the radio and missed her turn, ending up on the road near the cemeteries. She had stopped because of flashing headlights from a car as it came up behind her. Elizabeth vaguely remembered a red light that made her think it was a police car but couldn't describe the vehicle any better because of how dark the area was. By the time he got to the car it was too late. "I couldn't see his face at first. He kept moving the knife back and forth in front of me." She turned her head and closed her eyes.

"I could hardly breathe. When I saw the knife I realized he wasn't a policeman but when I heard his voice I knew it was Alex."

"What did he say?"

"He said, 'Remember me?' It was his voice. There was something in his voice that almost didn't sound human." She pulled the blanket close to her face as if to hide from the memory. "He was so close to the door and there weren't any lights. I didn't need to see his face to know it was Alex. He put the knife against my neck and I could feel it pressing into my skin." She began to cry, touching the side of her neck and pressing against the bandage.

Jamison waited, reaching for a tissue by the side of the bed and handing it to her. "May I call you Elizabeth? It might make it easier if we were less formal. I'm Matt."

She squeezed the tissue but didn't put it against her face. "Beth. My friends call me Beth."

Jamison concentrated intently on her reactions. "I know it's hard to talk to strangers about things like this, Beth, but . . ." Jamison hesitated, trying to frame the question as gently as he could. "Were you sexually assaulted?"

She studied Jamison for a few seconds before answering. Her voice was flat and emotionless. "I don't think Alex raped me but I was unconscious most of the time. I felt like I was drugged. I really don't remember much. He touched my face. I don't remember anything else until I woke up in a dark room. It was completely black. I only remember bits and pieces. I really only remember waking up on the bed and then Detective Garcia coming through the window, all the glass flying and the shouting."

When she said "Alex" there was something that Jamison couldn't quite identify about her tone. The way she said it seemed out of place with the circumstances. He decided he needed to know now.

"Beth, we understand you knew Alex St. Claire before this happened." He said it as a statement of fact. "Something happened between the two of you years ago when you were in high school. We need to know about that."

She seemed momentarily startled at the mention of their awareness of the previous relationship. Beth turned her face toward the window as she answered, her words a whisper. "Yes, I knew Alex when I was in high school. He was in college."

She turned back, looking closely at Jamison before the words spilled out of her in a torrent. "It was stupid and foolish of me but I was so young then. He was handsome and brilliant, and he wanted to be with me. I was flattered and vulnerable. I knew my parents wouldn't approve. When they found out, that was the end of it.

"Then months later he asked to meet with me one more time. I agreed, and then he forced me to get in the car and go with him to Los Angeles. I didn't want to go," she said, turning her face back toward the window.

Jamison waited for more but she was silent. The almost sterile description of the relationship was in sharp contrast to the tears seeping from the corners of her eyes.

There was obviously more, a lot more, but she wasn't elaborating and he wasn't ready to press her for the details of the relationship. "Why didn't you cooperate with the authorities when he was arrested for what happened in Los Angeles?"

She stared at Jamison for several seconds. Her voice was as soft as a baby's breath. "I was in high school and thought I was in love. I had slept with him willingly before we broke up. If charges were pressed, it would have all come out. My parents wouldn't have understood." She was pleading with him. "You have to understand. In some ways I felt like it was my fault too. I never saw him again after the charges were dropped."

Beth's eyes searched his face, entreating him for understanding. Jamison nodded. Maybe that was what Ernie had noticed. Jamison didn't know, but it didn't matter. "Thank you, Beth." He knew she was waiting for him to say the words all rape victims want to hear. Her head settled back against the pillow as he said them. "I believe you."

It was what she needed. "We'll be over to see you again after you get out of the hospital. St. Claire has a lawyer and I'm sure he's going to have an investigator come by to talk to you. Whether you want to talk to him or not is up to you, but you need to remember that whatever you say is going to be recorded or written down. You don't have to talk to anybody if you don't want to."

As he stood back from the hospital bed, preparing to leave, she was watching him carefully as if trying to measure her words. "I don't intend to talk to anybody except you and your investigators," she finally said. Then she turned toward Ernie. "Thank you isn't enough. I'm not sure what else I can say. Thank you."

Once they were outside the hospital, O'Hara shoved an unlit cigar in his mouth and talked through clenched teeth. "Have you decided now what you think happened?"

Jamison's response came out more abruptly than he intended. "If we hadn't gone in there she'd be dead. But there's something she isn't saying and I damn well hope that it isn't going to bite us in the ass. Get everything we can get on that old case."

Chapter 16

The forensic tests came back negative. There were no signs of semen or prostatic fluids from the swabs taken from Garrett or the bed, or anywhere else. That didn't mean St. Claire didn't intend to rape Garrett. But without that proof there was no other physical evidence of sexual assault, like bruising or other trauma on her body.

On the positive side, they had found some hair in St. Claire's Lexus that they could identify as belonging to Garrett. Each piece of evidence pushed the finger of guilt one way or the other, but forensics had come up with nothing else in the car.

The circumstances alone were enough to create a suspicion of St. Claire's intent to sexually assault. Jamison made the decision after quick deliberation. He would file charges of kidnap, assault, and attempted rape. Just how long St. Claire would remain in custody after the arraignment would depend on the judge and McGuiness's machinations.

There was more disappointing news. No evidence linking St. Claire to the three other victims could be found in the house or the car. No hair, no fiber, and worse, no positive results yet for DNA. The crucial DNA tests, as always, would take longer than the others.

Juries had undergone a transformation in recent years—spoon-fed on forensic television shows that used simplistic explanations and contrived situations that made it look as if DNA and other evidence was plastered all over crime scenes with blinking fluorescent signs. True reality was mostly hard-nosed detective work with a smattering of plain luck. Sometimes there was simply nothing. And if there was DNA evidence, it often took weeks of laborious, time-consuming, complex testing and retesting to locate it.

So if any of the other victims had been at St. Claire's house or in his car, his investigators had, so far, nothing to make a case. A similar pattern of criminal activity might raise suspicion, but without physical evidence of some kind, *any* kind, Jamison knew they had nothing and were nowhere.

Puccinelli, along with Detective T. J. Longworthy, walked the reports over to the DA's office. The pile of paper on the three murders was being given to Jamison with no written recommendation as to the charges requested by the sheriff's office, but the face sheet concerning potential charges did say "Kidnap, Assault with a Deadly Weapon and Murder." After a cursory glance at the pile of reports, Jamison recognized that Bekin was putting it all on him.

If Jamison refused to file charges, the sheriff could say he sent all the information over and it was the DA who refused. If there wasn't enough evidence, Bekin could say that it was the DA's call, not his. Bekin might look like a Freightliner truck but there was a wolfish brain inside that massive head.

Puccinelli said very little. Most of the talking came from Detective Longworthy. The reason was fairly transparent. Even though they had the same boss, T. J. Longworthy was carrying the water for Sheriff Bekin but Pooch wasn't. T. J.'s argument was all suspicion and assumptions based on years of experience.

Finally Jamison asked Puccinelli for his opinion. With a resigned expression, Pooch shrugged before saying, "Sheriff Bekin says it's your call."

Jamison took a deep breath and let it out with a show of disgust. They had to see they were going too fast. He gave the two sheriff's detectives a choice. They could take the case back and continue to work on it or he would write NCF, no charges filed, across the request for murder charges. Hard stares, mostly from T. J., went back and forth but neither side budged.

"Okay, so that's the way it's going to be," Jamison thought. He wrote "NCF" for murder and handed back the paperwork. He would go with kidnap, assault, and attempted rape. The look on Detective Longworthy's face didn't conceal his contempt, but as for Puccinelli, although he didn't say a word, it was clear to Jamison that he understood. But Jamison wasn't going to put Pooch on the spot by asking him to agree with his decision in front of an angry and unrealistic colleague.

An hour later, after he saw Jamison's decision, District Attorney Gage didn't ask him for an explanation. He simply said it was his case and his judgment. As rumors swirled in the courthouse community about the murders and whether Dr. St. Claire committed them, Gage handled the press inquiries by saying since it was now a formally charged case, he didn't want to add to the publicity, or as he self-righteously put it in the sound bite, "After all, Dr. St. Claire deserves a fair trial in a courtroom and not in a newsroom."

Jamison waited until Elizabeth Garrett returned home from the hospital the next morning before sending Ernie back to the house for another interview. But her statement remained unchanged. She didn't remember anything except scattered images until the moment he came crashing through the window. But some bits and pieces were becoming sharper. She now remembered St. Claire putting something over her face and that it had a peculiar odor, but she had almost no memory of anything after that until she woke up tied to the bed.

They were still waiting on the results of Garrett's blood tests but they did know there was no sign of any heroin or barbiturates, unlike the other victims whose blood had been described by a forensic technician as a "toxic stew." And like DNA testing, the blood results might come back right after the commercial break on television shows, but in real life detectives were lucky if it took days. With the arraignment staring him in the face the following morning, Jamison didn't have days.

He maintained contact with Garrett by phone, but left the interviews to Ernie. The more interviews they did, the more they had to turn over to the defense in terms of discovery, and this reality was always a frustration because it wasn't a two-way street. Jamison had to give full discovery of everything he had to the defense while the defense could bide its time until trial before making its disclosures. And for how St. Claire would testify, the defense wasn't obligated to give any disclosure at all because of his Fifth Amendment rights under the Constitution.

At this stage he didn't expect any surprises. Arraignment was generally a perfunctory thing. Charges were read, a plea was entered, bail was set, and a preliminary hearing was calendared. The trial would be a different matter.

St. Claire was officially represented by Tom McGuiness who, from the moment he had been hired, had cut off all questioning by Jamison's investigators with his client. Jamison knew the arraignment of St. Claire would be a circus. McGuiness had already made the assertion in front of the cameras that all the prosecution had was an allegation by a woman who had a "history" with a respected doctor in the community. The veiled reference to an earlier relationship between the victim and St. Claire predictably whetted the appetite of the press and their readers that maybe, after all, Elizabeth Garrett wasn't a "total" innocent, just as McGuiness intended. And the hints of the relationship to the murder cases kept the rumor mill grinding despite the fact that both Jamison and the sheriff's office were trying to keep a lid on that investigation.

And while Jamison anticipated that McGuiness would try to sow seeds of doubt in the minds of prospective jurors, as any good defense attorney would do, more importantly Jamison knew McGuiness was sure he wouldn't respond—not that McGuiness wanted or expected him to. The defense attorney didn't want a response.

A gauntlet of reporters and cameras confronted Jamison and O'Hara as they made their way toward the master calendar arraignment court run by Judge Frederick Kane. McGuiness was already seated in the front row of the spectator section. St. Claire sat in the "in custody" section dressed in a red jail jumpsuit. Other prisoners sat next to him, each chained to a floor bracket that couldn't be seen from the public seating area. The rattling of the chains was background noise to the murmur of the spectators as Jamison walked toward the front of the courtroom.

McGuiness leaned over, catching Jamison's attention as he walked by. "Matt, you are making a serious mistake, and thanks for not returning my phone calls." McGuiness had in fact left three messages. "Which is more courtesy than you've shown by dragging my client down here bundled up in chains."

"Tom, it isn't personal and you know it. Your client wasn't treated any differently than anybody else would be with these charges. You want to talk before the arraignment or after?"

The defense attorney replied, "I don't want to talk at all. I want everything you've got and I want an honor release. And if you have any other charges I want to know. There's no reason for him to have to post bail. He isn't going anywhere and you know it. I want you to agree to a bail reduction. A million dollars is ridiculous." McGuiness paused before adding, "Unless you have more charges. You don't seriously think my client is also guilty of murder, do you?"

Jamison didn't respond to the bait. "Send your assistant over later today and we will have copies of everything you are entitled to."

"I'm entitled to everything."

"You're entitled to what I have that isn't in the middle of being analyzed further. I'll give you what I have, and as soon as I have more, you'll get that too."

"What about the honor release or the bail reduction?"

Jamison rubbed his face, shaking his head. "No honor release, Tom, and no bail reduction. Make your pitch to the judge. St. Claire posts bail or he sits in a cell just like everybody else who's a kidnapper and a rapist."

McGuiness took a long look at Jamison. "I'm warning you again. You're making a mistake with this case and it's going to be a career ender for you. Just remember when you hit the bottom of that crater you're digging for yourself that I tried to warn you."

McGuiness walked through the swinging gate that separated the public area from the counsel area. He looked back, raising his voice enough so that the reporters straining to hear would be able to make it out. "Just remember I tried to tell you. What happens from now on isn't personal either." McGuiness shook his head as if he had tried to do the right thing and failed.

Jamison had seen that disdainful expression before and heard those warnings from other lawyers in other cases. But one thing McGuiness didn't say hadn't escaped his attention. McGuiness hadn't asked a single question about discussing a plea. McGuiness had something, and Matt wasn't going to know what it was until it dropped in the courtroom right on his head. Whatever it was, Jamison had no doubt it was going to hurt.

When St. Claire's case was called, McGuiness immediately asked for a bail hearing.

After waiting until McGuiness was through, Jamison responded, "Your Honor, the People object to a bail reduction. First thing, Your Honor, the defendant hasn't entered a plea yet. This defendant has been charged with kidnapping, assault with a deadly weapon, and attempted rape. The charges qualify as violent felonies and will result in a state prison commitment when he is convicted. I don't need to explain . . ."

A man of few words, Judge Kane interrupted. "No, you don't need to explain. Based on the charges, the request from the defense is denied at this time, but the matter will be referred for consideration of a bail reduction or an honor release. Bail will remain at one million for the time being. After the report from the honor release officer comes back I'll be prepared to reconsider it."

During the exchange between the lawyers, St. Claire was standing in the custody area, a belly chain draped around his waist and legs, his hands manacled with cuffs that ran through the belly chain. His face showed no reaction to the mention of prison but St. Claire's expression remained oddly inquisitive, as if he were taking in a play performed in front of him.

Kane turned his attention to Jamison. "Anything further before we finish the arraignment?"

"Yes, Your Honor. We recognize the court's heavy calendar but we will request this case be set for preliminary hearing as quickly as possible."

Usually the defense would request an extension to drag out the proceedings and get as much information from the prosecution as possible. Jamison wanted the judge to know that he wasn't going to agree to a long extension of time prior to the preliminary hearing.

Before the court had the opportunity to inquire as to the reason for Jamison's position, the defense attorney spoke up. "Your Honor, I am, of course, disappointed by the district attorney's decision to charge Dr. St. Claire, as well as the speed by which the State wishes to—"McGuiness looked over at Jamison, infusing his voice with as much disdain as he could muster—"rush to *injustice.* It is a move obviously intended to prejudice my client's case further, just as parading Dr. St. Claire into the courtroom in custody was designed to prejudice his case.

"However"—again McGuiness looked directly at Jamison—"in the district attorney's request for a speedy preliminary hearing, I concur. Dr. St. Claire also requests to have this matter settled as quickly as possible. He wishes to clear his reputation and is confident, as I am, that this case will result in the charges being dismissed either because they should never have been brought in the first place, or my client being rightfully acquitted.

"Dr. St. Claire has nothing further to say except for entering his plea and he will not be requesting an extension or waiving time for the preliminary hearing. We request that the preliminary be held within the statutory time and want the court to know that if it was possible to proceed today we would be ready."

Jamison's instincts had already prepared him to expect the unexpected, but for McGuiness not to seek more time was a surprising response.

Judge Kane had a bemused expression as he watched the prosecutor and defense attorney circle each other like two dogs getting ready to fight. "I appreciate your fervor, Mr. McGuiness, but we will not have a preliminary today. I will set it for a week from Monday, which is within the defendant's statutory time."

The judge turned to Jamison. "Acceptable to the People?"

He hadn't expected the quick setting but Jamison was in no position to object, and now Alex St. Claire himself spoke up.

"Your Honor, am I permitted to speak?" he asked as McGuiness moved next to his client, holding his palm out, signaling that St. Claire should not say anything further. St. Claire continued to look at the judge waiting for his response.

Jamison knew that a highly experienced trial judge such as Kane would view this as a potential problem no matter what he did. "Dr. St. Claire, you have a right to speak, but I advise you that you should not do so until you have spoken to your attorney. It's not in your best interest to make statements at this time."

St. Claire lowered his head and raised his manacled hands in acknowledgment. "Your Honor, I appreciate the court's solicitude. I would simply like the court to know that I am innocent of these charges. Mr. Jamison's conduct in charging me is a shameful miscarriage of justice, and I am disappointed that I am being treated like a common criminal." St. Claire looked at the other inmates chained next to him. "No offense intended, gentlemen."

One of the defendants seated with St. Claire in the in-custody area laughed. "No offense taken, Doc. I'm innocent too."

There was a ripple of laughter from the other in-custody defendants as Kane rapped his gavel on the bench.

In an orchestrated display of concern for the rights of his client in front of the members of the press who were present, McGuiness turned toward Jamison and asked, "What hard evidence do they have other than this one woman's word against my client's?"

Before Jamison could do anything more than open his mouth to protest, the judge held up his hand. He was used to posturing from attorneys. With a resigned expression, Judge Kane said, "Mr. McGuiness, your comments are noted, but are more appropriately addressed to a jury than to me. A plea of not guilty will be entered to each charge. Anything else from either counsel?"

St. Claire and McGuiness answered simultaneously. "No, Your Honor."

In the first skirmish, McGuiness had clearly won the war of perception. The only positive result was that for the time being, the bail remained high, and Jamison was able to watch St. Claire shuffle slowly from the courtroom in handcuffs and a belly chain.

Chapter 17

When the arraignment ended, the only person in the courtroom without an elevated pulse, Jamison thought, was Alex St. Claire. That thought alone raised the prosecutor's heartbeat. He had seen only a few individuals like that and all of them were like reptilian predators.

What set St. Claire apart was his uniqueness. Not only did he think he was smarter than everybody else in the room, he was probably right. But Jamison knew that even the smartest people make mistakes and the person who caught the mistake didn't have to be as smart as the person making the mistake—as long as he was determined and had a little bit of luck. At this moment, Jamison didn't feel very lucky, but he was determined as hell.

With less than a week to go before the preliminary hearing, Jamison's objectives were limited because it wasn't like a trial. It was simply a proceeding to decide if there was enough evidence to justify a trial. He didn't have to prove his case beyond a reasonable doubt. The ultimate question of guilt or innocence was for a jury to decide.

But McGuiness would be permitted to cross-examine Beth Garrett. Other than that, Jamison expected no surprises. If McGuiness had anything to reveal he wouldn't do it at the preliminary hearing. He would save all his evidence for the trial where there would be little time for the prosecution to investigate or respond. To Jamison, the process was like playing cards when the other guy got to look at your hand while keeping his own cards close to the vest. Worse, guys like McGuiness only played those cards when all the bets were down and there were no second chances.

With the preliminary hearing now only days away, Jamison sat with O'Hara at the long table in the sheriff's office waiting for the detectives assigned to the murder investigations to arrive. Detective Washington stuck his head in, walked over to the side table, poured a cup of coffee, and settled his bulk into a chair across from Jamison. Longworthy dropped his lanky frame into a chair, flopped a yellow legal tablet on the table, and yawned. He didn't say anything, but his face had the haggard look of a man who was finishing a late shift.

Longworthy nodded to O'Hara and Ernie, moving his eyes past Jamison. Jamison noticed the snub just as he had noticed it the last time they had gathered around the table. He was also aware that Longworthy intended for him to recognize it. Maybe it was because he had refused the murder charges. Maybe it was simply because he was a lawyer and it was obvious Longworthy didn't like lawyers. Whatever the reason was, Jamison recognized there was nothing he could do about it.

Slowly Jamison looked around the table at each detective. He took his time before he spoke, and then spoke deliberately to insure there would be no mistaking the gravity of what he had to say. "Gentlemen, I need your help on this case." First, he had to assure them he was on their side.

"I think St. Claire committed all the murders," he began. "But right now we have no physical evidence that ties St. Claire to any of those victims. All we have is a similar pattern to the Garrett case.

"We haven't turned up a relationship, not social or school or doctor–patient, nothing that will help us prove that St. Claire even *knew* our other victims. Clearly he had a history with Garrett, but we don't have anything that shows that the other crimes were based on a relationship of any kind either with St. Claire or Garrett.

"All the DNA tests are negative except for Garrett. So we have no evidence that Ventana, Johnson, or Symes were in St. Claire's house or his car. And topping all that off is that Garrett's blood tests came in negative for the heroin-barbiturate cocktail found in the other murder victims, and there were no similar narcotics found at either of his houses. So there it is. We don't have squat that I can see.

"I got this back a few days ago." Jamison reached into his file folder and pulled out several pages from the state crime lab. "There were two separate types of hair found on each body. The good news is that the hairs on each body all match in terms of texture and color. And we know one other thing." Jamison looked around the room. "The hair doesn't match St. Claire. It didn't come from him. One strand on each body came from an African American person. The other strands came from a dog. And that, gentlemen, is a piece of evidence that we can't explain, but Tom McGuiness will be more than happy to. He'll put his hand on the shoulder of his lily-white client and tell the jury that St. Claire doesn't have a dog. The second thing he'll say is that maybe the crimes were committed by a black man who has a labradoodle."

Detective Washington broke into laughter. "Well, you can blow a hole through that. No self-respectin' black man would be caught dead with a labradoodle. That's a white boy's dog. Black man would have a dog that takes a piece out of your ass just lookin' at him."

Jamison leaned back in his chair. "Yeah, thanks, Washington. I'll keep that in mind when I call you as an expert witness on black men and their dogs."

Washington kept the grin on his face. "Just tellin' you, my man. Just tellin' you. You asked for help."

Longworthy pulled his legal tablet closer to him and began drawing circles on it while speaking. "The hair doesn't mean shit. The most important thing is that it was planted. And we know that one woman stopped in the middle of nowhere just like Garrett, and she had to have a reason. We know that two other women left with somebody they opened the door for, and they had to have a reason. Best guess is that they either knew the perp, or he was somebody they thought was a cop or someone like a cop."

Longworthy stared at Jamison as if the conclusion was obvious. "Garrett stopped because she thought she had to, because she thought St. Claire was a cop and that damn well explains why these other women let him in the door or stopped for him. You don't have to be Sherlock Holmes to . . ." His voice trailed off as he looked at them.

The silence lingered for a few moments before O'Hara decided he needed to assert himself. "T. J., that isn't going to nail him and you know it."

O'Hara stole a quick glance at Jamison to be sure it was all right to push his point. "Remember, the other victims were all killed by a combination of heroin and barbiturates. Nothing like that was in Garrett's system and we didn't find anything like that in the search. Don't forget, this guy has Tom McGuiness for a lawyer and all of you have gone up against him before. Without real proof that nails St. Claire to each case, you know McGuiness will get the murder charges thrown out and walk St. Claire out the door before the ink is dry on the order."

O'Hara's eyes lasered in on Longworthy. "T. J., maybe you're right and the hair was planted. That would be my guess too, but we still have to show *St. Claire* planted it so that Matt can make this case hang together. So let's stop pissing on the DA's office and piss on St. Claire. Can we all do that?"

Just then the door to the conference room opened and Sheriff Bekin stuck his head in. "Thought you boys might like to know St. Claire has posted bail. He's walking out of the jail right now. Big television bunch are waiting outside. Guess they got the news before you did."

Relishing Jamison's startled expression, Bekin was unable to conceal a tight little smile as he eyed the prosecutor. "Maybe the DA's office ought to have the newspeople give you a call when they find something out about your case?" he added sarcastically before pulling his head back from the open door.

Longworthy picked his pen up from the legal tablet he had been drawing circles on and stalked out of the room. Jamison started to say something when O'Hara put his hand on Jamison's arm. "T. J.'s all right. He's just pissed that we can't seem to nail St. Claire."

But Jamison's mind had already moved beyond T. J. and Bekin. He was mentally plodding through what he had to make his case and what he didn't have. Jamison sat back. The list of what he didn't have was far longer. Unless they came up with more, a lot more, the only way they could win the murder cases was to win the Garrett case—the pattern was there and they all knew it. What Jamison didn't know was how much St. Claire's lawyer knew and what he would do about it. As quiet as the investigation had been, three savage murders made a lot of legal noise.

Chapter 18

There was no way for Jamison to keep Elizabeth Garrett from being questioned in detail at the preliminary hearing. Not only was he concerned about the emotional trauma to Beth, he knew McGuiness's primary objective would be to damage her credibility as much as possible while revealing little about the defense case.

This left him with no options. Without her testimony, he had no case. He decided to outline the basic essentials of the charges with her testimony and wait to see how McGuiness would attack her. Mercy and compassion were not part of the deal.

Alex St. Claire walked confidently into the courtroom as if he was preparing for surgery. He had a swagger to him that projected confidence; he knew he was the principal actor and all eyes were on him. His carefully tailored dark blue suit and subdued maroon silk tie contrasted with his tan, which hadn't seemed to fade during his days in custody, the very image of a man who had no need to drag any woman into submission.

Tom McGuiness followed his client and settled himself at the counsel table. McGuiness gave a nod to Jamison and opened his briefcase. He handed a blank legal tablet to St. Claire. It was a common defense practice that allowed the client to keep busy and the attorney to avoid the distraction of the client constantly pulling on the attorney's sleeve, trying to offer his thoughts. But Alex St. Claire wasn't the usual client and McGuiness wasn't going to treat him like one. He would pay attention to what his client wrote.

St. Claire leaned forward trying to get a clear view of Jamison and O'Hara, who sat next to him as his chief investigator. "Good morning, Mr. Jamison, Investigator O'Hara." Jamison acknowledged him. O'Hara ignored him.

When Judge Patrick Sullivan had been assigned the preliminary hearing, Jamison didn't object. Sullivan was neither a really good nor a bad choice. He would do his job and everybody knew what was going to happen at the end. When Jamison finished presenting his evidence the defendant would be bound over for trial. The only issue was how much damage would be done to Jamison's case before the hearing ended. From his chair behind the bench, Sullivan called the case for purposes of the record. "Everybody ready to proceed?" Jamison and McGuiness answered they were. "The People may present their case."

Jamison stood. "The People call Elizabeth Garrett."

O'Hara left the courtroom and signaled to Ernie. Within a minute Ernie escorted Elizabeth Garrett from the hallway into the courtroom, whispering into her ear to raise her right hand. Elizabeth tried to keep her eyes on the judge as the oath was administered, but, as if magnetically drawn, when she caught the profile of Alex St. Claire she turned her head to face him.

St. Claire would not fail to miss any opportunity to burnish himself in the eyes of the court and tarnish Elizabeth. Instead of outrage at the ordeal she was putting him through, St. Claire's expression was one of compassion for the woman accusing him. Matt Jamison knew it was all for show, and for the moment the show belonged to Alex St. Claire.

Elizabeth walked slowly to the witness chair. The collective intensity focused on her by each person in the courtroom must have been almost suffocating. She looked like a cornered animal.

Jamison moved quickly to the events leading up to her abduction. Elizabeth Garrett related to the court what she remembered. Nothing in her opening testimony differed from what she had said previously and repeated to Jamison when he had gone over the details with her the day before. But McGuiness made a point of establishing what she couldn't remember. He followed the basic rule of a careful defense lawyer: don't concentrate on the strengths of the DA's case, only the weaknesses. His final question slid out of his mouth like the tongue of a rattler. "One more thing, please, Ms. Garrett. You and Dr. St. Claire had a previous relationship, didn't you?" McGuiness waited politely until Garrett nodded her head. "By nodding I take it your answer is yes?" He waited just a beat. "That was a romantic relationship, wasn't it?"

Garrett looked down. "Yes, but I was young and—"

McGuiness interrupted, his voice polite but firm. "A simple yes or no, please. I'm sure Mr. Jamison will give you the opportunity to give a further answer . . . if he decides to go into that."

McGuiness returned to the counsel table and flipped though his notes, leaving Garrett on the stand to watch him. He then looked up at her, followed by a glance at the members of the news media sitting in the front row, a practiced apologetic look on his face for making Garrett go through any further embarrassment, but Jamison knew it wasn't over.

"And that romantic relationship included sexual intimacy with Dr. St. Claire. Is that right, Ms. Garrett?"

Garrett's face reddened. Her parents were sitting in the back of the courtroom. "Yes, but again—"

McGuiness held up his hand. "We don't need the details of the liaison, Ms. Garrett. I have no desire to embarrass you. Thank you." McGuiness started back toward the counsel table and then turned to face her once more, as if he had forgotten something. "One more thing, please, Ms. Garrett." McGuiness allowed his gaze to slide toward Jamison and then to the press. "Those relations with Dr. St. Claire? They were all consensual, weren't they?" He waited, allowing Elizabeth's long silence to permeate the courtroom. "You must answer, please."

"Yes."

McGuiness repeated the answer as if it needed clarification. "Yes they were all consensual?"

"Yes."

"Thank you." McGuiness sat down at the counsel table, turning his face toward Jamison. "Nothing further, Your Honor."

Jamison recognized that McGuiness wanted him to open the door and explain the previous relationship, which would justify the defense attorney's coming at the witness, slowly opening her up. It was a temptation to allow her to talk about what really happened, but it wouldn't solve anything because it would allow McGuiness a chance to take more blood. One time going through it all was going to be bad enough. He decided he would wait until the trial.

"Nothing further of this witness, Your Honor. Ms. Garrett may be excused. The People are prepared to submit the case subject to any evidence the defense wishes to present."

McGuiness rose from his chair. "We have no wish to prolong this hearing but will the prosecutor stipulate that no physical evidence of sexual activity was found, no semen or prostatic fluid or any hair from my client's body?"

"We will agree, Your Honor, that at this time we have not received back any test results that would conflict with the proposed stipulation."

McGuiness acknowledged the stipulation. "Your Honor, it's clear that this case involves two people who have a long romantic history and we all know how complicated that can be. We realize the court has a very limited role here and it isn't your job to decide guilt or innocence. Still, the weakness of the People's case is quite evident. It would seem obvious that no sexual assault took place. We would ask the court to find insufficient evidence to support the charge of attempted rape. With that, we will submit the case to the court to determine if there is sufficient evidence to set a trial."

Jamison stood. "Your Honor, while it is true there is no physical evidence, the circumstances are not only consistent with intent to sexually assault, there is also no reasonable alternative explanation. Certainly the evidence would support a strong suspicion of attempted rape. I will submit it." Jamison sat down heavily.

The motion to dismiss the attempted rape charge was denied, but Jamison had seen the judge look at him over the top of his reading glasses. Judge Sullivan didn't have to say anything. His expression telegraphed the message that Jamison better have something more for trial to make his case. The lines were drawn.

Sullivan addressed McGuiness. "The trial date, Mr. McGuiness? Have you and Mr. Jamison discussed a date that works with your schedule given that your client is out of custody?"

McGuiness glanced over at Jamison, then delivered his blow. "Your Honor, Dr. St. Claire has been exposed to this terrible experience and the emotional toll on him has been substantial. He is the victim of vicious rumors of which I am sure the court is well aware. He wants this over with as quickly as possible and so do I. We request the earliest possible setting within the minimum statutory time. I am sure the prosecution wants this over quickly as well, although I suspect not for the same reasons."

The judge frowned. "Mr. Jamison, Mr. McGuiness, I have an open date in a little over three weeks. It is well within the statutory time." Sullivan knew he was calling McGuiness's bluff. It was too little time to get ready in a case of this magnitude and he felt certain that McGuiness would quit posturing and accept a more reasonable date outside the statutory time.

McGuiness spoke up before Jamison was able to respond. "Your Honor, we appreciate the court's effort to accommodate the concerns of Dr. St.

Claire. That date will be acceptable to the defense." He turned to Jamison. "I am sure that Mr. Jamison also wants to get this trial over with so that the cloud is lifted from Ms. Garrett?"

Jamison felt his stomach flip. The short setting on the preliminary hearing was one thing, but with St. Claire out of custody he did not have any reason to expect that McGuiness would try to set the trial so quickly. Three weeks was barely enough time for the Garrett case, and he needed more time for the murder cases to come together if possible so he could gain real leverage against St. Claire. Despite efforts to keep the suspicion quiet that St. Claire committed the murders, rumors had been churning in the community and press that St. Claire was the focus of suspicion. The linchpin of the murder cases was the Garrett case—that was what linked St. Claire because of the pattern. Prove St. Claire kidnapped Garrett and it would be clear that St. Claire was the primary suspect in the murders. Jamison knew if he lost the Garrett case, then without more evidence he wouldn't be able to make the modus operandi connection to the murders.

He understood the tactic. McGuiness suspected he was trying to connect the dots with the murder cases and he also realized that Jamison needed to prove his client was guilty of the Garrett kidnap in order to prove that he used the same conduct to commit the murders. Get an acquittal on the Garrett case and he would drive a massive hole in the murder cases because he would realize if Jamison had the evidence to charge the murders he would have done it already. Both sides needed to win—Jamison to prove St. Claire was guilty of the murders and McGuiness to deprive the prosecution of the one thing they needed to prove St. Claire was guilty.

Jamison also knew that McGuiness had something damaging and the defense attorney didn't want to give him time to discover what it was, but Jamison couldn't say that. He had said he had a case and he had charged it. With more confidence than he actually felt, Jamison said, "Your Honor, the People are prepared to go forward tomorrow if that suits Mr. McGuiness."

Sullivan pulled his lips into a deeper frown. "Fine, the case will be calendared for three weeks from today. I hope you gentlemen are ready and remember the adage to be careful what you ask for because you just got it."

Whatever McGuiness had, he was saving it for the trial. This was going to be an ambush and Jamison knew it. The only question was whether he could anticipate when it would take place at the trial and what McGuiness would have as his weapons besides surprise.

Part Two

Chapter 19

The trial was now a week away. As Alex St. Claire drove into the gravel driveway of the house in the foothills, he felt some of the strain of the past two weeks begin to drain away. This house had been his private refuge, the place that always restored him. When his parents died he had inherited it as part of the trust that allowed him to live as he wished. The bills, the taxes, everything was paid for by the trust. Unlike the farmhouse where he had gone with Elizabeth, there was no paper trail that would allow anyone to link him to this house or lead anyone to find this place. Nothing was in his name.

He closed the car door quietly even though there wasn't anyone close enough to hear. St. Claire had a cultivated dignity that he wore at all times like a cloak. He stood in the quickening chill of evening, his car making the settling sounds of heat dissipating into the cold night air. The house always looked the same to him. The windows were shuttered and seldom opened to the daylight. It had been his grandparents' vacation home, and he had left everything in place, just as they had left it.

These days he didn't spend much time in the house itself and indeed right now what he wanted was to visit the barn, which held other objects that restored him—but in a different way. He thought perhaps later he would walk the dark rooms of the house.

Most of the last two weeks St. Claire had spent with his lawyer, going over details that seemed to absorb McGuiness but held only detached interest for him. He had driven here to be alone. He preferred the carapace of his own carefully created persona. Rarely did he allow others the compliment of emotional intimacy.

He knew the sideways looks of hospital staff and his physician colleagues' awkward efforts to offer words of support barely concealed their doubt and suspicions. It wasn't that *he* didn't understand why they looked at him, it was because *they* didn't understand. They would never understand him and that ground on him like a pharmacist's pestle as he tolerated their clumsy solicitude.

He had to get away from them, from their averted eyes and whispering. They bored him, and whether he frightened them bored him as well. He had taken a leave from the hospital. Under the present circumstances he knew he made people uncomfortable and the time off hadn't been difficult to obtain.

St. Claire really didn't care what his lawyer thought either. He knew himself intimately, what stirred him, touched him, and made him feel alive—and different than other men. What he was he had long ago accepted. As for why, it didn't matter to him. As a child, when he realized he was different he considered the difference a gift. He had no desire to be like those who moved through life reacting to it instead of, like him, creating the reaction.

It was what lay ahead that would make the difference, the trial and the slow dance with Elizabeth. It was still a game. His whole life had been a game played out against what always proved to be lesser men, always testing himself, only his intellect helping him keep his balance on the cutting edge of the blade upon which he walked.

That was the game. Walking the blade. That was where he felt alive. Without it the hours and days were simply hours and days. *But Elizabeth,* the thought of her had drawn him back—back to the cutting edge of the blade. And now with the trial ahead, a new game. All the pieces to be moved, every move anticipated like a chess match with the eye on the queen. The thought made him shudder slightly with anticipation.

His mind jumped back to that moment with Investigator O'Hara's knee in his back. He hadn't forgotten that, nor would he. He dismissed O'Hara. O'Hara was as refined as a battle-ax.

The prosecutor, however, was different in St. Claire's mind. He did not have the street cunning of his investigator, but St. Claire could sense a relentless and dangerous mind when he saw it, not an insurmountable challenger, but a challenger nonetheless. He also saw the prosecutor's weakness. As he watched Matthew Jamison in the courtroom, he could sense it. Elizabeth was the prosecutor's weakness.

St. Claire had seen the way Jamison looked at Elizabeth, the way he moved around her, like a moth. But like a moth, St. Claire contemplated that Jamison had no idea that he was circling a flame.

He walked across the lawn toward the barn, the grass softly crunching under his feet as he broke the frost-stiffened blades with each step. Pulling the switch inside the door, the cold fluorescent light reflected off the stainless steel table in the room, his grandfather's favorite place. As a child he had watched with fascination as his grandfather worked at that table, dissecting tissue pulled from glass jars. The time away from his own father, so distant and critical, was a welcome respite, and the hours spent with someone who really cared for him aroused a passion.

Unlike his father, his grandfather's indulgence of his fascination with death and pain made him feel like his inquisitiveness about the morbid was natural. It was why he had become a physician—to learn the secrets that his pathologist grandfather discovered in bits of flesh and microscopic slides.

His father had been a surgeon who looked upon his only son as an obligation and his curiosity as a reflection of some flaw in the genetic inheritance. The realization of his father's feelings—which St. Claire recognized from an early age—justified the satisfaction he took when his father's life ended. As for his mother, she accepted him, and her death mustered a flicker of regret that he did not feel more at her passing.

He had not acquired a taste for the unrefined work dissecting a human body, but he had developed an appreciation for the body's secrets and the power a physician held over a human being.

His breath hung in shapeless puffs; the room had long gone unheated. As he turned on the electric radiator, his eyes ran over shelves with rows of jars that still held lumps of tissue in varying shades of pink to gray. There was intellectual challenge in them, just as there was challenge for him as an anesthesiologist in submersing a human being into the depths of unconsciousness, holding them there at his will. Sinking them to near death levels and slowly retrieving them took him almost to the edge of where lesser men dared not go, an edge that constantly tempted him to cross.

He ran his hand along the side of the stainless steel table, feeling its ever-present chill, reminding him that now that table was where *he* worked. He took pleasure in the thought of the seamless transition of generations and of the work he now did at this steel platform.

But tonight there was no work to be done. He walked across to the wall of shelves and bent down to the lowest shelf, moving several specimen jars. The edge of the wooden wallboard was smooth from the countless times in his life that he had pulled it open, revealing the space in the wall. As a child it was where he had kept his secret things, mementoes of his small triumphs over the living: a cat's collar, a twisted bird's wing, the remnants of his furtive childhood experiments with pain and consciousness. As a man it still held his secrets. He pulled out a small box and stood up. The gleam of a computer thumb drive caught his eye. He pulled out the compact digital memory stick and walked over to a laptop computer, inserting it. He carefully typed in a password to open the encrypted memory on the stick. As the digitally concealed photographs on the thumb drive revealed themselves on the computer, the collage of images spoke to him, as they always did.

St. Claire relished the moment as he revisited each photograph, each memory, the anticipation building until he came to the photographs of Elizabeth. He traced his finger along the curve of her face and her body, held still in the digital image. His mind transported to his fingertips the memory of the warmth of her breasts, her torso, if only imagined, the photograph portraying the essence of the queen of this game.

Chapter 20

Jamison pored over the reports in the file for the St. Claire case. Their contents were now memorized through the repetition of reading and rereading the same pages. The trial was less than a week away. He had a case that looked like it should be open and shut—victim disappears and is later found tied to a bed. Yet he was troubled by his nagging, vague concerns that the case still held secrets that only heightened his anxiety. What had he missed? What didn't he know?

With his investigators he spent hours questioning Beth Garrett, but only a few new details emerged. Jamison listened to her and tried to take a detached view, but it didn't come as easily as it had in other cases. He had a growing unease arising from his gut intuition that she was holding something back, something that was going to come straight at him at trial like an oncoming truck. And he was also very certain that McGuiness knew precisely what Beth was holding back and was keenly aware that he didn't.

He dropped the file and looked up at the sound of the door creaking open; O'Hara never knocked. He came into Jamison's office, sat down, and put his feet up on Jamison's desk. He knew how much Jamison disliked anyone doing that, so Jamison knew O'Hara was obviously trying to irritate him.

"Boss, I've been on the phone with T. J."

"So? Did he call to ask me again when I was going to get my head out of my ass and file murder charges or just to wish me good luck on the trial?"

O'Hara grinned. "He called to tell me that St. Claire made a mistake."

"What mistake?" Jamison sat up in his chair.

"They got a lab report back on some evidence. I don't have all the details yet. After I talked to T. J., I spoke to Washington. They got some physical evidence out of St. Claire's car and Washington says that it's enough to put the needle into St. Claire's arm."

"What physical evidence? The forensic boys went through his Lexus and didn't turn up a damned thing other than a strand of Garrett's hair."

Signaling Jamison to be patient, O'Hara said, "Apparently T. J. went back to the car because he couldn't believe there was nothing. Washington was with him and so was one of our forensic people."

"So? Come on, Bill."

"Near the passenger side, under a floor mat, they found a few strands of fiber that didn't match the carpet in the car. I don't know how our guys missed it, but Washington said that T. J. found it. The fiber is identical with individual carpet fibers from the carpet in Johnson's house and individual carpet fibers from the carpet in Symes's apartment."

Inhaling deeply, O'Hara paused before saying anything more, and the slow smile appearing on his face told Jamison that there was more. O'Hara was seldom subtle. "And they found another strand of hair. It's identical to Ventana's hair in color and texture, although the hair doesn't have a root ball on it so there's no way to test for blood. But we got enough off of the hair that we can say it's definitely hers."

He removed his feet from Jamison's desk and leaned forward. "Two separate carpet fibers that are identical to the carpet fiber in different places that belonged to two of the victims and a strand of hair that is identical to the hair of the first victim. McGuiness can argue all he wants, but you know and I know that can't just be a coincidence. You wanted a connection between St. Claire and all three victims. There it is."

Feeling a spurt of euphoria, Jamison stood up, pacing in the area between his desk and the window. Each piece of evidence by itself wasn't enough to convict St. Claire but together it couldn't be explained away. Those women had all been in St. Claire's car or in some way somebody who had been in St. Claire's car had been in the residences of those women. With the hair from Garrett that was in his car and the circumstances of her abduction they finally had something that would place the murder victims with St. Claire.

With a wolfish smile, O'Hara asked, "So do I get the pleasure of snapping the cuffs on Dr. St. Claire one more time when we arrest him for murder?"

For weeks, all Jamison had been able to think about was what he would do once he had more evidence, and now he had it.

He reached for the phone, turning to O'Hara as he started to punch in numbers. "Tell T. J. and Washington to keep their mouths shut about this. At least for now nobody talks. You get to the forensic people to make sure there are no leaks. The only warning Alex St. Claire and Tom McGuiness get will be when you make the arrest." O'Hara's grin disappeared as soon as Jamison finished his thoughts. "But no arrest just yet."

A dark cloud suddenly over his face, O'Hara leaned forward. Jamison held up his hand before the torrent spilled out of his investigator. "We still haven't found the link between St. Claire and those three other women. Why did he pick them? There has to be something. Get their personal medical records from their doctors. There has to be some way that St. Claire picked them and I'm guessing it has to do with medical records. We know these weren't random. This guy watched these women. He knew how to find them and he had a reason for picking them."

The conversation wasn't going to end with that. Jamison could tell. "You have something you want to say, Bill? So get it out."

"Yeah, I do. What the hell? We have the evidence T. J. found. You already said as much that we got enough to make an arrest, so why not do it? And another thing, there hasn't been another murder since we arrested St. Claire, has there?" O'Hara lowered his voice as he stared at the younger man. "Matt, this isn't going to go down well with Mover and the rest of the boys. You have to know that."

"I know that, but *everything* turns on the Garrett case. Win that and we have St. Claire. Lose that and if all we have is those bits of fiber and hair, then we got shit. I need more. You have to get it and those cops need to keep their mouths shut until we're ready. That's your job. Now find me the link."

He walked around his desk and put his hand on O'Hara's shoulder. Jamison had never done that before any more than he would put his hand on a pit bull. Still, he let his hand rest there for a moment. "Bill, I've thought about this. You and Ernie keep working on the murder cases and as soon as we have a case we can try, that's when we make an arrest. Okay?"

Still glowering, O'Hara's face softened a bit. "Just tell me what you're thinking."

"Okay, what I'm thinking is that I can't question St. Claire at all about the murders because he's lawyered up and there is no way McGuiness is going to let him talk to us. I do know that McGuiness has to put St. Claire on the stand in order to defend him in the Garrett case. He has no choice.

"I'm going to wait, and during the Garrett trial when St. Claire is on the stand I'm going to figure out a way to ask him questions that will help me prove the three murders. I'm not sure what they are yet, but we're going to go after St. Claire *during* the Garrett trial."

"And if the judge won't allow you to do that?"

"That's my job, to figure out how to ask questions that give us bits and pieces without McGuiness being able to stop me. You use a hammer. I use a scalpel. Okay?"

"Yeah, okay, but you want me to take the heat from T. J. and the rest without explaining any of this? That's not going to be easy."

Jamison didn't respond. He was thinking about the evidence the two detectives had found. It was perfect. He couldn't help thinking to himself, Maybe too perfect.

O'Hara spent the rest of the day visiting the family physicians of two of the murdered women and the gynecologist of the third. He avoided any indication that the information might be related to St. Claire. The doctors were cooperative, although O'Hara had to listen to several comments about what his office was doing to poor Dr. St. Claire.

Apart from the doctors' sensitivity about one of their own being caught in the vise of police and prosecutors, not a single doctor would turn over the medical records of the women who had been murdered without a court order for fear of violating some legal privilege. They could use a search warrant but that would require probable cause, and in the face of such a request any judge would say they were just fishing. And O'Hara knew that was exactly what he was doing, fishing with not much to use for a hook and no bait.

Late in the afternoon O'Hara returned to Jamison's office. "I can't get the records for our victims without a court order, so what do you want me to do?"

Jamison thought for a moment. "We'll use a grand jury subpoena. We'll call a grand jury for the purpose of investigation into the murders, but we don't target St. Claire. That way there's no public case. It's all confidential and there are no leaks. It will take a few days but you'll get the records. Fair enough?"

O'Hara gave a crooked grin as he turned to leave. "Okay, it looks like I've maybe helped turn you into something more than a worthless piece-of-shit lawyer. Now you're starting to think like a cop." He gave a small wave of his hand. "That's a compliment, by the way."

Flashing his gold shield long enough to overcome any hesitation at his demands, O'Hara badged his way into the University Hospital lab. He'd spent hours studying the records once the grand jury subpoena had ordered them to be produced. He read and reread and then read them for the third time. And there it was.

Soon he was sitting with Stanley Hill, the supervising technician, a balding fiftyish man in a stained lab coat that hung open. O'Hara didn't want to think about the source of the stains that covered most of the front. It looked as if he used his coat to wipe his hands. His shirt was unbuttoned near the belt and it was obvious from the paunch hanging over his belt that walking out to meet O'Hara was the most exercise he planned to get that day.

"You are Investigator O'Hara, I understand? What can I do for you?" Hill's voice maintained a preciseness that went with someone who relished the security of accurate tests and indisputable results.

O'Hara shoved his bundle of lab reports across Hill's desk. "I'm investigating a series of murders involving the women in these medical reports. Each of these women had some type of medical procedure requiring lab tests of tissue that your people performed here. What I would like is for you to look at these reports, and tell me what were the tests involved and what the results revealed."

The lab technician slowly separated the individual reports before looking up. "And when would you like me to get back to you on this?"

"Now." O'Hara didn't blink.

Hill slowly inhaled. He shuffled through the three reports involving Symes, Johnson, and Ventana, moving his finger down each page before looking up to see if O'Hara was still there.

"Each of these women had minor skin procedures done by their physicians that involved removal of tissue. We looked at the tissue to see if it presented any problems in terms of cancer. Nothing was found of significance." He shoved the reports back at O'Hara. "Does that help?"

"Not particularly." He hadn't come in with any intention of bringing up St. Claire's name but it was becoming clear that was unavoidable; O'Hara needed to know if there was any link.

"Are you familiar with the name Alex St. Claire? Dr. Alex St. Claire? Would Dr. St. Claire have had any reason to have access to these reports?"

Anxiety and concern registered clearly on his face as Hill shook his head. "Dr. St. Claire is an anesthesiologist here at the hospital. He isn't a lab technician or a skin or cancer specialist. There is no reason he would have been furnished with these reports." Hill pushed his glasses back up to the bridge of his nose, appearing satisfied he had answered O'Hara's questions. He hadn't.

"Let me put it this way, is there anything in these reports Dr. St. Claire might have been interested in?"

Hill pursed his lips and shook his head. "As I told you, nothing in these reports would have concerned Dr. St. Claire." Hill hesitated. "Except, well . . ." Hill looked at the reports again. "Perhaps. Yes, each of the test procedures used involved a new type of topical anesthetic. I know Dr. St. Claire is interested in that anesthetic and had been doing some type of study. Let me check with our lab secretary."

He excused himself, returning within a few minutes. "Dr. St. Claire requested that he be notified whenever we had any lab work that involved this anesthetic. He had a list of anesthetics that he was interested in. Part of a study I suppose he was doing. Our lab would send over the names of patients on whom this anesthetic had been used. So yes, Dr. St. Claire would have been aware of these patients. Our lab secretary has a log book that would show all notifications that were routinely sent to him and others. Presumably those notifications were made with the patients you have asked about."

Unclear about the implications, O'Hara asked, "So did they send over the reports to Dr. St. Claire?"

"No, just the names and patient ID information such as the type of procedure, sex, age."

"How would that help St. Claire?"

Hill's response was impatient and terse. "With the patient ID information, Dr. St. Claire could access our files and look at the patient file if he was interested in doing any follow-up work with the patient's physician."

"I see. And that would allow him to look at all the information in the file?"

"Of course." Hill shrugged dismissively. "Despite the problems your office has created for Dr. St. Claire, he is a highly respected physician in this hospital and can have access to any reports he wants to see."

O'Hara laid his business card in front of Hill, at the same time tapping his finger on the gold-embossed badge on the side of the card to emphasize his point. "Mr. Hill, this conversation is confidential. You will not discuss my questions or my visit with *anyone*." O'Hara hesitated. He needed Hill to understand. "Obstruction of justice doesn't just happen because you don't talk. Sometimes it happens because you do. Any questions?" Hill shook his head.

Satisfied that he had made his point with Hill, O'Hara walked over to the hospital's records office, pulling his badge out. "I would like to see the hospital files for these women."

Even as he uttered the words, he knew this wasn't going to be easy. The administrator of the patient files walked out, looked at his badge, and shook her head. "No, they're confidential," she said before she turned and walked away. He would have to get a subpoena or a search warrant. Everything was taking time that he didn't have. He put a call into Jamison, explaining what he had found.

O'Hara wanted access now and he didn't want copies like he would get with a grand jury subpoena. He wanted the original paperwork because oily residue on hands would transfer to paper and there was a chance they might find a print of St. Claire's. While it was becoming more and more difficult to get prints off paper because most things were computerized, most of the individual records of the victims had not yet been converted because they contained handwritten notes. O'Hara's recognition of the loss of a common investigative tool reminded him that not all progress was beneficial.

To get the original records instead of copies, O'Hara would have to get a search warrant, and usually that wouldn't be easy. However, three murders would make almost any judge bend a little. Four hours later he had the warrant.

With the trial starting in less than five days, including the weekend, O'Hara would have to pursue the investigation without Jamison's help. In the meantime one thing was clear as O'Hara went through the records.

Nothing was there for Elizabeth Garrett except her most recent hospital admittance after the kidnap.

When he heard that, Jamison wouldn't need much time to think about why. It was obvious that St. Claire already knew all he needed to know about her.

As O'Hara paced back and forth in the sheriff's office forensic lab, each page of the medical files of the three murdered women was meticulously sprayed and then heated using a common household iron. Numerous prints appeared on the pages, but most were smudges and fragments. The office fingerprint expert examined each sheet, quickly looking at any usable purple print and comparing it to the booking prints of Alex St. Claire.

After three frustrating hours sifting through sheets of paper, Jessie, the print technician, looked up. "Detective O'Hara, I've found one. St. Claire left this print on the Symes file. I'll keep looking." O'Hara was gleeful, promising the diminutive print technician that he would buy her dinner, which earned him a reproachful look because she was aware of his reputation.

This was just what Jamison needed. He could prove Alex St. Claire had looked at one of the files, at least, and that file had all of the personal information he needed to pick her as a potential victim. Late in the day he got one more break. There was a partial print from St. Claire on Ventana's file, although nothing on Johnson's.

In the few days left before trial was to begin, Jamison worked ceaselessly. He arrived at the office in the dark and he left in the dark, hoping to grab a few hours of sleep before he had to be back in the office to prepare his trial book, which contained his questions and legal memos and collated reports that matched them to witnesses and interviews. He put any presentation to the grand jury regarding the murders on hold. He wasn't ready for that yet and the pending trial consumed all his time.

The priorities for each remaining day before trial grew in number and intensity. He had to pay another visit to Dr. Gupta to get some very specific questions answered *and* he had a trial setting conference on the Garrett case *and* he had to have another talk with Beth Garrett. But first he had to talk to Gupta. He had a hunch. Maybe O'Hara was right. He was starting to think more like a cop.

Chapter 21

Gupta was not in a good mood. He considered the repeated questions about the blood samples as a challenge to his competence. Neither Jamison nor O'Hara really cared, but they were sensitive to Gupta taking offense. They needed his cooperation and they knew that Gupta could be difficult if he got his back up.

Glowering at both men standing in front of his desk, Gupta responded with irritation. "I have told you before that I was the one who initialed the blood samples and what the lab results were. It is not going to change simply because you keep asking me."

O'Hara was conciliatory but he also knew what buttons to push. "Dr. Gupta, we know you are very careful with your work. What we suspect is that somebody may have tampered with your results."

The pathologist became indignant. "Tampered? Do you mean that someone may have interfered with my tissue and blood samples? I have signed for everything. It is not possible." Gupta shook his head emphatically, repeating himself. "It is not possible."

Sensing Gupta's defensiveness, Jamison interjected. "Doctor, you've acknowledged that Dr. St. Claire was present during parts of the other autopsies. In fact, I was there once when he came in and I saw him handle the blood samples that you drew."

"Yes, that is true, but I initialed those blood samples. All I remember Dr. St. Claire doing was placing them in the tray for lab analysis. He did that in other autopsies too. So there is nothing that could have been done to them." As Gupta convinced himself that there were no lapses in his procedure, his relief was visible, and a smile erased his defensive expression.

"Yes." Jamison nodded sympathetically. "But suppose Dr. St. Claire switched the blood samples? When did you actually initial them?"

"After I finished with the blood draws they were placed in the evidence tray, perhaps by Dr. St. Claire. I don't remember. Then when I finished the procedure I stripped off my gloves and signed the blood vials. They were right there." Gupta's dark face grayed slightly. "You are saying you think Dr. St. Claire switched the vials of blood from each of those women? It would have been difficult. I think I would have seen it."

Offering a possible explanation, O'Hara suggested, "Of course you would have seen it if you had reason to suspect something was wrong. But you had no reason to suspect Dr. St. Claire, did you?"

Uncertain, Gupta hesitated. "No, I would not suspect a fellow physician of doing that. Why would I? I cannot say that it is not possible but I do not believe it."

Not wanting Gupta to linger on the thought that he may have been taken advantage of by St. Claire, Jamison said, "Dr. Gupta, is there any way you can tell if the blood that was tested actually came from those three women? I mean, if the blood vials were switched, then what was tested would not have shown what was actually in the blood of each victim, correct?"

Gupta was pensive; he seemed lost in thought as he considered the possibilities. "If the blood vials were switched before they were tested for drugs, we would naturally conclude that the drug results were those of the victims. But the person switching the blood would have to know in advance what the blood type was for each of the murder victims and substitute contaminated blood of the same blood type as the victim's. There is routine blood typing done with the toxic screen so if the blood type was different than the patient records, the technician would immediately know something was wrong and the blood did not come from the victim. That did not happen here."

The implication was clear to Jamison. St. Claire had the patient records. He would have known in advance what blood type to obtain. It was really quite clever. All he had to do was procure the blood samples from another person with the same blood type and substitute them before Gupta signed them, or even after, if he could replace the blood in the vials. He just had to make sure the blood he substituted would show massive doses of the heroin-barbiturate combination.

Jamison quickly concluded that knowing the blood types of the murder victims, St. Claire had obtained blood of a matching type from junkies who probably overdosed from a fatal dosage of the heroin-barbiturate combination that had been killing addicts in the community. Then he just switched the blood in a way that would make it appear that the samples with the contaminated blood were marked as belonging to the murder victims. And he would know that nobody would check the blood samples to see if they actually came from the victims.

As Gupta examined his copies of the autopsy reports, he offered, "If the combination of heroin and barbiturate did not cause the heart stoppage, then something else must have, and I do not know what it was. But I do have another way of determining whether heroin and barbiturates were actually present in each patient. When I do an autopsy in a suspected homicide I routinely save a piece of the liver in case further analysis needs to be made."

Before Jamison said anything, O'Hara asked, "How would that help us?"

Gupta allowed a sly smile. "Because, Detective O'Hara, the liver is our body's garbage disposal. All things we put into our body pass through it. With certain exceptions, the liver should normally have traces in it of what actually killed these three women unless the heart stopped immediately, which I doubt. It will also tell us if the blood samples we have are those of the victims.

"Of course, it would be best if we could get more blood samples but that is not possible now." The reality was that the bodies had long been released to the grieving families. One had been embalmed and buried, the other two cremated. There was no blood sample that could be compared.

Jamison asked his final question. "Would Dr. St. Claire know you took a liver sample?"

"I doubt it. He would have no reason to know, and I would have no reason to give him an explanation. The doctors in other fields of medical expertise depend on pathologists but they do tend to look upon us as not that fastidious because our methods are sometimes, shall we say, rather brutal to those who do not appreciate what we do. I will conduct lab analysis on the liver samples I have. As soon as I receive the results I will contact you."

O'Hara placed his card on Gupta's desk. "And you will not share our conversation with anyone?"

"No, Detective O'Hara. I will keep our conversation confidential."

~

As they rode back to the office, O'Hara acknowledged that Jamison's hunch had been right. "How did you figure out that the blood samples might have been switched? St. Claire could have just injected those women with the drugs. Wouldn't that have been easier?"

"I kept thinking about the fact that everything involving the murders was about misdirection. I remembered that at the Symes autopsy I saw St. Claire do those blood draws and put the vials in the tray. He was present at the other autopsies also. It just occurred to me that he had to have a reason to be at each autopsy and maybe the blood had something to do with it. Yeah, he could have injected those women with the drugs, but then there would be the chance that somebody would track the heroin or barbiturates. Those are restricted drugs and records are kept. I didn't think St. Claire was the type to go buy that shit. So it just occurred to me that maybe he switched the blood. There are plenty of junkies that have been overdosing on it. As long as he knew the blood type and got the blood from a junkie with the same blood type, he could do it."

O'Hara offered, "You would've made a good cop."

"I've watched a few good cops. I even work with one or two."

Chapter 22

Jamison needed one last interview with his star witness to make sure he knew everything she would say in her testimony, and to watch her tell the story so he could see what the jury would see.

Beth Garrett sat across from Jamison's desk. As she gazed at him today, he could see a level of nervousness, but she nevertheless held her body erect, composed. Jamison didn't feel the same level of confidence himself that she was trying to maintain. It didn't help that his first thought every time he saw her wasn't about the case. It wasn't any different this time even though he still had the nagging thought that she was holding something back.

Some of the heads in the office turned when they saw her walk in. There was no question she was beautiful. He wasn't sure how a jury would react, but he knew how he reacted to it. He wanted a victim in a case like this to look attractive, but not provocative. He made a mental note to bring that up later, about how she should dress.

"Beth, I want to talk again about your relationship with St. Claire when you were younger. This is going to come up in the trial. You have to be ready for it and I need to know everything because St. Claire is going to tell McGuiness everything." He kept his voice as gentle as possible. He didn't want Beth to feel cornered by him.

"Mr. Jamison." It was important that she didn't slip and call him Matt during the trial. He had emphasized that. "As I said before, we met when I was in high school. I broke it off because it was wrong. It was out of control. I was out of control."

"Out of control how? You've used that term before. Was there something unusual about your relationship, something, well, different?"

"It was my first time with a man. I didn't know what to do. Alex—"

"Beth," Jamison interrupted, "I know it's normal for you to call him that but it personalizes him in front of the jury. Be sure to call him 'the defendant.' Avoid calling him by his first name."

"I'm sorry. After we broke up, the defendant asked to meet with me and that's when he took me to Los Angeles. He took me to a motel. I've tried but I can't remember the name of it. The next day he said we were going to run away, maybe to Mexico. Then he stopped at a light and I got away. I ran to a house and pounded on the door. A woman answered, and she called the police. My parents came and took me home and Alex—I mean the defendant—was arrested."

"At the motel you had sexual intercourse with him?" Jamison hesitated. "St. Claire's attorney will ask you if you consented. He is going to imply that you went willingly to Los Angeles and that any sexual activity was consensual."

The tone of her response was edged with anger. "He made me go with him. I didn't consent. I didn't have a choice. I told you, he had a knife. I don't know what else to say." Jamison noticed that she didn't directly answer his question about sexual activity, but when she said she didn't consent to going with him it was emphatic.

He changed the subject. "I have the police report from LA. The woman, a Mrs. Mary Saxelby, said it was midafternoon and that you ran up to her door crying and hysterical. LA didn't do much of a report, even though you were seventeen, a minor, because you said nothing happened and claimed it was all a misunderstanding. They simply turned their reports over to the police here. Why is that?"

"My parents. I know I should have told my parents and the police, but it was my fault. I should never have gotten in the car with him. I didn't want my parents to know what I'd done. I was seventeen." She looked at him for understanding. Jamison had seen it before—that look that said sometimes people just do stupid things.

He tried one last time with as much emphasis as he could manage without sounding doubtful or intimidating. "Look, Beth, when I walk into that courtroom I need to know everything. It may be embarrassing. It may be something you've never told anybody, but I need to know. I can't afford to hear it in court for the first time. Think carefully. Is there *anything* about your relationship with Alex St. Claire that can come out in that courtroom that differs from what you've told me?"

The look on her face made him stop. He could see it in her eyes, pleading with him. When her eyes began to brim with tears he stopped. "Okay, Beth. I'll be there for you. I will do everything I can to make sure that Alex St. Claire never comes near you or anybody else."

Beth sat there for a moment. Jamison could tell she wanted to say something more. He waited. "Mr. Jamison, the newspapers, my parents, everyone keeps saying that you're investigating Alex about murder, the murders of those women. Is that true?"

"I can't talk to you about that, Beth. But it is true that your kidnapping and the pattern with those murders have remarkable similarity. I just can't discuss it unless there's something you haven't told me that St. Claire said to you or makes you suspicious. Is there?"

"No, Alex never said anything to me. I don't know. I just don't think he would do something like that."

"Think about what he did to you. If he could do that, there's no telling what he is really capable of."

"But you don't know—you don't know if he murdered those women?"

"I don't know enough—yet. Right now we need to get through your case. If you are worried about St. Claire coming back for you, I don't think he would be that stupid but please tell me if you see or hear anything. Alex St. Claire is unpredictable and unpredictable people can do stupid and dangerous things. Is there anything, anything at all that you can tell me that might help prove St. Claire had something to do with those crimes?"

"No, I've told you everything."

Jamison focused on Beth's eyes. He sensed that he still hadn't heard everything but there was no point in asking Beth to go over her history with St. Claire again. If there was something else, it would be a horrible mistake for her not to tell him, and he had tried to make that clear. But maybe there just wasn't anything else. Maybe he was seeing shadows that weren't there.

With insecurity borne of experience, he watched her walk out of the office. If she was holding anything back, then Jamison knew that a jury would see it also under the unrelenting cross-examination of a defense attorney who, if she was hiding anything at all, had the advantage of knowing what it was. And Jamison knew Tom McGuiness would ruthlessly use every advantage available to him. He picked up his file to head down to court to confirm the trial was going forward.

The Friday trial confirmation conference, a routine procedure meant to address last-minute trial details with the trial judge, Judge Wallace, did nothing to assuage his concerns.

Jamison had estimated the trial would take three to four court days.

Wallace had looked over at McGuiness and asked whether he had anything to add to that. McGuiness had said, "Your Honor, with all due respect to Mr. Jamison, we believe the trial will be more complicated than his estimate allows. Our estimate is not less than seven to ten days of trial."

Wallace had caught the prosecutor's slightly raised eyebrows as Jamison slowly turned his body to face McGuiness. "Mr. Jamison. It appears there has been a communication gap. Have you and Mr. McGuiness discussed this case?"

"Well, Your Honor, as usual I expect Mr. McGuiness will be producing witnesses that haven't shown up in our investigation of the case, but he hasn't shared those names with me. I will accept his estimate but I have a right to know his witness list and he hasn't given me anything." It was a common defense strategy to stonewall discovery until the last minute to keep the prosecution off-balance.

In response to the not-so-subtle implications, McGuiness shot back, "You'll get my witness list when I know what witnesses will be called. I'm still investigating this case and so far I haven't decided whether it is worth calling defense witnesses. I'll decide that when I hear what you have to say."

The judge in return had admonished both sides not to test him with theatrics that might jeopardize the trial before ordering the lawyers to be ready to begin jury selection on Monday morning.

Now, O'Hara followed Jamison back to his office. Jamison closed the door before saying a word. "What the hell? What has he got that is going to take at least seven days to put on? I'm going to have to walk into court and still not know the answer?"

The older investigator put his hand on the younger man's shoulder. "I've never seen a case yet where we had all the answers going in."

"Maybe so, but when McGuiness puts on his case we're going to have answers and right now I feel like I'm the one who won't be able to explain."

Chapter 23

No matter how many times he did it, walking through the courtroom doors on the first day of trial always hit Jamison with a heavy dose of reality. He didn't feel stage fright or fear. That was long behind him. He often thought it was probably what a pitcher might feel before a big game.

Jamison stood when the case of the People versus Alex St. Claire was called. "Matthew Jamison, ready for the People, Your Honor." At that moment all eyes were on him. The wait was over. He looked behind him at the panel of prospective jurors.

Jamison watched as the parade of jurors looked at Alex St. Claire, dressed in his meticulously tailored suit, exuding an air of confidence. No matter how skillfully he attempted to reveal the truth about the defendant, he knew that jurors thought doctors wore a patina of integrity, unlike people they thought of as criminals, let alone rapists and kidnappers. Still, by the end of the *voir dire*, a day and a half later, he had seven men and five women as jurors, with two alternates who would sit in if they lost a juror during the case. Opening statements would be in the morning.

Fourteen people fixed their eyes intently on him as Jamison rose from behind the counsel table and looked first at Judge Wallace, saying, "Your Honor," and then at the jurors, who sat expectantly.

He walked to the well of the courtroom, the open area between the judge's bench and the counsel table with the jury box on one side, and stood silently for a moment, allowing his mind to focus on his opening statement. Whether the jurors wanted to be there or not, one could always sense their anticipation of the first words in a case.

"Ladies and gentlemen. You have heard bits and pieces about this case during jury selection. Now is the time for me to explain what I expect the evidence to show. First I will present my case, and then Mr. McGuiness has the opportunity to present his case. This is because the People bear the burden to prove Alex St. Claire guilty beyond a reasonable doubt of the crimes of kidnapping, assault, and attempted rape.

"The defendant is a highly educated man and as a physician he is a member of one of our most revered professions. We all trust our doctors. But doctors are people, and people sometimes make mistakes, even the best and most educated of us."

He hesitated for a few seconds and added, "And sometimes, like other human beings, they do things that are not just mistakes, they are crimes. Criminal acts, even despicable criminal acts, are not constrained by education but by morality. And, ladies and gentlemen, morality is individual to each of us and so are our deepest and darkest thoughts, which we conceal unless we act on them. The evidence will show that Alex St. Claire did act on his darkest thoughts.

"I will not refer to Alex St. Claire as Dr. St. Claire. In this courtroom he is a defendant and he is a defendant because the evidence will show that he was a man obsessed with the victim in this case, a young schoolteacher, Elizabeth Garrett. She will tell you that many years ago she had a relationship with the defendant. Then she was a young woman in high school and the defendant was in college, a gaping span of maturity. To Elizabeth Garrett, the defendant was a fascinating and irresistible older man.

"The defendant is not on trial because of that relationship. He is on trial because once it had ended he could not get over that relationship. He could not get over his feelings for Elizabeth Garrett and one day his feelings could no longer be controlled.

"One night Elizabeth was driving to her parents' home where she lives, completely unaware that Alex St. Claire was following her. While listening to music she made a mistake, missed her turn, and ended up having to take a remote road to get home. It was a mistake that would place her in great jeopardy. To force her to stop her car, the defendant used flashing lights, pretending to be a policeman. And just as each of us would do if we thought a police officer was behind us, Elizabeth stopped, anxious and frightened, trying to figure out what she had done wrong.

"The evidence will show that the only thing Elizabeth did wrong was to stop. The defendant came up to her car and used a knife to subdue her. He cut her on the neck, and then he used some type of drug or anesthetic to kidnap her. Elizabeth will tell you she has no memory of how she got to the defendant's house, but she will tell you that it was not by her own choosing.

We don't know what drug the defendant used to overcome Elizabeth Garrett. But you must remember, he is an anesthesiologist, a specialist in drugs that control and render people unconscious. There are many drugs he had access to that he could have used.

"You will hear investigators from the district attorney's office and from the sheriff's office who, on the following day after a frantic search, found Elizabeth tied naked to a bed, in a home, a home that as we will show you the defendant kept secret. And, ladies and gentlemen, the last witness I will call in this case will be Elizabeth Garrett."

Jamison had made the strategic decision that he would lay out all the evidence that pointed irrefutably toward a forcible abduction and a sexual motivation before he put Elizabeth Garrett on the stand. He would build the drama of the case, and then put her before the jury with the credibility of the physical evidence already reinforcing her.

Jamison stood for a moment in front of the jury before he approached Alex St. Claire, seated behind the defense table. His words resonated in the silent courtroom. "You will hear about what those officers saw when they rescued Elizabeth from the defendant." Jamison paused and let the word "defendant" settle on St. Claire before finishing his sentence.

"And at the end of this case, as hard as it may be for many of you to believe that an educated man, a doctor who has sworn to do no harm, could abduct, terrorize, and brutalize a young woman, the evidence will show that is exactly what he did." Jamison raised his hand and pointed. "And you will conclude that Alex St. Claire is guilty."

"Mr. McGuiness." Judge Wallace leaned forward in his chair. "Do you wish to make an opening statement or reserve your statement until the conclusion of the People's case?" Wallace usually gave defense attorneys a moment to gather their thoughts after the prosecution made their opening statement. It was not unusual for a defense attorney to wait until after the prosecution presented their entire case before they made an opening statement. Defense attorneys preferred to see what the prosecution would actually be able to prove before deciding what to explain to the jury about their defense. "Would you like a brief recess?"

"Thank you, Your Honor. A recess will not be necessary. I will make an opening statement and it will be very brief." He walked from behind the counsel table and stood a few feet from the jury box, close enough so that he would fill their field of vision and far enough back that he would not appear threatening.

"Ladies and gentlemen. First, on behalf of my client, Dr. Alex St. Claire, I would like to thank you for your time and willingness to be here. Mr. Jamison has given you one perspective of what he believes the evidence will show. There is another perspective and it is quite different. Dr. St. Claire is a brilliant man, a highly regarded physician, an anesthesiologist. Mr. Jamison is right about one thing. You would not expect a man like Dr. St. Claire to do what he has been accused of.

"And your assumption would be correct. The evidence will show that he did not do what he has been accused of. When we get to the end of Mr. Jamison's case you will have heard one side, but I believe you will have begun to wonder whether there is another side, another explanation. I assure you that there is another side, another explanation, and you will hear it from us.

"No, Dr. St. Claire may not have used the best judgment and perhaps he was the victim of his deep feelings for Elizabeth Garrett. If there is one thing that human experience has shown it is that love and passion take many forms and frequently can lead to poor judgment.

"But at the end of this case, regardless of whether you find the explanation to be one of passion or poor judgment, the final explanation and the only reasonable conclusion will be one of total innocence of any crime except, perhaps, the crime of loving too deeply and trusting too much. On behalf of Dr. St. Claire, I ask, we ask, that you keep an open mind as you have promised to do."

McGuiness walked past his client, momentarily placing his hand on Alex St. Claire's shoulder before turning back to the court. "Thank you, Your Honor. My client is prepared to proceed."

Jamison leaned over to O'Hara, seated next to him at the counsel table as his chief investigator. "He's going all in with the consent defense," he whispered, "but he wouldn't have made that opening statement if he was just going to rely on his client. God only knows what it is because I sure as hell don't."

The first witness for the State was the Garrett's neighbor, Ron Costa, who testified he saw the car abandoned by the side of the road as he drove home and became concerned. He had parked behind what he recognized as Elizabeth's car, walked over, and found there was no one inside the vehicle.

He had run his hand over the engine compartment but it was barely warm, so he knew the car had been sitting for a while. The door was unlocked and he had looked inside. As soon as he opened the door, the interior light came on and he saw what looked like a smear of blood on the driver's seat. Then he immediately called her father.

Cross-examination by McGuiness was brief. An accomplished trial lawyer, McGuiness knew that effective cross-examination only highlighted the point you wanted the jury to remember. Simply asking questions, allowing a witness to repeat what had been said in direct, accomplished nothing except to emphasize detrimental testimony. He moved quickly to the point he wanted.

"Mr. Costa, you live near the Garrett family, correct?"

"Yes, for many years. I've known Elizabeth since she was a little girl."

McGuiness made a show of flipping through his notes as if he was searching to make sure he asked all of his questions. Jamison watched, knowing that McGuiness had every question firmly in his mind and the show of looking at his notes was simply to diminish any impression that the defense was a well-oiled machine with every question planned in advance.

"Mr. Costa, when you walked up to Ms. Garrett's car was the door open?"

"No. I opened it. But it wasn't open when I first saw the car."

"So did you leave it open?"

"When I opened it the interior light came on. As I said, I saw what looked like blood on the seat. I don't know if I shut the door. Like I told the detectives, I may have left it open. I don't remember. I was in a hurry to call Elizabeth's father."

"At the time of night that you saw Ms. Garrett's car were you coming home from someplace specific?"

"Yes, I had been working late. Sometimes I have to."

"Yes." McGuiness turned to the jury with a smile. "We all understand that. So let me ask you. This route that you took that night." McGuiness paused as if carefully considering his words. "Is this the road you normally take home?"

"Yes, it is the fastest way home for me."

"And are you familiar with the restaurant known as the Packing Shed?"

"I know where it is. I've never been to it but I know young people go there."

"If you were going home *from* the Packing Shed"—McGuiness paused, placing emphasis on the word "from" to make his point—"would the fastest way to your home near the Garrett family, would that take you past the place where you saw Ms. Garrett's car that night?"

"Oh, no, it would be out of the way. There's a much more direct road that you would take to get to where we live if you were coming from town."

"So, you would not expect a person familiar with the community who was coming from the Packing Shed to take the road where Ms. Garrett's car was found if they were going to the Garrett house?"

"No, not really. It's very dark out there, you know."

"Yes, it's very dark out there, but I want to make sure I understand. A person familiar with the roads out there and coming from the Packing Shed, then, wouldn't take that road where Ms. Garrett's car was found unless they were lost or . . ." Again McGuiness hesitated, letting several seconds pass before he finished his question. "Unless they intended to take that road, even though it was not the most direct route to the Garrett home?"

Costa was puzzled. "Why would you want to take a longer way to get home in the middle of the night if you didn't have to?"

"Yes, Mr. Costa, that is an excellent question. Thank you for asking it. Your Honor, I have no further questions. Perhaps Mr. Jamison will want to ask Mr. Costa's question?"

Jamison sat at the counsel table with his hands folded on his yellow legal tablet. "Thank you, nothing further of this witness, Your Honor."

Clearly Elizabeth Garrett had not taken the most direct route home. Jamison had given Elizabeth's explanation, but McGuiness had effectively planted a question in the minds of the jurors about that explanation. It was a point Jamison had anticipated. It just sounded much worse when he heard it in court.

Elizabeth's father made his way to the witness stand and took his oath without looking to the left or the right. Jamison knew it was evident to everyone in the room from his body language that he was an angry man. Garrett testified that Costa had called him and he had gone to find his daughter's car. He described what he saw and said it wasn't like Elizabeth to leave her car by the side of the road or to not call.

When the direct was over Mike Garrett looked stonily at St. Claire and then at McGuiness as the defense attorney walked from behind the counsel table and approached him.

"Mr. Garrett, I realize this is very difficult for you. I only have a few questions.

"You're aware that your daughter and my client, Alex St. Claire, had a relationship when they were much younger?"

"I wouldn't call it a relationship."

"Isn't it correct that you have always disliked my client and disapproved of your daughter seeing him?"

Barely suppressed anger seethed to the surface. "My daughter was in high school. He took advantage of her. He—"

"I'm sorry, Mr. Garrett," McGuiness interrupted, "the question is whether you disliked my client and disapproved of your daughter seeing him. Yes or no?"

"Yes. He's older than her. He ruined—" McGuiness looked at the judge.

Judge Wallace interrupted this time. "Mr. Garrett, please simply answer the question asked."

Through clenched teeth, his answer came out with a hiss. "Yes, I dislike your client. As a matter of fact, I hate him. Does that answer your question?"

Glancing over his right shoulder toward the jury, McGuiness stepped back. "Yes, sir, it does. I have only one other question. Was your daughter, Elizabeth, aware that you disliked Alex St. Claire and that you didn't want her to see him?"

Mike Garrett glared straight at St. Claire's emotionless face. "Yes, she knew. But, you know, children don't always listen."

Slowly McGuiness walked back to the counsel table, again resting his hand briefly on the shoulder of his client. "Yes, sometimes young people don't listen. I do have one more question. I'm sorry. Did it puzzle you that your daughter's car was where you found it? I mean, did it seem unusual to you given that she was coming from the Packing Shed Restaurant in town?"

"It was out of the way if that's what you mean, but you could drive that way and get to our home." Garrett cocked his head slightly, as if trying to determine what McGuiness was getting at. "It was just a longer way to drive."

“A longer way for a young woman to drive in the middle of the night on dark country roads if she wanted to get home as fast as possible? Is that right?”

The contempt in the answer was barely concealed. “There are all kinds of roads out there that will get you to our home. My daughter wouldn’t have left her car like that unless somebody forced her to.”

McGuiness returned to the counsel table and stood directly behind St. Claire. “Or unless she intended to meet someone there?”

“My daughter didn’t plan to meet anyone and you know it.”

Judge Wallace held up his hand as he addressed Elizabeth’s father. “Mr. Garrett, we all understand this is difficult for you. Please just answer the question.”

Pausing to allow the implications of his last question to be drawn by the jury, McGuiness said, “Your Honor, thank you. Mr. Garrett doesn’t need to answer. I have nothing further.”

Judge Wallace excused Mike Garrett, reminding him that because he was a witness he wouldn’t be permitted to be present in the courtroom during the trial, a fact that from his expression only further inflamed the father.

Jamison sat through the last series of questions by McGuiness, his face a study in the indifference cultivated by trial lawyers for the excruciating moments when they were getting hit in the gut. McGuiness had taken the first swing of his ax and he had made a noticeable cut.

“Your Honor, the People call District Attorney Investigator Bill O’Hara.”

As he walked past the jury box, O’Hara smiled. His large frame was carefully tailored into his trial suit. He believed it made him look less intimidating, but he was probably the only one in the courtroom who thought so. Or, as Ernie would say, “You can take a grizzly bear and put him in a tuxedo but he isn’t going to fool anyone.” He took his seat in the witness box after taking the oath, looking exactly like Ernie’s description.

Through initial questioning, O’Hara recounted his experience as a homicide investigator for the sheriff’s office as well as his time as a district attorney investigator and his two awards for bravery in the line of duty. O’Hara answered quietly, his rumbling voice commanding attention as Jamison asked his next question. “Investigator O’Hara, were you assigned as lead investigator for the district attorney's office to assist the sheriff's office when Elizabeth Garrett's car was found?"

"Yes, I responded with you that night and we went to the location of Ms. Garrett's car."

"Subsequently, is it correct that you concluded that the defendant might have information about the disappearance of Ms. Garrett?"

"Yes, after talking to her parents, our investigative team, including you, learned that Ms. Garrett and the defendant had a relationship years ago that had, shall we say, ended badly."

"And why did that cause you to conclude that the defendant might have information about Ms. Garrett?"

Before the trial, O'Hara had been told by Jamison to avoid any mention of the homicides because it would result in a motion for mistrial by raising uncharged crimes in front of the jury. "We had become aware of the past relationship between the defendant and Ms. Garrett. It seemed like normal follow-up. I had met the defendant in the course of other investigations involving the hospital where he worked, so I knew him."

"So you went to his home to talk to him?"

"Yes, the four of us, you, Sheriff's Detective Arthur Puccinelli, DA Investigator Ernest Garcia, and myself."

Meticulously Jamison guided O'Hara through the events at the house, the refusal of St. Claire to answer the door, and the decision to break it down when he heard the screams from the back of the house.

"And did you ultimately see Ms. Garrett?"

"Yes, after we cuffed the defendant, I ran down the hall. I saw Ms. Garrett wrapped in a blanket. The window was broken and Investigator Garcia was shielding her behind him with his gun drawn."

"How did Ms. Garrett appear to you?"

"She was almost incoherent and there was some blood on her, possibly from cuts of her own or because of cuts sustained by Investigator Garcia."

Jamison then took O'Hara through the rest of the investigation. He nodded at McGuiness. "Your witness."

Any perfunctory pleasantries were disregarded as McGuiness immediately attacked. "Investigator O'Hara, you didn't have a warrant when you broke in my client's door?"

"I didn't need a warrant. When I heard him running and a woman screaming we were afraid for the life of the victim."

"That assumes, does it not, that Ms. Garrett was a victim?"

"Yes, counselor, it assumes that. It's my job to decide when to act. If I make mistakes somebody can get hurt or die. My job was to protect Ms. Garrett."

"Did you see my client attempt to harm Ms. Garrett in any way?"

"No, but when I went through the door your client was running down the hall. I saw where she had been tied to the bed."

"You saw that after you threw Dr. St. Claire on the floor and both you and Detective Puccinelli put your knees into his back, isn't that correct?" McGuiness's tone was biting.

"Yes."

"And when you did that, twisting Dr. St. Claire's arms behind him, he was screaming something, wasn't he?"

"Yes, he said a number of things."

"And you said a number of things to him, I believe, such as calling him"—McGuiness gestured apologetically—"'fucking asshole' while you had a gun pointed at his head, isn't that correct?"

"Yes, I did use words to that effect and, yes, both Pooch, Detective Puccinelli, and I had our weapons drawn and pointed at the defendant when he was subdued. It was a chaotic situation. It wasn't a ballroom dance, counselor. It was a potentially very violent situation and you try to gain control. The objective is to avoid hurting anybody physically. It isn't about trying to avoid hurting someone's feelings. We didn't hurt your client physically. He was appropriately subdued."

"And while he was being 'appropriately subdued' as you put it, one thing Dr. St. Claire said to you was that you were making a mistake, isn't that correct?"

"Yes."

"As a matter of fact, Dr. St. Claire repeated several times that you were making a mistake, didn't he?"

"Yes, he did. I've arrested a lot of people, Mr. McGuiness, and it isn't the first time I've heard one of them say that. It isn't like television where they say, 'You've got me. I did it.'"

McGuiness paused, tilting his head as if he was taking the full measuring of O'Hara. "No, Investigator O'Hara, it isn't like television, is it? But sometimes on television things aren't what they seem, are they?"

"Is that a question?"

"No, that's not a question. But let me ask you this. When you heard the footsteps running down the hall, you also heard the window crashing?"

"I heard the crashing of the window and the footsteps very close together."

"Can you say which you heard first?"

O'Hara hesitated a moment before answering. "No, it all happened very quickly."

"So would it be fair to say that it's possible that Dr. St. Claire heard the glass breaking and Ms. Garrett screaming at the same time you did?"

"I would have to make an assumption, counselor. I don't know what he heard."

The expression on McGuiness's face reminded O'Hara of a snake trying to decide where to strike. "Let me ask you this, Investigator O'Hara. The breaking of the window and the screams of what turned out to be Ms. Garrett, that's what made you break through the door, is that correct? That's what made you run into the house and down the hallway?"

"That and my sense that your client was running away from the door."

"Isn't it fair to say, Investigator O'Hara, that Dr. St. Claire could also have been running toward the room where Ms. Garrett was screaming to rescue her from a threat?"

"We weren't a threat."

"That must be why Ms. Garrett screamed." McGuiness let his comment hang in the air for a moment. "Thank you, Investigator O'Hara. I have nothing further." The defense attorney turned back toward the counsel table and then paused as if caught in further thought. "Oh, yes, there is one more thing. You questioned Dr. St. Claire, didn't you?"

The question made O'Hara uncomfortable. He had enough experience to know that it was improper for a prosecutor to tell a jury that a defendant had asked for a lawyer, but McGuiness wasn't a prosecutor. He looked warily at McGuiness. "Yes."

"And my client told you that things weren't what they might appear. Isn't that correct?"

"Yes."

"But that didn't cause you to question your arrest, did it?"

"No, I don't usually find people tied to a bed after their car is left by the side of a road."

"I suppose not, but let me ask you this. At the time you crashed through that door and arrested Dr. St. Claire was it possible that she might have been cooperative with being tied to the bed?"

O'Hara rubbed his mustache, debating with himself as to how to answer. "Are you asking me whether it was possible that Ms. Garrett was emotionally involved with the defendant and had allowed herself to be tied to the bed?"

"I am asking you whether at the time you went crashing into that house and saw Dr. St. Claire and Ms. Garrett if there was anything about the circumstances that was inconsistent with the possibility this was a consensual situation."

"We spoke to Ms. Garrett—"

McGuiness interrupted. "You didn't speak to Ms. Garrett until later, after all of this happened, did you?"

"No."

"So I take it the answer to my question is that based on what you saw after you broke down my client's door and handcuffed him and saw Ms. Garrett, that you assumed this was not a consensual situation. Would that be a fair statement?"

O'Hara's face turned darker and his mouth drew into a hard line. "Mr. McGuiness, I've been a cop for over twenty years. Is what you are suggesting possible? Yes. But did I think this was a consensual situation? No."

"So while you had your knee in my client's back and he was screaming that it wasn't what it looked like, you didn't believe him, did you?"

"No."

"Thank you, Investigator O'Hara. You're a police officer and a very good one. We all appreciate that, but as a highly experienced investigator, you know sometimes things just aren't what they appear to be, are they?" McGuiness held up his hand. "You don't have to answer that."

Judge Wallace indicated that O'Hara would be the last witness of the day. Trial would resume in the morning.

Jamison, O'Hara, and Pooch returned to the district attorney's office. After he took Garrett home, Ernie joined them. They went over the day's testimony and the cross-examination, trying to divine what evidence McGuiness might have or the direction he was going. Jamison did most of the talking while the others listened.

"So we already knew that the location of Garrett's car was out of the way if she was going directly home. Her explanation is that she was listening to music and she missed her turn and came back using the road where her car was found. So where is McGuiness going with that?" He already suspected the answer, but he just wanted to hear their thoughts.

"Well," O'Hara began speculating, "our case is that St. Claire was following her and stopped her when he saw the opportunity. My guess is that McGuiness is going to argue that they met there. It would be consistent with consent and that she went to that location *because* it was off her normal route home. But whatever McGuiness does, her story makes a lot more sense than his as far as I'm concerned."

Ernie nodded in agreement. "My kids listen to music and forget about everything around them. You could drop a bomb outside their door and they wouldn't notice. She wasn't paying attention and he had to be following her. If she was going to meet St. Claire there are a lot of other places they could go instead of leaving her car in the middle of a deserted cemetery road. Besides, there's still the blood on the seat. How's McGuiness going to explain that? Sometimes defense attorneys just have to explain *too many* things. McGuiness has raised a little dust, that's all."

As he listened quietly, Jamison knew everything they said was true, but there was one thing that he understood as an experienced trial lawyer. No good lawyer asked questions unless he had answers that worked for his benefit.

The next morning Art Puccinelli took the stand and recounted everything he had seen. He identified photographs of the car, acknowledging that footprints and tire tracks were disrupted by the number of people who had approached the vehicle before the forensic crew arrived. He described the smear of blood on the driver's seat and ended by describing the frantic scene at St. Claire's home.

McGuiness stayed behind the counsel table and wrote on his legal pad, letting Puccinelli remain in the witness chair in silence for a moment. He looked up.

"I have just a few questions of this witness, Your Honor." McGuiness flipped again through his notes. "Detective Puccinelli, did you supervise the investigation of Dr. St. Claire's car, a 2006 dark blue Lexus sedan?"

"Yes, I did."

"And what did you find?"

"We found a strand of hair that belonged to Ms. Garrett."

"No blood?"

"No."

"Did you find any special modification of the vehicle?"

"Modification?"

"Yes, like flashing lights or a red light?"

"No, we found nothing like that."

"But isn't that what Ms. Garrett claimed she saw?"

"Yes, she said there were flashing lights and she thought she saw a red light. That's why she stopped."

"But you didn't find anything like that in Dr. St. Claire's vehicle, did you?"

"No."

"Or in his home?"

"Which one? He has two."

"In either home."

"No."

"Thank you, Detective."

Jamison remained seated at the counsel table. "Detective Puccinelli, is it that complicated to make a flashing red light?"

"No. All you need to do is put red cellophane over a white flasher and you have a flashing red light. Same thing people do when they break a taillight and don't want to pay for a new one. They just tape red cellophane or plastic over the taillight so it looks red at night or when you hit the brakes."

Jamison looked at the jury and shrugged as if to emphasize his point that it wasn't that hard to do. Besides, it was the only explanation he had.

"Your Honor, the People call District Attorney Investigator Ernest Garcia."

Jamison took Ernie through the preliminary investigation leading up to the approach to St. Claire's home. "Investigator Garcia, can you describe the situation when you approached the defendant's home?"

"We believed that it was possible the defendant may have kidnapped Ms. Garrett and was holding her against her will in the house. If that was true, then it was clearly a very volatile situation, one with a high degree of risk to the hostage. On the other hand, it was possible that the defendant, Dr. St. Claire, was not involved in the disappearance of Ms. Garrett and we wanted to avoid any unnecessary violence."

"So you were preparing for either situation, a hostage situation or a situation where Dr. St. Claire was simply another person to be interviewed?"

"Yes. After a situation develops it's too late to decide what you should have done. You have to be prepared for all possibilities. That's what we did."

"Describe what you saw when you approached the side of the defendant's home."

"I crouched outside a window near the back of the house. I thought it was probably a bedroom and looked through the slightly open curtains."

"Did you see anything?"

"Yes, I saw Ms. Garrett. She was lying on a bed. She was naked. There was a camera on a tripod at the end of the bed."

"Could you see her face?"

"No, because of the curtain and the angle from where I was looking."

"Was she moving at all?"

"No, she looked like she was tied in such a way that she couldn't move much but I couldn't tell if she was unconscious."

"What went through your mind?"

"I could hear Investigator O'Hara's voice at the front of the house and I could make out the voice of another man. My concern was the safety of Ms. Garrett. So I went in."

"You mean you broke through the glass?"

"Well, yes. It was real fast. I rolled onto the floor and got away from the glass. Ms. Garrett was screaming and thrashing around, and I was yelling at O'Hara that I had her."

"Did you hear anyone coming down the hall?"

"Honestly, all I could hear was Ms. Garrett screaming. I was trying to untie her and pull her off the bed but she was hysterical. I kept saying 'police' but she was pulling away."

"Then what happened?"

"I had a knife in my pocket. I pulled it out and cut the ropes where she was tied. I only got one knot untied and I cut the rest and pulled her to the floor while I tried to cover the door to the bedroom."

Jamison walked over to the clerk's desk and picked up a clear plastic bag, handing it to Ernie. "Do you recognize the contents of this bag?"

"These are the ropes that were used to tie Ms. Garrett to the bed."

"Now, you use the term 'ropes.' For the record, when you say 'ropes' can you describe what these bindings look like?"

Ernie reached inside the bag and removed a strand about two feet long. "They aren't like regular rope, like a clothesline or twine. They are more like braided rope that looks decorative. They're kind of a gold color."

Jamison passed the strand to the jurors and watched while they passed it among themselves. When it was handed back to him he focused on bringing the jurors back to the events in the house. "After you came through the window, did you hear anything from the front of the house?"

"I heard O'Hara yelling, and then I heard a crash and O'Hara yelling at who I assumed was Dr. St. Claire to not resist."

"And Ms. Garrett? What was happening?"

"I pulled off a sheet or blanket from the bed and tried to cover her. She was still kicking at me so I kind of laid on her and kept my gun up covering the doorway until O'Hara and you looked in. There was glass and a lot of blood from my coming through the window. But then she began to calm down. I think she went into shock of some kind because she just stared ahead, like she didn't know where she was."

"And, Investigator Garcia, would you please tell the court what happened after that?"

"Backup officers came in and then paramedics. I was pretty cut up myself. I kept talking to her but she seemed like she didn't know what was going on. She was crying and I kept telling her it was okay and that we were the police."

McGuiness stood back from Garcia before he began his cross-examination. "Investigator Garcia, please allow me to acknowledge your heroism in going through that window. Regardless of what may have actually happened we are all grateful that men like you are there to protect us. I don't have many questions. When you looked through the window you did not see Dr. St. Claire, is that correct?"

"Yes, he apparently was at the front door where Bill, Investigator O'Hara, was."

"So you never saw Dr. St. Claire do anything harmful to Miss Garrett?"

"You mean other than tying her to the bed? No."

McGuiness allowed a slight smile as he shrugged, looking over at the jury and raising his eyebrows to acknowledge what seemed obvious. "In fact, all the cuts and bruises on Miss Garrett were caused by flying glass from the window and when you tried to pull the ropes off her hands and legs?"

"Other than the cut on her neck, I can't say for sure about the cause of other injuries."

McGuiness stared at Ernie briefly as if slightly unsure of himself. "Yes, the scratch on her neck, but you have no personal knowledge as to how that was caused, do you?"

"Not other than what Ms. Garrett said."

"Correct, not other than what Ms. Garrett said. And what about the ropes?"

"I can't answer whether the ropes injured her. I pulled them off. As for the other cuts and bruises on her, I can say that some of them, maybe most or all of them, were probably caused by the flying glass and when I pulled her onto the floor where there was more glass."

"Yes, now those ropes. Would you describe them as made from some kind of cloth?"

"They are pieces of something like cotton or silk, kind of shiny, like pieces of what you might call braid or material like that."

"So, they aren't ropes like you would use to bundle things, more like something decorative?"

Catching the implication, Ernie responded, "They weren't something that a person could pull apart."

"Were you able to remove them fairly quickly or was she tied tightly?"

"Well, she wouldn't have been able to get out of the ropes so, yes, they seemed fairly tight but I can't say now exactly how tight. When it was over I could see ligature marks on her wrists and ankles so they had to be pretty tight."

"Is it possible, Investigator Garcia, that when you were cutting the ropes off that you may have accidentally cut Ms. Garrett? She was thrashing around quite a bit, correct?"

"I was holding her." Ernie shook his head emphatically. "I didn't cut her."

"I'm sure if you did, it was accidental. Investigator Garcia, would you explain to the jury what ligature marks are?"

"Ligature marks are the marks that are left on someone's body where they are restrained by, for example, handcuffs or a rope that is very tight."

"So if there were any ligature marks on Ms. Garrett from being tied, meaning marks left by the ropes being tight on her ankles or wrists, those could have been made as you frantically pulled at the ropes to try to get her free?"

"I don't know. Maybe."

"Thank you, Investigator Garcia. Oh, one more question. When you looked through the window, was Miss Garrett screaming at that time or only after you crashed through the window?"

"I didn't hear any screaming until after I went through the window."

"Thank you. Nothing further."

Jamison looked up from his notes. "Investigator Garcia, of course Ms. Garrett had no reason to scream if she didn't think anybody would hear her?"

"No."

McGuiness was on his feet. "Objection. Speculation, Your Honor."

"Sustained. The jury will disregard the question and the answer. Is there anything further, Mr. Jamison?"

"No, Your Honor. The witness is excused subject to recall."

Jamison called witnesses from the forensic bureau to identify various pieces of physical evidence that McGuiness stipulated could be received.

He had run out of witnesses that he wanted to put on before he got to Garrett. He needed time. Jamison stood up. "Your Honor, we anticipated this taking a little longer than it has. With the court's indulgence I would ask the court to recess until tomorrow. Our next witness will be the victim in this case, Elizabeth Garrett. I would like to start with her in the morning."

Back in his office, Jamison sat with his two investigators. As usual, O'Hara spoke first. "Look, I don't think any jury is going to believe that girl consented to all of this. Its total bullshit and we all know it. Besides, St. Claire's not just a kidnapper, he's a murderer. We've got the hair and fiber samples in St. Claire's car from the other victims. McGuiness doesn't know about that."

Jamison's gaze moved between the two men and settled on O'Hara. "You're right. McGuiness doesn't know about that and I'm not ready to tell him about it until we have what we need to make a murder case. But you know as well as I do that McGuiness doesn't have to prove St. Claire is innocent. All he has to do is raise a reasonable doubt about whether he's guilty.

"He knows that Beth Garrett's the key to this case so I'm guessing something is coming. Whatever it is, he has it and we don't. And the worst of it is that we're not going to know what it is until we hear it in court and my guess is it's going to come from St. Claire along with some kind of evidence."

O'Hara asked, "So you think he's going to put St. Claire on the stand when he doesn't have to?"

"Bill, he doesn't have a choice. Just because a defendant has a right not to testify doesn't mean a jury won't wonder why he doesn't. McGuiness can raise all the possibilities he wants, but a jury is still going to be looking to his client to personally deny that he kidnapped Garrett.

"But I think St. Claire is a cool number and I'll need to shake him. St. Claire and McGuiness know we suspect him for those murders. They just don't know what we've got. I need him thinking about that when he's on the stand and I need to find a way to make him think about it."

O'Hara pulled his lower lip up over the edge of his mustache. "We got the fiber and hair that T. J. found. We know he looked at those files for those women. The MO is the same. What more do we need?"

"That isn't going to make this case." Jamison snorted derisively. "I told you that. And it isn't going to convince Wallace to let me put the murders into evidence to help prove he kidnapped Garrett. Ernie, I want you to call Gupta and pin down those blood samples. Something's wrong here. I can feel it."

The next morning Jamison glanced impatiently at his watch. He hadn't heard back yet from Ernie about the blood samples but, other than taking one less thing off his mind, whatever the blood might show it wasn't going to help him with what he had to face now. He had a half hour before Elizabeth's examination was going to start.

He needed a few minutes to clear his mind. Then as he was putting papers into his briefcase, Ernie arrived.

The news raised more questions than answers. Ernie said that Gupta found no trace of heroin or barbiturates in the liver of any of the victims and that they didn't die as a result of overdose. Gupta wasn't sure what killed them. He was sending his tissue samples to the FBI to get something more definitive.

"But there's more. You were right, amigo. Gupta says that the blood samples that were examined after the autopsies didn't come from the victims. Nobody bothered to do separate tests to see if the blood actually came from the victims because there was no reason to."

Jamison was used to Ernie stringing out a story but his patience was thin. "C'mon, Ernie, bottom line, what did they find?" Ernie's smile told him that there was some good news.

"Apparently Gupta was able to do some kind of enzyme comparison between the fluid in the livers of the victims and the blood samples. The blood types in the vials matched the blood types of the victims, but the blood in the vials came from somebody else who had toxic levels of drugs in their blood.

"St. Claire switched them." Ernie's face took on a colder expression. "The blood probably came from a junkie. All St. Claire had to do was find somebody with the same blood type that overdosed on that shit that is hitting the streets and then put that blood into the vials marked as for the victims. He knew nobody would have reason to check to confirm if it was actually the blood of the victims."

Excited about the possible explanations, Jamison's mind began to race. He could feel the noose of guilt beginning to close in on St. Claire. "We need to check with Gupta and see how many of these OD autopsies he's done on junkies recently. See if any blood types match with the victims, and then see if we can get a match on the blood we have. Then, we'll find out if St. Claire had any access to the blood or to those dead junkies."

He pushed down on the pencil, breaking the lead. "We need to find that shit, Ernie. It's there somewhere. You meet me in the courtroom as soon as you talk to Gupta."

"Okay, *patron*, but this time *I* get to snap the cuffs on Dr. St. Claire."

Chapter 24

"Your Honor, the People call Ms. Elizabeth Garrett." Elizabeth entered the courtroom doors and walked hesitantly across the well of the courtroom, stopping when Wallace asked her to be sworn in.

The witness chair sat almost directly in front of the jury. She looked like an animal on display in the zoo being observed by strangers—the jury, the judge to her right, the prosecutor, and the defense attorney in the center of the courtroom were protected by massive tables.

So that his voice would come from the side rather than from him standing in front of the jury, Jamison walked behind the corner of the jury box. He wanted the jury's attention only to be drawn to his witness. She was dressed in a simple navy blue suit with pearls around her neck. Her light brown hair framed her face and fell around her shoulders.

Jamison watched as Elizabeth's gaze moved across the counsel tables and stopped at Alex St. Claire. The prosecutor glanced over at the defendant. St. Claire's finely drawn features betrayed nothing as he stared back at her. The image flashed through Jamison's mind of Elizabeth's description of St. Claire standing in the bedroom in front of her, controlling her.

It was apparent to everyone in the courtroom that Elizabeth's eyes were riveted on St. Claire. It seemed to Jamison that of all the people in the courtroom, in some incomprehensible way St. Claire was the one to whom she felt the greatest connection. He wondered at the feeling of vulnerability that must have given her.

Jamison had decided he needed to bring the previous relationship with St. Claire out into the open. He knew McGuiness was going to bring it up anyway. Remaining at the far corner of the jury box, he quickly moved directly to the issue. "Ms. Garrett, how long have you known the defendant, Alex St. Claire?"

St. Claire watched Elizabeth intently as she answered. "I've known him for over ten years. We met when I was sixteen, almost seventeen. He was twenty-one."

"Did you have a relationship with the defendant while you were in high school?" Jamison kept his voice softly modulated.

"Yes, at first we would just talk. He would come by a small store where I worked on weekends and after a while he started to wait for me. We would go for coffee and it went from there."

"Did your parents approve of him?"

"I didn't tell my parents at first. He was older. When I did tell them, they didn't want me to see him anymore."

So far Jamison's questions were designed to fill in the details about their relationship before turning to the question about why she kept seeing St. Claire after her parents had forbidden it.

"You kept seeing him even after your parents told you not to?"

"Yes, we saw each other in secret. Looking back I know how it sounds but I was young and I thought I loved him."

"I realize this is very difficult for you to talk about in front of strangers, but were you intimate with him?"

Beth's face reddened. The jurors' eyes were fixed on her and her eyes were fixed on her mother, who was sitting in the front row. "Yes. I had never been with a man before."

"Do you recall how often the two of you would be intimate?"

"I'm not sure; he would meet me sometimes twice a week. Sometimes it was less. He was always studying. We did other things too. I mean it wasn't all . . . We talked. We walked."

"Was there a time when you decided to stop seeing him?"

"After my parents found out, they said they would send Alex to jail if I continued to see him. I told him we couldn't see each other anymore."

"And did the relationship end then?"

Before any answer could be given, McGuiness objected. "Your Honor, may we approach the bench?"

Wallace motioned them forward and addressed the jury. "Ladies and gentlemen, we will take a short recess." After the bailiff escorted the jury from the room, Wallace signaled both attorneys to step back. "So, where are we going with this, Mr. Jamison?"

"Your Honor, Ms. Garrett and the defendant had a previous relationship. It's our position that the nature of that relationship is relevant to why she would not have gone willingly with the defendant on the night in question."

"Mr. McGuiness?"

"Well, Your Honor, actually I just wanted to make sure I understood why Mr. Jamison was bringing this up at this time. I haven't alleged that there was consent but I can say to the court that I intended to bring it up, so whether it's now or later makes no difference to me."

Jamison returned to his seat, sipping from a paper cup full of cold water. It was clear that McGuiness was being far too accommodating. *But why?* The jury returned and he resumed his questions. "Ms. Garrett, the last question was 'Did the relationship end then?'"

"It ended for about a month. He would come by the store but I wouldn't see him. Sometimes he would leave a note. Then one day he said he had to see me. He said it was important and to meet him near the park where we walked."

"Did you meet him?"

"I saw him. He was in his car. I got in and we talked. Then suddenly he began driving."

"Then what happened?"

"He said he was taking me away. He said he wanted to marry me. It was like he was crazy. I told him I wasn't going with him. Then he pulled out a knife. He told me we were going to go south, maybe across the Mexican border, and get married. He wouldn't stop. He drove to someplace in the Los Angeles area and he got a motel."

"Why didn't you run away?"

For several seconds she remained silent, and when she answered her voice was so soft that jurors strained to hear it. "I've asked myself that a thousand times. I was terrified. He had the knife. I don't know what to say. I just didn't run. I was so afraid. He waved the knife in front of my face."

"Did you stay at the motel?"

"Yes, we spent the night there. He wouldn't let me call my parents or anyone to tell them where I was. He kept saying we were going to get married. He kept saying it was all going to be all right, I would see."

"Did anything happen while you were at the hotel?"

"He forced himself on me." Elizabeth looked down, the words coming out in a whisper.

"By 'forced himself on me' do you mean that he made you have sexual intercourse?"

"Yes."

"Did he hurt you in any way or threaten you?"

"The knife was right there on the nightstand. It was always in reach for him. I didn't resist. I couldn't. I was too afraid. Looking back I know someone might ask why I didn't try to escape. All I can say is that I was seventeen and I was terrified."

Jamison paused to allow the jury to focus on Elizabeth. Her head was down and her hair covered her face as she stared at her lap. When she looked up tears were streaming down her face. Jamison glanced at the jury box; several of the female jurors were wiping at their eyes and stealing glances at St. Claire.

"The next day, what happened?"

"He said we were going to Mexico, that we would get married. We drove all over the area, and then he stopped at a light—I don't know; I suddenly realized I had to get away and this was my chance. And so I jumped out of the car and ran to the nearest house. I was banging on the door and a woman let me in. That was when the police were called and she called my mom."

"Was this in the daytime?"

"It was early afternoon, maybe one or two if I remember correctly."

Jamison moved over to the counsel table and picked up a stapled set of papers, looking over at McGuiness, who nodded and said, "Your Honor, Mr. Jamison and I have stipulated that if called to testify, the officer who responded from the Los Angeles Police Department would say that he contacted Ms. Garrett at two thirty in the afternoon."

"Thank you, Mr. McGuiness," Jamison replied. He stepped back around the counsel table and stood near the jury rail while he continued his direct examination of Elizabeth Garrett. "What happened to the defendant?"

"I don't know. He drove away and the next time I saw him was in court back here when my father had him arrested."

Jamison went back to the counsel table and looked at his notes. "Now, Ms. Garrett, you refused to cooperate with the authorities about that incident. Is that correct?"

"Yes." Her voice was barely above a whisper. "I knew they thought I ran off with him. I didn't tell anybody about what happened at the hotel. I just wanted to put it behind me. I felt like part of what happened was my fault.

What he did was wrong but I wasn't hurt. I didn't want to ruin his life. I just wanted him to stay away from me. So I told my parents that I didn't want to think about it anymore. And that was that. The police said that unless I cooperated they had no case. I didn't see the defendant again for ten years, until right before this happened."

"Please explain how you came to see him again?" Jamison could see the jurors leaning forward.

"I was shopping at the Fashion Mall. He walked up behind me and tapped me on the shoulder. I turned around, and I think I screamed a bit. I know people were looking. But he didn't do anything. He said he saw me and wanted to say hello and that he was sorry about everything. He said he had been crazy about me. He thanked me for not pursuing the charges. He said he was a doctor now, an anesthesiologist, and that he'd been studying someplace in Europe. Now he was back and at the county hospital. I kept backing away, and then I walked off. That was it."

"Did you tell anyone about this?"

"Only my girlfriend Cheryl, Cheryl Ewing."

"Did you see the defendant again after that?"

"It was a little over a week later when I saw him that night on the road by the cemetery."

"Tell us what happened that night by the cemetery."

Jamison had instructed Elizabeth to face the jury when she answered this question. She moved forward in the witness chair, pushing her hair back, and paused before answering. "I was driving home around nine o'clock at night. I had been at dinner with Cheryl. I was going to stay at her place because I didn't have to teach the next day, but I changed my mind and decided to go home instead. I was listening to the radio and I guess I wasn't paying attention because I missed my turnoff. That's why I ended up where I did. I turned off of Olive onto the road between the cemeteries. It was out there when I saw flashing lights behind me and what looked like a red light. There aren't any streetlights out there and it's very dark. All I could see was the red light and the headlights, which flashed."

"Was there a siren?"

"No, I didn't hear any siren. I pulled over. I didn't know what I had done wrong but you know, you see the red light and you stop." Several of the women jurors were nodding. "I reached into my purse for my license and rolled down the window. That's when I saw him."

"By him, you mean the defendant?"

"Yes, the defendant. He was just standing right next to the window. As soon as I heard his voice I knew it was Alex."

"What did he say?"

"He said, 'Remember me?' And he had this knife. He just moved it back and forth in front of my face. It was like I was paralyzed by fear." Her voice broke as she brought her hand up to her neck. "He cut me."

The courtroom was completely silent. The jurors, the audience, and the judge sat, rapt. Jamison let the silence build before asking his next question. "Ms. Garrett, when you say the defendant cut you, would you describe for the jury exactly what he did?"

She closed her eyes, breathing more rapidly as her hand again brushed her neck. "He moved the knife closer and closer to my face, swinging it back and forth before my eyes, and then he put it on my neck. I could feel the blade sliding down my skin. He held the knife in front of me and I could see the tip. There was blood on it." Elizabeth's voice trailed off to a whisper and she began to cry. "I was petrified. I thought he was going to kill me. I remember he reached in. There was something in his hand but I don't know what it was. I kept looking at the knife. That's all I remember until I woke up later."

Again, Jamison let the silence fill the seconds before he asked his next question. "Elizabeth, what was it like when you woke up?"

"It was black. Everything was black. I tried to move but my hands and legs were tied somehow. The only light I saw was when the defendant came in. He gave me something but I don't remember much except that it was so black. I could hear a kind of humming sound, like a refrigerator, but I couldn't see anything. I really don't remember much except I was lying on something hard, like a table. There was plastic under me. I could feel it but I never saw it. When I woke up again I was on the bed and my arms and legs were tied. My clothing was gone. There was a camera on a tripod. It was at the end of the bed."

"Elizabeth, Ms. Garrett, while you were held captive, did the defendant, if you remember or know, ever have sexual relations with you?"

"I was unconscious most of the time. I can say that when I was awake he only touched me. He put his hand on my leg and my thigh. That's all I remember."

Jamison retrieved from the clerk's desk several photographs that had been removed from St. Claire's camera and printed by the forensic crew, and handed them to Elizabeth.

"I show you now People's Exhibits One through Five. Can you tell us what they depict?"

Elizabeth held them in her hands for what seemed like a minute before looking up. Her face flushed at the thought that pictures of her unclothed would be passed around. "They are each pictures of me on the bed."

"Are you looking at the camera in any of them?"

"This one. I have my head lifted up."

"That is Exhibit Five, for the record. Can you describe the expression on your face?"

"There is no expression. My face is blank."

"And in the other pictures can you describe your face?"

"My eyes are closed in most of them and in one I have my face turned toward the side. You can't see my eyes."

"Do you remember these photographs being taken?"

"No, I'm sorry. I don't remember much of anything until Investigator Garcia came crashing through the window."

"When Investigator Garcia came through the window, can you tell the jury what happened?"

"I didn't hear anything until the window broke and the glass flew in. I started screaming. I didn't know who he was. He kept pulling at the ropes. He had blood all over him. He pulled me off the bed. That's all I recall until I woke up in the hospital."

Jamison walked to the side of the jury box, his voice projecting from behind the jurors as they looked at Elizabeth. "Ms. Garrett, on that night when you left your car by the side of the road, did you go voluntarily with the defendant?"

Elizabeth looked at Jamison, startled. "No, no, Mr. Jamison. I told you, he had a knife."

"And, when you were tied to the bed, did you consent to any of that?"

The convulsive sound of words bursting out of Elizabeth filled the corners of the courtroom. "I *never* wanted to see you again! You should have left me alone, Alex! You should have left me alone!"

Elizabeth began to cry softly and Jamison said, "Your Honor, we have no further questions."

McGuiness stood up from behind the counsel table. "Your Honor, perhaps a short recess for the sake of the witness?" Wallace excused the jurors, who shuffled out of the courtroom, several stealing glances at Elizabeth, who was still crying as Jamison helped her off the stand.

Usually McGuiness walked to the front of the witness stand when he cross-examined. Part of it was intimidation. Part of it was so he could concentrate on the face of the witness, watching for any small sign that indicated the witness was not being truthful, looking for a place to slip in a barbed point. But with a witness like Garrett he knew that would be a mistake. A jury would resent it, and they would resent him.

He had thought very carefully about how to conduct this cross-examination. Intimidation was not what he was after and he did not expect surrender. His objective was destruction, but he intended to make Elizabeth Garrett destroy herself.

"Perhaps, Your Honor, this would be an appropriate time for a stipulation that Mr. Jamison and I have agreed to?" McGuiness turned toward Jamison, who nodded. "I believe the prosecutor will stipulate that no evidence of sexual activity was found after medical examination of Ms. Garrett?"

"We will stipulate to that, Your Honor." There was no point in Jamison arguing about it. The stipulation simply removed from dispute what the evidence would show if a medical examiner was brought in. All McGuiness had done was put the stipulation in front of the jury before he asked Elizabeth a single question.

Elizabeth waited for McGuiness to begin his questions. Jamison had reminded her during the fifteen-minute recess that she should try to remain calm, only answer the specific question asked, and keep her answers as short as possible.

"Ms. Garrett, I understand this is very difficult for you. It isn't my intention to upset you, please understand. If you need a recess just let me know and I certainly will have no objection to giving you a moment. All right?" Elizabeth nodded.

McGuiness was a master at lulling the witness, dancing around the area where he would inflict his wound, creating a false sense of security before he stuck in the blade.

Every trial lawyer knew the worst thing a witness could do was lie about something that can be irrefutably disproven. And Thomas McGuiness believed that Elizabeth Garrett was going to lie. He believed she already had lied indirectly. And now he had every reason to believe she was going to lie directly.

"Ms. Garrett, you have acknowledged that you used to have a relationship with Alex St. Claire, is that right?

"Yes."

"And you've told the court that your parents told you not to see him anymore, is that true?"

"Yes."

"But you continued to see him, didn't you?"

"Yes."

"So you lied to your mother and father about your relationship?"

"I thought I was in love. I thought they wouldn't understand."

"Okay, you told Alex that you loved him, isn't that true?" McGuiness was encouraging Elizabeth and the jury to think of his client as "Alex" and not "the defendant." There was nothing Jamison could do as he watched McGuiness subtly personalize Alex St. Claire.

"I didn't understand what it meant."

"Well, Alex told you that he loved you also, didn't he?"

"But he was older . . ."

"I understand. But let's talk for a moment about the time when you say you broke up with Alex. You testified that after your parents found out that you were still seeing him, you told Alex that you couldn't see him anymore?"

"Something like that."

"Well, what exactly did you tell him?"

"I told him that my father had forbidden me to see him anymore and that it had to be over."

"And you also told him that you still loved him, isn't that so?"

"Yes."

"You and Alex slept together numerous times during that relationship, didn't you?"

"Yes. I had never been with a man before. I testified to that."

"You also testified that Alex asked to see you after you broke up. And that you agreed to see him even though, according to you, you had done what your parents said?"

"I don't understand what you're asking."

"Well, Ms. Garrett, isn't it true that it was *you* who asked Alex to come and see you?"

"No, it is not."

"Isn't it true, Ms. Garrett, that you told Alex St. Claire that you were pregnant?"

The response was adamant. "No, I never said that. I wasn't pregnant and I never told Alex that."

"I'm going to ask you that question again, Ms. Garrett, and I ask you to think carefully about your answer. Isn't it true that you told Alex St. Claire that you were pregnant and you didn't know what to do? Isn't it true that he said he wanted to marry you and that's why you left with him? It was to get married, wasn't it?"

"I object!" Jamison was on his feet trying to stop the questions. "Mr. McGuiness is asking repeated questions without allowing the witness to answer. He's testifying instead of the witness."

Wallace looked over the top of the bench at McGuiness. "The objection is sustained. Mr. McGuiness, you will allow the witness to answer before asking your next question."

"Yes, Your Honor, I apologize. Ms. Garrett, isn't it true that Alex St. Claire said he would marry you because you told him you were pregnant?"

"He said he wanted to marry me but I never said I was pregnant and I didn't leave with him voluntarily. He had a knife."

Spreading his arms apart as if willing to embrace an explanation, McGuiness said, "So let me see if I understand this. You went with my client to Los Angeles and you spent the night in a motel somewhere and you never tried to escape. Is that your testimony?" The defense attorney's voice was incredulous.

"Don't you hear me?" Her voice began to rise as she became emotional. "He had a knife. I was terrified. He was like a possessed person."

"You stopped to get something to eat, didn't you?"

"Yes. We went to a drive-through, a McDonald's or a place like that."

"But you didn't scream then either, did you, or try to run away?"

"I told you, he had a knife."

"Ms. Garrett, isn't it true that when you ran away from the car that it was because you wanted to call home and Alex didn't want you to? You had started to cry about your parents?"

"I escaped from his car!"

"Ms. Garrett, you didn't press charges against Alex, did you?"

"No, I just wanted it to be over. Part of it was my fault. I shouldn't have become involved with him. I didn't want to put my parents through the publicity of a trial—everybody knowing all of it."

"Isn't it true that you didn't want to press charges, in fact were uncooperative with the police, because you knew Alex didn't kidnap you at all? Isn't that true?"

"I have told the truth."

"And you weren't pregnant?

"I was not pregnant and I never said I was."

Shaking his head as if measuring the credibility of the witness, the defense attorney began to cut carefully. "All right, Ms. Garrett, let's move on to the events surrounding the allegations you have made against Dr. St. Claire when you *again* claim he kidnapped you." McGuiness allowed just enough inflection to the word "claim" that anybody listening would understand the sarcasm. "Earlier you testified that one day this year Alex, Dr. St. Claire, a respected member of the medical community, just showed up behind you out of the blue on the floor of a shopping mall and apologized for what he had done."

"That's right."

"What day was that?"

"It was a Saturday, in the early afternoon. I remember that. In October."

"Could it have been the twelfth of October?"

"That would probably be right. I would have to look at a calendar."

"Well, can we agree that it was the same day you called him?"

As they cross examine a witness, skilled trial lawyers all exhibit a measure of a predator's DNA. But they also have a keen subliminal sense of the reaction of the lawyer at the other counsel table, a heightened awareness that their opponent's blood is slowly turning icy cold. McGuiness knew what Jamison was thinking, *had* to be thinking, as he listened to McGuiness's questions and kept his face expressionless: *What call? She said she had no contact with St. Claire.*

Jamison would know McGuiness wouldn't ask the question unless he had something more than St. Claire's word, just like he wouldn't ask about a pregnancy unless he could back that up. McGuiness didn't have to look to know Jamison's sphincter was beginning to tighten.

Elizabeth's voice fell to almost a murmur. "I called him at the hospital after I saw him at the mall. I didn't know how else to get hold of him. I wanted him to stay away from me."

McGuiness snapped out his next question. "No, Ms. Garrett. Isn't it true that on the day you saw Alex St. Claire at the mall it was you who called and told him that you wanted to see him?"

"No, it's not true. I called him later and told him to stay away from me."

"Are you aware that the hospital keeps a sign-in book for medical staff so they know who is in the hospital?"

Her head moved back and forth as she remained silent. "Miss Garrett, would it surprise you to know that the hospital also logs the calls that come in to the doctors? Let me put the question this way. If I brought in the hospital sign-in book and it showed Alex St. Claire in the hospital between eight thirty-five a.m. and two forty-five p.m. and a call from you at two p.m. would that surprise you?"

Elizabeth looked around the courtroom, her eyes darting to the back, looking for her mother, for somebody. "I called him but not until after he came up to me at the mall. If you have some book that says differently, then it's wrong."

"I see, so the hospital log would be wrong?" McGuiness paused. "Never mind. Let me ask another question. On the night you left your car out by the cemetery, you stopped because you knew Alex was behind you, didn't you?"

"I saw a red light. I thought it was a policeman."

McGuiness stepped from behind the counsel table and walked into the well of the courtroom. He looked at Judge Wallace for permission. Wallace nodded, giving the silent approval that attorneys ask for before closing in on a witness. "Ms. Garrett, isn't it true that there was no red light behind you?"

Elizabeth shook her head emphatically. "I said I thought there were red lights, a red light. There were flashing lights. Why else would I stop?"

Lowering his voice just enough so that the jurors would have to strain to hear it, but clear enough so they could hear the bite of his question, McGuiness asked, "You stopped because you planned to meet Alex. Isn't that the real reason?"

"I had no intention of meeting the defendant. I was afraid of him."

McGuiness's head and body bent forward. It reminded Jamison of a cobra sizing up his victim. "You called Alex after you left the Packing Shed, didn't you?" The tone of his voice had lost any conciliatory pretense.

"No, I told you I didn't have his number."

"Are you *sure* that's what you want to testify to?"

"That's what happened. I didn't know it was him. I would never have stopped if I knew it was him."

Abruptly switching to the evidence at the farmhouse, McGuiness asked, "Miss Garrett, you are aware that the police found no physical evidence of you being on that steel table in Alex's garage, aren't you?"

"Yes, but I was there. It was a metal table. There are pictures of it."

"Isn't it true, Ms. Garrett, that Alex showed you that room and told you that is where he worked sometimes when he just wanted to be alone? You never were on that table, were you?"

"He put me on that table, and then later I woke up on the bed where Investigator Garcia found me. Your client kidnapped me and he tied me to that bed."

McGuiness shook his head, drawing his face into an expression of regret at what the witness was forcing him to do. "Ms. Garrett, I am sorry to have to ask this, but isn't it true that you asked Alex St. Claire to tie you to that bed? Isn't it true that you and Alex had once made that part of your sexual activity?"

Elizabeth's mouth curled with revulsion. "That's not true. I never asked him to do that to me. We had no relationship. How many times do I have to say that?"

Turning again toward the jury with a resigned expression on his face as he slowly walked back to the counsel table, McGuiness reached into a file folder and withdrew two sets of photographs, handing one set to Jamison. "Your Honor, perhaps Mr. Jamison should have a moment to look at these photographs before I show them to the witness? I was hopeful it would not come to this but Ms. Garrett has left me little choice. While the prosecutor is looking at them, I request that they be marked for identification as Defense Exhibits A through E."

After looking at the first photograph, Jamison barely glanced at the others, sliding them over so O'Hara could see them as well.

Jamison only heard the almost imperceptible whisper of "Shit" that came out of O'Hara because he was sitting right next to him. Jamison fought to retain his composure. There was no objection to be made. McGuiness was under no obligation to show them to the prosecution before the trial and he had waited for the right moment like a lion stalking its prey.

His stomach churning, Jamison fought to keep his expression impassive. He could object or he could ask to approach the bench. Neither would do any good. Anything he did other than remain seated at the counsel table would give the impression that he was afraid of the evidence or, worse, that he had never seen it before. He felt all of those things but he couldn't let the jury see it.

He shrugged indifferently; he knew what was coming and he also knew he couldn't stop it.

"Ms. Garrett, I am showing you now Defense Exhibits A through E. Do you recognize those photographs?"

Elizabeth's mouth began to quiver. For what seemed like interminable seconds she couldn't bring herself to look at the pictures. Instead she looked beseechingly at Jamison as if he were her life raft.

He could see her growing despair and helplessness. There was nothing he could do. He had warned her to tell him everything and what would happen if she didn't. At this point he had to think about damage control because he knew how the jury would react. Jamison couldn't let the jury think this was unexpected. He could scarcely look at her as he tried to maintain his own strained composure.

Elizabeth turned her face to look directly at St. Claire. "Why, Alex? Why would you do this to me?" All eyes were on St. Claire.

St. Claire's eyes were filling with tears. Jamison couldn't help cynically thinking that the tears almost made St. Claire look like he cared. Then he realized that the jury couldn't tell the difference. To them it looked like he cared a great deal. Jamison then felt the chill that came with his own momentary flash of doubt that maybe St. Claire really did.

Before he asked his next question, McGuiness let Elizabeth hold the photographs in her hands to make sure the image was firmly planted in the minds of the jurors.

"Ms. Garrett, who are those photographs of?"

Elizabeth didn't respond until McGuiness repeated his question and stood in front of her, waiting for her answer. She had no choice. "They are pictures of me."

"Do you recall when they were taken?"

"Alex took them when we were seeing one another back when I was in high school. He said that he destroyed them." Elizabeth looked toward the jury. "I don't know why I did it. I loved him . . . Alex asked me . . ." Her voice trailed off.

McGuiness's voice was gentle but firm. "Ms. Garrett, I won't ask you to describe what is in those pictures." He turned to Judge Wallace. "I would like the jury to see the photographs, Your Honor, if Mr. Jamison has no objection."

Jamison had to act as if it made no difference to him. "No objection."

As he passed the pictures to the jurors, McGuiness stepped back, waiting as he moved toward the counsel table and put his hand on his client's shoulder.

One by one each juror stared at the photographs. After passing them to the juror next to them, each juror looked at Elizabeth and then at St. Claire. The photographs were of a young woman in a provocative pose with her hands and feet bound. She was nude and very little about Elizabeth Garrett was left to the imagination.

McGuiness waited until the last juror looked at the photographs and handed them back to the bailiff. Standing behind Alex St. Claire, McGuiness began softly, slowly raising his voice as his questions came in rapid fire. "Ms. Garrett, the photographs—you didn't want your parents to know about the details of your relationship with Alex, did you? You didn't go forward with any charges because you didn't want your parents to know what really happened, did you? You knew Alex didn't do what you accused him of and you were desperately looking for a way to explain why you had run off with him. Isn't that the truth?"

Jamison was on his feet, objecting in an attempt to disrupt the staccato barrage of questions.

Judge Wallace's gavel came down. "Mr. McGuiness, allow the witness to answer. And Mr. Jamison, please lower your voice."

Grabbing at the folds of her skirt, Elizabeth stared at her hands. There was no question in front of her, only the echo of the torrent of insinuation from McGuiness. She didn't look up as she responded in a voice that was barely above a whisper. "I didn't want them to know how I'd behaved. I was terribly ashamed of myself." She raised her head and looked at McGuiness. "I wanted it all to be over. But I told the truth about what Alex did. He forced me go with him when I was still in high school and he did the same thing all over again the night all of this happened. He did and he knows it."

McGuiness approached Elizabeth, standing close enough so that each juror could watch both of them at the same time, the prey and the hunter. He paused, allowing the tension to fill the space between them. "Ms. Garrett, isn't it true that you met Alex St. Claire that night by the cemetery as part of a sexual game that the two of you enjoyed?"

"No! That is not true! He knows what he did to me!"

McGuiness let her words hang in the air before he backed up and looked over at the jury, his voice almost a whisper. "Isn't it true, Ms. Garrett, that everything that happened between you and Alex St. Claire was consensual?"

Tears ran down Elizabeth's face as she looked around the courtroom. "No, no, he had a knife! He had a knife!"

McGuiness stood, staring at her for almost half a minute before he returned to the counsel table. "All right, Ms. Garrett. I have no further questions, Your Honor."

~

Jamison glanced discreetly at his wristwatch. McGuiness had timed the conclusion of his cross-examination to end at three thirty. He knew that Judge Wallace would require him to begin redirect instead of recessing for the evening. Wallace did not like to waste even a half hour of trial time if he could avoid it. Jamison drew in a deep breath, took a sip of water, and rose from his chair. He would have to try to repair the damage or simply let Elizabeth walk off the witness stand and deal with the damage later.

"The People ask that Ms. Garrett be excused subject to recall, Your Honor. We have a forensic witness that we can call or, if it pleases the court, we can proceed in the morning."

A former trial lawyer himself, Judge Wallace evidently sensed that Jamison had been blindsided and was doing his best to keep himself under control. Wallace softened. "The court will recess for the evening." Wallace admonished the jury once again to keep an open mind and not discuss the case. As the wooden symbol of judicial authority rapped the bench Jamison felt a small flicker of relief.

Jamison didn't move from the counsel table. His eyes were fixed on the empty judge's bench. He needed to have a better sense of what was going on before he allowed Elizabeth to be questioned further by anyone, including him. He needed time. And time was something he had very little of.

He heard all too clearly the growing silence as the courtroom emptied and the jurors left their seats, moving slowly through the fog of emotion shrouding the courtroom. None were looking at Elizabeth Garrett, who remained alone on the witness stand.

Chapter 25

Jamison entered his office, threw his briefcase down on his desk, and sank into his chair. The plan was for O'Hara to bring Elizabeth up by the back elevator to avoid any reporters lurking around asking questions. Ernie wasn't back yet so he had no idea what more Gupta had to say.

Needing a few minutes to calm down as well as think clearly before talking to her, Jamison walked down the hall to the men's room and splashed cold water on his face. When he returned to his office, Beth and O'Hara were sitting in front of his desk.

Before Jamison could say anything the words tumbled out of Beth. "I know what you're thinking, but it isn't true."

He hesitated a moment before carefully framing his response. "Beth, I have questions. I don't have answers."

"I can explain."

"Why didn't you tell me about the phone call and the pictures?"

"The pictures were a long time ago. They were the reason I didn't want to press charges. Well, at least part of the reason. I didn't want my parents to know about all of that. At that time, I would have done anything Alex asked. I did do anything Alex asked. I didn't tell you about the pictures because I knew if I did you would never believe me that when he stopped my car by the cemetery he forced me to go with him. I can see it on your face right now."

His normally impassive demeanor with witnesses shattered as Jamison snapped, "If you can see it on my face, then don't you think the jurors have the same questions? Look, if I had known about the pictures I would have brought it out. I would have prepared the jury for it. I would have been prepared for it. You need to tell me the truth no matter how bad you think it sounds. I can't try this case unless I know the truth." His voice softened. "Beth, I have to ask. Did you tell St. Claire that you were pregnant and is that why he took you to Los Angeles? Tell me now."

"I never told Alex or anyone that I thought I was pregnant. Never."

He could feel the first throb of a monstrous headache as he rubbed his temples. "And the phone call? You called him and you didn't tell me? Just like you didn't tell me about the pictures?" Jamison's voice rose in barely controlled anger. He knew he needed to calm down or she would shut down.

"I called him just like I testified. I called him after he came up to me at the mall. Not before. I didn't know where he was working until he told me."

"But you didn't tell me."

"All I did was tell him to stay away. I didn't think that would be used like it was. I know how it looks but I really didn't think I was keeping something from you. I'm sorry, but that's the truth. I didn't see him again until that night by the cemetery and I never called him. I don't know what his lawyer is talking about." Elizabeth looked at him, her eyes wide and pleading.

There was no point in saying anything more to her right now. It wouldn't change anything. Jamison wondered how much else she hadn't shared. "All right. I'm going to have one of our investigators drive you home. Investigator O'Hara and I need to talk. One of our people will pick you up tomorrow at eight thirty and bring you down here. Get a good night's sleep. I'm not sure I'm going to put you back on the stand until maybe later, but we have to be ready."

Jamison rose and walked around his desk, placing his hand on her shoulder. "Get some rest. I'll deal with it." He made his voice sound more confident than he felt.

After arranging a ride for Elizabeth, O'Hara returned to Jamison's office. He sat down heavily, his face reflecting his mood, which wasn't good. O'Hara trusted his own instincts and his instincts would have led him to ask Elizabeth more questions, probing questions, on redirect to explain or rehabilitate her after the damage McGuiness had done. But that was because he was used to interrogating people and Garrett was a victim, not a suspect.

"We got dumped on in there," Jamison exploded with frustration. "I thought about asking her more questions, but I didn't know the answers. She was unraveling up there."

He turned his chair to face the window, his back to O'Hara as he considered the situation. "Right now there are three possibilities. Either Elizabeth is telling the truth and the defense is throwing up as much smoke and innuendo as possible or she's not telling the truth and St. Claire didn't do what she says he did . . . or . . ."

"Or what, Matt?"

"Or the truth is somewhere in between."

"So what're you going to do?" O'Hara was suddenly deeply concerned that both the case and Jamison were coming apart.

"The only thing I can. I'm going to assume she's telling the truth and that's how I'm going to cross-examine St. Claire when he gets on the stand. He has to take the stand."

"You think you can break him on the stand?"

"I never count on cracking a guy on the stand," Jamison admitted. "That only happens on television. No way is that going to happen with St. Claire. What we have to do is take every piece of evidence he brings in and prove it's a lie. If we can't do that, then we're going down. I'm going to rest our case and see what they have. Then McGuiness will have to make a decision whether to put on a defense or not. But I'll bet he won't risk not putting on a defense. He can throw all kinds of dust in the air but if his client doesn't testify that jury isn't going to give him a pass. They are going to wonder what he has to hide. We see what McGuiness has got, and then we'll react to it. I'm not putting her back on the stand until we see what we have to deal with. It's the only way I'll know what to ask."

"Matt, people are going to have questions about why she didn't jump out of St. Claire's car when he took her to LA, why she didn't scream. Right now, my bet is that the jury thinks she's lying." It wasn't a question, and O'Hara didn't say whether he himself thought she was lying.

"Maybe she is, Bill, maybe she isn't. It's pretty obvious she didn't tell us everything. But people behave in different ways. She was seventeen. She should have done a lot of things, showed better judgment. The jury doesn't know that we think he murdered three women and was about to murder one more." Jamison stared out the window into the diminishing light of dusk. "It isn't over, yet."

When Ernie entered Jamison's office the first thing that was obvious to him was the silence. Clearly the day hadn't gone well. O'Hara had given him a blow-by-blow of what had transpired while he was out talking to Gupta. He and Gupta had been tearing through files all day, he explained, but they managed to find all the autopsies that Gupta had conducted on people who had died from drug overdoses in the past year. It didn't take long to check the blood types and to match them to the blood types of the victims.

There were seven possible matches of consistent blood types. Gupta had gone back into his lab storage to retrieve the blood samples that he maintained for at least a year. He routinely maintained three vials of blood from each autopsy. None were missing.

Sliding into the chair next to O'Hara, Ernie said, "Gupta and I have been going through the autopsy files. Guess what?" Jamison waved his hand with an impatient motion, obviously not wanting to play the game. Ernie's lips parted, showing his teeth. "Three of the blood vials for junkies that Gupta did the posts on didn't show any heroin or barbiturate levels, although they should have according to the records. At first Gupta couldn't tell who it came from. But then Gupta did enzyme matches. The blood that was supposed to be from the junkies came from our three victims and the blood in the file that was supposed to be from our victims came from three addicts who OD'd. None of our victims ingested any narcotics. Matt, this is huge. Somebody switched the blood samples."

O'Hara slammed his hand on Jamison's desk. "I knew that son of a bitch would screw up. They all do, no matter how smart they think they are."

Ernie shared O'Hara's exuberance. "Gupta is furious. He wants to go to the medical board, the hospital, and God only knows who else. I told him to sit tight. We'd get back to him." Ernie tilted his chair back. "We got St. Claire's *cojones* in a vise, Matt. Now we get to squeeze."

"Can we show that St. Claire had access to Gupta's tissue storage?" Jamison felt a weight come off his shoulders.

"I asked that. Gupta said that the key is in his desk. Some of his technicians have access because they remove samples for testing. He never worried about leaving the key there because he trusts his people. St. Claire could have walked in anytime and opened up the tissue cold storage. It would have been simple. All he had to do was switch the blood samples from the victims with the blood samples from junkies whose blood type matched theirs. Nobody would have known the difference and nobody would have reason to check. Gupta said you just remove the stopper, flush the vial out with saline, and then pour the blood in from the other vial. So the blood vial has Gupta's signature on it and the victim's name on it. We did exactly what St. Claire would have expected, took the test results and assumed that the blood sample was accurate."

Drawing circles on his legal pad before speaking and trying to keep his excitement in perspective, Jamison sat silently for a moment. The news wasn't going to do them any good in the Garrett trial unless they could get it into evidence. But it would help close the door on the murder cases. "So we know somebody switched the blood and that St. Claire had the opportunity to do that. We know he had access to the records and we have the hair and fiber matches. Now we squeeze."

"Ernie, talk to Bill and he'll fill you in on the testimony about the hospital call logs. I need you to get me copies."

He lifted the receiver to call the district attorney and then hesitated before putting it back down as a realization struck him. "Without the heroin and barbiturate levels we don't know what killed these women. Does Gupta have any ideas? I'm going to have to come up with something."

Ernie was smiling. "Well, Matt, I think you need to talk to Gupta. He has an idea, but what he thinks is going to make the shit hit the fan when the press finds out."

Chapter 26

When Jamison and O'Hara entered Gupta's office the diminutive pathologist's head barely showed above the mound of paper and books stacked on his desk. He looked disheveled and disturbed. His normally rosy complexion was a slightly gray color and his sparse strands of hair stuck out at odd angles. Gupta picked up a piece of paper and wordlessly handed it to Jamison, who quickly scanned the document, stumbling over the strange word.

"Succinylcholine? What the hell is that?"

Gupta took the paper back and put it on his desk. "Succinylcholine, Mr. Jamison, is the perfect murder weapon in the hands of the right person. Especially if no one knows what to look for. Let me tell you a little story. In the 1960s a physician, Dr. Carl Coppolino, was charged with two murders. His attorney, Mr. F. Lee Bailey, was the most famous lawyer of his day. Doctors in my specialty are familiar with this case because it is a curiosity and because it involves a physician. Dr. Coppolino, it seems, claimed that his wife had died of a heart attack and at first that was the way it appeared.

"But after questions were asked about his relationship with a woman whose husband had also died suddenly, she admitted that she had an affair with Dr. Coppolino, and that he had helped her kill her husband. And, this is the crucial part for you, Mr. Jamison. He did this with an injection of succinylcholine. For months nobody could find the cause of death until the New York City Chief Medical Examiner Dr. Milton Halpern figured it out.

"You see, Mr. Jamison, Dr. Coppolino was an anesthesiologist and it was not uncommon for such specialists to use succinylcholine to relax the muscles in the throat so that an endotracheal tube could be inserted more easily through the nose or mouth. Because the drug metabolizes quickly in the body it was impossible to detect using standard methods. However, Dr. Halpern devised a test that found a metabolite of succinylcholine in the brain tissue of Dr. Coppolino's wife.

"Given in sufficient quantities, succinylcholine will paralyze all the muscles in the body. What makes it a perfect murder weapon is the fact that in sufficient quantities it mimics the appearance of a heart attack. It would also look exactly the same as the effect of a massive drug overdose stopping the heart. In simple terms, I concluded the cause of death was consistent with drug overdose because of the blood results and the physical manifestations. Why would I have suspected that the blood vials had been switched? Who could even imagine such a thing? We don't routinely test for things like that.

"So I had no reason to look for something else because the drug levels would have produced death and were consistent with my examination. If succinylcholine was used by the killer of these women then I would expect it was injected where I found the puncture wounds, where I assumed the heroin-and-barbiturate cocktails were injected."

Jamison digested the startling information. A rush of new questions raced through his mind. "I would think this succinylcholine is not something that is readily available?"

Gupta agreed. "It would be something that only a physician or a veterinarian would have access to normally. Veterinarians use it for the same reason as physicians."

"And I take it this succinylcholine would be here at the hospital?"

"Yes, it is something that is accessible."

"Including to Dr. St. Claire?"

"It is something anesthesiologists use under certain circumstances."

"So when can you do this test?" Jamison suspected that if Gupta could have done it he already would have, but hoped his assumption was wrong.

"Sadly, Mr. Jamison, I cannot. You see it requires brain tissue of some quantity. I do not normally maintain large tissue samples of the brain . . ." Gupta's voice was apologetic. "It is a space problem and it simply did not seem to be an issue in the case of these deaths given the appearance and blood tests. However, I do have a small specimen of brain matter from the Symes girl. As you know she was cremated, as was the Ventana girl. Johnson was buried according to my records."

"If we can get the body exhumed, you can remove the brain. Can we test it, then?"

"There is no brain," Gupta answered. "I removed it and did a gross examination as well as made some tissue slides, but the slides are not enough to do that kind of test." His voice trailed off into a mumble. "I did not return it before the body was released."

O'Hara's face darkened. "What does that *mean*, 'did not return it?'"

Holding up his hands in a gesture seeking understanding, Gupta said, "I'm saying that I disconnected the brain tissue and removed it from the body. I examined it later. I cannot do everything immediately. Let us simply say that after I obtained my tissue samples, I disposed of it." O'Hara's expression caused Gupta to shrink even more into his chair. "Respectfully, please understand this is our normal procedure, but not everything is returned to the body except to the extent it affects appearance."

Recoiling at the implication of Gupta's statement, O'Hara exclaimed, "You disposed of her brain?" The revulsion on his face didn't require further questions.

Gupta's voice became defensive. "I kept one piece from Ms. Symes's brain tissue because of the pattern of activity of multiple murders but it is not substantial. That must be sent to the FBI. They have more sophisticated testing methods. If succinic acid is present, hopefully they will find it. As for the other victims, all I have are slides. There are no gross tissue samples."

"So you can't be sure that this succinol . . ." Jamison stumbled over the word.

Gupta pronounced it for him. "Succinylcholine."

"Right. That this stuff is what killed these women?"

"Looking at everything I would say it is a very likely cause. It would be consistent with what we found and the injection site would be where I thought the drugs were administered. None of these women died of a drug overdose. It is clear to me that they were dead at the time of the infliction of the wound. There are very few drugs that would have the paralytic effect I believe occurred here and not be readily detectable. There are some extremely rare paralytic agents that are neurotoxins but obtaining them is very difficult. Succinylcholine is easily obtained by the right person, virtually undetectable, and fits all of the physical manifestations of the bodies."

Jamison asked, "So this succinylcholine was injected and you assumed it was the injection site for the drugs because the blood tests showed a drug overdose. Is that it?"

"Yes, my conclusion is that the victims had some kind of anesthetic that they inhaled rendering them unconscious before the injection of the paralytic. I will keep running tests, but at this moment I am offering the opinion of succinylcholine as likely cause of death." Gupta hesitated. "Particularly if Dr. St. Claire is the suspect, which is most disappointing to me."

Jamison asked Gupta, "When you send the tissue to the FBI lab, how long is it going to take to confirm?"

Gupta was constrained. "I believe it should be done within two weeks, maybe less, but this is not something easily tested for."

"I don't have two weeks, Dr. Gupta."

"I am not a magician, Mr. Jamison." Gupta shrugged. "Even the FBI cannot do this test in less than maybe a week."

O'Hara's face showed disappointment and apprehension matching Jamison's. Each of them knew Jamison didn't have a week and he definitely didn't have two weeks. He didn't have twenty-four hours. He had to be in court, and when he cross-examined St. Claire he would be flying blind.

~

The next morning Jamison sat alone in his office with the door closed. He needed quiet to think. Ernie had obtained copies of the hospital call logs and they showed exactly what St. Claire testified to. Elizabeth had called St. Claire, and the time was right there in black and white.

He would have to explain it somehow, but he would be on the defensive because Beth hadn't told him about it in advance and now it sounded like she was lying. At the very least, she hadn't been completely truthful and her explanation would sound weak. If the cross-examination was any indication, McGuiness was still holding cards he hadn't played.

Jamison had some serious choices to make and he would have to make a very aggressive move. There was a reason he hadn't been willing to charge St. Claire yet with the three murders and it centered on lack of evidence. But now with the new evidence and a little luck, maybe, just maybe, if he handled it right he could make the murder charges stick and use them in the Garrett case. Second, the Garrett case was key to making them stick because the Garrett case was the only one where they had a living witness.

If he could get evidence of the murders introduced in the Garrett case, he knew that a jury would find St. Claire guilty because the evidence would shatter St. Claire's credibility. Without that murder evidence in the Garrett case he realized his chances of convicting St. Claire were rapidly slipping away.

While he had a lot of faith in his ability to cross-examine St. Claire, he also knew he wasn't a magician. Getting evidence of the murders admitted in the Garrett case was going to be difficult at best. There was only one way to make that happen.

It was becoming increasingly clear that McGuiness was arguing that everything that happened between Garrett and St. Claire was consensual. Jamison could argue the evidence of the murders helped prove that St. Claire had the same intent with Garrett because the pattern of the crimes was the same. He would argue that the only difference was that they had rescued Elizabeth Garrett before St. Claire could do to her what he had done to the other victims.

But getting Wallace to allow that uncharged murder evidence into the trial was a very big if. He was going to have to be very patient and wait until McGuiness had finished his case. He needed to let St. Claire testify first and see where that went and what he could get out of him.

The allegation of murder was explosive and would force Judge Wallace to make a very difficult decision. This was the kind of evidence that got cases reversed if the trial judge made a mistake. And trial judges didn't like getting reversed. The easy call for Judge Wallace would be to keep out any evidence of the murders.

His cross-examination of St. Claire would weigh heavily with Wallace and it was also Jamison's opportunity to ask St. Claire questions that he wouldn't be permitted to ask outside of the courtroom. If he handled the cross-examination carefully, he might get answers that he could use later to prove the murders in a future trial. It was a high-stakes lawyer game and he knew it.

There was also one other possibility that could influence the outcome. If Wallace said he was going to let the evidence of the murders into this trial, most lawyers would ask for a mistrial and take the continuance to prepare for the murder charges. But McGuiness wasn't most lawyers and St. Claire wasn't most clients. Neither of them suffered a lack of confidence, and Jamison was counting on St. Claire's arrogance. He had a strong feeling that St. Claire's inflated sense of self would make him go all-in, demanding that the trial go forward despite the murder evidence. And McGuiness was a risk-taker who believed his skill and his instincts would carry him over any hurdle. Jamison had been humbled enough times in court to know that overconfidence was the worst enemy of a trial lawyer.

Jamison sighed, picked up his briefcase, and walked downstairs to the courtroom. First he had one more decision to make. McGuiness expected Garrett to retake the stand. What would he do if she didn't?

Chapter 27

McGuiness and St. Claire were already seated at the counsel table when Jamison walked into the courtroom. He took his seat, carefully laying out his legal tablet and file. Jamison acknowledged McGuiness and ignored St. Claire when he said, "Good morning." The twelve jurors and two alternates filed in and took their seats.

Judge Wallace settled himself behind the bench and peered over at Jamison. Given yesterday's events, he was curious to learn what Jamison would do. How a lawyer reacted to unanticipated attacks on his case separated the good trial lawyers from the rest. Judge Wallace caught the smile on the prosecutor's face. "Mr. Jamison, you may proceed."

After hours of rumination, Jamison had concluded that if he rested the prosecution's case, McGuiness had only two choices. He could also rest his case, present no evidence, argue reasonable doubt and remind the jury that his client had a constitutional right not to testify, or he could put St. Claire on the stand.

The chances of a jury giving a defendant the benefit of the doubt without his testifying was always a significant gamble for the defense. Clearly McGuiness had drawn blood with his cross-examination of Garrett, but other than the pictures, there was no evidence to back up any of his implications. Elizabeth had denied it all. Therefore McGuiness *needed* St. Claire on the stand to win his case. So did Jamison, but not for the same reason.

McGuiness wouldn't expect him to rest his case without bringing Elizabeth back to explain questions the defense had raised. In trial, sometimes doing the unexpected was the best weapon.

"Your Honor, the People rest." The expression on McGuiness's face told Jamison he had indeed taken him off-guard. Perhaps nobody but a trial lawyer or a judge would know it, but Jamison did. He was also hoping that Wallace would react to form and confront McGuiness immediately to start putting on his case.

McGuiness stood slowly before addressing the court, gathering his thoughts. "Your Honor, I had expected that Mr. Jamison might be calling a few additional witnesses. There will be a delay before my first witness is available."

The judge didn't disappoint. "Counsel approach the bench." Wallace motioned both lawyers to the side of the bench. "Mr. McGuiness, are you planning to put your client on the stand?"

The defense lawyer shifted uncomfortably. "Yes, but I had planned on putting an expert witness on first as well as another witness regarding the phone logs."

Immediately Jamison said, "Your Honor, as this court is aware, Mr. McGuiness has given no indication of witnesses other than his client. If he has such a witness I have a right to know who it is and an opportunity to talk to them."

Wallace held up his hand to stop him. "Mr. McGuiness, you know my rules. You are to have witnesses ready to go. You have a witness ready to go. Let's at least get on with that."

McGuiness opened his mouth to respond and then obviously thought better of it. "Yes, Your Honor." He walked back to the counsel table. "The defense calls Dr. Alex St. Claire."

St. Claire stood, deftly buttoning his suit jacket with one hand as he walked to the center of the courtroom. He moved his body slightly, causing the French cuffs of his white shirt to extend just beyond his suit sleeve. It was the gesture of a man accustomed to wearing expensive clothing with no hint of self-consciousness and who was used to being in control and accustomed to deference. He raised his right hand to take the oath.

Jamison didn't need to look over at the jurors to know that right now St. Claire had their sympathy. Jamison suspected that St. Claire was aware of this as well.

McGuiness waited until his client was comfortably seated before asking his first questions. He carefully established that St. Claire had completed his college education at the University of California at Berkeley with high honors, and then obtained his medical degree with honors at the University of London Imperial College School of Medicine in England. He had done research in Europe on the effects of anesthesia before returning to the United States and doing a residency in Chicago. While he had been in Europe his parents had died. The loss of his family and the fact that he had been raised in California made him want to return.

Jamison saw no point in trying to halt the effort to polish St. Claire in the eyes of the jury. It would only make him look petty. But he also knew that the more academic status and acclaim that McGuiness layered on St. Claire, the more a jury would be inclined to give him the benefit of the doubt. Before he uttered one word about the charges, he would be perceived as a humane man of distinction, working in the most noble of professions, and the jury would think, "Why would a man like this do what he had been accused of?" That was the question McGuiness wanted them to have stuck in their heads.

What was in Jamison's head was that as far as he was concerned they were all looking at a multiple murderer who wore French-cuffed shirts and two-thousand-dollar suits.

"Dr. St. Claire, do you know Elizabeth Garrett?"

Turning his face toward the jury, St. Claire answered quietly. "Yes, I met Elizabeth when I was a college student here before I transferred to the University of California."

"And how old were you when you met her?"

"I was almost twenty-one, and she was, I found out later, nearly seventeen. I thought she was older, but I wasn't that old myself."

"You have heard testimony that the two of you had a relationship. Is that true?"

"Yes, but the truth is we fell in love. There is no other way to put it." Jamison found the precision of St. Claire's speech irritating and affected. The slight hint of British accent seemed to give him a patrician air. Jamison wasn't sure the jury would be as put off by the accent as he was or put off at all.

Carefully, McGuiness threaded St. Claire through the days and months and finally the years of their relationship before asking the questions that moved toward the heart of the case. "During this time did you and Elizabeth become intimate?"

St. Claire looked down, hesitating before answering. He raised his head and kept his eyes on McGuiness. "Yes, we both were inexperienced. It just happened. And then we couldn't stop. It was the first time for both of us."

"You heard Ms. Garrett testify yesterday about some photographs. Where did those photographs come from?"

"I kept them all these years. I should have destroyed them. I told Elizabeth that I would, but the truth is I couldn't destroy anything that reminded me of her. I am embarrassed by the pictures, but we experimented with our sexual activities. Everything was new and different. She liked certain things and, I confess, so did I.

"It's hard for people to understand, I suppose, but we would play games, little personal games. It was part of our relationship, but it was just between us. You understand? We didn't hurt each other. It was just a game. I would never do anything to hurt Elizabeth."

Jamison shifted his eyes to take in the jury. This was Tenaya County, it wasn't Hollywood. Even though bondage might no longer seem shocking, it still would alter, if only slightly, the crafted image of St. Claire as a man without mortal faults. Jamison tucked that fault line away as something he would work on and turned his attention back to McGuiness's questions.

"So Ms. Garrett was a willing participant in this game shown in these photographs?"

"Yes, she was. I would never do anything that Elizabeth didn't ask me to do or agree to do."

"At some point did your relationship end?"

"Her parents were behind that. Elizabeth was underage and her father was quite specific about what would happen to me. I was afraid. I tried to stop seeing her but it didn't work. We saw each other in secret."

"You recall that she said you kept coming to her place of work and she told you to stay away? Is that correct?"

"I did keep coming to where she worked but she didn't ask me to stay away. We were just trying to keep it from her father. And then she told me she was pregnant. I didn't know what to do. Both of us were scared. We were so young. That's when I decided that we would get married. We would run away. We talked about it. Looking back on it now, it sounds immature and dramatic but we didn't know what else to do."

"Did you know if Elizabeth was actually pregnant? Did she have a test?"

"All I knew was that she told me she was pregnant. I believed her. Why wouldn't I?"

"Elizabeth testified that the reason she went with you to Southern California was because you had a knife and forced her to go with you. Is that true?"

"I did not use a knife." His modulated tone broke and rose in indignation. "It is true that I kept a small knife in my car. Elizabeth knew it was there but I never threatened her with it. She wanted to come with me as much as I wanted her to. It wasn't just my idea to get married. It was hers too."

"I drove us to Los Angeles," he continued, his composure restored. "I didn't know where we could get married. She was not yet eighteen. We stayed at a motel and talked. Then I thought of Mexico. Looking back on it I realize that it was totally unrealistic. I didn't think about how we could get across the border. We didn't think about any of that."

"Elizabeth left you? She ran away?"

"After we left the motel and we decided to go to Mexico she became very emotional. We drove around and talked. We decided to see a few things, you know, like tourists. We stopped a few times and I thought it was going to be okay. But at the end of the day she said she wanted to see her mother; she wanted to go back. I didn't want to go back. We argued. I said she would feel better after we were married. She became hysterical.

"She jumped out of the car and ran to a nearby house. I hoped she would come back out, but I got scared. I'm not proud of it, but I drove off. I did return, but when I did, I saw a police car so I drove away."

"When did you next see Elizabeth?"

"I didn't see her again for a long time. Her father wouldn't let me see her and my lawyer told me to stay away. I came to court after I was arrested, but then the charges were dropped. My lawyer said Elizabeth and her parents didn't want to press charges. He made it clear that I needed to stay away from her for my own good. I didn't see her again until all of this happened."

McGuiness walked over to the counsel table and retrieved a bag from a briefcase. As he walked back to St. Claire, he held the bag out so that all eyes were on it. "Dr. St. Claire, Alex, do you recognize this bag? It has Sears printed on it, the department store?" He handed it to St. Claire.

St. Claire took the bag and looked inside it. "Yes."

McGuiness took the bag back and moved close to where Jamison was sitting. Only Jamison could see the look in McGuiness's eyes as he turned the bag on end, dumping its contents out on the counsel table directly in front of Jamison and O'Hara. Baby clothing tumbled out in a small pile. Jamison looked down at the pile as McGuiness pulled a receipt from the bag and laid it in front of him. McGuiness waited so that everyone could see the clothing. He held up a piece to St. Claire. "Alex, what is this?"

"It's part of the baby clothes that we bought while we were driving around in Los Angeles. We stopped at a Sears store. I noticed the baby clothes. I don't know why, but Elizabeth picked some out and we bought them for the baby."

"And this?" McGuiness held up the receipt.

"That's the receipt for the clothes."

"Does the receipt have a date on it?"

"Yes, it has a cash register stamp for the day we were in Los Angeles."

McGuiness handed the receipt to Jamison. "Would you stipulate that the date on the receipt is the same as the date when Elizabeth testified they were in Los Angeles?"

The dates were the same. Jamison didn't have a choice. "I agree."

McGuiness retrieved the receipt from Jamison and picked up each item of baby clothing individually, making a display of dropping the items carefully into the bag so that all the jurors could see it. As he did so, McGuiness turned his head just enough so that Jamison alone could catch his expression. His eyes read, *I told you so.*

"These are the baby clothes you and Elizabeth purchased?"

"Yes, again, I realize it probably doesn't make much sense, buying clothing for a baby before it is born. We didn't know whether it would be a boy or a girl or how big . . ." St. Claire's voice trailed off as if his focus was on the memory of that moment instead of on the courtroom.

McGuiness returned to the counsel table and removed from his briefcase a piece of paper encased in a clear plastic folder. He showed it to Jamison. It was a cash register receipt for the same day. Jamison shoved it back across the counsel table toward McGuiness, who picked it up, returned to the witness box, and handed it to St. Claire. "Dr. St. Claire, do you recognize this piece of paper?"

St. Claire looked at it briefly and gave it back. "Yes."

"What is it?"

"It's a cash register receipt from the *Queen Mary*, the legendary passenger ship that is down in the harbor at Long Beach. We visited the wax museum that was on the ship. It has the date on it for the same day."

The defense attorney laid the receipt on the flat wooden rail in front of the jury box. “So you and Elizabeth went to the wax museum on the *Queen Mary*? Were there a lot of people there?”

“There were people all over. It’s a major attraction. She wanted to go.”

“And it was after you went to the *Queen Mary* that she ran away?”

“Yes, we drove around some more. She was becoming more and more upset and that’s when I stopped at an intersection and she jumped out of the car.”

“This was over ten years ago, wasn’t it? Why did you keep these things?”

Inhaling deeply before answering, St. Claire stared up at the courtroom ceiling. “I suppose there is some complex answer for it but the truth is I’m not sure why.” St. Claire turned his head toward the jury. “The only thing I can say is I held on to every part of Elizabeth. I put these things away. I kept them because they were part of her, part of us. They were just stored at the house when I went away to school. When all this happened you asked me whether there was anything that might explain our relationship. I remembered these things and I gave them to you.”

“Dr. St. Claire, let’s talk about these charges you have been accused of. Elizabeth testified that she hadn’t seen you in ten years, and then all of a sudden at a shopping mall you walked up behind her and frightened her. She says she had not seen you since the charges were dropped. Is that true?”

“It is true that I had not seen Elizabeth since then. I may have let my emotions get the better of me and made some costly mistakes in my life, but I’m not a fool. I stayed away. The day I saw her at the mall was no surprise to her. She phoned me at the hospital. She said she had heard I was back in town and that perhaps we could talk over coffee.”

“What time was it when you got that call?”

“I don’t recall exactly, but it was in the early afternoon. The call logs from the hospital would show what time. They keep a record of all calls that go into hospital extensions. You have to go through the main switchboards.”

“And what did you do in response to the call?”

Inhaling audibly, St. Claire’s voice cracked as he spoke. “I suppose maybe I am a fool. When I heard her voice I wanted to see her. I knew better, but I did it anyway. I left the hospital and met her at the mall.”

McGuiness continued with his orchestrated examination. “What happened at that meeting?”

Jamison felt a cold sensation in his stomach. He could see St. Claire had the jurors in the palm of his hand. They were riveted.

St. Claire wiped at the corners of his eyes. "We talked. She said she was sorry about what had happened. Seeing her again brought everything back. We spent the afternoon together. We went to my house to talk some more and—to be alone."

"And when you went to your house to be alone, did anything happen?"

"It was like we had never been apart. I drove her back to her car at the mall. I had to be out of town for a conference, but I was coming back on the day all this happened. She had planned to have dinner with a friend and agreed to meet me after. She didn't want her parents to know, nor did I."

"While you were at your home that day, were you and Elizabeth intimate?"

"Yes," St. Claire said softly. "The answer is yes, we were."

McGuiness placed a photograph in front of Jamison. It was a picture of Elizabeth turning her head as she got into a car. Her hair was swirling around her face. McGuiness picked up the photograph and showed it to his client. "Do you recognize this?"

"Yes, it's a photograph that I took of Elizabeth after we returned to her car at the mall. She had a camera with her and we took some photographs. We were teasing each other. She didn't want me to take it and she turned her head away as I snapped the picture. She gave this to me later."

"You said she asked you to take 'some photographs.' Do you have the others?"

St. Claire shook his head. "No, it was Elizabeth's camera. This is the only one she gave me."

"Let's move to the night Elizabeth testified you stopped her car by the cemetery. So did you follow her car that night and stop her? Did you have a red light on your car?"

"I did drive my car to that location. It was where we agreed to meet. She was waiting. I didn't have any red light on my car. That's ridiculous. Why would I need that? I walked up to her car and she had the window down. I did say, 'Remember me?'"

"Did you have a knife?"

"Why would I need a knife? She came willingly with me and we went to my home out in the country where I do some of my work sometimes. It wasn't far. I showed her around. We talked."

Jamison made a quick note for his cross-examination. *If there was no knife, then how did the blood get on the seat?* That would have to be explained. He refocused as McGuiness continued.

"Did you have sexual relations?"

"I'm not going to say I didn't want to. I did. But she fell asleep on the couch. We were both very tired. I was going to take her back to her car but it was late."

"She stayed and slept all night?" McGuiness asked.

"Yes. Then the next day I went into the office for a while and returned home as soon as I could. She said before I left that she wanted to wait for me. Otherwise I would have driven her back to her car. I didn't stay long at the hospital. I wanted to be with her as much as she wanted to be with me. We started playing our old game and she wanted to be tied up. That's when Mr. O'Hara came to the door."

"And you didn't let him in?"

"I didn't want to let him in for obvious reasons, to protect Elizabeth as well as myself. I refused. Then I heard Elizabeth screaming and the glass breaking. I ran back down the hallway to her and that's when Mr. O'Hara broke down the door and tackled me. I tried to tell him the circumstances were not what he thought but he wouldn't listen."

"So, the camera that was in the bedroom and Elizabeth tied up, that was all part of a sexual game between you and Elizabeth?"

St. Claire stared down at his hands. "As humiliating as this is to discuss in front of everyone, the answer is yes."

"How did Elizabeth get cut on her neck?"

"That happened at home right before I tied her up. It was an accident. I did have a knife. It was just part of our game. I didn't mean to cut her. I had the knife and she moved and I wasn't paying attention. Thank God it was just a scratch."

McGuiness paused, allowing the silence to intensify the moment before he asked his next question. "Dr. St. Claire, after all of this happened, you are aware that Elizabeth told a very different version than what you have told us today?"

St. Claire's voice was inaudible. McGuiness stepped farther back and raised his voice. "Dr. St. Claire, did you hear me? Do you have anything to say about why Elizabeth would say something so different from what you have testified to today?"

St. Claire looked down. "I can't answer that, only Elizabeth can. My guess is that it's her parents again. Even so, I love her. I still love her. What kind of a fool does that make me?" Several of the women were wiping away tears. Jamison drew circles on his legal pad, trying to appear as if none of it was affecting him. At least now he knew what he was facing.

As he walked back to the counsel table, McGuiness said, "Your Honor, I have no further questions of Dr. St. Claire at this time." He looked over at Jamison. "Your witness, counsel."

Jamison sat silently for a moment and then rose slowly from his chair at the counsel table. "Your Honor, may we have a short recess? I would like to examine further some of the evidence that Mr. McGuiness has introduced."

Aware that Jamison had not seen any of the evidence before St. Claire's examination, Wallace responded, "We'll take a twenty-minute recess. Be prepared to proceed when we return."

St. Claire left the witness stand and walked back to where McGuiness was seated. There was no lack of confidence in his stride.

Several jurors gave St. Claire sympathetic looks as they filed out of the courtroom. Jamison whispered to O'Hara, "I'm going to take a closer look at that evidence. Meet me in one of the empty jury rooms in the back hallway." O'Hara nodded. His expression was grim.

Jamison had the bag and the *Queen Mary* receipt in his hands. He laid them on the empty jury room table in front of O'Hara. "What do you think?"

O'Hara picked up the two pieces of paper. "They look legitimate to me. I mean, how could you forge something like this? The only thing that went through my mind was why the hell would he have kept this stuff? Who keeps this kind of stuff?" O'Hara put them back down on the table. "What are you going to do?"

"The first thing I need to do is talk to Beth." Jamison picked up the receipts and told O'Hara to return them to the clerk in the courtroom. "I need to make a call."

He pulled out his phone and waited impatiently until Elizabeth answered. "Beth, I have some questions and not much time. When you went to Los

Angeles with St. Claire, he testified that you told him you were pregnant and—"

"I never said that," Elizabeth blurted out. "You have to believe me."

"Okay, but he said the two of you bought some baby clothes. Beth, he brought them to court and there's a receipt for the day that the two of you were down there. He also has a receipt for the same day for a tour of some attraction on the *Queen Mary* in the harbor." Jamison could hear labored breathing on the other end of the phone. "Beth, I have to know the truth. Did you purchase any baby clothes when you were with him? Did you go to the *Queen Mary*?" Jamison was trying to keep his voice calm but he couldn't keep the agitation out of it. There was a long silence at the other end of the line.

"I don't know what you're talking about. I don't know what he's talking about. None of that happened." Jamison could hear her starting to cry.

"Beth, St. Claire had a photograph of you that he said was taken in the parking lot at the mall the day you testified he surprised you. He said you asked him to take it with your camera."

He could hear the catch in Elizabeth's voice as her words tumbled out. "I don't know anything about photographs. I don't know how he obtained a photograph of me, but I didn't know it was being taken."

Jamison took a deep breath. "All right, all right. Beth, I had to ask. I'll talk to you later. I have to go back to court." Jamison hung up and ran back to the courtroom.

Judge Wallace and the jurors were already seated. Wallace gave him a hard look as he rushed in. "It looks like we can get started now. Are you ready, Mr. Jamison?"

Jamison didn't immediately answer. He scribbled a note and handed it to O'Hara, telling him to have Ernie go to the hospital and check the log books. "Yes, Your Honor."

Wallace nodded to the defendant. "Dr. St. Claire, please retake the witness stand. I remind you that you are still under oath."

Jamison looked down at his notes. He didn't have much. Either St. Claire was telling the truth or Beth was telling the truth. Either the baby clothes had been purchased as St. Claire said or they were purchased to create an alibi. He had to cross-examine St. Claire based on the assumption Beth was telling the truth. The worst part was that while he really wanted to believe her, he couldn't shake off his own nagging doubts. He also knew that if he had doubts then the jury was already halfway down the road to walking Alex St. Claire out of court.

Jamison took a deep breath to slow down his heartbeat, picked up his notepad, and glanced at his outline. Before he tried any case he always decided on his objectives in cross-examination of likely witnesses. He had learned a long time ago to stick with those objectives and to never go fishing if he didn't know how deep the water was.

With St. Claire, he knew he had no idea what might be coming at him. His objective was clear. He had to shake St. Claire's credibility, find a crack and then drive a wedge into it. The problem was finding the crack.

"Dr. St. Claire," he began deliberately, "let me see if I understand what you say happened the night Elizabeth Garrett's car was found abandoned by the side of the road. Ms. Garrett agreed to meet you after she finished having dinner at the Packing Shed?"

"Yes."

"Was there some reason why she could not meet you at your home?"

"No, Mr. Jamison, there was not. As a matter of fact, that was my suggestion: my home. Elizabeth is the one who asked me to meet her at that location. I was there waiting for her when she drove up. How else would I have known where she was going to be? That was not the most convenient way for her to drive home." St. Claire paused. "At least according to your own witnesses. Your implication that I followed her to that location would mean that Elizabeth would take a different route than she has taken perhaps several hundred times before, in the middle of the night, and I would follow her?" St. Claire let his answer hang in the air. "Mr. Jamison, Elizabeth called me and told me she was leaving the Packing Shed. How else would I have known when she would be driving home?"

Jamison didn't want to answer but he had no choice. "By following her from the Packing Shed would seem the most logical explanation. Isn't that what you did?"

St. Claire smiled before answering. "It is what I could have done had I wanted to sit in my car waiting for her to leave the restaurant and follow her some ten miles out into the country. That is your suggestion, isn't it?"

"It isn't simply a suggestion, Dr. St. Claire, it is exactly what you did, isn't it?"

"I believe the logs of the hospital will reflect that I did not leave the hospital until after nine thirty that evening. Isn't that the time Elizabeth testified she left the restaurant? She called me, Mr. Jamison. I didn't call her. Perhaps you should look at the logs at the hospital?"

Jamison kept his composure. He could feel his shirt begin to stick to his body. He wasn't making any headway with St. Claire and McGuiness had let him walk again right into the log books. He didn't have to see them to know that somehow they would reflect what St. Claire said. Again, there were only two explanations. He couldn't cross-examine in that area without walking blindfolded through a mine-field. He decided to shift.

"You testified that the cut on Ms. Garrett's neck occurred when the two of you were at your home?"

"That's correct. It was an accident."

"I assume she bled?"

"Yes, there was a small amount of blood."

"Did any of that blood get on the sheets or the pillowcase?"

"I believe there may have been some. Actually I went and got some tissues. The cut was really more of a scratch. There wasn't much."

"Was there enough to have left a smear of blood on the seat of Ms. Garrett's car?"

St. Claire didn't flinch. "Perhaps, I really don't know."

"You heard the testimony that there was a smear of blood on Ms. Garrett's driver's seat with the outline of a knife tip?"

"Yes, I heard that. And I heard Elizabeth say I put it there."

"Didn't you?"

Momentarily, St. Claire stared straight at Jamison and then moved his head slightly toward the jurors, speaking slowly with emphasis. "*If I had done what Elizabeth said*, then I suppose the answer would be yes. But I did not do that. I don't know how it got there. Perhaps you should ask Elizabeth when you ask her about the clothing we bought for the baby? Besides, how many knives did you find in my home?"

Jamison quickly evaluated St. Claire's answer. The defense couldn't admit that he had used a knife at the scene where the car was found because that would make Elizabeth's version more credible. St. Claire's answer was the alternate version, but it was an unexplained hole in their story. Jamison walked over to the counsel table and picked up a manila envelope, removing a plastic bag with a knife in it. He took the bag to the clerk and asked her to put an exhibit number on the bag. Then he held the bag in front of St. Claire. "This is your knife, isn't it?"

St. Claire reached for the plastic bag that Jamison held slightly out of reach. "May I see it, please?" He examined the knife through the clear plastic.

"Would you describe it please, Dr. St. Claire?"

"It is a knife with a four-inch blade."

"It is a switchblade, isn't it, Dr. St. Claire? A spring-loaded knife that flips open when you press a release switch on the side?"

"Yes."

"Are you aware it is illegal to possess a switchblade knife?"

"Yes."

"Whose is it, Dr. St. Claire?"

"It's mine."

"And it is also sharpened on both sides, isn't it, like a dagger?"

"Yes."

"And you kept this switchblade in your car?"

"No, the knife in my car is rather small, more like a pocket knife. You didn't find it when you searched?"

Jamison answered the question. "No, there was no knife in your car that I am aware of. This is the only knife we found. Is this the knife that cut Elizabeth Garrett?"

"I said it was an accident."

"Your answer is yes?"

"Yes."

Jamison reached into the bag and pulled out the knife. He flicked the switch on the side, allowing the blade to snap open and holding it in front of St. Claire. He had deliberately not put the knife into evidence earlier during his case, anticipating that cross-examination might be the right moment. "Why would you have a knife like this, Dr. St. Claire?"

"I have had it for many years. It's a curiosity, and I don't carry it. I keep it in my home. Isn't that where you found it?"

"We found it in the room where Elizabeth Garrett was tied to the bed. Isn't it true that this was the knife you used when you stopped Elizabeth's car that night?"

"I told you I did not stop her car. But the answer is no."

"Then can you explain, Dr. St. Claire, why the tip of this knife exactly matches the outline found in the smeared blood on Elizabeth's driver's seat?"

Before Jamison finished asking the question, McGuiness was out of his chair. "Your Honor, I object. Mr. Jamison is asking my client to speculate. There is no evidence the knife matches any outline on the driver's seat. The question is—"

Wallace ruled before McGuiness finished. "Objection sustained. Mr. Jamison, you will rephrase your question. There is no evidence before the court regarding the outline on the seat of the car."

"Thank you, Your Honor. I agree there is nothing in evidence *yet* as to the outline of the knife on the seat. I don't expect that rephrasing will produce a better answer than what we have received."

McGuiness stood again. "Your Honor . . ."

"I'll move on. But before I do"—Jamison waived his hand toward McGuiness—"will you stipulate that the blood found on the side of the driver's seat was Elizabeth Garrett's?"

McGuiness nodded. "We will agree that it is Ms. Garrett's blood."

"Thank you." Jamison turned back toward St. Claire. "Since you have been so helpful in providing explanations to my questions, do you have any explanation for how Elizabeth Garrett's blood got on the driver's seat?"

"You would have to ask her. I do not."

"Or why she would wipe a knife stained with blood on that seat?"

St. Claire's expression was impassive. "That seems to assume that it was left by a knife or . . . by that knife."

Jamison hesitated. There was something here and he could ask or he could wait. He decided to wait and switch gears, hopefully to get St. Claire off-balance. He walked over to the clerk's desk and picked up the bag of baby clothes. "Dr. St. Claire, these baby clothes that you testified you and Elizabeth Garrett purchased while you were in Los Angeles. Isn't it true she was not with you when they were purchased?"

"No, Mr. Jamison, it is not true." St. Claire's expression was incredulous. "Why would I do something like that? Elizabeth told me she was pregnant. It was her idea to buy the clothes. I was trying to make her happy."

"Why would you keep them all these years when they represent such an unhappy memory?

"Why do people keep love letters from relationships that ended many years ago? I have no good answer. I put them away. I didn't look at them. When this happened, I was told that the accusations regarding Los Angeles would come up, and Mr. McGuiness asked if I had anything that might help prove we went down there as I said. I remembered that I might still have these packed away, as was the receipt for the *Queen Mary*."

Jamison picked up the *Queen Mary* receipt. "You were not with Elizabeth Garrett when you purchased this either, were you?" His voice had a harsh biting edge to it.

St. Claire shook his head. "Mr. Jamison, if your girlfriend jumped out of your car under these circumstances and you saw the police come as I testified, do you think I would have been in a frame of mind to go sightseeing?"

"I am not suggesting you were going sightseeing, Dr. St. Claire. I am suggesting that you purchased these items to create an alibi. Isn't that what happened?"

St. Claire turned slightly toward the jury before answering. "Mr. Jamison, I was young. I wasn't sophisticated and I wasn't a criminal. All of it was foolish and immature. I'm sorry. I don't have a better answer than that." His voice carried indignation that was hard to ignore.

Back at the clerk's desk, Jamison laid the receipts back down. He knew that he didn't have a single piece of evidence to disprove anything that St. Claire said about what happened. All he had was Beth Garrett's word. The photograph of her was lying in the center of the counsel table. He picked it up and studied it for a moment before realizing the jury was looking intently at him. He walked over to St. Claire and handed him the photograph. "Dr. St. Claire, this photograph, which you testified you took of Elizabeth, you took it from a distance, didn't you?"

"What do you mean, 'from a distance'?"

"What I mean is that you were standing far enough away when this photograph was taken that she might not have been aware it was taken. Isn't that correct?"

St. Claire considered the implication of Jamison's question. "Mr. Jamison, if you are attempting to subtly imply I was hiding somewhere and took this photograph, you are wrong. It was Elizabeth's camera, not mine. Your investigators seized my camera when you ransacked my home. You didn't find any photographs of Elizabeth and me at the mall, did you?" St. Claire held out the photograph.

Jamison took the photograph back from St. Claire and examined it again. "Well, Dr. St. Claire, we didn't find this photograph either."

It was time, Jamison decided, to abruptly change the questions. "Dr. St. Claire, what is succinylcholine? Are you familiar with that?" St. Claire's mouth tightened almost imperceptibly. Jamison sensed that he had hit a nerve. There *was* a reaction. It was overshadowed by McGuiness rising up from his seat at the counsel table.

"Your Honor, may we approach the bench?"

McGuiness was at the side of Wallace's bench before the judge could answer. Jamison took his time walking over. McGuiness kept his voice low but the fury in it was evident. He turned toward Jamison. "What is this about?"

Keeping his voice at a whisper, Jamison explained, "Your Honor, succinylcholine is an anesthetic. We believe that an anesthetic was used to subdue Ms. Garrett. This is an anesthetic that is available to physicians."

Wallace wasn't as inclined to accept Jamison's explanation as he hoped. "Mr. Jamison, this drug, you have some basis for believing it was used to induce unconsciousness in Ms. Garrett?"

"Your Honor, Ms. Garrett's testimony supports that a drug was used. I have looked into the types of anesthetics that Dr. St. Claire has access to and this is one of them."

"Do you mean to say there are other possibilities too?"

"Well, Your Honor, it could have been one of a number—" Wallace held up his hand to stop Jamison's dissembling.

"You don't know, do you?"

"No, Your Honor, all we know at this point is that we have reason to believe this might have been the drug."

"And what is that reason?"

"Your Honor, it is a very long explanation and if the court would give me a little latitude to ask this question, I will explain at the first opportunity."

Wallace turned to McGuiness. "Mr. McGuiness, anything further?"

"No, Your Honor, I object. Mr. Jamison has as much as admitted he's on a fishing expedition and this is just a waste of time."

Wallace's normally impassive face gave way to a smile. "Well, Mr. Jamison, I'll give you a little latitude, but I won't forget that you say you have an explanation. I'll want to hear it. Go ahead."

Perspiration running down his back. Jamison sensed that Wallace realized that he needed this and decided to give him a break. He nodded his appreciation. "I won't take long, Your Honor."

"Dr. St. Claire, I will repeat my question. Are you familiar with the drug succinylcholine?"

"Yes."

"And what is that drug?"

"It is a paralytic. It is used to relax the muscles of the throat so that a tube can be placed in the throat for purposes of breathing during surgical procedures."

"And is it something you utilize as an anesthesiologist or in your experiments with anesthetics?"

"It is something I have used, yes."

St. Claire was no longer relaxed. His posture had perceptibly stiffened and his eyes were fixed on Jamison. Jamison waited, hoping that St. Claire would do what he needed. It only took a few seconds of silence. "I'm not sure I understand your point, Mr. Jamison?"

"My point, Dr. St. Claire, is that Elizabeth Garrett testified that something was done to her causing her to have no memory of how she came to be tied to your bed. Some type of anesthetic or other drug was used to subdue her."

"Mr. Jamison, *if you believe her* that she was not conscious from the time that she left her car until the time she was in my bed, then that is untrue."

Deciding to skirt the edge of his own rules when he didn't know the answer, Jamison asked, "Yes, but if you believe her, and that is her testimony, then that would mean a drug had to have been used. You have access to succinylcholine and that is a paralytic drug, correct?"

"Yes, but it does not induce unconsciousness, at least not initially. Other drugs are used for that."

"But it could induce unconsciousness?"

"Mr. Jamison, succinylcholine must be administered very carefully because it can induce paralysis and even death if not given correctly."

"Yes, that is correct, Dr. St. Claire, if not given correctly it will cause the patient to essentially asphyxiate, but more importantly, if that happens it looks no different than a heart attack from, let's say, a massive drug overdose. Isn't that correct."

St. Claire leaned forward. "Yes, that is correct. Did you find any trace of succinylcholine in Elizabeth's drug screens?"

"No, but then you wouldn't expect there would be those traces, would you?"

"I did not do anything like that to Elizabeth."

"But you did have a vial of that drug in your refrigerator in your garage where you kept an examination table, isn't that true?" Jamison was guessing.

St. Claire lowered his head slightly in acknowledgment. "Yes, that is possible. I do not recall; it wouldn't be unusual. But that is not a drug I would ever give in anything but controlled circumstances."

"Because?"

For just a brief moment, St. Claire's eyes glinted like ice crystals. "Because it might kill her, Mr. Jamison." He allowed his answer to fill the silent courtroom before adding with a smile, "Or do you think I am a murderer also?" No one in the room except Jamison could see the taunting flicker in St. Claire's eyes.

"Your Honor, I have no further questions at this time." McGuiness's head jerked back just enough to reflect surprise. Jamison sat down. He had nothing else. He had planted the seed. Now he would have to wait.

Despite his many years of experience, Wallace seemed to be taken off-guard by the abrupt termination of the prosecutor's cross-examination. For a few seconds he said nothing, then coughed and announced they would adjourn.

McGuiness stood again. "Your Honor, before the court adjourns for the evening, I would like to ask Dr. St. Claire a few additional questions." Wallace nodded.

From his seat at the counsel table, McGuiness asked, "Dr. St. Claire, perhaps you could answer a question that Mr. Jamison did not ask. When you accidentally cut Ms. Garrett while she was on the bed at your home, was there blood on the pillow?"

"Yes, a small amount."

“Was that blood still there when Investigator Garcia came crashing through the window?”

“Yes.”

“I’m showing you now photographs of the pillow on that bed. Is there more than one spot of what looks like blood on it as well as spots on the sheet?”

“Yes.”

“You are aware that Ms. Garrett was surrounded by flying glass when Investigator Garcia broke through the window and pulled her off the bed?”

“Yes.”

“And other than the spot of blood left when you accidentally cut Ms. Garrett, were these other spots of blood on the pillow or the sheets before Investigator Garcia broke the window?”

“No.”

“So, would it be correct to state that had Investigator Garcia regrettably not crashed through the window, causing flying glass to cut Elizabeth, the only blood on the pillow would have been from that scratch. But with all of the blood spots caused by the flying glass, it is now impossible to show that there was blood on the pillow from the scratch.”

“Yes, I would have to agree.”

“Now, Doctor, I am showing you now the photograph of the smear of blood on the driver’s seat of Elizabeth Garrett’s car. Would you examine it, please?” St. Claire took the photograph and carefully examined it before handing it back. “Dr. St. Claire, I realize you are not an expert in knives but please take the knife removed from your home and place the tip over the outline of the smear. Would you tell us please, does the knife fit perfectly within the outline?”

“No.” St. Claire’s voice seemed at first hesitant, as if he wasn’t sure what he was being asked. Jamison didn’t know either but he was certain that St. Claire had been prepped for this and what he was watching was a carefully crafted show.

McGuiness laid the knife and the photograph on the flat rail in front of the jury box, allowing enough time so that all twelve jurors were fixated on it. “You have also had surgical training, have you not?”

“Yes, I spent considerable time both in my medical training in Europe and here in the United States doing general surgery as part of my residency.

I also do a form of surgery in my examinations of animals in my studies of the effects of various anesthetics."

"So would it be fair to say you are familiar with surgical instruments, including extremely sharp knives?"

"Yes."

"Do you wipe these knives off?"

"Of course, depending on the circumstances."

"And when you wipe the knife off, do you move it at all?"

"You mean do I move it across whatever I am using to wipe it with? Yes, if I don't have both hands free, of course I have to slide the knife against the cloth."

"Please put the knife over the photograph again." McGuiness handed the exhibits back to St. Claire. "Now do you see anything unusual?"

"At the top of the outline there is a flat spot instead of a sharp tip."

"And what does that suggest to you?"

Jamison was on his feet. "Your Honor, I object. Dr. St. Claire is not a forensic expert and he certainly is no expert in blood smears."

Before Wallace had the opportunity to rule, McGuiness turned toward Wallace. "No, Your Honor, Dr. St. Claire is not an expert in blood smears, but if Mr. Jamison wants to look carefully at this photograph, what he will see is exactly what our expert in blood smears saw. If a knife made this impression, it was moved slightly and it is impossible to say that this knife left that impression simply because the outline of this knife generally fits the outline in the photograph. But I'm perfectly happy to leave further testimony on this until our expert testifies. Thank you, I have nothing further."

Despite the tangle of questions twisting through his mind, Jamison's face showed no reaction. "Nothing further, Your Honor.

Chapter 28

O'Hara and Jamison weaved their way through the crowded halls in silence. Too many people were around for either of them to express what they were thinking. Bad news traveled fast in a courthouse. The first reports were that Jamison was getting his ass kicked by McGuiness. Rather than asking how it was going, several prosecutors just gave supportive smiles and a few slaps on the back as Jamison walked by.

As soon as the door to Jamison's office shut, O'Hara opened his mouth and then appeared to think better of it. Jamison dropped the file on his desk and stared out the window, his back to O'Hara. "You want to know why I didn't go after him more, right? The simple answer, Bill, is that I didn't have a damn thing to touch him with. McGuiness has sandbagged us all through this case. Going over everything St. Claire testified to and asking him if it was true wasn't going to do anything to help us."

It was clear to Jamison there were only a couple cards left to play. He had looked carefully at the receipts and they didn't look phony. Either St. Claire was telling the truth and Elizabeth was lying or St. Claire obtained the receipts later in order to create an alibi. Jamison had made the only choice he could and went with St. Claire trying to create an alibi. If he couldn't crack that alibi, then he would lose. It all came down to that. Asking St. Claire over and over whether he'd kidnapped Beth and had drugged her and cut her wasn't going to crack him, and it was just going to give St. Claire another opportunity to tell the jury that he loved her and would never hurt her.

"Bill, get Elizabeth's cell phone records." They had to break St. Claire and the only way to do that was by proving that something he said, anything at all, was a lie; then his whole veneer of credibility would crack. McGuiness would be forced to explain why the jury should believe St. Claire when he had lied.

O'Hara voiced what they were both thinking. "Except for the knife you didn't lay a glove on him. There was one thing, though. When you asked that question about succinylcholine. He reacted to that. And it appeared McGuiness didn't know what the hell you were talking about."

As he faced the window, Jamison could see his own uncertainty reflecting back at him. "No, he hasn't explained the knife imprint on the seat or the blood, but he has made a possible argument that it wasn't the knife that we have. It all comes down to making Beth out to be a liar. Their argument is going to be that they don't have an explanation for the blood on the seat, and we should ask her. They don't have to prove he put that knife on the car's seat. We do. And if we don't put her back on the stand to answer the questions they've raised, then we're going to get pounded in their final argument because they're going to say they asked the questions and we didn't give an answer.

"If we do put her back on the stand, they're going to say she's lied about so many things, how does the knife prove anything? But about the succinylcholine, you're right. McGuiness doesn't know what we're talking about. St. Claire does, however. You could see the look in his eyes. St. Claire knows we know or at least suspect how he did it. But that isn't going to mean anything unless we can prove it and St. Claire knows that too."

O'Hara's face softened. "Look, I don't think he's smarter than us. There has to be something."

Jamison sat quietly, thinking. "Well, so far he's proved that he *is* smarter than us. But even smart people make mistakes. Bill, you and Ernie get on the phones. Call a Sears store and call the *Queen Mary*. See if there is any way we can find out when those two receipts were made. If we can show the time of day, if we can show anything about them that's inconsistent with what St. Claire has said, then we'll know who's telling the truth."

"Matt, those receipts are ten years old."

"You've got cases still open that are older than that." Jamison laughed at the thought. He was surprised that he could find anything humorous at the moment. "And get those damned phone records and the hospital logs. I need to know what's in them." Jamison knew he didn't really need to see them. McGuiness wouldn't have brought them up unless he already knew.

Jamison drew a long sigh. It was almost seven o'clock in the evening. He was still at his desk trying to figure out what kind of closing argument he was going to make. And then there was the decision about whether he should put Beth back on the stand after McGuiness finished his case.

The ringing phone was a welcome distraction. It was O'Hara. The Sears receipt came from a branch in Torrance, which was only twenty minutes from Long Beach and the *Queen Mary*. The receipt had no time check and the original tapes were long gone. But O'Hara had checked with a clerk at the store who told him that the clothes he described were for winter. Elizabeth would have known that she needed summer clothes. Jamison immediately understood the point. A woman would have realized that. A guy just walking in and buying baby clothes would not.

Jamison thought about it. It wasn't much but it was something. It might make an impression on the female jurors. "What about the *Queen Mary*?"

"Ernie's working on that. He made some calls and then took off for LA. The ship is supposed to be open until nine. They told Ernie they had to see the receipt so he had to go down there with a copy."

Finally Jamison had to bite the bullet and ask the question he didn't want to ask. "And the cell phone and hospital records?"

"We'll have the cell phone records in the morning. I pulled some strings. One of the retired guys from the sheriff's office handles security for the phone company. He said he would get them, but it's going to take a while since almost everybody has gone home for the night."

"What about the hospital records?"

"McGuiness has them. I couldn't get them, but I do know that he has the record custodian subpoenaed. We won't know the answer until tomorrow."

Jamison hung up the phone. He already knew the answer.

He was lying in his bed still wide-awake when his cell phone rang again. It was Ernie. He'd been at the *Queen Mary* trying to find out if anybody could help them with the receipt. He'd finally gotten the manager to come down. "Matt, the manager said that he couldn't tell what time the tickets were purchased simply by the receipt and without the original cash register tape, but he could say that this receipt was for one ticket and not for two. So unless St. Claire bought two tickets separately, then he only bought one ticket.

"When I asked if he had the cash register tapes from ten years ago he told me I was crazy, but that he would look when their warehouse opened tomorrow. He wasn't even sure that they still had them going back that long, but they do keep them at least until they run out of room. So now we know for sure he didn't buy two tickets and he's lying about that. We won't know about anything else until tomorrow."

It wasn't much, but Jamison felt his spirits lifting. They were making hairline cracks in St. Claire's story. "Good work, Ernie. Call me as soon as you know something. If I'm not in my office, have one of the guys bring a note to court so I'll know what you have. Whatever you do, get the manager up here and bring him with you. I'm going to need him right away if McGuiness decides that he's got all the momentum and rests his case."

Chapter 29

In his office by 7 a.m., Jamison hadn't slept most of the night and his stomach was already starting to sour from the three cups of coffee he had sucked down to get his body moving. Ernie called to say that it would probably be late morning before he could have anything new. Jamison didn't have until late morning. In his gut he knew what McGuiness was going to do. He was going to put on a few cleanup witnesses and then rest his case. He knew that because that's what he would do if he was McGuiness.

He was staring at his fourth cup of coffee when O'Hara burst through the door carrying bundles of papers. "Got the phone records."

"And?"

"And it shows that she did get a call and we know it was from St. Claire's phone. It was very short, less than a minute and it was around the time Beth testified she left The Packing Shed. Then it shows she made a call back to the same number. It was also very short."

Jamison looked at the number. "Did you call Beth?"

"Yeah, I figured it was best to get the explanation as soon as possible. She said that she did get a call. She says she answered it but then the person hung up, she thought because she didn't answer quickly. She says she didn't recognize the number and she called back but whoever answered didn't talk and then hung up. But it does confirm that he lied when he said Elizabeth called him."

"Maybe. All St. Claire's going to say is that he made a mistake and he was the one who made the call, and then she called him back. But it's also consistent with our theory that St. Claire was watching her when she left the restaurant and that's how he knew when to call. It also explains how he was able to follow her home." Jamison shook his head with frustration, realizing the implications if St. Claire was nearby watching Beth when she left. "This guy is three steps ahead of everyone, including us. Ernie better come up with something because right now we aren't going to get him on what we've got."

Deep in thought, O'Hara rubbed his mustache. "But why would he call her? Why not just follow her?"

The realization had just flashed through Jamison's mind. *Nothing here was done without thinking it through.* "For the same reason he did everything else. He called her so he could make it look like they had a conversation. He had to call her because she wasn't going to call him. He bet she would call back. People can't resist returning a missed call. The baby clothes, the tickets, all of it is to set up an alibi and use printed records as proof to do it. He knows we can't attack records. So what you and Ernie have to do is figure out how he did it. The hospital phone records, all of it. And I have to buy time while you do it."

"That's all? We just have to figure that out today? You want it before lunch?"

"I know what I'm asking, Bill. Yeah, I want it before lunch. I want it as soon as I can get it, but I need it before McGuiness stands up in court and rests his case. And if we don't get it, St. Claire is going to waltz out of that courtroom.

"But I have an idea about how to bring his little parade to a halt for a while. At least for most of this morning. I've got to go."

Jamison didn't have time to explain. "Just get those records for me, Bill. If anybody can, you can, you and Ernie. Just get it for me and get the answer from Ernie on those tickets."

His yellow legal tablet was filled with circles. The Garrett case and the murders were intertwined. He knew it for sure, but how everything linked up was still lost in fog. He tried to focus on Garrett, but his mind kept coming back to the murders. He asked himself whether there was any kind of vehicle that St. Claire had access to at the hospital. Check the hospital, he realized. There had to be something. Jamison suddenly sprang out of his chair. "I gotta go down to court."

What Jamison intended was to stall as much as possible with McGuiness's witnesses, and then make his motion to introduce the murder cases. Everything would stop then so Wallace could hear his arguments. It would buy time, but would it be enough? Wallace might listen and he might not. So far the evidence hadn't gone his way. And no judge was going to let Jamison bring in three circumstantial evidence murder cases unless he could make a better case that St. Claire was lying. He would have to wait for Ernie and then make his motion. For Jamison this was like waiting for a stay of execution when you were the condemned.

Minutes later he could feel the tension in his neck as he sat at the counsel table waiting for the next shoe to drop. McGuiness obviously couldn't help himself. As he walked by he leaned down and muttered, "I tried to warn you."

Jamison felt himself recoil, thinking, Prick. He shrugged, holding in his reaction.

McGuiness called one of the hospital records custodians to the stand. She had the logs of the calls coming into the hospital as well as the logs of staff checking in and checking out. Before she testified McGuiness stood. "Your Honor, to save time perhaps Mr. Jamison would stipulate that these are the hospital logs of October twelve and they show a two p.m. call from someone identifying themselves as Elizabeth Garrett asking to speak to Dr. Alex St. Claire. I also have the sign-in sheets for hospital physician staff."

Jamison stood up. "Your Honor, I appreciate Mr. McGuiness's concerns about time but I would like to question the witness so we will not be stipulating." He could see the slight frown on Wallace's face, but he didn't care. He needed to delay as much as he could until he heard from Ernie.

Quickly McGuiness established that the sign-in log of the hospital for the day Beth said St. Claire surprised her at the mall showed Dr. St. Claire arrived on October 12 at 8:35 a.m. and checked out at 2:45 p.m. that afternoon. A separate call log showed that a hospital operator had put through a call to Dr. St. Claire at 2 p.m. that same day. The person listed as making the call identified herself as Elizabeth Garrett. It also showed that on the day St. Claire was accused of kidnapping Beth that St. Claire left the hospital at 9:32 p.m., the time he had testified he left to meet her after she left the Packing Shed.

Jamison preferred to make his point through cross-examination testimony. Beth had admitted she called St. Claire but it was after he had surprised her at the mall. Either St. Claire had somehow managed to create false record entries or Beth hadn't been truthful about the time of her call, which was the point McGuiness was making.

When McGuiness wrapped up his direct examination, Jamison smiled at the hospital record custodian, Mrs. Lopez, then picked up the log books and made a point of examining them before asking whether it was possible for these logs to be inaccurate.

Mrs. Lopez reacted with consternation. "No, these are very accurate. We are a hospital. Records must be accurate. The doctors put it down themselves. They fill it in with their name when they come in, and then they put down the time when they leave. That way we have a record of who was in the hospital and when they left."

"I see. But if a doctor put down the wrong time, how would you know?"

It took repeated questioning of Lopez to establish that when a doctor checked in, the time on the log sheet would have to be consistent with the times around it or an incorrect later entry would be apparent. However, the checkout times could be completely different. The checkout time for each physician did not have to be sequential because it simply showed when a doctor indicated he or she had left the building.

Jamison emphasized this point with Lopez, establishing that if St. Claire wanted to, he could leave without putting down a time and then return and fill in a time that looked like he had never left.

Maria Lopez appeared flustered. Jamison picked up the call logs. "This call log from October twelve shows a two p.m. call from someone identifying herself as Elizabeth Garrett and asking to speak to Dr. St. Claire. Is that correct?"

Lopez testified that if a person asked for a doctor, they would put the call through unless the doctor was unavailable.

"But no message was taken?"

"No, if there was a message we would have a record of it. The call log shows that the call went through to Dr. St. Claire."

"I see. So based on your knowledge of the records, Dr. St. Claire could have left the hospital without checking out and returned in time to have received this call from Elizabeth Garrett at two p.m. and you would have no record that he was gone unless he put it down on the log for checking in and checking out?"

"That is possible, but that would mean that he hadn't filled out the log properly."

"I suppose that's right, isn't it, Mrs. Lopez? Thank you. I have nothing further of this witness." Jamison hesitated. "Your Honor, I do have one more question that occurs to me. Ms. Lopez, if a doctor left by a back door, he could simply call and ask the desk clerk to fill out the checkout log for him?"

"Yes."

"So, is there any record as to whether the doctor signs out personally or just calls and has the staff put down the sign-out time?"

"No. The log is simply intended to show what physicians are in the hospital. We depend on the word of the doctors."

Jamison laid the log book on the counsel table in front of McGuiness. "Yes, you depend on the word of the doctors. Thank you. I have nothing further."

McGuiness rose quickly, picking up the log book from the clerk's desk where Jamison had left it. "Mrs. Lopez, you have never had a reason not to trust Dr. St. Claire, have you?"

"Oh, no. He is always very nice to all of us. Not all of the doctors appreciate how important my records are, but Dr. St. Claire does."

McGuiness turned slightly toward the jury with his brightest smile. "Thank you.

"We call Dr. St. Claire's assistant, Donald Wilson."

Wilson sat uncomfortably on the witness stand. McGuiness quickly led Wilson through a description of his duties and then asked whether he had been to Dr. St. Claire's home in town or to his home in the country.

"I haven't been inside his home in town. I have been to the house out in the country several times to deliver animals and lab specimens that Dr. St. Claire has worked on."

"Are all of those animals alive?"

"The ones I take to his home have already been euthanized or have died for various reasons. We use all kinds of lab animals and only euthanize them if they are sick. Dr. St. Claire really tries to avoid killing anything unless it is absolutely necessary for the experiment. At the house he has an examining table in the garage. Sometimes I help him as he removes tissue. Then I take the remains back to the hospital."

"Do you know why he doesn't do all of this work only at the hospital?"

"Dr. St. Claire is a very busy man. He works in surgery also and his work in the lab depends on when he is available. Sometimes I apply anesthetics to different animals and monitor the results. He prefers to remove tissue himself and taking it out to the house allows him to work on it at his convenience, I guess. Oh, and I clean the area up when he's finished. I know he's concerned that his neighbors in town would be upset if they regularly saw our truck at his house in town."

McGuiness smiled. "Thank you."

From his seat at the counsel table Jamison immediately asked, "Your truck?"

"I guess I should call it a van. You know, we use the coroner van from the hospital and it makes some people uncomfortable."

Pausing as he thought about the coroner van, Jamison decided to open the door. "What does the van look like?"

Wilson shrugged. "It's dark colored and has Coroner written on the side. It's basically like a cargo van, no windows."

"Is it used for any other purposes than just by you and Dr. St. Claire?"

"Well, it's the coroner's van so they use it for picking up bodies for autopsies, homicide scenes, things like that. It has a radio. Of course, the coroner has priority on it if there is a body that has to be picked up."

Jamison nodded. "Of course. By the way, does the coroner van have emergency lights?"

"You mean like a police car, flashing lights and stuff? Yeah, it does."

"So in some respects it would look like a law enforcement vehicle?"

"I suppose."

He made a note before deciding to shift his questions based on his memory of the garage after Beth's rescue. "The garage has soundproofing on the walls, is that correct?"

"Yes, I helped Dr. St. Claire put it up. You see the space is like at the hospital lab. Animals make noise. They bark. He said he didn't want to disturb the neighbors."

"I thought you never take any live animals out to that location?"

"That's correct."

He thought about asking whether Wilson saw any need for soundproofing if he never took live animals there, but decided he'd wait for his final argument. He was about to sit down when something Wilson had said flashed in Jamison's mind. "Mr. Wilson, when you transported animals to and from Dr. St. Claire's house in the country, did you wrap them in anything?"

"Wrap them? You mean did I put them in anything? Yes, we use body bags to transport. We have some of the older ones and we use them. The coroner disposes of body bags after they have been used and we take some of them. Otherwise they are destroyed."

"How are they destroyed?"

"They get burned in the hospital incinerator along with tissue samples and biohazard material."

"Are you personally aware of whether Dr. St. Claire ever drove that truck?"

"I know he used it a few times. We keep a spare set of the keys in the lab. It isn't used that often so we just borrow it."

"And do you have a log sheet that you use to sign the van out?"

"There is a log, but usually I just say I'm going to use it for a while. I don't sign a log normally. It just isn't necessary."

"You said you clean up at Dr. St. Claire's house after he does his examinations. What do you use?"

"To clean up? I use disinfectants, basic cleaning supplies."

"Do you use bleach?"

"Yes."

"Thank you, nothing further."

The next defense witness was a forensic criminalist who had examined the bloody imprint on the seat of Elizabeth's car. It didn't take long for him to testify that the imprint could not be positively established as having been made by St. Claire's knife because it was smeared. Jamison had already been over it with his forensic people. The best he could do was establish that the defense witness couldn't say with certainty that the impression hadn't been made by St. Claire's knife.

McGuiness stood, looking first at the jury before turning to Judge Wallace. "Your Honor, the defense rests." He glanced over at Jamison and raised his eyebrows. Jamison didn't need an interpreter.

It didn't take long for Wallace to respond. "Mr. Jamison, you may proceed with rebuttal."

"Your Honor, may we approach the bench?

Both lawyers crowded near the corner of the bench where Wallace leaned over. "What is it, Mr. Jamison?"

"Judge, I would like to speak to you in chambers. Perhaps we could take a recess?"

Wallace pursed his lips, looking at the clock in the back of the courtroom. "All right." He turned to the jury and announced he would be conferring with counsel.

The judge led the way into his office, and motioned to the attorneys to sit down. "What's the problem, Matt?" he asked.

"Your Honor, I would ask the court for a little time before we put on a rebuttal case. As you know we weren't told in advance about the pieces of evidence that Mr. McGuiness produced and we are working on that. We have a few witnesses that we are going to be bringing in and I need to get them here."

Immediately, McGuiness was out of his chair. "What witnesses? You haven't given me any notice."

"Well, I didn't get any notice from you about baby clothes or the *Queen Mary* either, did I?"

"I don't have to give you notice as to my client's testimony."

"No, you don't but I shouldn't be expected to respond immediately to evidence and witnesses I've never heard of either. The People have a right to a fair trial too."

Wallace interrupted. "How much time? You know I don't like to delay juries."

Jamison could feel his stomach roiling. "Your Honor, I know that but we have only had one evening. I need at least a day or two more." Jamison hesitated, swallowing the acid that was rising up from his stomach. "And I'm not feeling well."

McGuiness snorted. "Well, that's what happens when you find out your case is coming apart at the seams. I tried to warn you."

Instead of replying, Jamison bolted for the judge's bathroom. Both the judge and McGuiness could hear him throwing up. He cleaned his mouth in the sink and wiped his face with a paper towel before walking back in. His face was a pasty color and he looked like he might throw up again at any moment. Wallace shook his head. He wasn't sure whether Jamison was actually ill, but he did look sick. "All right, Mr. Jamison," Wallace decided. "I hope you feel better tomorrow. Please call my office this afternoon and let us know if we can resume tomorrow when you're better. Let's tell the jury."

O'Hara sat across from Jamison's desk in his office. "You actually threw up? How did you manage that?"

"I have no idea. Wallace was talking and that asshole McGuiness was rubbing my nose in the case. I was asking for time and I could sense Wallace wasn't going to give it to me. All of a sudden I could feel everything coming up."

"Well, you got to admit your timing was perfect. Can you do it again? We may need to stall." Rumbling laughter came out of O'Hara's throat.

"It isn't funny. Anyway, we've got until tomorrow and that's it. Anything from Ernie?"

"I got a note that says he's going to call later. He did say that maybe we've gotten a break but the note doesn't say what."

O'Hara started for the door and then turned. "Matt, why did you ask those questions of Wilson about transporting dogs?"

"Because, it suddenly dawned on me that if St. Claire's lab assistant moved dogs in body bags, then maybe that's how some of our victims were moved. It's never made any sense to me how St. Claire could have moved those women and there wasn't any hair or anything else in his car. What if he used the coroner's van and just put them in a body bag? We never looked at the coroner's van. I need you to get me information on that truck." Jamison tried to restrain his anticipation of a possible break in the murder cases.

"Let me guess. You need it in an hour?"

"No, I need it yesterday."

An hour later, Jamison picked up the phone. It was O'Hara. "Here's the story. The coroner kept the transport van out at the hospital with the keys in his office and there was a log but the assistant out there said that if St. Claire's staff wanted to use it they usually stuck their head in the door and said they were going to take it. The assistant admitted that sometimes he wrote it down and sometimes he didn't and that St. Claire's staff had their own keys. Oh, and there was nobody in the office at night unless they got a call to do a pickup. The van could have been used by St. Claire or even the janitor who cleaned the office and there wouldn't be a record. There was another truck there that apparently was also used. It had a camper-type shell on the back and was dark colored with lights." O'Hara had already called forensics to have them go over both vehicles.

Jamison listened to the rest of O'Hara's speculation. The coroner's van had emergency lights on it but so did the truck. Jamison sensed that maybe there was an explanation beginning to poke through the haze of confusion in the murder cases.

~

It was almost noon when Ernie called Jamison's office. He had already had several visits from other prosecutors asking him if he could show them how to throw up on demand. There were suggestions about him being the entertainment at the next office party. He knew this was going to be a running joke for a long time. Jamison answered on the first ring. Before he could say anything, Ernie began, "First off, amigo, I want a raise because you owe me."

"I owe you for what?"

"The guy found the cash register tape. He had to look through piles of stacked boxes but he found the tape. It's got mouse shit on it and it isn't real clear, but guess what?"

"Come on, Ernie. Just give."

"Okay, like I said yesterday, the ticket was for only one person. Even better, it was purchased right before six p.m. The manager knows because the next ticket was for six people, and then the cash register was cleared. He bought the ticket after Garrett jumped out of the car at two or two thirty in the afternoon. He's lying and we can prove it."

Chapter 30

By late afternoon Jamison's phone rang. It was McGuiness. The first thing he mentioned was that Jamison was already the talk of the local bar association about his ability to vomit on demand. Jamison didn't reply to the jibe. "What can I do for you, Tom?"

"You said yesterday that you had witnesses that weren't on the list you gave me. What witnesses and what reports do you have? I have a discovery order and Wallace isn't going to let you get away with not giving me the information."

"Yeah, yeah, it isn't a two-way street. I have two witnesses."

"And who are these people?"

Jamison hesitated before answering. "Robert Marchand is the manager of the wax museum on the *Queen Mary* and Shirley Peterson manages the children's clothing section of the Sears store in Torrance."

"And they are going to say what?" McGuiness could feel a sense of dread building.

"Marchand is going to say that your client is lying when he says that Elizabeth Garrett was with him at the *Queen Mary* wax museum and Peterson is going to testify that the clothing your client says he and Elizabeth bought was not something that would have been purchased for a baby due in the summer."

Feeling a flood of relief, McGuiness laughed. "This Marchand is going to say that Dr. St. Claire is lying? From ten years ago he remembers that Elizabeth Garrett wasn't with St. Claire?"

"No, he's going to testify that receipt you threw in my face in court was not for two tickets but one." He stretched out the pause. "And it was purchased right before six p.m., several hours after Elizabeth Garrett fled your client. Your client perjured himself and I can prove it. See you tomorrow."

McGuiness held the phone in his hand, the dial tone a flat buzzing after Jamison hung up. He slammed the phone back down on the cradle. He understood what Jamison was going to do. McGuiness had built his entire case around the credibility of Alex St. Claire. The receipt, the baby clothes, all of it undermined Garrett's credibility with unimpeachable physical evidence. But now Jamison had something showing clearly that St. Claire was lying about that evidence and from that Jamison would argue that he was lying also about the rest. McGuiness needed to think.

O'Hara woke Jamison at five the next morning. It took him a moment to register what O'Hara was saying. "We got something! We've got some hairs and fiber in the coroner van that can be identified as coming from Symes and from Ventana."

They agreed to meet at the office in forty-five minutes. O'Hara was waiting for him when he walked in. But the look on Jamison's face wasn't the smile O'Hara had expected.

"What's the problem? I told you we have hairs from two of the victims in the van. Think about it."

"Yeah, I am thinking about it. But you think about it. I'm not surprised that we have hair and carpet fiber from Symes and Ventana. They were both picked up at the crime scene using that van. McGuiness will have an easy explanation for that." His voice was rising, but Jamison couldn't help himself. The frustration was getting to all of them.

O'Hara thought about it for a moment, rubbing his mustache several times. "Matt, they vacuum that van fairly frequently. We were lucky to find what we found. If he used the coroner's truck to move the victims, then even if we found some hair or carpet in it, what you're saying is we wouldn't be able to prove anything because it was used to transport the bodies of those same victims from the crime scenes."

"You got it. When you think about it, St. Claire had access to that van, and a body moved from a crime scene might have evidence drop on the floor of the van. If St. Claire used the van to dump a body and the same van was used to remove that body from the crime scene, we couldn't say when any hair or fiber got in that van. St. Claire would know that too. McGuiness would just say the victim's hair and the carpet fiber got in the van when the coroner picked up the body. And if he used a body bag, then he could move his victims to where he dumped their bodies, pull off the bag, and any forensic evidence would be on the bag that would get burned. What makes everything work at this point is the hair and fiber T. J. *says* he found in St. Claire's car." The tone of Jamison's voice made it clear to O'Hara that he had an issue with T. J.'s discovery.

"*Says* he found?" O'Hara was incredulous. "Now you have a problem with that, Matt?"

"Yeah, I have a problem with that. As much as I want to believe it, the more I thought about it, the more concerns I had. You think McGuiness is going to overlook the fact that everybody missed it, and then all of a sudden one of our boys turns up some hair that ties St. Claire to the three murders?"

O'Hara took a deep breath. "Matt, you need to back off on T. J. He found that evidence and you know as well as I do that St. Claire did this. Nothing we've found contradicts that."

"Nothing we've found yet. I'm not saying St. Claire's innocent. I'm saying that I need to prove he's guilty and all McGuiness has to do is find one hole in this and we have a major problem. Any word on the succinylcholine results?"

"Gupta said he has been calling but we aren't likely to know anything for maybe another two days at best."

"We don't have two days. I have to be in court by nine."

McGuiness was waiting for Jamison as he walked into court. There was nothing pleasant about the expression on his face. "We need to talk to Judge Wallace."

"Why? I gave you my witnesses."

"We need to talk to Judge Wallace. I'm going back to his chambers now."

The door to Wallace's chambers was open. McGuiness knocked and Wallace waved the two of them in. He smiled at Jamison. "Feeling better today, Matt? I'm guessing you felt a lot better when I gave you some time away from this courtroom. I was once a trial lawyer too." He laughed at his own observation.

"Your Honor, I do feel better this morning, thank you." Jamison could feel his face turning red.

"So what can I do for the two of you? I'd like to get started."

"With the court's permission, Your Honor," McGuiness said, "I want to re-open my defense case. I want to put Dr. St. Claire back on the stand before the prosecutor begins his rebuttal case."

"Wait a minute"—Jamison flushed with anger—"you rested your case and I have witnesses ready to go from out of town."

Wallace's face wrinkled in frustration. "What's this about, Mr. McGuiness?"

"Your Honor, the prosecutor has some evidence that maybe my client wasn't completely candid about."

"Candid about?" Jamison was so angry he was sputtering. "Your client lied and he got caught."

Wallace raised his hand and faced Jamison. "What witnesses do you have? What are they going to say?"

Before responding, Jamison took a deep breath to calm himself. "Your Honor, I have two witnesses that will prove that Dr. St. Claire perjured himself regarding what happened when he and Ms. Garrett were in Los Angeles."

Wallace drew his fingertips together and thought for a moment. "Sometimes clients don't tell their lawyers all the truth. When I was a trial lawyer it happened to me more times than I like to remember. If I let Mr. McGuiness put his client back on before you bring in these witnesses, can't you just cross-examine him?"

"I could, Your Honor, but what Mr. McGuiness really wants is to take the sting out of his client's perjury before I can put my witnesses on. I wasn't the one that put on perjured testimony."

McGuiness interrupted. "You put on Elizabeth Garrett, didn't you? She's lied throughout this case."

"Enough. I've heard enough." Wallace stood up. "Mr. McGuiness I'm going to let you put your client back on." The judge looked over at Jamison before he could say anything further. "I appreciate your anger over this, Mr. Jamison, and if you had actually started your case I wouldn't allow it. I'll give you ample latitude in your cross-examination. That's it. Now let's call the jury."

Jamison recognized he needed to calm down. McGuiness had all night to think about how to present this. He could feel himself fuming but that wasn't going to do any good. He had to clear his mind.

Chapter 31

The jury was completely unaware of what was coming as McGuiness called St. Claire back to the stand.

Jamison noted that St. Claire didn't look quite as confident as he had before, but he also caught the smiles several of the jurors gave as St. Claire walked by them to the witness stand. Jamison was on the defensive. He knew the next minutes would make or break him.

"Dr. St. Claire," McGuiness asked, "when you testified before you made some statements that you want to correct. Is that true?"

St. Claire cleared his throat, looking at the jury. "I said something that wasn't true and I regret it. I want to be completely honest with everyone."

"What do you want to correct?"

"The ticket to the *Queen Mary* wax museum—I, we, Elizabeth and I didn't go together like I said. I bought it later after she had left. I didn't know what to do. I was wandering around and I just went there. I really don't remember what was in there."

"And when did you tell me that you had not been accurate about the receipt for the *Queen Mary*?"

"I told you last night when you called me and said that Mr. Jamison had a witness." Jamison could sense several of the jurors turning to look at him, then looking back at St. Claire.

"Why did you tell us that you had gone to the *Queen Mary* with Elizabeth if it wasn't true?"

"Well, I was a little frightened. I'm on trial and Elizabeth has accused me of kidnapping her when we went to Los Angeles. I let my fear get in the way of better judgment. This whole thing has been a terrible nightmare for me emotionally." St. Claire leaned over the railing in front of the witness stand, speaking softly to the jurors. "I don't have an excuse. I can only apologize."

Thumbing through papers on the counsel table, McGuiness slid out a sheet of paper encased in a clear plastic folder. He handed it to Jamison who examined it and handed it back. It was a letter. Jamison asked to approach the bench.

"Your Honor, I'm not sure what this letter is, but we're now going beyond what I thought was going to be covered. I object. I don't see the relevance of the letter. There isn't even a front page."

"I'm going to allow it." Wallace waved both men back. "When you cross-examine I will give you the latitude, Mr. Jamison, that I said I would."

"Do you recognize this?" McGuiness handed the letter to St. Claire to review.

"Yes, it's a letter I received from Elizabeth, earlier this year, several months after I returned to the community and before she called me at the hospital."

"Would you tell us what's in it, please?"

"It says that she misses me and that she wants to see me as soon as possible. It's signed, 'Love, Beth.'"

"Why did you not discuss this letter before now?"

"There was no first page and you said that would be a problem because it didn't show when it was written. I don't know what happened to the first page."

"Did you respond or write back?"

"No, I did not. I still had feelings for Elizabeth but I knew she wasn't good for me. I should have listened to my instincts, but when she called . . . and I heard her voice . . ." He dropped his head and handed the letter back.

"Your witness." McGuiness walked back to the counsel table.

Jamison picked up the letter. He knew he shouldn't do it but he was tired of being at the receiving end. He was flirting with the edge in terms of misconduct, but he wanted the jury to know that it wasn't a two-way street in terms of evidence and he was having to react to things he had not been shown.

"Your Honor, may I have a moment to read this letter since I have never seen it before today, as the court is aware. I'm not questioning Mr. McGuiness's motives, of course, but for this to show up now . . ." Jamison waited for McGuiness to erupt.

"I object! Mr. Jamison is well aware that I am not required to disclose my client's testimony prior to trial."

Jamison had gotten what he wanted. He nodded his head. "Your Honor, no implication was intended. Mr. McGuiness is correct. The defense is not required to share his client's testimony with the prosecution even though we must give all information to the defense. I certainly do not mean to imply that this letter is a fabrication like the wax museum receipt."

Wallace halted any response from McGuiness. "Mr. Jamison, you've made your point. Please proceed without further editorial comment."

"Of course, Your Honor. Thank you." Jamison turned to McGuiness. "I apologize if I offended you. I assure you and the court it was not intentional." Jamison could see the veins bulging in McGuiness's neck. He walked closer to St. Claire. "Dr. St. Claire, let us make something very clear. When you testified before that you and Elizabeth Garrett went to the *Queen Mary* wax museum you were under oath?

"Yes, but I—"

Putting a steel edge into his voice, Jamison said, "I didn't ask for your explanation, Dr. St. Claire. I asked whether you understood you were under oath. You've answered that question. Now, you come to this jury and you are still under oath but you have a different answer? Is that correct?"

"It isn't a different answer. I was scared. I admit that what I said was wrong."

Feeling his anger taking hold, Jamison pushed it back, trying to take control of himself. "So when you testified before, you lied to this jury? Yes or no, Dr. St. Claire?

"I did not tell the truth."

"You lied, didn't you?" Jamison's voice snapped back at St. Claire.

"Yes, but like I said—"

Cutting St. Claire off, Jamison's voice resonated with contempt. "You've answered my question, Dr. St. Claire. You also lied about Elizabeth being with you when you bought the baby clothes, isn't that true?"

"No, I was telling the truth. We bought them together."

"You didn't tell Mr. McGuiness that you had lied until he informed you that my investigators found a witness who could tell us that receipt for the wax museum was not purchased when you said it was, isn't that correct?"

"Yes, but as I said—"

"Did he also tell you that the baby clothing was for a child born in the winter?"

"Yes, but I'm not sure what I'm supposed to say. Elizabeth picked them out. I don't know anything about baby clothes."

Jamison walked over, grabbed the Sears bag and poured its contents over the counsel table. "Isn't it true, Dr. St. Claire, that you bought those clothes without Elizabeth Garrett and you didn't realize they were winter clothes? Isn't that the truth?"

"No, Mr. Jamison. Elizabeth told me she was pregnant. I believed her."

"You believed her? Isn't it true that you were perfectly willing to sit in court and let the jury believe she was lying when she said you took her to Los Angeles against her will, forcing her to escape? You wanted it to look like you both were wandering around and that she could have left at any time. Isn't that what you wanted the jury to believe? You knew she was telling the truth and yet you wanted the jury to believe she was lying. Isn't that the truth, Dr. St. Claire?"

"I wouldn't put it that way."

Placing both hands flat on the counsel table, Jamison leaned forward, the words coming out with measured disdain. "I'm sure you wouldn't put it that way, Dr. St. Claire. But you *knew* she never went to the wax museum. Isn't that the truth?"

"Yes, about that, but—"

Jamison held up his hand before St. Claire could continue. "And you wanted the jury to believe she was lying when *you* knew she was telling the truth, isn't that true?"

"I said I panicked."

"So when you get caught in a lie you admit that you made a mistake, but if there is no witness but Elizabeth to contradict you, then we're supposed to believe you?"

McGuiness was shouting, "I object, the question is argumentative."

"Your Honor, I withdraw the question. Now, Dr. St. Claire, that photograph that you said you took when you and Elizabeth left the shopping mall that afternoon after *you* say she called you." Jamison held it up. "Isn't it true that you took this photograph but from a considerable distance away? You used a telephoto lens, didn't you, Dr. St. Claire? Elizabeth Garrett had no idea you were taking her picture, did she?"

"I took it just as I said I did. I don't know what you are talking about. I didn't use any special lens. It was her camera. She asked me to take her picture."

Jamison held the picture out directly in front of St. Claire. "Dr. St. Claire, if I was to tell you that an expert could look at this photograph and tell whether a regular or telephoto lens was used, would that surprise you?"

"I know nothing about photographs. Maybe it's possible that I was farther away when I took the picture, but we were walking out to the car. It was an impulse."

"Where did you get this letter?"

"I told you. Elizabeth sent it to me."

"You saved everything else from your relationship with Elizabeth, including ten-year-old receipts and a bag with baby clothes, but not the first page of a letter from her?"

"I'm not sure how that happened."

Jamison laid the letter down on the rail in front of the jury. "Well, Dr. St. Claire, let me ask you. Isn't it true that you don't have the first page of the letter because that page would show that the letter wasn't to you but to someone else?"

"It was to me." Jamison could see St. Claire's hands rubbing against his thighs, although he knew the jury couldn't see it."

"You stole that letter, didn't you?"

"That's ridiculous. I'm a physician, not a thief."

Jamison walked over to the side of the jury box so that his voice came from behind the jurors. His question came out like a pistol shot. "Not a thief, Dr. St. Claire? But you are a liar, aren't you?"

McGuiness was on his feet, arguing that Jamison was badgering the witness. Wallace was tapping his gavel harder and harder to stop the murmuring in the courtroom. "Mr. Jamison, rephrase your question."

"Yes, Your Honor. Dr. St. Claire, isn't it true that you watched as Elizabeth Garrett left the Packing Shed restaurant, and you called her and then hung up the phone knowing that she would call back?"

"I did not call her and how would I know she would call back?"

"Didn't you say she called you? Did you forget that you called her first?"

"What difference does it make? She called me and we were going to meet. I don't recall who called first."

"Dr. St. Claire, you followed Elizabeth Garrett home from the Packing Shed Restaurant and made her believe you were a police officer, didn't you?"

"No, we agreed to meet. I didn't have to stop her."

"You have been stalking Elizabeth Garrett for years, haven't you, waiting for an opportunity. Isn't that true, Dr. St. Claire?"

"No, it's not true. We had a relationship we both couldn't deny. That is the truth."

"What *is* the truth, Dr. St. Claire? Is it that you had an obsession and you could not let this young woman go? Isn't that the truth?"

"No."

"I see. So now that we know you lied under oath we are supposed to believe you are telling the truth?"

"I am telling the truth."

"And you are under the same oath that you violated before." Jamison sat back down at the counsel table. "I have nothing further."

The courtroom was silent as stone. Jamison surveyed the jurors' expressions. Some of the jurors were looking away. Others looked confused. Jamison noted with satisfaction that none of them were smiling at Alex St. Claire.

A tie for the prosecution doesn't win in a criminal trial. But Jamison had pulled his case back from disaster by impeaching St. Claire. Now he had to break it apart. The hard decision was going to be whether or not to put Elizabeth back on the stand. The other hard part was finding a photographic expert to justify his cross-examination. He had been guessing. He hoped he had guessed right. And he hoped he had guessed right about the letter.

Chapter 32

The People's rebuttal case consumed the rest of the morning, filled with the testimony of the witness from the wax museum and the clerk from the children's department of the Sears store in Torrance. Marchand testified that he was able to pinpoint the time the wax museum ticket had been purchased because there was a large purchase right after it and then the cash register was cleared so that a new tape could be put in. The time was written on the master tape when it was removed.

McGuiness didn't bother to ask any questions of the witness from the wax museum. He knew that asking more questions would only emphasize that his client had not been truthful. But as to Shirley Peterson from the Sears store, he brought out that the store made both summer and winter clothes available but the floor displays emphasized the clothing seasonal for that time of year. Jamison countered that a woman would understand that if you bought baby clothes you would pick clothing the baby would be wearing at the time of year when it was born. It was a small point but the women on the jury would understand.

It was the first time that Jamison walked out at the end of the day feeling like he was in control. But he also knew that tomorrow was another day and he still had to corroborate that his guesses about the photograph that St. Claire said he took of Garrett, which she said she wasn't aware of, were correct. At this point, everything was important.

O'Hara had scrambled all evening and most of the morning to find a photographic expert. After he found one, Jamison learned his guess had been only partially right when O'Hara slipped him a note with what she would say. There was no time for him to ask questions. He would have to go with what O'Hara had told him.

The expert would testify that the photograph introduced by McGuiness could have been taken at a distance without Garrett knowing it, but it also could have been improperly focused. He knew the testimony wouldn't be clean but he had no choice. He had alluded to the expert in his cross-examination of St. Claire. Without the expert McGuiness could argue that Garrett had posed willingly for St. Claire and that would dramatically undercut her testimony that he had stalked her. So Jamison had to put the expert on and hope he could wring out something positive.

"The People call Professor Cynthia Stafford." A surprisingly young woman walked quickly to the center of the courtroom and raised her right hand. Jamison established Stafford's education and experience. She taught photography at the university and was a self-described "experimental photographer."

"Dr. Stafford, have you examined this photograph of a young woman?" Stafford nodded and then answered affirmatively as she took the photograph of Elizabeth Garrett and stared at it. She testified that because the photograph of Garrett was slightly blurred and the background was clear, it was most likely that a telephoto lens feature was used when the photograph was taken, or that Garrett moved and the camera auto-adjusted on the background.

McGuiness quickly pounced. "So, Professor Stafford, it's possible this photograph was taken close to the woman in the photograph, say ten or fifteen feet away?"

"I cannot exclude that as being possible."

McGuiness held up the photograph. "So if my client said he was standing ten or twenty feet away and simply pointed the camera at the person in the photograph and snapped the picture, then the result here is possible?"

"Depending on the camera, yes, and because the person was moving the camera refocused on the background when the person moved out of the specific line of focus. But it's also possible the person was a greater distance away and with a telephoto lens you could also get this result."

"Dr. Stafford, is it your experience that if a woman sees a camera and doesn't want her picture taken that she will frequently turn and move away?"

Stafford laughed. "Women are all alike. If they don't want their picture taken, they turn away. Or," she added, looking at the jury, "if they don't know their picture is being taken they don't pose."

As he leafed through his legal pad during the lunch recess, Jamison flinched at the scribbled reflections of his case—two steps forward and one step back. He had taken a risk with his cross-examination of St. Claire that a photography expert would confirm what his questions implied and broke a basic rule of cross-examination: never ask a question unless you knew what the answer was. He had done the same thing with the letter. But as he recognized, when the ship is underwater, going by the book isn't going to help. All he had effectively accomplished with the photography expert was to establish that Elizabeth's version was possible and that she could be telling the truth. McGuiness had accomplished the same thing, that St. Claire might be telling the truth. The letter was a different issue.

For most of the hour-and-a-half break, Jamison and O'Hara had been at it trying to decide whether to put Beth back on the stand. O'Hara was against it. McGuiness had popped the letter out of nowhere and he might have more that he would spring on her.

Jamison listened carefully. He trusted O'Hara's instincts, but this was a credibility contest. The letter *was* a problem. He had been guessing when he accused St. Claire of stealing it. If he hadn't stolen the letter, then the only other way St. Claire could have gotten it was if it did come from Elizabeth. And if that was true it would wedge the cracks in his case wide open. So he had taken the only course consistent with his case, and he had done it hoping he was right.

He had shown the letter to Elizabeth, and she said it was her handwriting. He had listened as she told him the letter was to a college boyfriend, but didn't recall if she had mailed it. She was adamant that it hadn't been written to St. Claire and she had no idea how he had gotten it.

Reassured that he had made the only move he could in cross-examining St. Claire about the letter, he still was faced with the crucial hurdle of convincing Wallace to let him bring in the murder evidence that neither Wallace nor McGuiness knew anything about. At least he didn't think McGuiness knew anything about it, but there was no real assurance of that either. He needed to buy time, to hear conclusively from the FBI on the presence of succinylcholine, and to get rid of the nagging concern in the back of his mind about the hair and fiber samples that T. J. had found in St. Claire's car.

He just couldn't buy that T. J. had got so lucky with finding the single hair from Ventana and the carpet fiber from Johnson's home and Symes's apartment. He had sent Ernie out to go over St. Claire's car one more time to see if there was anything, anything at all that might give him some assurance. He needed that answer before attempting to get Wallace to allow in the murder evidence.

He was still unsure of how to handle all the unresolved questions when he returned to his place at the counsel table. "Your Honor, may we approach the bench?"

"What is it?" Wallace waved both counsels forward.

"Your Honor, there's something I would like to discuss with you in chambers."

Wallace walked into his office, sat heavily in his chair, waiting for Jamison's explanation. "I'm afraid I need some time. Some issues have come up. This letter is something I need to do more investigation about and there is other evidence that we have been developing that I am not prepared to discuss at the moment."

McGuiness hadn't sat down and he moved right in front of Jamison's face. "What evidence? You haven't told me about any other evidence."

Jamison's face flushed as he sought to control his own anger. "What are you whining about? Yesterday I walk in here and you lay that letter in front of the jury after your client got caught perjuring himself. You don't think I need to look at that?"

"You had time to look at it. I don't hear you saying it isn't her handwriting."

Wallace interrupted. "Now I can see this letter caught you off-guard, Matt, but what other evidence are you talking about? I expected to get this case to the jury by tomorrow. Apparently Mr. McGuiness has not been told about this evidence?"

"No, Your Honor, Mr. McGuiness has not been told. I didn't know whether this evidence would be relevant and admissible until after I heard the defense case. It's clear that Mr. McGuiness is taking the position that Ms. Garrett is lying about everything and his client is innocent." Jamison glanced at McGuiness. "Judge, I would prefer not to discuss this evidence at this time. If you give me a little time I can be prepared to discuss the evidence, but I'm waiting for more information."

Wallace kept silent for a few seconds, then stood up and looked out his window. "If you have other evidence, then I want to know right now what it is. If you expect me to give you more time at all, then it had better be damn good. I'm going to require that you hand everything over to Mr. McGuiness and I make no guarantees about whether I'll let it in. I have to know first what it is. It's your choice. Tell me now or I expect you to finish tomorrow, but I will give you some time to look at the letter. I know you didn't expect that. So, what's it going to be?"

"Your Honor, what Dr. St. Claire has said is that he *did do* the acts he has been accused of *but he did it* with innocent intent. He did take Ms. Garrett, but she consented and it wasn't kidnap. He tied her up, but it was with her consent. We argue that her version is correct and that Dr. St. Claire is lying. What's at issue is Dr. St. Claire's intent, as opposed to the usual case when the defendant says somebody else did it but it wasn't him and leaves his identity in issue."

Wallace's eyes were narrowing. He could sense that something was coming that was going to force him to make a ruling on which the whole trial would turn and maybe there would be a basis for an appeal. He began to tense. "Your point, please?"

Jamison swallowed hard, anticipating the explosion from McGuiness and the judge when he finished. "My point, Your Honor, is that Dr. St. Claire has made his intent the issue and therefore all relevant evidence is admissible to prove that his intent *is* what Elizabeth Garrett said it was. He kidnapped her and he tied her to the bed. What we have not said is that we know he didn't rape her, but we are sure he intended to kill her."

His face furrowing, Wallace leaned over his desk. "What? Where's this coming from?"

"Your Honor, it's coming from evidence that we have that Dr. Alex St. Claire murdered three other women before he kidnapped Elizabeth Garrett." He could feel the blood rushing to his ears as McGuiness started yelling about due process and his client's constitutional rights, lack of discovery, and misconduct by Jamison.

His voice was a low rumble as Wallace told McGuiness to sit down while he listened to what Jamison had to say. "What evidence?"

"Your Honor, the basic evidence is that the three murders of young women followed exactly the same pattern that was used in the kidnap of Elizabeth Garrett. We have now tied Dr. St. Claire to all three of those women. We also have evidence that Dr. St. Claire used his position at the hospital to switch blood samples on those three women to make it look like they died as a result of an overdose of heroin and barbiturates."

"Then what did they die of?"

"Your Honor, we have tissue samples that are still being tested at the FBI lab in Washington. We believe they may have died as a result of injection of a drug called succinylcholine, which can be used to induce respiratory failure and cause the heart to stop. We know Dr. St. Claire had access to this drug."

Before making his next statement Jamison hesitated. "We have hair and fiber samples from Dr. St. Claire's vehicle that we can show are related to these murder victims. We believe that this evidence will show Dr. St. Claire murdered these three young women, and we believe that this evidence demonstrates that he kidnapped Elizabeth Garrett just as she said."

Wallace stared coldly at Jamison. "Now is a hell of a time to try to bring this kind of evidence in, especially without any warning to the defense, and you know it."

In order to have any chance of getting the evidence in, Jamison had to hold his ground. "Your Honor, we've been working day and night on those murder cases and we were pushed to go to trial on this case before our investigation was completed. We are asking the court to hear the evidence and then make its own decision."

McGuiness's face was almost purple from anger. Wallace immediately said, "Tom, before you have a stroke, let me say this. I'm very disturbed that something like this would come up now. I'm going to hear this evidence outside the presence of the jury. Then I'll decide."

The judge turned his focus to Jamison. "If you want me to even consider allowing you to do this, then you need to turn everything you have over to Mr. McGuiness and I mean everything. I'll give the jury a long weekend, and then I'll hear your arguments the day after tomorrow." Wallace paused. "And they better be damn good because if that evidence comes in and Dr. St. Claire is convicted, we all know the court of appeal is going to go over it looking for any sign there was an abuse of discretion."

"Your Honor, I understand. I wouldn't be asking the court to do this if I didn't think that not presenting it would cause a bigger injustice by allowing Dr. St. Claire to get away with what he did to Elizabeth Garrett and . . . get away with—"

Before Jamison finished, Wallace rose and pushed his body halfway across the desk. His voice held an unmistakable warning. "That may be, but even if Dr. St. Claire is acquitted, you can still bring murder charges. And if he's convicted of those murders, then he will get what he deserves even if he's acquitted in this case. But on the other side, if he's convicted of the charges in this case because of my error in allowing in evidence of uncharged murder, there is injustice in that too, isn't there?"

"Day after tomorrow, gentlemen, and, Mr. Jamison," Wallace said, his eyes penetrating Jamison's, "if I think for one minute you're playing fast and loose with me, I'll have you in front of the state bar on charges. Don't think I won't."

The judge stood, facing both attorneys. "And another thing. If you think you have enough evidence to convince me that Dr. St. Claire committed three murders, then you have enough evidence to charge him and arrest him. Why haven't you done that?"

Because Jamison had been concerned that Wallace would ask this question, he had an answer. He knew it wasn't a good answer but it was an answer. "Your Honor, we have been doing the investigation while this trial has been going on. I didn't want to risk a mistrial by arresting Dr. St. Claire in the middle of this trial. It was my decision."

As Jamison and McGuiness walked out of Wallace's chambers, the defense attorney spoke up. "So, are you planning to arrest my client when we walk back into the courtroom, because if you are, then you can expect I will be making a motion for a mistrial." McGuiness looked over at Wallace, who didn't appear at all surprised that he made the threat.

Jamison didn't hesitate before answering. He knew what his options were. "No, I'm not going to do that. But both you and your client have some hard decisions to make. Even if this evidence doesn't go in now, St. Claire had better get used to sitting in the defendant's chair."

Chapter 33

With O'Hara trailing behind him, Jamison raced back to his office. He had bought a little time to put together a murder case. But in fact, his explanation to Wallace sounded far more confident than he felt. He had bits and pieces but no smoking gun.

He sagged into his chair and the air came out of his mouth like a deflating tire. "Bill, we don't have it. I can feel it, and now my ass is on the line."

O'Hara shook his head. "We have it. You know that bastard did it. We have the evidence that he looked at the medical files for those three women. He had access to the blood samples that were all switched. He had access to the blood with the heroin and barbiturates. He used that coroner's van and we have hair and fiber samples."

"Yeah, those hair and fiber samples of T. J.'s. I don't have a good feeling about that and neither should you."

O'Hara pushed his big fingers across his mustache. "Good feeling, bad feeling. I'm telling you, Matt, you need to just take what you got."

"Yeah, I know you're right, but my gut is telling me something's wrong. You get the reports together, everything we've got. All of it goes to McGuiness. Start sending part of it over this afternoon and keep sending it. If we have any shot at getting this in, then we have to make sure we've done everything we can to make sure we don't give Wallace the slightest excuse to turn us down."

He looked at the papers covering his desk, shook his head, and pushed them aside, leaving a bare spot. "Now I have to sit here and start thinking about how to present a triple murder case by the day after tomorrow. That's two days to put together a case that we would normally put together in two months." Jamison hesitated before finishing his thought. "And that assumes that Wallace doesn't grant a mistrial even if he decides to let it in."

"Well, relax. At least we have two days. It could have been worse."

"How?"

"He could have said no without even listening to what you have."

Jamison shot his investigator a grim smile. "Tomorrow, you and Ernie, seven a.m. Be ready. And tell Ernie to go over St. Claire's car again."

When the three of them gathered the next morning Jamison could tell by Ernie's face that what he had wasn't good. He didn't waste any time. "Matt, I went through St. Claire's car again. I found a receipt in the glove compartment for some repair work. I had to go to the garage to check it out. Long story short, St. Claire's car was in the shop at the time of the Ventana kidnap. I don't know how that hair from Ventana got in there, but it didn't happen because she was in that car. Maybe he had it on his shoe or something. That could explain how it got there along with the fiber samples from Johnson and Symes."

Jamison's stomach sank. "Right. And they were all found in exactly the same spot. T. J. put that hair and those fiber samples in that car. I knew everybody couldn't have missed it." His hand slapped the table so hard it stung. "T. J. just couldn't leave it alone."

O'Hara reacted. "Matt, you don't know that. St. Claire must have tracked that evidence into his car on his shoes. That's how it got on the floor. T. J.'s a good cop. He is."

Whether T. J. had been around a long time wasn't going to explain the garage receipt. "Bill, you and I both know what happened here. Get T. J. over here right now. Don't warn him of anything. I need to know."

As O'Hara started to get up, Ernie put his hand on O'Hara's shoulder to keep him seated, and said, "Matt, you bring T. J. over here and you know what you're asking?"

"This is a murder case. It's not about opening a trunk and then remembering some bullshit about consent to search. Get T. J. over here. This is his problem to answer."

T. J. sauntered into Jamison's office. The expression on his face said it all. T. J. Longworthy had been around a long time and he had broken more men in interrogation than Jamison could ever dream of. He wasn't afraid of the prosecutor. "You wanted to see me?" His tone was defiant as he glanced over at O'Hara and Ernie. Neither man said a word.

Jamison took a deep breath. His voice was firm. He knew it had to be. "Sit down, Detective Longworthy. I have a question, and *you* need to think carefully before answering. Ernie did a search of the glove compartment in St. Claire's car. He found a receipt that matched the time of the Ventana murder. The car was in the shop. St. Claire didn't have it when that crime was committed. So can you tell me how that hair sample got into St. Claire's car?"

T. J. didn't flinch. "The same way the fibers got in his car. The same way every perp screws up. They walk through the evidence and it gets stuck on their shoe. That's how." T. J. leaned back and put one foot up on Jamison's desk.

"First of all, Detective, get your foot off my desk. Second, is that the story you're sticking with, that St. Claire had Ventana's hair stuck on his shoe and that just happened to be right near the carpet fiber samples from the Symes and Johnson murders and all our forensic people missed it except you?"

"I don't miss much."

"You're sure you want to go with that?"

Longworthy stood up, the rapid movement slamming his chair backward as he pointed his finger at Jamison's face. "You listen, Jamison, and you listen good. St. Claire killed those women. You know it, and so do I. You said you needed evidence and I got the evidence you needed. You want to go after somebody? Then go after him. But you stop riding my ass."

Longworthy walked toward the door and then turned. "That's the trouble with you lawyers. Nobody ever told you in law school that this is a dirty business. These aren't nice people, Jamison, and nice people don't catch them."

After Longworthy left, Jamison sat silently. O'Hara was drumming his fingers on the arm of his chair while Ernie shuffled through the papers in his lap. Both men knew when to keep their mouths shut. Finally O'Hara broke the silence. "So, Matt, what are you going to do? T. J. is willing to testify to what he found. You know St. Claire did it, and you haven't got any proof that T. J. planted that hair and fiber in St. Claire's car. You're letting your suspicions get the better of you."

"Maybe, maybe not. Listen, you and Ernie go see if T. J. had any access to that stuff that he found in the car. Anything at all. And I need to know by this afternoon. Get it for me if it's there. I need to know."

Jamison was at his desk diagramming the evidence argument that he would make to Wallace in the morning. He wasn't going to have the test results back from the FBI on the succinylcholine. So he would have to go with arguing that he didn't need to show what killed the women, only what *could* have killed them. If he could show St. Claire had access to the medical reports and to the blood and tissue samples, he could make the argument, but what would turn the case was the hair and fiber samples that T. J. found in the car. If he had those, then he knew it would be enough. A big if.

A few hours later, O'Hara and Ernie walked into his office. Both men were grim. Ernie had checked with the manager at Symes's apartment and with Johnson's boyfriend. T. J. had been to see both of them and had access to the carpets. Neither investigator knew whether he had taken a carpet sample but clearly he'd had the opportunity.

O'Hara's news was even worse. T. J. had gone to Ventana's apartment and asked if she had a hairbrush. O'Hara had to acknowledge that T. J. could have taken hair from it.

The look on Jamison's face was enough for O'Hara to offer his thoughts. "I know you're not asking us, but T. J. said he'll testify that it happened the way he said it did. Sometimes you just need to let it go. Let the jury decide."

Listening and drawing endless circles of frustration on his legal pad, Jamison was subdued. "Well, I'm not McGuiness and I like to think my job is always based on me doing what I think is right rather than what I think I can get away with. I need to think about my argument to Wallace."

Alone in his apartment, Jamison sat in an armchair. He hadn't moved for several hours. The apartment was dark. He hadn't gotten up to turn on any lights. He kept going over it all in his mind, sure that if he put in T. J.'s evidence he could dance around the explanation of how Ventana's hair got in the car. But that wasn't the problem. Putting on that evidence meant that he was vouching for it.

For the first time Jamison understood something that one of his law school professors said—that consequences didn't dictate ethics; ethics dictated consequences. He was a prosecutor. It came down to a matter of his personal sense of integrity. He had to do what was right but what was right under the circumstances was still unclear.

Besides, T. J. could be telling the truth and O'Hara had a point. It was a jury decision in the end. But Jamison also knew that juries depended on him to only offer evidence that he didn't doubt himself.

He leaned back in the chair, tired of debating with himself. He might as well remain where he was. There were only a few hours before sunrise and he wasn't going to sleep either way.

When Jamison entered the courtroom, McGuiness looked at him but didn't say a word. Jamison sat his file down on the counsel table as the bailiff walked into the courtroom.

"All rise. Court is now in session, the matter of the People versus St. Claire."

As Wallace moved up several steps to the elevated bench, it didn't look as if he had gotten a good night's sleep either. "Mr. Jamison, Mr. McGuiness, before I call the jury into the courtroom, I would like to discuss this matter in my chambers rather than open court. I'm sure you understand." Wallace walked off the bench without another word.

Both lawyers picked up their files and followed Wallace into the judge's chambers. It made sense. Wallace didn't want everybody in the courtroom to hear what Jamison was about to say.

The court reporter set her machine up in the corner of the judge's office and waited for him to make a statement. Wallace looked at all the parties. Jamison stood. "Your Honor, I have something I would like to say." He had made his decision. Before he could continue, Judge Wallace raised his hand for him to stop.

"Mr. Jamison, before you say anything, I've spent considerable time thinking about this. What you said troubles me deeply, but I don't see any way I can allow you to put on the type of evidence you have told me about without giving Dr. St. Claire the opportunity to prepare adequately. I can't send a jury out for two months while Mr. McGuiness prepares and that assumes that two months is enough time.

"I've thought about what is the most just thing to do. A mistrial would mean that everything that has been done in this case with this jury would be wasted. On the other hand, I recognize that the evidence you have discussed, if you can prove it, would most likely be enough to convince any jury to convict.

"The only problem with it is that if I were on the court of appeals looking at this case with a cold record, I would have serious questions about abuse of discretion. Maybe I would vote to reverse and maybe I wouldn't. But I'm not on the court of appeals, and unlike three justices on the appellate court who can talk it over among themselves for hours, I am one judge, and I have to do what I think is the right thing under the circumstances.

"So I've decided I'm not going to allow it. If you have the evidence, then you can charge Dr. St. Claire and try him for murder but he will have a reasonable opportunity to prepare to defend himself against those charges.

"I take you at your word that you have been trying to put all of the evidence together and I understand your frustration, but sometimes things don't happen just the way we want them to happen. I've made my decision. Monday be prepared to finish this case and argue it."

Jamison silently considered Wallace's statements before responding, wondering whether he would do the same thing if he were sitting in the judge's chair. "Thank you, Your Honor." In some ways Jamison meant that more than Wallace would ever know.

Jamison wasn't listening as McGuiness started rambling about sanctions and delay. He was thinking about Monday when he had to make everything come together. He knew the first thing he had to do was phone Beth Garrett. They needed to talk. When he walked out of Wallace's chambers he saw the questioning look on O'Hara's face. He shook his head and leaned in close to O'Hara, his voice low. "I'll explain later. Call Beth and get her down to our office."

Monday morning, Jamison rose when court was called to order. "Your Honor, the People recall Elizabeth Garrett to the stand."

Jamison handed an exhibit to Beth. "Miss Garrett, I show you now a letter that has been received into evidence. Is this your handwriting?"

Beth turned the pages in her hand. Her face flushed. "Yes."

Jamison watched her reaction intently. "There is no face sheet indicating specifically to whom the letter was written. Do you know who this letter was written to?"

The answer came out softly. Elizabeth seemed to be distracted, as if recalling the past was an effort. "It was written to Bobby Allison, a young man I dated when I was in college at Tenaya State, here in town."

"Do you know how this letter came to be in the hands of the defense?"

Her eyes wandered around the courtroom and then focused on St. Claire. She seemed resigned to the reality that there was nothing unknown of her life. "No, this letter was either mailed or it was part of my personal possessions and it was kept either at my parents' home or my apartment before I moved home or maybe my car."

"Did you send it to Mr. Allison?"

"I don't recall. Probably, but I haven't seen it since it was written and that was almost seven or eight years ago."

"If you mailed it, would you drop it off at a post office?"

"No. I would have put a letter in the mailbox in front of my parent's home for the mailman to pick up."

"And if you did that, would it be correct that anybody would have access to that mail until the postman picked it up?"

"That's true. We, my parents, live in the country and the postman picks up the mail. We don't worry about somebody stealing the mail from the box."

"Have you ever been the victim of a burglary, someone breaking into your home or apartment?"

"When I was in college my apartment was broken into but nothing of value was taken. There were papers scattered around. We just assumed whoever it was heard something and left before they could get our stereo and television. That's all we had that was worth anything as we were college students, you know?"

"Was that at a time after you dated Mr. Allison? In other words after you would have written this letter?"

"Yes, it could have been there at the time but I never realized it was gone."

"I have nothing further." Jamison returned to his seat at the counsel table. He didn't have a choice. He had to put Elizabeth in front of a jury to explain the letter and now McGuiness was going to have another chance to tear into her.

McGuiness picked up the letter. "Miss Garrett, this letter says that you miss the person you are writing to and want to see him again. Is that right?"

"Yes."

"You deny writing this letter to my client, Alex St. Claire?"

"I had no contact with your client after I returned from Los Angeles."

McGuiness quickly moved toward the witness stand, putting an envelope in front of Garrett. "Do you know what this is?"

Beth picked up the envelope with a puzzled expression on her face. "It's my graduation announcement from college."

"Who is it addressed to, Miss Garrett?"

"It's addressed to Alex St. Claire, but that isn't my handwriting. I didn't address this and I didn't send it."

"So somebody, you have no idea who, sent my client the announcement of your graduation from college?"

Elizabeth began to cry. "It wasn't me. I didn't send him anything. I just wanted him to leave me alone. This isn't my fault! It's *his* fault! I hate you, Alex! I *hate* you! Just leave me alone, you bastard! Leave me alone!" Her voice trailed off as McGuiness stepped back, surprised at the outburst.

"I have nothing further."

Jamison walked toward the witness stand and took the paper from Elizabeth's hands. He looked into her eyes. He was so close it was as if no one else was in the courtroom. As she returned his gaze, he could see her eyes searching his, as if she was saying the only thing that mattered was that he believed her. Jamison leaned in. "It's over, Beth. You can step down."

He could ask more questions of Elizabeth but the result would be the same, her saying she told the truth and insisting St. Claire was lying. If the jurors believed her, then saying more wouldn't change that and if they didn't, then he knew that saying more wouldn't change that either. He put out his hand and helped Elizabeth down. All eyes followed her as she walked out of the courtroom.

O'Hara handed him a slip of paper from Ernie. Jamison looked at it, but he kept his expression neutral as he turned to face Judge Wallace. "Your Honor, the People rest."

McGuiness stood. "Nothing further, Your Honor."

Wallace shifted his bulk in his chair as he turned back toward the jury. "Ladies and gentlemen, thank you for your patience in this case. It has been a long trial. Tomorrow we will hear the closing arguments of counsel." Wallace moved his head slightly so that he could focus on Jamison and McGuiness. "Gentlemen, court will resume tomorrow at nine a.m."

Jamison reread the slip of paper O'Hara had handed him. Ernie's usual scrawl had been replaced with block letters. It read, SUCCINYLCHOLINE INCONCLUSIVE.

Chapter 34

Jamison spent the rest of the day thinking about what he was going to say to the jury in the morning. It was almost 5 p.m. and he was still searching for the focus of his argument. A yellow legal pad was directly in front of him. The page was as blank as his mind. Jamison couldn't put his thoughts down on paper until he knew himself what he believed. Finally he picked up the phone.

"Dr. Levy? This is Matt Jamison. May I come to your office? I'd like to talk."

~

Aaron Levy watched as Jamison fidgeted with his file and tried to make himself comfortable in the same chair that Levy's patients sat in.

Before Jamison said anything, Levy asked, "This Dr. St. Claire you are prosecuting. I have been following the case in the paper. You think he's the murderer you've been looking for, don't you? But you have another reason for being here. Am I correct?"

Levy sensed that his insight made Jamison both uncomfortable and wary. It was disconcerting to have someone look at you intently, and know that the person knew more about you than you had ever disclosed. Jamison's answer was circumspect. "Yes, there are pieces of both that fit together, but then again nothing in this case fits exactly."

He spread the photographs out on Levy's desk of Garrett tied to the bed.

"And what does not fit, exactly?" Levy's eyes narrowed, looking at the pictures. "Is it that you cannot believe a physician would do such a thing? Or does it trouble you that these two people have a past? That's what I've read in the papers." Levy gently delved, "Or is there something here that you personally struggle with?"

Levy didn't probe further as Jamison went over the evidence in the trial, moving back and forth as the questions he had kept confined in his brain during the trial rolled out of his mouth. He waited for Jamison to finish before asking the question that had been clear to him from the beginning of the conversation.

"You have doubts in your mind about her? She may be telling the truth. If so, then you have your answer. But if he's telling the truth or some form of the truth, then whether she's telling the truth or not is a much darker question."

Watching the younger man, Levy paused to let his words sink in. He had spent years probing the hidden recesses of the human mind, quickly learning early in his career that logic often had nothing to do with motivation and obsession.

"Psychopaths are very manipulative, Matt. And they frequently seek out compliant companions to help them act out their fantasies. They may not hurt these people and they may live what appears to be outwardly normal lives while at the same time have this entirely separate existence, a dark side that everyone else is entirely unaware of. But there is something more here that troubles you, isn't there?" Levy's observation didn't sound much like a question.

"I think it's because I want to believe her and yet there are things that cause me to question myself."

Levy kept his voice conversational but probing. "I am inferring that you maybe have doubts about your objectivity?" Jamison didn't respond. "I see." Levy's mind began to fill in the spaces in his understanding.

"I cannot answer, of course, who is telling the truth." His countenance became more thoughtful than usual. "She may be entirely truthful and a complete victim of Dr. St. Claire. Psychopaths, as I said, can be incredibly manipulative. And if he did what you suspect, then he is clearly a complete psychopath.

"That she may not have been completely truthful could be explained as a defensive explanation, her way of trying to make sure she's believed. She wants you to believe her. Often the truth is much more ambiguous than we would like. If you have trouble accepting her explanations, then surely a jury will have the same problems."

Levy slid the photographs around of Elizabeth Garrett tied to the bed. "When you look at the development of a person's character, there can be events in a woman's life that cause her to have a fantasy of being abused. It's a fantasy because it isn't real. Something like people getting on a roller coaster because they really know it won't come off the tracks. They can be safely terrified."

Jamison's response was questioning. "Safely terrified?"

"Games of bondage and sexual submission can be part of that. It is a fantasy in which the abuse is not reality," Levy explained. "The reality is that Elizabeth Garrett may be a complete victim *or* she may be a willing victim *or*"—Levy stared directly at Jamison—"as hard as it is to believe, she may not be a victim at all. That is what you must ask yourself and that is what the jury must decide. First, you must decide what you believe. But the fact that at one time she willingly engaged in this type of behavior does not mean she willingly did so *this* time. *And* it does not mean she did not."

He understood the consternation on Jamison's face. It wasn't a definitive answer, but then very seldom in his line of work was there a definitive answer when you were looking for *why* things happened. About the only thing definitive was *what* happened.

"Matt, you should trust your judgment. If you have questions, then you should look at the reasons, but don't lose sight of who is the master manipulator here. It's possible Ms. Garrett may not have been entirely truthful, but that doesn't mean that she isn't the victim. What we see is still the best indicator of what is likely. What we may suspect can often obscure reality."

Levy became silent, waiting for Jamison to digest what he'd said. He knew the young man well enough that he could envision the kaleidoscope of evidence flashing though his mind as he processed the answer.

"I think she's a victim."

Levy nodded. "Then you've answered your question. What I've explained are simply possibilities. What is clear is that your good doctor is most likely a murderer. I will tell you if that is so, then Elizabeth Garrett is extremely lucky to be alive. I will also tell you that somewhere there are pictures that Dr. St. Claire has of his victims. These people always keep mementoes. They revel in the memory of what they've done. I cannot tell you where they are, I can only tell you that they exist and you will have to find them. But for now, Matt, you must clear your mind and satisfy yourself with what you believe because for your argument to the jury to be believed, *you* must believe it yourself. We'll talk again. This case isn't over."

Before Jamison left, Levy put his hand on the young prosecutor's shoulder. It was a fatherly gesture born of their long friendship, one that began in earnest years before when Matt's father, a very successful but personally flawed criminal defense lawyer, abandoned the family. Roger Jamison's sense of control came with his mastery in the courtroom but outside that forum he was master of very little, including himself. Years of his infidelities and alcoholism had imprinted their pain on Matt's childhood. Levy, his father's friend, had stepped into the fatherless boy's void. He had come to love Matt, his intensity almost like a coiled spring. As a psychologist he knew it to be an effort on Jamison's part to assert control over his life.

As Matt rose to go, what Levy left unsaid was his realization that what St. Claire was to Elizabeth Garrett, a dominant and overwhelming force in her life, was just as he had known Jamison's father had been to Matt's mother.

Levy understood very clearly that what was unconsciously troubling and confusing Jamison emotionally was his empathy for Elizabeth Garrett, an empathy he had gained at an early age for women who were not in control of their own lives. And on a conscious or subconscious level, Jamison wanted to believe she was a victim because he couldn't understand it if she wasn't.

Chapter 35

In any criminal trial, the prosecution bears the burden of proof because they brought the charges. They go first.

If the defense wishes, they don't even have to argue. But they always do. And they always argue that the prosecution hasn't proven its case beyond a reasonable doubt. Jamison knew when he walked through the swinging gate to the counsel table what his job was. He was a prosecutor.

He could feel the tension of the courtroom. Adrenaline pulsed through his body. His criminal law professor had said that great lawyers are born, they aren't made. And it was in final argument that the pitched sea of emotion that is a criminal trial is crossed or not crossed successfully. Whether Jamison was born to be a great lawyer was not on his mind. What was on his mind was that this was his final chance to make his case.

Standing in front of twelve people in final argument was like standing on a dark stage and delivering a soliloquy in a pinpoint of light. Jamison rose from his seat at the counsel table, walked to the well of the courtroom, and stood alone in front of the jury rail.

The eyes that looked back at him were neither sympathetic nor antagonistic. They were simply expectant. He left his notes at the counsel table. He began to pace. He always paced. He went over the evidence and testimony in minute detail before he stopped pacing and stood quietly in front of the jury, reaching for the words he wanted to leave them with and to think about when McGuiness gave his arguments.

"Ladies and gentlemen, a criminal trial is sometimes described as a search for the truth. I would describe it more accurately as a search for certainty. But there is only one way we can provide that certainty: it is by presenting you with the evidence and the witnesses. You, the jury, alone determine the credibility of witnesses. You, the jury, alone decide what you believe or don't believe. You, the jury, alone decide what you can be certain of. It is never easy. It is never simple.

"I am not going to talk about each piece of evidence in this case. You know and I know that the only thing that decides certainty in this case is whether you believe Elizabeth Garrett or if you believe Alex St. Claire.

"How do we decide who to believe? We look at the logic of what the witness says. We look to see if anything supports what the witness says. We look to see if something the witness says can be proven to be true or untrue. We look to our own experience as men and women, human experience, because it is human experience by which we make our judgments every day and measure the judgments of others. Every day.

"You saw Elizabeth Garrett testify. You saw her come into this courtroom and expose herself to humiliation and attack. You saw her stand up to that and you saw her dignity. Mr. McGuiness is an excellent lawyer. He is very good at what he does. Every aspect of Elizabeth's life was dissected, moved around, peeled away, and exposed for twelve strangers. But she took it. She looked you in the eye. She looked Mr. McGuiness in the eye and yes, she looked Alex St. Claire in the eye, a man who has been a specter hanging over her entire young life.

"Elizabeth Garrett is no competition for Alex St. Claire in terms of sophistication or education. Not many people would be. She is only competition in terms of character.

"She has been stalked and she has been harassed and she has survived. I do not think many young people, male or female, could do what she has done.

"And to you, ladies and gentlemen, Mr. McGuiness will argue that *you* hold Alex St. Claire's future in your hands. But I will argue that you hold Elizabeth Garrett's character in your hands.

"I want you to think about the logic of this case. If Elizabeth wanted to meet Alex St. Claire as he maintains, then why meet him on a darkened road near her home? She could easily have gone to his home or met him at a restaurant or coffee shop 'to talk' as he testified. Does it make any sense that a young woman would stop near a remote and darkened cemetery to conduct a conversation?

"Alex St. Claire says that Elizabeth and he had a relationship that was unusual. Think about it. This young woman is found tied to a bed. There aren't many explanations Alex St. Claire can give for that except that she did it willingly. But think about that. This young woman knew that her parents would be frantic. She knew people would be looking for her. This wasn't early the next morning. It was in the afternoon of the next day. Do you get any sense from watching this young woman, from listening to her answer every single question, no matter how humiliating, that she would do that? Did she strike you as that irresponsible and insensitive to others?

"The defense evidence in this case has been a puzzle to me and I am guessing it has been a puzzle to you as well. I examined the baby clothes and the receipt for those clothes. I looked at the ticket receipt for the *Queen Mary*. They looked real. There were only a few explanations. *Either* the receipts were obtained as Alex St. Claire said they were and Elizabeth was lying, *or* they were obtained to provide an alibi. Well if, as I argue to you, Elizabeth is not lying, then they were obtained to provide an alibi, to provide a veneer of truthfulness and credibility for Alex St. Claire.

"You heard him deny that. You heard him insist that they did these things together. Why did he do that? He did that so that you would doubt Elizabeth. Why would anybody keep these items for as long as the defendant did? He kept these things for ten years. And what do we now know about them? We know that they are a lie. They were obtained and held on to *for years*, to create an alibi, an alibi not only for what he did in the past, but for what, in the dark recesses of the mind of Alex St. Claire, he planned to do in the future. This young woman was his obsession.

"You didn't hear any admission from Alex St. Claire that he lied to you until he was caught. And when he got back on the stand and admitted he lied, he looked you in the eye just like he did when he wanted you to believe that he was telling the truth. He is a liar.

"But Alex St. Claire is more than that. It is frightening to believe what he really is. He has stalked this young woman. Think of it. Everything has been done to provide him with an explanation that makes her look like she is lying. But the only person who has lied and who has been proven to have lied is Alex St. Claire.

"There are the pictures of Elizabeth when she was a teenager that she was humiliated with on the witness stand. You all saw them. You heard her say why they were taken. God knows that we all have done things when we were young that we regret. But she admitted it. Is it any wonder that she didn't want anybody to know? Is it any wonder she didn't want to press charges back then if it meant that those pictures would be shown not only to her parents but to the entire world? Do any of you have any doubt about the way she felt when you looked at those pictures?

"It is frightening to think of what Elizabeth has had to endure at the hands of Alex St. Claire. He has been there all these years, waiting, watching, and planning. Look at the photograph of her in the parking lot introduced by the defense, her hair swirling as she turns her head. You heard the photographic expert testify she was moving and that it was consistent with being taken from a distance. You heard her testify she didn't know anybody was photographing her. She wasn't posing for a photograph as the defendant wants you to believe. She was being stalked. And now in this courtroom the defendant used that image stolen from an unaware young woman as proof that she was with him, just like he used those receipts that he had kept all those years.

"What Alex St. Claire described as love for Elizabeth Garrett is not love, ladies and gentlemen, it is obsession. The defendant is obsessed with Elizabeth Garrett and he has waited like a hawk circling its prey, waiting for the right moment to hurtle to the ground and rip its talons into an unsuspecting victim.

"Alex St. Claire may be a physician, a man trained to heal, but concealed inside him is the mind of a remorseless predator. He did what Elizabeth said he did and he will not stop unless you find him guilty."

Standing silently for a moment, Jamison's eyes scanned the twelve people who had listened intently. Some were looking back at him. Others were glancing furtively over at Alex St. Claire. They were thinking about what Jamison had said. He walked back to his chair and sat down. He could feel the spreading wetness under his shirt. In some ways the damp chill of perspiration was reassuring. It told him that he had argued what he believed.

McGuiness remained seated, his pen appearing to slash across his legal pad. Jamison knew it was simply for show. McGuiness already knew what he was going to say and where he would start. Finally McGuiness walked across the courtroom and placed his hands on the jury rail, leaning in as close as he could get to the jury. He slowly recounted his client's impressive educational background and the lack of independent evidence other than Elizabeth Garrett's word, tearing at each vulnerability in the evidence, each inconsistency. Then he moved directly in front of the jury to make his last point.

"Mr. Jamison is impressive, isn't he? But there is one thing he didn't talk about and that is the one final thing we *have* to talk about. He said that a trial is not so much a search for the truth as it is a search for certainty. I agree with that. Sometimes we just don't know what is or is not the truth because we can't be certain. And in a criminal trial, if we cannot be certain of what the truth is, then the judge will instruct you that you are obligated to find an accused person not guilty.

"The burden of proof in determining whether you are certain is called proof beyond a reasonable doubt. It simply means that if you can't be certain, morally certain, beyond any doubt that is reasonable, then you are obligated to find the accused not guilty.

"In most cases, the truth is fairly clear. We can look at logic and we can look at evidence, and depending on the case we can reach a conclusion with a very high degree of confidence. But this is not most cases. This is a case where everything, *everything*, ladies and gentlemen, rests on the only thing of which we *can* be certain—and *that* is that this was a tumultuous relationship from the beginning.

"No matter how you look at it, what we have seen is two people who have run the emotional gamut, the ecstasy and the degradation, of an intense and complex human relationship. And what we all know is that what human relationships present to the world and what they present in the privacy of that relationship often are completely different. What we have seen is a tragic human relationship stripped of all privacy and all dignity for both people—for both Elizabeth Garrett and Alex St. Claire.

"One of the reasons you twelve people are here is because of your maturity and human experience. You've been around. You've seen people fall in and out of love, experience the euphoria and the despair. You have seen people behave irrationally for emotional reasons. But if there is one thing that is obvious to anybody who has ever been in love, it is that logic has nothing to do with it.

"The prosecutor says that my client planned all of this for ten years. That he bought those baby clothes on his own. That he contrived the hospital log. He implies that he stole the letters and the graduation announcement. That he took photographs from a distance.

"He says that because he has no other explanation that is consistent with Elizabeth Garrett telling the truth. Well, I'm going to say something that will surprise him and maybe you. Is that possible? Yes, it is possible because almost anything is possible. But is it realistic to believe?

"To believe Mr. Jamison's theory you have to be certain not just that it is possible, but that it *is* what happened. And you have to be certain beyond all reasonable doubt. You can't make a mistake. You have to be sure today, tomorrow, next week, next month, and when you are sitting in your car driving to work next year. You have to be that sure. You have to believe that everything, *everything* Alex St. Claire said is a lie. Because the reality is that if you believe even one thing Alex St. Claire said may be true, then that means that Elizabeth Garrett is not telling the truth.

"Is that possible, that Elizabeth Garrett is not telling the truth? In the swirl of emotion that is this case? In the swirl of emotion that is created by love? Ladies and gentlemen, when it comes to what is or is not true in the emotional relationship between two people only these two people know what is or isn't true, and perhaps even they don't know it. Nothing is so unquestionably true or untrue that there can be no reasonable doubt.

"Mr. Jamison would have you believe that if you find Alex St. Claire not guilty, then you are deciding Elizabeth Garrett is not telling the truth. I would say to you that if you find Alex St. Claire not guilty the only thing you are deciding is *that you aren't sure what the truth is.*

"Ladies and gentlemen, Alex St. Claire is entitled to your verdict of not guilty. Do that and you will sleep well because you will know that whatever may be the truth in this case, it will never be clear beyond a reasonable doubt.

"Your responsibility isn't to make sure that all guilty people are found guilty. Your responsibility is to make sure that only people who you are certain are guilty, are found guilty. And in this case, nothing is certain except the tangled mess made by two people. Find Alex St. Claire not guilty and tonight and tomorrow and next week and next year, you will know that you did the right thing because uncertainty in this case is the only thing you can be sure of tonight, tomorrow, next week, and next year."

Jamison rocked back in his chair at the counsel table. He stood slowly and buttoned his suit jacket while he walked back to the center of the courtroom for his closing argument.

"Ladies and gentlemen, Mr. McGuiness is right that the burden is on me to prove Alex St. Claire guilty beyond a reasonable doubt. I ask you to look at the evidence and consider whether you believe Elizabeth. If you believe her, then that is enough. There is only one proven liar in this case and that is Alex St. Claire. Does anyone think for a moment that he would have gotten back on the stand if he hadn't been caught in his lie?

"Yes, he has an explanation for everything. He saved the evidence for years. He is the victim of a cruel and conniving woman. He loved her but his love was unrequited. Still, he loved her, despite all she had done to him. And according to him, years later when this woman called he went running right back, and she did the same thing again as he claimed when she falsely accused the defendant of kidnapping her and taking her against her will to Los Angeles. Let me break this case down this way. If Alex St. Claire is lying when he says Elizabeth went willingly with him to Los Angeles ten years ago, then he is lying now. And lie he did.

"If you believe his explanation for why he lied you have to believe he was so distraught over Elizabeth, the mother of his child, the woman he loved to distraction leaving him, that he went to a wax museum.

"And when this same woman, this woman who once had him arrested, who once falsely accused him of kidnapping and rape, calls him ten years later, he goes running out to a shopping mall to see her and then agrees to meet her on some dark road out in the country so they could once again play what he describes as 'their little game.'

"And he would have you believe that this young woman—who is so afraid of what her parents think that ten years ago she refused to testify against him because they would see those pictures, who still lives with her parents, this schoolteacher—that this fragile young woman would meet him on a dark country road and leave her car door open.

"And I remind you, Elizabeth said he had a knife and that he cut her. How did the blood, Elizabeth's blood, end up on the seat of her car along with an unmistakable knife silhouette left on the upholstery? When you walk into that jury room, I want you to think about that. How did Elizabeth Garrett's blood get on that seat and how did that outline of that knife happen to that seat? There is only one way that happened that makes any sense and that is the way Elizabeth Garrett said it happened.

"Alex St. Claire planned everything he did. That is the only explanation. This young woman is the victim of a man with an obsession that knew no bounds. As frightening as it is to believe, for years the defendant has thought about her, lusted after her, and on that cold night at the border of a cemetery he took her.

"Only you can bring this to its proper end. Give Elizabeth Garrett freedom from a life of fear of this man. Find him guilty because that is what he is."

Jamison searched for more words, something that would end it more forcefully. But all he could think of were the same words. "Find him guilty." He let his gaze move from juror to juror before he walked back to the counsel table.

Chapter 36

Waiting for a verdict was always a time of excruciating uncertainty. Time took on a presence of its own, the ticking of the clock, the silent phone, and the etching of stomach acid rising up in a dry throat. Second-guessing every question asked during the trial and every strategic maneuver filled the minutes as time took its pleasure in slow drips. There was nothing for Jamison to do but wait.

His two investigators kept him company. They had as much invested in the case as Jamison did. O'Hara had waited through hundreds of jury verdicts, so many that he couldn't remember more than a handful. He didn't need to. Whether the time spent waiting was measured in hours or minutes, it always felt as if the wait was longer than his patience could accept. As usual, Ernie sat quietly, thumbing through a magazine. Because he had nothing to say, he said nothing.

When Jamison looked at him, frowning, O'Hara realized the thrumming of his fingers on the desk thundered like hoofbeats in Jamison's silent office where they had gathered. Jamison hadn't said much all afternoon and even less as the hours stretched into evening. A used and reused paper coffee cup sat on his desk, sagging from the saturation of cold dregs.

Jamison kept going over the case in his mind, day by day, witness by witness, word by word. As he had argued, he could feel his confidence in the truthfulness of Elizabeth Garrett building and with that, the anger rising as he realized he was all she had to convince people about what happened.

Now as he sat waiting, he began to detach himself from the argument. Emotionally he believed everything he had said. Logically he knew that emotion clouded judgment. The question was one of certainty for the jurors. Unlike the jury, he didn't have to be right beyond a reasonable doubt in what he believed. He just had to believe it.

The ringing phone startled him even though he had been staring at it and waiting for it to ring for hours. He hesitated momentarily before lifting the receiver. It was the court clerk. "Judge Wallace wants you to return to the courtroom. He's releasing the jury for the evening."

The courtroom was almost empty when Jamison arrived. He was immediately confronted by a reporter from the newspaper as well as a local television reporter hoping for a comment, which he declined to give. They all sat in silence until McGuiness arrived with St. Claire. McGuiness ignored the reporters' questions and pushed St. Claire past them. Jamison couldn't tell if St. Claire was nervous or relieved that after five hours there was still no verdict. He always looked the same, as if he had just walked away from a full-length mirror after making sure his tie was straight.

Every lawyer tries to read the faces of jurors like tea leaves and with the same level of success. Jamison was no exception, but now he sensed there was some emotional distance between the men and the women on the jury, a subtle indication that telegraphed that the two genders had separated in some way. The women moved around the men without acknowledgment. Wallace excused the jurors for the evening and the jurors shuffled out the same way they had shuffled in, moving as a group but with visible separation. Other than that there was nothing on their faces to read.

The three men waited until they were back in Jamison's office before saying anything. O'Hara spoke first. "That jury's deadlocked and it's the women against the men. You could see it. Reminded me of my second wife." He paused. "Reminded me of my first wife too. When women are pissed at you they have a way of walking around you like they're stepping around dog shit."

It wasn't what he wanted to hear but Jamison knew O'Hara was right. He nodded. "I think the women believe her, and the men either believe him or aren't sure. Either way, unless something happens, we'll have to go at this again."

Ernie's face took on a thoughtful expression. "Maybe a hung jury isn't a bad thing. Next time we'll know what's coming and we'll have more time to break down his alibi."

Jamison accepted that Ernie might be right. "Okay, but this case turns on the credibility of both of them, Garrett and St. Claire. There's no in-between. You either believe her or you don't. Sometimes why that happens isn't all that clear."

"Amigo, it's too soon to do this Monday morning quarterbacking. We have to wait and see. Let's go home. Get some rest. Tomorrow we can start looking at what we got left, including the murder cases that we've been working on, and trying to find holes in St. Claire's story."

The continued lack of acceptance of the impact of the Garrett case on the murder cases underlaid the frustration in his voice as Jamison responded, "Without this case we have no murder case. Nobody seems to understand that. Okay, you two go home. I'll leave in a minute. First I need to call Beth." He waited until O'Hara and Ernie left before he picked up the receiver and dialed.

The next morning Jamison sat at his desk picking through stacks of reports on the murders that Ernie had put together while he and O'Hara had been in trial. He studied pictures of the victims, searching for something he hadn't seen before. When he told O'Hara they needed the Garrett case in order to make the other murders provable, he meant it.

As their only victim who had survived St. Claire, she could provide testimony as to St. Claire's modus operandi. Her testimony could provide the explanation of what had happened in the other cases. But without her case they only had speculation. Unless the evidence tightened considerably, they couldn't walk into the murder cases without a conviction in Garrett's case; McGuiness would eat them alive, ripping apart the gossamer-thin strands of the circumstantial case that depended on Garrett to pull it all together. Jamison knew it. His gut wasn't just roiling from a quart of coffee and churning stomach acid. He pushed more paper around his desk. He was always like this until the verdict came in.

As he continued going through papers, the lunch hour came and went, and still nothing had come out of the jury room, not a question, not a sound. Then at two o'clock the phone rang. It was the court clerk. "Mr. Jamison, we have a verdict."

He put the phone down and picked up his file. There was no hurry. The clerk would have to call McGuiness at his office and it would be at least a half hour before everyone was ready. Jamison walked out into the hallway. Already his colleagues' heads were sticking out of their offices with wishes of good luck. As he turned down the hall O'Hara was already walking toward him, wrestling his frame into his coat. Ernie met them at the top of the stairs.

Some people said the pitcher's mound was the loneliest spot on earth. It couldn't be any lonelier than the counsel chair for a lawyer waiting for a verdict in a big trial. Prosecutors weren't supposed to take the verdict personally, but the people who said that either weren't trial lawyers or they were on Valium. It was always personal.

Ignoring St. Claire, Jamison acknowledged McGuiness out of politeness. He knew that McGuiness felt no differently than he did. The trial had been a gun-fight and they both knew there could be only one winner.

The twelve people who would decide the final answer filed into the courtroom. Wallace asked his bailiff to take the verdict forms from the foreman and began to go through them, shuffling them around and discarding pages that weren't applicable. Like most judges, Wallace never showed much emotion when he was looking at verdicts. But Jamison caught a moment's hesitation when Wallace pulled the verdict forms apart and dropped them into separate piles.

Finished with his housekeeping, the judge turned to the jury. "Are these your verdicts?" It was a question that every judge asked. Jamison never understood why they asked that before the verdicts were read. Who else's verdicts could they be? But much of what happened in a courtroom was ritual and much of the justification was simply that was the way it had always been done. The forewoman nodded and then managed to get out a barely audible yes. The word seemed stuck in her throat.

Jamison placed his hands flat on the counsel table. It was his ritual. His hands would stay there until the verdicts were read. When he turned his head slightly, he could see St. Claire at the other end of the counsel table, his face almost serene. If there was any sense of uncertainty or insecurity, it didn't show. Jamison felt himself involuntarily swallowing hard as the stomach acid crept into the back of his throat.

Wallace handed the verdict forms over to his clerk. "The clerk will read the verdicts, please."

Wallace's clerk quickly scanned the verdicts before reading them. Jamison caught a subtle glance at him before she began reading. "In the case of the People of the State of California versus Alex St. Claire, to the charge of assault with a deadly weapon in Count One, we the jury find the defendant not guilty." The words rang through the silent courtroom like a funeral bell.

"To the charge of attempted rape in Count Two, we the jury find the defendant not guilty.

"To the charge of kidnapping in Count Three, we the jury find the defendant, Alex St. Claire, guilty of the lesser included charge of false imprisonment."

As the sound of the clerk's words slowly faded, there was a gap when silence filled the courtroom. Then a sudden jumble of sound began to grow around him, but it was lost on Jamison. He could feel the blood pulsing through his body. He lifted his hands from the counsel table and looked down at the puddle of water in the shape of two handprints.

They had lost everything, the assault, the attempted rape, the kidnap. False imprisonment had been a lesser charge that Wallace had insisted be put into the verdicts. Judges did that when they felt the evidence was susceptible to a different interpretation and one could not commit the greater charge without committing the lesser one. One could not kidnap a person without falsely imprisoning them, but a person could falsely imprison someone, hold them in one place against their will, without moving them and thereby kidnapping them. It was a minor charge.

The jury had found that all they were sure of was that Elizabeth Garrett was tied up without her consent. Now Jamison understood he was right when he detected a split in the jury. The women had held out for some form of guilt, something that was supportive of Garrett.

But compared to the rest of the charges that St. Claire was acquitted of, the false imprisonment was nothing. St. Claire would walk out of the courtroom a free man and McGuiness would give a sound bite to the reporters that would portray the false imprisonment charge for what it was, nothing but a slight blemish on St. Claire's good name.

He had lost. Jamison felt the blood draining from his body and heard the sounds of the courtroom returning as his mind refocused. St. Claire was thanking McGuiness.

Wallace's voice could be heard over the courtroom reaction, asking him if he wanted the jury polled, asking each juror if that was their verdict. Jamison looked vacantly around the courtroom, trying to regain his composure. "Yes, Your Honor." He could feel O'Hara's hand on his back. None of it mattered at that moment. The loneliest spot on earth had just become lonelier.

Out of the corner of his eye he saw Alex St. Claire looking at him, his mouth turned up ever so slightly into the faintest trace of a smile. Jamison knew it was meant for him alone to see.

Chapter 37

Everyone stood while the jurors filed out of the courtroom. Some of the women looked back at Jamison and gave him a nod or a sympathetic smile. None of the men looked at him. He could pretty well figure out what had happened. The women were not going to go along with any verdict unless Alex St. Claire got punished for something and the men weren't going to go along with anything unless he got acquitted. The jury had compromised on the minor charge of false imprisonment. It happened a lot more than the public realized.

"Gut justice" O'Hara called it. The women knew St. Claire did it or at least did part of it, and the men were just as convinced that it was all Elizabeth Garrett's fault. They had found common ground by agreeing on the false imprisonment but it wasn't much. It was only better than nothing, but it wasn't much better.

Jamison waited until the door to the back of the courtroom was shut and all the jurors gone. He already knew the answer but he had to ask. "Your Honor, in light of the jury's guilty verdict of false imprisonment, the People request that the defendant be remanded to custody pending sentence."

McGuiness started to stand but Wallace spoke before he could say anything. "Am I correct that there are no other charges pending?"

"No, Your Honor, there are no other charges pending." Jamison knew that Wallace was asking about the murder charges he had said were under investigation.

"Then your motion is denied, Mr. Jamison. I see no need to do that given the verdict. Sentencing will be set for a week from today." Wallace dropped his gavel against the top of the bench. The sharp rap of wood on wood punctuated his words as he rose. "Dr. St. Claire may remain free pending sentence. Court is adjourned."

A few of the deputy DAs still at work stopped by Jamison's office to offer support. None of them said anything about the verdict. They had all been there. He picked up the phone to call Beth Garrett. Her disappointment was palpable. He tried unsuccessfully to reassure her and said he would stop by soon to talk to her personally.

While Jamison was on the phone with her, O'Hara quietly stuck his head in, then slid into a chair and waited while Jamison finished the conversation.

Slowly he laid the phone back down in its cradle. The strain of the last few days and the struggle to accept the finality of the jury's decision showed in fatigue lines drawn across his face. "Bill, I don't know what more we could have done. Through this whole trial I've felt like a bug crawling across a barn floor getting shit dropped on me. I keep going over and over it in my mind. McGuiness clipped me and I couldn't stop it."

"McGuiness didn't take you down." O'Hara shook his head. "Think about it. St. Claire has been two steps ahead of everybody all along. He had an alibi prepared for this case. If we hadn't broken part of his story it would have been a straight acquittal. What you got is more than anybody else would have gotten. Just remember, we got a murder case to make. This isn't over."

He heard everything that O'Hara said, but it didn't change what Jamison already knew. "Bill, we don't have a murder case. Without the Garrett case we can't make the murder cases. She was our only surviving victim and she's the MO link. Without her, all we have are three dead women and a lot of suspicion. To prove those murders we have to put Beth Garrett back on the stand and we have to do it after a jury has walked him out the door on everything she says happened. The only way we make those murders is to come up with something that directly ties him to them, and it has to be something that he can't explain. We need hard evidence that puts him at the crime scenes and we don't have it.

"Oh, but what we do have," he added, his voice edged with irritation, "is the shitstorm we're going to have to face with that evidence that looks like it was planted in St. Claire's car. T. J. put that evidence there, and you and I both know it. We use that evidence and everything we've got will be made to look like a frame of Dr. Alex St. Claire. Like we're trying to get even because we lost this case. That evidence in the car was the one independent link. There was no defense explanation for it and we can't use it."

"We can try." O'Hara stood up abruptly. "T. J. will deny doing that and whose word is a jury going to take? You know St. Claire did those three women."

"Bill, if Wallace or any other judge thinks that evidence was planted, he's going to come after everybody. The first thing he'll do is sanction us by telling the jury that planting evidence can be considered by them in deciding whether to believe our case. He could even dismiss our case. Then on top of that a jury is going to find out that another jury didn't believe Beth Garrett and walked St. Claire out the door."

"I thought an acquittal wouldn't be admissible?"

"It isn't." Jamison coughed derisively. "But don't think because it isn't admissible that McGuiness won't find a way to drop that little bomb in front of a jury. Another thing. If St. Claire walks on the murders, we can't retry him because of double jeopardy."

O'Hara pushed his chair against the desk. "So you're saying we let him walk?"

"I'm saying that we need more evidence." Jamison stood and grabbed his jacket. "I need to go home and get some sleep. Tomorrow we've got to start figuring out how to get Wallace to send St. Claire to prison on the false imprisonment. I'm not holding my breath on that."

~

With the short setting from the verdict to sentencing, Wallace had implicitly told Jamison what to expect, but he would still argue. He sat at the counsel table and could not stop his sideways glance sufficient to take in the tranquil face of Alex St. Claire. That composure agitated him even more.

When Judge Wallace asked for the position of the district attorney on sentencing, Jamison rose and argued for a felony commitment and then sat silently while first McGuiness and then Wallace picked through the wreckage of his case.

When Wallace asked if there was anything further before sentence was pronounced, Jamison asked if the matter of the murder cases could be addressed. Wallace started to rebuke him, assuming he was going to try to use the murder cases to argue that a felony sentence was appropriate. McGuiness jumped to his feet too, raising his voice.

Jamison stood silently until everybody stopped talking. "Your Honor, I know the court is aware of our investigation and our discussions regarding arresting Dr. St. Claire for murder. I am also aware that matter may be on the court's mind. Therefore I believe it is appropriate that I indicate to the court that we will not be proceeding against Alex St. Claire at this time for reasons of insufficiency of the evidence and without prejudice to filing those charges in the future."

Wallace gave Jamison an appreciative nod and started to speak. As Wallace explained his sentence, Jamison could feel himself deflating as the breath slowly drained from him. The judge reduced the felony charge of false imprisonment to a misdemeanor, only slightly more serious than a traffic ticket. He said it was evident that the jury rejected all the serious charges and that in his view what was left didn't merit felony treatment. It was obvious to Jamison that the judge didn't believe St. Claire had tied up Garrett against her will either, but that he accepted the jury's finding of fact. His sentence was probation and credit for the time St. Claire had served when he had been in custody. In the end, his sentence was only the inconvenience of the trial.

Slowly rising from his seat at the counsel table, Alex St. Claire adjusted the cuffs of his shirt as if he had just sat through the boredom of a long meeting.

O'Hara sat in the front row of the courtroom, watching as he turned and left the courtroom. As he passed O'Hara, St. Claire inclined his head slightly. "Have a nice day, Investigator O'Hara. Perhaps we will meet again under more pleasant circumstances." The words came out with the air of a man who was dismissing a servant.

All his life, O'Hara had chased down dangerous men. He silently acknowledged a commitment to himself. One way or the other, Alex St. Claire wasn't going to make him stare again into the sightless eyes of another young woman.

Chapter 38

After the sentencing, Jamison dropped the file in his office. He didn't talk to anyone. He needed to talk to Beth. They had spoken intermittently between the verdict and sentencing but he had not seen her. She had returned to teaching, saying it was the best therapy to "get on with my life." He had spent much of his time trying to recover from the wreckage left to his caseload while the trial was in progress. But there was no question the trial had taken an emotional toll from which he hadn't recovered.

Now as he drove up in front of the school where she taught, he tried to sort out what he would say to her. For a survivor of a violent crime, for any victim, a not guilty verdict was received as a rejection that they had been telling the truth, and, as repugnant as the idea was, that the jury didn't care. Legally Jamison knew that wasn't true. The verdict meant that the jury wasn't absolutely sure what the truth was. But explaining that to Beth Garrett wasn't going to assuage her pain. She wouldn't accept some ivory tower legal concept. She would take it personally.

Jamison parked and walked toward the school entrance, stepping around children as they straggled into the parking lot. Some walked by themselves to the front of the school where buses awaited them. The younger children were herded out by their teachers. Jamison saw her helping several children board a bus.

She was silent for a moment as she examined his face. Then she asked, "Is it over?"

He smiled but he knew his expression was not reassuring. "Yes."

"Nothing happened to Alex, did it?" She didn't seem surprised or resigned.

Jamison followed her to her classroom. There was no place for him to sit. The tables and chairs were perfectly proportioned for someone who was six or seven years old, but not for an adult. Beth smiled as she recognized his discomfort. "They don't put chairs in here for grown-ups."

"Alex St. Claire is out, Beth." Jamison looked directly at her. "I couldn't stop that. I wish I could tell you that you have nothing to be concerned about but I can't. St. Claire is a dangerous man. He could be vindictive."

She took a deep breath. "Alex will leave me alone, don't you think?" Her eyes sought reassurance, a reassurance Jamison wasn't sure he could give.

"If you see him at all, call me. I'll make sure that somebody is there for you."

There was hesitation reflected in her eyes. He knew what she was going to ask. They all asked it. "Do you believe me about what happened?"

He had thought about the answer to that question. The trial and the verdict had been a roller-coaster of belief, doubt, and questions. In the end he had argued she was a victim. But he couldn't easily disregard the doubts that had recurred throughout the trial, and stubbornly lingered even now.

What he saw in front of him was a woman who wanted to be believed, who he wanted to believe, and who he had argued *should* be believed. Beth's eyes searched his face. He knew what she wanted to hear. What he hoped she couldn't tell was whether he believed it himself.

Beth reached across the space between them and placed her hand on his arm. Jamison felt the warmth of her hand as he absorbed the intimacy of the gesture. She was looking directly up at him. He had never really thought about how small and fragile she was. "It's very important to me that you believe me."

He hoped she would not perceive the moment of hesitation before he answered. During the trial, as he struggled with the conflicts in the evidence and the insidious creeping doubt that undermined his confidence in his case, Jamison had flashes of memory of when he was a boy and a singular moment when he stood in front of his mother with a clarity of vision that had stunned his adolescent mind.

His mother was a woman trapped by her dependent submission to an overpowering husband who was neither a good husband nor a good father. She had survived, he had come to realize in the stroke of an instant, because she rationalized her world and herself in order to keep a sense of dignity. At that one moment, even though he was a child and she was an adult, Jamison had realized that sometimes people create their own reality so they can cope with the world as they would have it, rather than the world as it really is. And he had known that such people need to be protected, not just from themselves but from the ones who saw that weakness and used it to their advantage. It was why he became a prosecutor.

As Elizabeth Garrett stood in front of him, asking him to believe her, the insight of his childhood gave him his answer. Whatever Elizabeth Garrett was and why didn't make any difference to his answer. Regardless of what the truth was, regardless of his doubts, in Elizabeth Garrett's world she was telling the truth. He looked down at her hand still on his arm, looked into her eyes and said what she wanted to hear. "I believe you."

Part Three

Chapter 39

O'Hara liked to tell himself that he was past being surprised by verdicts or sentences or being affected by them, but not this time. The sly smile of St. Claire stayed with him every waking moment.

He'd gone over and over each detail of the case in his mind. He couldn't let it go. Nothing had come together. It was like pieces of a puzzle where parts from another puzzle had been mixed in. O'Hara didn't like it when puzzles didn't come together. The murder cases were still out there, and as long as St. Claire was still out there O'Hara knew *he* needed to be still out there. Eventually he would get him.

In the week since the sentencing, O'Hara kept an eye on Elizabeth Garrett's school from his parked car down the street, waiting for her to go home. She usually stayed later than the other teachers but was gone by dusk. Now it was almost dark and she still hadn't left. As he sipped at a cup of long cold coffee, he reached for his cell phone to call Ernie Garcia, who also agreed with him about St. Claire, and then put it down. There was no point in calling other than to let Ernie know nothing was happening.

Ernie was aware O'Hara was keeping an eye on things. Ernie had a family. He didn't. Besides, O'Hara heard about the officer-involved-shooting call over the radio. He knew that Jamison would call Ernie out to investigate the police shooting because it was Ernie's turn. O'Hara knew that was where Ernie and Jamison would be. He was tempted to go himself, but not just yet. Not until Garrett left the school.

O'Hara hadn't said anything to Jamison about watching out for Elizabeth Garrett. He had his reasons and decided it was probably best to not share them. But O'Hara had been doing this line of work too long. He had only seen a few people like St. Claire, but he knew them. His instincts told him it was just a matter of time. Just a matter of time.

He shifted uncomfortably in the seat, the butt of his nine-millimeter automatic digging into his kidney, another reason he didn't wear the heavy automatic unless he had to. He preferred the less bulky Walther .380 in his ankle holster, but he was required to carry his department-issued nine-millimeter. The Walther was just a backup weapon, what some cops called a "throwaway." Nobody was authorized to carry one, but he did anyway. Most cops did. You only needed the backup gun when the shit hit the fan or when you had some reason you couldn't use the department-issued weapon—or didn't want to.

O'Hara yawned. Once Elizabeth was in her car, he would follow her home from a cautious distance. If he didn't see St. Claire, then that was fine. St. Claire's car was still impounded, so he didn't know what that asshole would be driving. He had tried to familiarize himself with the school neighborhood's cars, so if a car looked like it didn't belong there, he would be sure to spot it.

He knew he couldn't keep this up much longer, watching evening after evening. O'Hara's eyes strained as he scanned the school parking lot, looking to see if anything was different. Her car was the last one in the lot, caught now in the shadowed edge of a pool of illumination from the parking lot lights. Everyone else had gone home when it was still light, which was, as far as O'Hara was concerned, what Elizabeth should have done.

He reached for his coffee and then thought better of it. His bladder wasn't what it used to be. There once was a time when he could sit on a stakeout for hours without needing to find a bathroom or a discreet tree. Not anymore. He could feel growing discomfort. Sooner or later he was going to have to take a leak.

He had hoped she would have come out already. St. Claire hadn't been seen by anybody for nearly a week, nor had he shown up at the hospital. Supposedly he was taking a short leave "to get over the stress of the trial." O'Hara had run by St. Claire's home in town and the one in the country where they had found Elizabeth almost three months before. There were no signs of activity. Maybe St. Claire really was gone.

Or maybe his instincts were getting stale. O'Hara could feel the growing urgency in his bladder. Perhaps it was time to call up the doc for another prostate check. Lately he had been getting up more than once in the middle of the night. He yawned again.

Finally, O'Hara saw Elizabeth walk across the parking lot. He barely caught the movement before he saw the figure approaching Garrett's car from the side. O'Hara opened his car door. He had turned off the interior light, as he always did from old habit on a stakeout. As long as he was quiet he didn't expect anyone to see him. He moved as quickly as he could, reaching down his leg to his ankle holster before moving toward the circle of light in the parking lot. The Walther .380 came up into his target line of sight with trained precision.

Chapter 40

The body lying in the parking lot of the convenience store was covered with a yellow plastic sheet. Jamison and Ernie Garcia stood nearby. The young man beneath the yellow shroud didn't make much of a mound, his skinny legs sticking out at an odd angle from under the rumpled plastic cover. His first mistake had been walking out directly in front of a police officer who was responding to the silent alarm sent by the store clerk as he had handed over the cash in the register. His last mistake was turning toward the officer with a gun in his hand.

Police-shooting investigations rotated DA investigators and it was Ernie's turn in the box. Jamison didn't hear the radio traffic about the shooting in the parking lot at Elizabeth's school and neither did Ernie.

~

Art Puccinelli was sitting in his office at the sheriff's department when his sergeant assigned him the shooting call at the school. Realizing it was Elizabeth Garrett's school, he was at the scene in less than fifteen minutes.

Puccinelli stared at the body lying on the asphalt, oblivious to the intense forensic team lights and officers trying to control the crime scene. He couldn't honestly say that he felt any pang of sympathy. He punched in O'Hara's number on his cell and waited for voice mail to answer. O'Hara seldom picked up his phone. He would look at the message and decide whether to call back. This time was no exception. Puccinelli left a message to call and included a quick comment about the shooting. He scrolled farther up his contact list and called Ernie, who picked up after two rings.

~

"What you got, Pooch?" asked Ernie.

"Well, somebody's been busy tonight and they did us a favor."

Puccinelli wouldn't call him in the middle of an investigation just to pull his chain. He waited, but Pooch didn't make him wait long. "St. Claire waited for Elizabeth Garrett to leave school after work, or at least that's the way it looks."

Why hadn't O'Hara called? was Ernie's immediate mental reaction. He was supposed to be watching her at the school to make sure she got home safely. All of Ernie's senses went into high gear. "Shit. I'm with Matt. Is Garrett all right?"

"Yeah, she's okay. Very shaken up though. I asked her to wait in her classroom with one of the deputies."

"And St. Claire?"

Ernie detected a tone of satisfaction in Puccinelli's voice. "He's dead, Ernie. Somebody capped him twice. But they didn't wait around to admire their work. We're not sure yet exactly what happened."

Ernie took a few deep breaths to calm down. He immediately flashed on two things: O'Hara wouldn't have left Garrett's school without calling him and nobody would have gotten to Garrett without O'Hara seeing it.

Something was missing. Ernie waited for more information, but Pooch was silent. Ernie kept his voice as level as he could. "Somebody popped him? Who? Do you have any idea who? Did she see the shooter?"

"How am I supposed to know who? But whoever it was intended to get him. There's not much mistake about that. Look, there's something more. I'm assuming Jamison's with you?" Pooch hesitated. "You better get over here. Something's not right here."

Ernie recognized that what wasn't right was something Puccinelli didn't want to say, and Ernie also knew before he said anything else he needed to talk to O'Hara himself. He needed time to think. "I'll get Jamison," he told Pooch. "It might be a little while. There's been a robbery and an officer took down the perp. We've been at it for a couple of hours." He finally forced himself to ask, "Have you talked to O'Hara?"

"I figured you were busy. I heard about the officer-involved shooting, and I know you're on the DA team that handles those. I tried O'Hara first, but he isn't picking up, so I called you."

"I'll tell Jamison," Ernie said. Right now Ernie needed information. "Did St. Claire try anything?"

"No, and it doesn't look like he even got that close to her. It's not clear at this point why he was waiting for her. She's with one of our deputies right now. She wanted to call Jamison but I told her to wait. It looks like St. Claire came up to her in the lot. She heard him call her name and when she turned, there he was. That's when she heard several quick shots and St. Claire went down.

"According to her, St. Claire was at least ten to fifteen feet from her when he was shot. Whoever did it caught him square in the chest, popped him twice. Honestly, it looks like the shooter was waiting for him."

Ernie had to ask. "Did Garrett see the shooter?"

"No, said she was so scared all she saw was St. Claire. Is Jamison there?"

"He's here. I'll talk to him. We'll be there as soon as we can." Ernie waited for a dial tone and then punched in O'Hara's number. No answer. "Shit!" He approached Jamison, who was standing by the forensic people as they photographed shell casings in the area where the officer had told them he had been standing.

Ernie gently pulled on Jamison's shoulder and motioned for him to move away from the investigators working the shooting scene, even though Ernie knew that Jamison didn't like being interrupted while he was trying to put the image of a crime scene together in his mind.

"What's up?"

Before Ernie could finish, Jamison was on his own phone trying to call O'Hara. The look on his face told Ernie all he needed to know. Ernie hadn't told Jamison that O'Hara had been watching Garrett and now wasn't a good time. Ernie had a feeling it *really* wasn't a good time. Within minutes they were rolling to Garrett's school.

Jamison kept redialing O'Hara's phone while Ernie sped through the streets, his emergency lights flashing. "What the hell?" he muttered. "He must be with some woman. Otherwise he'd answer his phone if he saw that it was me or you."

Taking his eyes off the road, Ernie glanced to his right as he slowed for a jammed intersections before rolling through. "Yeah, you know Bill, probably a woman."

Then Jamison slapped his leg in disgust. "Dammit! I should have known St. Claire would come back after her. I didn't think he'd be that stupid. Bill told me that son of a bitch was supposed to be out of town."

Ernie's mind was racing. That O'Hara hadn't called spoke volumes and that the shooter hadn't been identified also spoke volumes. Right now he needed to learn about every bit of evidence that was found at the scene of the shooting. Then he would know what he had to deal with. He would try to call O'Hara again as soon as he could get away from Jamison. Normally,

O'Hara would answer the phone if he knew from caller ID that it was Ernie, but Ernie's first call had gone to voice mail, and O'Hara hadn't picked up, nor had he called back. He would try again when no one could hear. Ernie didn't know why he had a bad feeling, he just did, and for cops bad feelings seldom turned out to be for nothing.

The school parking area was lit up like a Christmas tree lot. The forensic team was already working and large lights flooded the parking area, washing out the graying asphalt to an almost white color. The flashing red-and-blue lights on patrol cars blocked the intersection leading into the school, and officers were standing in front of the milling crowd that always seemed to be attracted to flashing police lights like moths to a flame. Ernie slowed the car to a crawl as he threaded his way through the cluster of onlookers. Officers waved him by, nodding their recognition. His mind was a jumble. He had to talk to O'Hara.

Jamison was out of the car, sprinting across the parking lot toward an ambulance with its rear doors wide open. Elizabeth's silhouette was outlined by the lights from the inside of the ambulance. She was sitting in the back with a blanket wrapped around her.

Ernie watched Jamison hold his badge up as he pushed through the cordon of medical and police personnel and made his way to the ambulance. Then Ernie walked slowly to the perimeter of the crime scene where Puccinelli was standing, talking to a uniformed deputy. Brightly illuminated inside the circle of forensic staffers was the main attraction. St. Claire was lying on his back, both arms stretched straight out from his body as if he had been deliberately posed. His chest was covered with a large red stain spreading from the center like a tie-dyed shirt.

Ernie kept his focus on St. Claire for a moment before tapping Puccinelli on the shoulder. "So, Pooch, what you got?"

"Where's Jamison?" Puccinelli asked. Ernie nodded toward the ambulance. Pooch shook his head like it didn't surprise him. "According to Garrett, she saw St. Claire walking toward her just as the shots were fired. She isn't sure how many but it looks to me like two right in the chest."

Ernie asked, "And Garrett didn't see the shooter?" There was an edge of concern that was more than simple curiosity in his voice. Ernie wondered if Puccinelli's finely honed cop sense detected the nuance in his tone.

It was the second time Ernie had asked that question. Puccinelli looked at him carefully before shaking his head. "She says she was so frightened that all she could think about was protecting herself. A neighbor apparently heard the shots and called it in. All the officers on the scene found was her and, of course, him." Pooch pointed in the direction of the body.

"But get this," he said, lowering his voice to a whisper. "When those first officers arrived they told me she was rocking St. Claire back and forth."

The description stunned Ernie. "What do you mean, rocking?"

"I mean she was holding him and rocking him like a baby. She was hysterical. They had to pry her loose so they could check on St. Claire. It's possible that maybe she shot him. She had blood all over her dress and smeared on her hands, but that was consistent with her holding him. We've swabbed her hands for gunshot and metal residue, and that was negative. We haven't found a gun, although maybe she dumped it.

"But I don't think she capped him. My money's on her old man. I'm guessing he's the one that did it. Can't say I blame him. Whoever did it did the world a favor."

Ernie pulled out his phone and started walking away. He was going to try O'Hara one more time. "Did she say anything else?"

"Yeah, and you and Jamison aren't going to like it." Pooch gave a short laugh and shook his head. "She told the officer who pulled her away from St. Claire—and this is her exact quote—'Alex wasn't going to hurt me. He loved me.'"

Ernie could feel his blood pressure skyrocket. "That has to be wrong." Then he turned away and punched in O'Hara's number. He walked well outside the perimeter of police tape to get out of range of Pooch or anybody else who might hear too much. This time O'Hara picked up on the second ring.

Ernie didn't hear anything. All he could tell was that somebody answered the phone. After a long silence, O'Hara finally spoke. "Yeah, Ernie. What's going on?" From the sound of O'Hara's voice, Ernie could tell that he was fishing. Normally O'Hara would just say "What" and he didn't bother with names or greetings.

"Bill, where the hell have you been?" Ernie tried to remain calm. "Do you know what's going on?"

"Not a clue. Tell me." From the sound of O'Hara's voice, he didn't seem particularly interested. That wasn't the O'Hara he knew. Besides, Ernie knew Puccinelli had called him and left the message about the shooting.

"Tell me?" Ernie shouted into the phone. Surprised by his sudden burst of anger, he lowered his voice and continued. "St. Claire came to Garrett's school and somebody popped him as he walked up to her in the parking lot.

"No shit? Somebody got that son of a bitch."

It didn't sound to Ernie like O'Hara was asking a question or even that he was surprised. "Bill, where were you? You were supposed to be watching her."

It wasn't what O'Hara said. It was what he didn't say that put all of Ernie's senses on alert. "I had to do some stuff. We haven't seen St. Claire at the school or anyplace else for a week."

Ernie knew O'Hara wasn't leveling. There was only one reason Ernie could think of for that. He decided to back off. This wasn't the time to ask questions.

Carefully measuring his words, Ernie said, "Yeah, well you're missing the big show. He's lying in the parking lot like a rag doll with two rounds in his chest."

"What else? Did she see the shooter?" O'Hara's voice was unnaturally calm even for O'Hara. Ernie understood O'Hara was telegraphing he needed information, not questions.

"I haven't talked to her, but she told the first officers responding that she didn't see anything. She said that St. Claire walked up to her, and then she heard shots and that was it.

"Oh, and get this. Art Puccinelli is the on-scene detective. He says that when the first officers got to the scene, Garrett was holding St. Claire in her arms and rocking him. She kept saying Alex would never hurt her and that he loved her." He could hear O'Hara breathing but there was no response.

"Bill, you there?" Ernie wiped his face. He could feel the sweat even in the chill air. "I'm saying I think maybe we been played, brother." He waited to see if O'Hara would say anything more.

But O'Hara didn't react to the idea that something was still going on between Garrett and St. Claire. That was enough right there to tell Ernie that O'Hara already knew more than he was letting on.

"Yeah, I'm here." O'Hara's voice was cautious. He didn't say anything else.

Ernie's mind was a jumble, and he filled the silence with a rush of words. "Listen, let me get back to you. As soon as I know more I'll call you, okay?" Ernie decided he had to ask the next question. "You want to come here to the school and take a look?" He waited, knowing that the answer would tell him what he was already afraid of.

"No, you handle it. Just keep me in the loop, okay? I've got some personal stuff I'm dealing with," he said, then clicked off.

Ernie didn't need the answer tattooed to his forehead. O'Hara had been the one who shot St. Claire, and he didn't want anyone to know he was the shooter. There were only a couple of reasons why O'Hara would be concerned about an internal affairs investigation of his killing St. Claire, and neither of them were good. Ernie concluded that for now he needed to figure out how to protect O'Hara if he could or—and the question sat at the back of his mind—*if* he should. And he would have to do it without saying anything to anybody, especially Jamison. Ernie liked Jamison, but Jamison was a prosecutor and a lawyer. If Jamison knew that O'Hara pulled the trigger, he would do what prosecutors do, and that wouldn't be good for O'Hara. He made the decision quickly. It was better for the time being to leave Jamison out of it.

Ernie didn't hear Puccinelli walk up behind him. The tap on his shoulder startled him. Pooch's hands went up in silent apology when Ernie turned with the phone still against his ear. Pooch asked, "That O'Hara? Tell him that he missed his opportunity. Somebody else got that son of a bitch first." Pooch motioned for Ernie to follow. "We got something."

Pooch motioned for Ernie to walk with him to the edge of the lot. "Right there. See them?" A forensic technician was putting a small yellow flag next to a shell casing. A few feet away another casing was already marked along with a third. The brass casings glinted dully in the lights from the forensic van. Pooch leaned in. "Looks to be from a small automatic. My guess is a .380 maybe. Walther PPK or maybe a Beretta. The angle's right. Appears like three shots were fired and one missed. Hopefully we can match up the extractor marks made when the casings were ejected but we've got to find the gun. If we're lucky we can lift a fingerprint off of one of the casings, though I'm not sure how much enthusiasm I have about that. Hard to feel much incentive to get the guy that popped this asshole, but I guess that can't go in the report."

"Yeah, hard to feel much." Ernie could feel the lurch in his stomach. He didn't need to see the gun. O'Hara always carried that damn Walther PPK as a backup. Ernie had teased him that it was a pimp gun, but O'Hara would always say if it was good enough for James Bond, it was good enough for him.

Looking at St. Claire's bloodied body, it was clear that both rounds were closely spaced. Ernie mused that one round must have gone wide to explain the third casing. The slug could be anywhere out there. They wouldn't find it tonight and probably never. Ernie breathed a sigh of relief; at least Bill hadn't used his nine-millimeter. All of those were department-issue and everyone had ejected casings and fired slugs on file for matches. They would need to have the gun before they could make a match, although they wouldn't need the gun if they got a print match off a shell casing. He put his hand in his pocket and began fingering the cell phone nervously.

The fact that O'Hara did it and he didn't use his nine-millimeter also raised red flags. A cop didn't reach for his backup weapon unless he'd lost his main weapon or he didn't want to use it. And Ernie was damned certain that if O'Hara used his backup it was because he wanted to use it instead of his traceable department-issued nine-millimeter.

"We got something else too." Pooch pulled a plastic bag out of his pocket and held the bag up in the light. Inside it was a syringe with the needle capped. "It'll be interesting to see what's in it. Found it in St. Claire's pocket."

Pressing for information, Ernie asked, "Anything in St. Claire's hand, a weapon of any kind?"

"Nothing." Pooch shook his head. "If St. Claire was going to hurt Garrett or try and take her by physical force, that isn't apparent from anything we have so far."

All Ernie could think about was O'Hara. The picture wasn't clear in his mind, but he could already see the outline. Bill didn't want anybody to know he was the shooter, either because he saw something in Garrett's reaction that told him he had misinterpreted the situation after he fired and the shooting would be found unjustified, or—though Ernie cringed at the thought—maybe O'Hara just decided to take the opportunity and rid everyone of St. Claire.

But if it was just a bad shoot, Ernie felt like O'Hara should have stayed and weathered the internal affairs investigation. At the same time, Ernie couldn't fault him. He didn't know what he would have done himself, whether he would have stayed if he'd been the shooter. But Ernie also knew if O'Hara simply took the opportunity to rid the world of St. Claire, then the shooting would be impossible to explain away. A bad shoot, done without adequate justification for deadly force, was the nightmare of any cop. You made a split-second decision to shoot and a mistake could cost you everything. Fire too soon and it was unjustified; fire too late and the victim gets hurt and everybody asks why you didn't act sooner. Either way the cop took the fall. From what Ernie could see it looked at the very least like a bad shoot and at the worst—Ernie didn't want to think about that.

So far, it looked like what O'Hara should have done was yell at St. Claire to let him know he was there and that if St. Claire tried anything, he would shoot him. Then if St. Claire tried to hurt Garrett, there would be some justification. Even if you were a cop, especially if you were a cop, you had to have justification when you pulled the trigger. What rang more alarm bells in Ernie's mind was that there was no indication O'Hara yelled anything before he pulled the trigger.

If it wasn't a justified shoot, the least that would happen was that O'Hara would end up losing his job and maybe his pension. The worst that would happen is that he could end up being charged. And if it looked like he just took the opportunity to blow away someone, even a piece of trash like St. Claire, well, even being a cop picking off the worst kind of trash wouldn't help O'Hara.

Ernie shook his head. It was also likely that in a matter of seconds O'Hara would have realized from her actions there was a possibility that Garrett and St. Claire were still involved, and, if so, then she wouldn't back him up. If what O'Hara had really done was kill her lover, then O'Hara was going to end up on the short end. All Garrett had said so far was that she hadn't seen the shooter. What a sick, twisted mess this is, Ernie thought.

The sound of his name startled Ernie, but not nearly as much as the face of the man who called out to him from behind the yellow crime scene tape. Tom McGuiness stood there wearing a dark windbreaker. His hair looked like he had combed it in a rush with his fingers. Aside from his surprise, the second thought that went through Ernie's mind was that the defense lawyer didn't look anything at all like he looked in the courtroom. He looked like a regular guy.

What the hell is he doing here? McGuiness was motioning for him to come over. What lawyer bullshit, Ernie thought as he made his way to

McGuiness. Ernie thought with a flicker of satisfaction, Well, he won't be collecting any more fees from St. Claire.

Ernie followed the lawyer to an area away from the circle of milling gawkers and crowd-control cops. "What are you doing here, McGuiness? Are you guys just like vultures and no matter where you are, you can just tell when something goes down that you can feed on?"

The defense attorney's expression changed almost imperceptibly. Ernie could see that he had hit a nerve and that it stung. He regretted his comment. "I'm sorry. Long night. Look, what can I do for you?"

"Is that St. Claire over there?" McGuiness looked over toward the parking lot. "Did somebody shoot him?"

"That's right. How'd you know?"

"Let's just say I got a call. It doesn't matter. Do you know who the shooter is?"

"If I did, I couldn't tell you. Do you have something you want to tell me?"

"Look, Ernie, I know you guys think all defense lawyers are assholes." McGuiness sighed heavily. "Just tell me. Did she shoot him? Did Garrett shoot St. Claire?"

What difference did it make? Ernie thought silently for a few seconds. "It doesn't look like it. We'll know more later. They're still processing the scene. But I guess if anybody had a right to shoot the son of a bitch, she did."

McGuiness replied carefully. "Maybe yes, maybe no."

"What's that supposed to mean?"

"Look, Ernie, I do a job. You do a job. Give me credit that I don't always like everything I do either. Did you check her purse?"

"For what?"

"For a gun."

"There was no gun in her purse and they've swabbed her hands but I'm guessing that no gunshot residue is going to show." Ernie's eyes fixed on McGuiness. "Don't tell me you're here to see if you can pick up a client?"

"Take a breath, will you?" McGuiness continued. "Just listen to me. I have to leave before the press sees me. I don't want any connection to me. Just listen. She's not being honest with you. And its time you woke up to that. She's never been honest with you or Jamison."

Ernie stepped back and started to turn away from McGuiness. He'd heard enough of that crap during the trial. McGuiness grabbed his arm. "Listen for a damn minute. I'm saying that St. Claire's dead now, but even dead men still have the attorney-client privilege. So what I say to you stays with us. You can't use it and I'll deny it. Understood?

"What I'm trying to tell you is that there's something here nobody's seeing. I don't know if she shot him or not, but I'm saying that I wouldn't be surprised if she expected him to be here. You think about that. I can't say a lot and I have to get out of here. But, Ernie, I'm not the asshole you think I am. Don't think I didn't know what St. Claire was. St. Claire scared me more than any client I've ever had."

McGuiness walked a short distance away before turning his head. "Ernie? One more thing. Tell Jamison he needs to find out who Bobby Allison is. Got that? Tell him the one from the trial." He turned his back on Ernie and walked away from the crowd.

Ernie stood in the shadows thinking, Bobby Allison? He looked over at the ambulance and the two figures outlined by the lights from the inside of the ambulance. Garrett was leaning against Jamison. Screw McGuiness. Now wasn't the time to talk to Matt. He looked around for Pooch. One of the forensic technicians pointed and told him Puccinelli was looking at the victim's car.

Ernie could see flashlights moving around a black sedan. He walked over. Pooch was fingering keys that had been pulled from St. Claire's pocket.

"This is his car. It fits the keys. We'll take the car downtown. I want to be there when we look through it."

Ernie thought again about McGuiness. He pointed in the direction of Garrett's car. "Maybe you should impound her car also."

Pooch's face was hard to read in the dark. There was a pause before he replied, "If you think so."

It wasn't lost on Ernie that Pooch didn't ask why.

Chapter 41

It had been a long night for Puccinelli. After the coroner moved St. Claire's body, he had left the crime scene to the forensic people. There were reports to write and he had to put the situation together in his head. He hadn't made much progress. Now his third cup of coffee was cold. He rubbed his eyes. He was way too old not to feel the effects of all-night investigations, and he still had St. Claire's autopsy ahead of him later that morning. Jamison and Ernie were going to meet him there.

There was a partial print on one casing that had been retrieved from the scene, but prints hadn't been run yet. They were waiting for his directions. Pooch put the papers down and thought, That son of a bitch deserved what he got. Still, that didn't mean somebody could just shoot him. His logical focus was still on Garrett's father, and if the father did it, Puccinelli didn't blame him. He would want to do the same thing. But after the father arrived at the crime scene, Puccinelli observed Mike Garrett's stunned reaction for himself and decided to put off talking to him until later in the day.

But there were other things scratching at his cop instincts, things that were equally troubling, things he couldn't quite put his finger on yet. Puccinelli had fired at enough targets in his life, both paper and human, that he knew whoever fired those shots was someone who knew how to shoot, someone who had likely fired at a lot of targets himself, both paper and human. The other thing that was nagging at his cop instincts was that the shooter's hand had remained steady when he fired. A handgun wasn't a rifle; if it was pointed a hair off, or if the gun hand trembled a bit, or if the shooter was too far away from the target, the more likely the shooter was to miss. For most people, Mike Garrett probably among them, handguns were really only effective close in. Shots fired from more than ten or fifteen feet, even for an experienced shooter, often missed their target in actual shooting situations. Human beings weren't paper targets; they moved.

Only the most experienced shooter could hold a handgun steady enough in a shooting to place two rounds like that. Pooch's instinctive reaction told him that it was someone with the trained reaction of a person who could fire a gun with focused intensity, a man who could pull the trigger with the deliberateness that disappeared from most men under stress.

Pooch experienced a sickening stab of denial. He didn't want to know who pulled this trigger because he wouldn't like the answer. There were only a few people he knew who could fire a Beretta or a Walther PPK with that kind of accuracy and they were all cops, and only one of those cops had any purpose being out there when St. Claire got shot.

As far as Puccinelli was concerned, St. Claire deserved what he got but he knew there was a big difference between what St. Claire deserved and what the law would permit. Whoever did this wasn't going to be able to get away with arguing it was justified. The bastard deserving what he got wasn't legal justification. The fact that the shooter left the scene also told Puccinelli that whoever killed St. Claire knew that what they had done wasn't going to be excusable in the eyes of the law. In the eyes of gut justice maybe, but not in the eyes of the law. This had all the appearances of being what some cops referred to as .44-caliber due process—but in this case it was a .380.

Somebody would end up being St. Claire's last victim, either for making the mistake of firing too soon or for taking justice into his own hands. Either way it wasn't something Puccinelli could ignore, no matter how much he might agree with the result.

He picked up a routing memo for the forensic people, made a quick note, and walked it over to the detective division secretary. "Please give this to the lab." He had asked them to leave fingerprinting the casings alone for the time being. At first he wasn't sure why he did that. Maybe he didn't really want to know. He realized there was no "maybe" involved; part of him dreaded getting an answer.

He headed over to St. Claire's autopsy. Later he would have to talk again to Beth Garrett to get a more detailed statement. There were questions he wanted to ask, but he hadn't wanted to ask in front of Jamison. They could wait. Maybe it was better to wait. It was evident that Jamison had lost his objectivity. For now he was expected at the coroner's office. Usually Puccinelli hated autopsies but he had no qualms about seeing St. Claire on a steel slab.

~

At nine thirty in the morning Ernie picked Jamison up at his apartment for the trip down to the morgue. He still hadn't said anything to Jamison about Garrett's reaction at the crime scene, her rocking and cradling of St. Claire's dying body. He'd been waiting for a good time, but from Jamison's grim expression it still didn't seem like that might be now either.

Besides, at the moment Ernie's focus was on O'Hara. Personally at this point he really didn't give a damn about Elizabeth Garrett, and what he had heard the night before hadn't improved his opinion of her. He kept his thoughts to himself because he wasn't sure where Jamison's head was at.

Neither man said a lot as they drove to the morgue. Aside from the fatigue of being up most of the night, they were both absorbed in their own thoughts. After several minutes of silence, Jamison asked Ernie if he heard from O'Hara. Jamison said he had been calling but still hadn't gotten an answer.

The only thing that surprised Ernie was how long it had taken Jamison to bring up O'Hara. Concealing his apprehension, Ernie told him he had finally gotten through and that O'Hara just said he was catching up on "a personal relationship." Ernie regretted that he wasn't being candid and rationalized it as being in O'Hara's best interests. What Jamison didn't know couldn't hurt him—or O'Hara.

Jamison's eyes narrowed slightly at Ernie's explanation, but he kept to himself any questions he might have had about why O'Hara would miss this, the autopsy of the man who for almost two months had been their unrelenting focus, a man everyone knew O'Hara detested.

Ernie's instincts told him that Jamison's not asking more about his conversation with O'Hara was a deliberate decision. Both Ernie and Jamison could understand that everybody needed a little personal time, but everybody wasn't O'Hara—absence didn't fit with O'Hara. Then there was the secondary flash of cop cynicism. Maybe the kid knew more about this case than Ernie thought. Either way, he wasn't going to push to find out what Jamison was really thinking. Once he opened that subject there would be no turning back for Jamison. He was relieved that Jamison remained silent.

During the drive Ernie did mention his encounter with McGuiness. Jamison seemed surprised by the unexpected appearance of the defense attorney's seeking an off-the-record conversation. But, after all, it was his client—now former client—lying on the ground.

Aware that he was about to bring up a sensitive issue, Ernie hesitated before saying, "Amigo, McGuiness said some things that I didn't understand. He repeated several times that she wasn't what she seemed."

"That's it?" From the tone of Jamison's voice it was clear to Ernie that Jamison wasn't impressed by this information, but he went on. "McGuiness said something else, Matt. He said to tell you 'Find out who Bobby Allison was.' I don't know what he was talking about. Do you?"

"Bobby Allison?" Jamison looked at Ernie with a puzzled expression. "In the trial there was a letter that St. Claire claimed Beth Garrett had sent him, but it didn't have a front page. She said it had been written to a college boyfriend named Bobby Allison. I think St. Claire somehow got his hands on it and kept it all these years. It was just one more thing he used to twist everything." Jamison lapsed into silence and dropped the subject. Ernie said nothing more until they got to the morgue, but he could sense that the information from McGuiness seemed to unnerve Jamison.

When Puccinelli walked through the swinging doors of the morgue the body of Alex St. Claire was stretched out on the metal table, the handsome patrician features sagging with the flaccidity of death. He approached Jamison and Ernie, who had arrived before him. "St. Claire hasn't looked this good since the day we arrested him."

Dr. Gupta stood next to the autopsy table. He was unusually quiet but everyone assumed that he wasn't used to working on one of his own. The Y-shaped incision down the center of St. Claire's body had been made after the wound tracks had been probed and photographed. Ernie's only comment was that the grouping was good for what he guessed were "snap" shots, quickly fired rounds. Both rounds had torn holes right through the heart. The two .380 slugs were sitting in a stainless steel bowl. The pathologist straightened up and put down his scalpel.

Puccinelli offered his opinion. "I'd say the shooter was at least twenty feet away. He had to be closer than forty feet to make that shot with a Walther or Beretta, which is what I think he used. Since Garrett said she couldn't tell much about the shooter I'd guess that he was still in the shadows, so more than twenty feet but less than forty. Still a hell of a good shot, especially with a second so close to the first. You'd almost guess it was a pro."

Pooch's eyes drilled into Ernie when he made that last comment. "So how come we haven't heard anything from O'Hara? Not like him to miss something like this," Puccinelli asked pointedly.

Ernie shook his head, avoiding Puccinelli's direct gaze. "We think he's with some woman. Couldn't get anything specific out of him."

Puccinelli nodded absently. His mind drifting back to speculation he really didn't want to consider. He looked back at the two slugs sitting in the bowl. He looked at Ernie and caught him staring back at him before turning his head away. That brief exchange of glances between them told Puccinelli all he didn't want to know. Cops acquired a silent language that they all shared. If he wanted a direct answer, now he knew he would have to ask. But he didn't want to, and even if he did ask, he wasn't sure he would get an honest answer. The thought began to burn a hole in his gut.

Puccinelli motioned Ernie to the corner of the autopsy room, pulling him aside away from Jamison. He kept his voice down and leaned in. "You suggested we have Elizabeth Garrett's car impounded last night and you left without saying why. I'm going to have to go talk to her right after leaving here. I have a feeling you know more than I do."

Ernie looked back over his shoulder. Jamison was talking to Gupta but he kept glancing over in their direction. Ernie kept his voice down also, waiting until Jamison's focus moved back to the body. "Pooch, last night Tom McGuiness came to the shooting scene." The startled expression on Pooch's face told Ernie that he had caught Pooch unaware. Ernie did have a twinge of guilt. Withholding this from Puccinelli until this moment was inappropriate. They were in this together as investigators and they needed to share. "McGuiness said that we don't have the whole picture on Garrett and St. Claire. He's the one who tipped me that we needed to look in her car."

"Why would he do that?" his voice came out loudly.

"Something I should know?" Jamison's head snapped in the direction of the two men.

Ernie shook his head. "No, nothing. Just a few loose ends." His tone signaled to Puccinelli that this was a conversation that had to take place when Jamison wasn't around.

~

On the trip back to the office, Jamison was unusually quiet. He was deep in thought. When Gupta had pulled the .380 slugs out of St. Claire, he had dropped them into the steel bowl with a sound that reverberated in Jamison's mind. A Walther PPK fired a .380 slug. Cops carried nine-millimeter automatics. They didn't carry weapons that fired a .380. But he knew someone who did.

Following the autopsy, Puccinelli hadn't been in his office five minutes when Ernie arrived. "First off, Pooch, on McGuiness, I'm sorry I didn't fill you in right away on his being out there." He left the apology at that before continuing, grateful that Pooch was evidently willing to give him a pass. "McGuiness didn't say much except that maybe we don't have a complete picture of the relationship between Garrett and St. Claire. McGuiness isn't stupid. I don't think he believes winning is everything. I could tell he didn't like St. Claire and it's like he's telling us that if we look deeper we may find the answers we need. So that's why I suggested her car be impounded."

Puccinelli seemed surprised. "So you want me to get a warrant for her car? And I'm supposed to say what to the judge?"

"You say that we don't know who the shooter is. We don't have the gun and she was the last person to see St. Claire alive. If we can't get the warrant, then we ask her permission. But I'm not sure she'll give us permission. Warrant first, okay?"

It was only a momentary reaction but Puccinelli caught the shift in Ernie's eyes. Ernie was holding back just like a perp who was deciding how much to say in an interrogation. "And you're not going to say anything to Jamison? You're not going to tell him what we're doing?" Ernie shook his head.

Puccinelli had held back long enough. "You and I both know she didn't shoot him. Whoever did was an expert with a handgun. There's only one person I know who carries a Walther .380 and can use it that well. Where's O'Hara?" Puccinelli waited. Ernie's silence confirmed his suspicion. "Have you asked O'Hara?"

Before giving an answer Ernie hesitated and seemed to focus on some nonexistent spot over Pooch's head. "I'm not going to ask until I know the rest of the answers." And with that point emphasized, Ernie walked out the door without any further comment.

By midday, Puccinelli had the warrant for Garrett's car and was on his way to the fenced area next to the forensic lab. The car St. Claire had been driving the night before, a black Ford Crown Victoria, sat in the enclosed area. He walked over to the gate in the fence that surrounded the area. There were two other vehicles in there also. One was Garrett's. The other was St. Claire's Lexus, still unreleased even though McGuiness had been demanding it after the trial. They had hoped they could stall and not release it until after the murders were resolved. That certainly looked like a dead end now.

Charlie Faxon, a forensic tech, was waiting with the keys. He unlocked the gate and followed Puccinelli inside. Faxon handed Puccinelli a set of latex gloves to wear during the examination of the Crown Victoria. Charlie looked the large sedan over, observing, "It looks just like your duty car, Pooch. Or like one of the cars that the highway patrol drives."

Puccinelli acknowledged that Charlie was right. It looked just like one he drove himself except that his was white and highway patrol cars didn't have white door panels and a front license plate. So the thought occurred to him that if this was the car St. Claire used with Garrett or the others it might explain why they mistook it for a police car. But they had run a registration check on St. Claire and the only car that had shown up was the Lexus. So this was something unexpected. Maybe St. Claire always used a rental. He would see.

Puccinelli opened the door and did a quick visual search. There wasn't anything clearly visible. The car was very neat. He lifted the center console. There were what looked like bills. He shuffled through them. Several appeared to be tax assessor bills from the look of them as well as some utility bills. The obvious thought struck him that even people like St. Claire had to pay taxes—well, not anymore.

The glove box was clean, with current registration and insurance papers. Nothing else. Puccinelli looked at the vehicle registration. It was held in the name of something called the St. Claire Trust and the address was to a post office box. That explained why they hadn't picked it up when they did a registration check and found only one, the Lexus owned by St. Claire, under his name. Puccinelli sucked in his breath hard. "What the hell is the St. Claire Trust?"

He slid his hand under the seats. Nothing. Puccinelli pulled his body back out of the car and handed the keys to Faxon. "Charlie, open the trunk, will you?" He handed over the bundle of bills and the registration. "Bag these up. Have the forensic boys go over the car with a fine-tooth comb."

The trunk was just as clean as the car. Puccinelli pulled up the mat covering the spare tire, his gaze moving across the jack and lug wrench before he stopped. He turned to Faxon. "You see that? What's that?"

Faxon leaned into the trunk, keeping his hands at his sides to avoid touching anything unnecessarily. "It looks like an aerosol can for spray paint. But what's that thing on top?"

It looked to Puccinelli like the top had a rubber cup on it. When he got closer to it, he saw that it wasn't a cup. It looked more like one of those little masks that doctors put over their faces in surgery, only this one was rubber or plastic. He looked up at Faxon. "Do you know what this is?"

Faxon peered over Puccinelli's shoulder. "I don't, but whatever it is, it doesn't belong here." There were no markings on the can but when Puccinelli looked at it more closely it looked heavier, sturdier than a normal aerosol can. He told the tech, "Take some pictures of it. Bag it up also. Be careful with it. I want to see if we can get any prints off of it." He straightened back up. "Get me the pictures as soon as you can, Charlie. I want to show them to Gupta."

He had a feeling. Maybe Gupta would know what it was. Maybe it was nothing, but it didn't look like nothing. He pulled the trunk carpet farther back. There were black leather gloves and a box of latex gloves next to a light with a power cord that would go into a cigarette lighter. The light was just a droplight that you could buy at any hardware or automotive store except for one small change. The light had a red bulb. As it often turned out, the simplest explanation was usually the correct one. St. Claire could plug in the light and at night it would look like a red light. Ernie had guessed right when he testified at the trial. They just didn't have the right car. Nobody would question it because once people saw the red light they believed a cop was behind them. People didn't look at details. "Photograph it and check it for prints." He pulled out his phone to call Ernie.

Minutes later Ernie arrived to begin their search of Garrett's car in the impound lot. The discovery of the red light would help them close the case on St. Claire but it wouldn't help answer all the questions they both still had. Ernie said, "You got the warrant?"

Puccinelli held up the sheaf of papers in his hand. "Yeah, I went to the trial judge. Figured that would be fastest. Judge Wallace just flipped through the pages, looked up at me, and signed it. Never asked a question, just shook his head. So let's start digging."

~

After Ernie dropped him at the DA's office, Jamison had tried to work. It had been all Jamison could do not to lose his focus. He'd learned that

O'Hara had called the front desk saying he was taking some vacation time. Jamison had left multiple messages on O'Hara's phone, but nothing had been returned and now Ernie was treating him like a mushroom too, keeping him in the dark and feeding him bullshit. He decided to go check on Garrett to keep his mind off of his deepening concerns, and his mind off of what he might do if he actually knew the truth.

Jamison sat at the kitchen table of the Garrett home, watching as Beth's mother moved around making coffee. Beth was resting. The strain of the trial and now St. Claire's killing had taken a lot out of her. It would take a lot out of anybody. He felt guilty about doubting her pleas to believe her. St. Claire had come after her again. At this point the question was who had stopped St. Claire?

On his way over to Beth's, Jamison had replayed their conversation at her school before the shooting again and again in his mind. He had tried to be impersonal but it had been very personal. He hadn't spoken to her again until St. Claire's shooting. When he thought carefully about it, he knew that just as he had argued in court, everything Elizabeth said was possible, including her explanation about the photograph he had argued was taken from a distance. He also knew better than anybody that some of the things St. Claire used to prove she was a liar were themselves shown to be a lie. But one thing clearly wasn't a lie. St. Claire had returned and gone after her, in a darkened parking lot long after her work day had ended.

Ann Garrett moved with the practiced grace of someone who could close her eyes and still find everything in her kitchen. There were still questions, little things that nagged at Jamison for reasons only his subconscious might understand. He hadn't stopped thinking about what McGuiness had told Ernie about digging into who Bobby Allison was. Everything had happened so fast at the trial he hadn't questioned Beth's explanation. It had appeared at the time to be just one more suspect piece of evidence ginned up by St. Claire. But he didn't really think Tom McGuiness would have passed that on to Ernie for no reason, especially now that St. Claire was dead. While he didn't want to, Jamison planned to call McGuiness later in the day and see what he was talking about. But for now he decided he would ask Ann Garrett. If anyone would know who Allison was it was going to be her.

"So, Mrs. Garrett, does Beth ever hear from this former college boyfriend of hers, Robert Allison? Bobby Allison?"

Mrs. Garrett turned with a startled expression. "Who?"

"Robert Allison. I was wondering, is this guy still around?" Jamison smiled, hoping he had asked the question in a way that didn't seem like more than idle curiosity. He realized that neither the mother nor the father were likely to know about the name coming up during the trial because as witnesses they weren't permitted to be present during the testimony.

Ann Garrett shook her head. She looked like she might say something and then shook her head again. "That can't be right. You must be mistaken." She hesitated. "You should ask Elizabeth." Mrs. Garrett turned back toward the coffee maker and picked up a cup. Whatever she thought about saying, Jamison could tell she wanted to keep it to herself.

He got up from the table. His stomach was churning. "Mrs. Garrett, please tell Beth I was here. I need to get back to the office." There was something about the reaction of Beth's mother that told him he really needed to find out the answer to his question. But clearly it wasn't going to come from her, or from Beth either. The next question was why?

Chapter 42

Puccinelli and Ernie didn't want to tear Beth Garrett's car apart. Uncertain about what they were looking for, they quickly realized nothing was inside that didn't belong there—some clothes in an overnight bag and a few other personal items, nothing out of the ordinary.

While they searched her car they talked about finding the light and the aerosol can. Ernie was thoughtful. "I don't know. St. Claire was obsessed with her. Finding that light helps explain what she said happened." Ernie pulled at the trunk carpet to check the compartment where the spare was. A brown manila packet was slid into the tire well next to the tire.

Ernie lifted the packet out. He shuffled through the photographs it contained, holding them where Puccinelli could see. There were photographs from what looked like high school and some of Elizabeth and St. Claire. Puccinelli asked, "Why would she have any photographs of that asshole now?"

Ernie looked at each one individually. He studied several before he slid them back into the plastic packet. "Let me take the photographs. I want to take a closer look at them. Maybe it'll trigger something." Pooch looked dubious about releasing evidence. Ernie gave him a lopsided grin. "Hey, don't worry about it. St. Claire's dead and whoever shot him sure wasn't looking for anything else. I'll take care of them."

Puccinelli stood there watching Ernie, waiting for him to say something. Both of them knew that whatever was said at this point would take them down a road neither wanted to travel. Who the shooter was still had to be resolved. Pooch finally spit it out. "Look, I don't give a rat's ass about St. Claire, but O'Hara's another story."

Ernie's face was a blank. Puccinelli could tell there was no way Ernie would offer anything up without a direct question.

Finally, Puccinelli decided to ask it. "O'Hara was out there wasn't he?"

Ernie bit his lip, struggling to come up with an answer. "If he was, then you know it was to make sure nothing happened to Garrett."

He hesitated but Pooch had to ask. "If he was out there, would anybody else know?"

"Only me. He would tell me." Pooch didn't ask if O'Hara had told him.

Ernie avoided Puccinelli's gaze and looked at the pictures before he blurted out his thoughts, his voice raised in frustration. "That bastard got what he deserved. Maybe they thought they were saving her. Maybe they didn't. Either way, if they made a mistake, it would be a real screwed-up system if it meant that a good man would go down for killing a bad man a second too soon. Right?"

Silent for a moment while he mulled over the answer, it didn't take Puccinelli long to make a decision. "Good enough for me."

So there it was. They had forged an unspoken decision. There would be consequences, including some they knew they couldn't predict. Ernie felt like he could ask because they both needed to know. "Are there any prints on those shell casings?"

Puccinelli shook his head slowly. "There looks like maybe a partial print." It all depended on how the person had pushed the shell into the magazine of the weapon. He had looked at it already and caught the faint outlines of a partial print.

Puccinelli thought for a moment about what it would mean if O'Hara's prints were identified on the casing. He still had control of the casings. The answer came to him quickly. "I think I may have screwed up with the casings. Hey, shit happens. It's not like anybody really wants to find out who shot St. Claire."

Ernie nodded. Somehow the casings, or at least the one with the print, would get misplaced. He didn't need to hear anything else. "Somebody's got to talk to Jamison."

"He's your boy. You talk to him."

~

As he walked back into the forensic lab, Puccinelli saw Charlie Faxon, the forensic tech who had helped process St. Claire's car and was working on the crime scene evidence, including the spent casings from the parking lot. "I need to see those shell casings." Earlier he had told forensics to hold off on processing what looked like a partial print on the brass of one casing with enough print ridges and lines to possibly make a positive print and maybe not. Faxon shrugged and handed over the sealed plastic bag, the brass casings glinting in the fluorescent lights of the lab. "What do you need them for?"

"The DA investigator wants to see them. I'll have them back within an hour." He looked down at the evidence seal. His initials were on it but so were the technicians. "Don't worry. I'll be careful. When I get back you can run the prints."

"Nothing more to do." Faxon gave Puccinelli a knowing look. "I saw a partial and ran it. I saw that you wanted to hold up but I had the time and figured you just wanted to make sure we got to other stuff first." He held up the bag, the tarnished brass casings glinting inside the plastic evidence bag. "Tell O'Hara he needs to be more careful."

Puccinelli could feel a cold lump in his stomach. He forced himself to appear uninterested. "Why?"

"Because O'Hara screwed up at the crime scene. That partial is his, or I should say there are enough points of comparison on it that it fits his print, not enough to say absolutely, but who the hell else could it be? I couldn't believe that when the print came up. You guys know better than that. Why didn't he have gloves on?"

Puccinelli felt the tension diminish. Now he realized Faxon thought O'Hara had been working at the crime scene and picked up a casing without gloves on. That was how Faxon assumed O'Hara's print had gotten on the casing. Puccinelli's mind raced through the crime scene facts. It was an explanation that might work. Now that O'Hara's print had been identified, it would have to work. He could feel his heart thumping. "I don't know. He knows better." He paused, almost afraid to ask. "There were no other prints on the casings?"

"Nothing. No DNA either. So maybe it won't make any difference but he needs to be more careful. He really could have screwed up a piece of evidence."

"Look, you keep this." Puccinelli handed the bag back. "No reason to take this over to the DA's office and let them screw it up more." He kept his voice as steady as he could. "Just give me the report as soon as you have it. Don't have it typed, just your written memo will be sufficient."

Faxon smiled and shook his head again. "Okay, not to worry. I've known O'Hara a long time. He's a good guy. Don't want to get him in trouble for being so sloppy. Besides, everything else was clean. Here's my copy of the report but you know I have to put it in the file, right? I can't help that. Any leads yet on the shooter? Whoever he was did the world a good turn."

Pooch knew that Faxon, like most forensic technicians, never got to be in on the flashy points of the investigations he worked on, crashing doors or making arrests in cases. But he did like having inside information.

Puccinelli took the sheet of paper and quickly scanned it. "No, nothing yet. You do what you have to do and I'll make sure O'Hara hears about it. I'll also tell him that he owes you a couple of beers." He walked outside and pulled out his cell phone to call Ernie. He was about to cross another line.

"Can you talk?" Pooch could hear muffled voices and a door closing.

"I can talk now. I've been thinking about the casings. If they haven't run the print."

Puccinelli broke in. "One of our guys already ran it. They picked up a partial, not enough to positively make it but enough so it's consistent with a known." Puccinelli tried to keep his voice free of emotion. "It's O'Hara's."

Ernie was silent for a few seconds. "So the crime tech knows its O'Hara's? What'd he say?"

"He thinks O'Hara was at the crime scene and screwed up the casing by picking it up. He's making a report. He doesn't want O'Hara to get into trouble, but it will be in the report. Nothing I can do about it." Puccinelli paused. "That report's going to show up. When it does, maybe the sergeant or the lieutenant who reviews it won't jump to the conclusion that O'Hara was the shooter, but a lot of people know Bill carried a Walther."

For a few seconds Ernie said nothing. "I'll get back to you. Give me a couple of hours."

"To do what?"

"Don't worry about it. Look, Pooch, if anybody asks before I get back to you, tell them O'Hara should have known better and you aren't going to cover his ass. Don't say anything else. Just that. Okay? Say that. I'll be back to you."

Ernie disconnected and sat back in his chair. There was a crime scene log that documented all the people inside the yellow tape of the crime scene as well as reports of all people handling evidence. O'Hara's name wasn't on it, but there were a lot of people out there. Ernie thought about it. Maybe they should just let people think O'Hara really screwed up? Not that he killed St. Claire, but maybe he didn't sign the crime scene log? It might work. It had better. Ernie reached for his report forms. *Maybe I haven't finished my reports.* He thought about it. *Yes, I need to do that.*

Chapter 43

Puccinelli had stared at the wall for several hours, the anxiety beginning to take over his imagination. The sergeant already had been by. When the sergeant reviewed the forensic reports he caught that O'Hara's prints were on the shell casing. The sergeant was taking that to the lieutenant and the lieutenant would take it to Sheriff Bekin. So far everyone was assuming that O'Hara had been at the crime scene and contaminated evidence by picking up the casing. Nobody was connecting the dots to O'Hara's print being on the casing because it came from O'Hara's Walther.

Sooner or later somebody was going to ask the right question. When the sergeant pointed out that O'Hara had screwed up their investigation, Puccinelli simply repeated word-for-word what Ernie told him. After that he kept quiet and let the sergeant talk, chew on him for O'Hara's screwup and for not doing a better job of controlling the crime scene.

~

It was three in the afternoon before Ernie called Puccinelli. "You in your office? I forgot to give you all my reports." Now Ernie was telling him that he hadn't given him all his reports? He finally asked, "What reports?"

Ernie was guarded, his voice muffled. Nobody was around to hear him but this was no time to take chances. He whispered but bit down on each word for emphasis. "My reports from the crime scene. What I saw, what I did." Ernie's voice dropped down even more. "What O'Hara did. My reports. I'm sorry, I'll run them over. Anybody ask anything, yet?"

"My sergeant's already been in here," Pooch reported. "He took a bite out of my butt about O'Hara picking up evidence."

Ernie let out a derisive cough. "Well, O'Hara should have paid better attention. My report makes it clear that he was walking around the crime scene. I don't know anything about whether he picked up a casing, but he was there for a few minutes, so maybe he did. He'll have to deal with that. He just wanted a look, and then he left. I don't know what the hurry was, but he didn't hang around. Not like O'Hara." Ernie waited to see if Pooch registered what he was saying.

It took Puccinelli less than a minute, but he caught on. "So your report says that O'Hara was at the crime scene for a short time and left?"

"That's right." Then Ernie asked rhetorically, "Didn't you have him sign the crime scene log? That's going to get your ass in trouble with the sergeant."

Puccinelli let out a long and loud breath. It all came together. Ernie's report would put O'Hara at the crime scene, which meant O'Hara would have had the opportunity to pick up the casing. Pooch realized his own report wouldn't reflect seeing it happen because he could say he never saw O'Hara do it, and he could say he forgot O'Hara was there during the investigation and inadvertently left it out of his report.

Puccinelli felt a small stab of guilt. Ernie was stepping up big time, putting much more on the line than he was. Ernie's report would put O'Hara there, not his. It wasn't Ernie's job to keep track of who was at the crime scene. It was his. But he didn't have to make any report changes. Just acknowledge that if O'Hara was there, he should have made him sign the log. It might be enough. He answered Ernie. "And O'Hara?"

Ernie had obviously thought about it. "Well, O'Hara is just going to have to file a report and admit he screwed up. He shouldn't have picked up that casing." Ernie let that thought hang in the air. "Are we good?"

It was a risk. Puccinelli knew it. But who was going to question it? Report screwups happened all the time. Both Pooch and O'Hara would get written up. Ernie would file his report that bridged the gap. There weren't a lot of choices. "Yeah, we're good, but somebody may remember that O'Hara carried that Walther all the time. What if they want to see it?"

Ernie kept his voice level. "You know, I'm sure O'Hara's Walther won't match the extractor marks or firing pin impressions on those casings. Matter of fact, I'm positive. But I'll ask O'Hara if he *still* has *that* Walther in case somebody wants to check."

Puccinelli processed Ernie's comments. In so many words, Ernie was telling him that if O'Hara had any brains he wouldn't still have the Walther. "You do that. You talk to O'Hara." He put the phone down. If anything went wrong, it wasn't just Bill O'Hara that would go down. Both he and Ernie would go down too for a cover-up. There would be no way around that if this all fell apart.

~

There was no sound on the other end but Ernie could tell O'Hara had picked up the phone. "Bill, you there?"

There were a few more seconds of hesitation before O'Hara responded. As usual, there were no pleasantries. "Anything?" His voice sounded harsher than usual and Ernie could sense that O'Hara had spent a rough night, one that included a lot of bourbon.

Ernie bit his tongue. *Anything?* "Yeah, it seems that one of your fingerprints ended up on a shell casing from the gun that killed St. Claire." He waited for a response. There was only silence at the other end of the line. "Listen, Bill, and I want you to just listen." There was still no response. "I told Pooch that you were at the scene for a few minutes and I guessed that you didn't sign in. I had to tell him that I figured you picked up a casing. So you're going to need to make a report. You got it?"

Finally the silence broke. "You told him I picked up one of the casings at the scene?"

"That's right. I had to. We needed an explanation. I told him that was what I figured happened. You picked up a casing. One of the techs ran the print, and guess what? Your print, or at least a partial of your print, showed up."

"And that's what you told Pooch?"

"Pooch said if you filed a report about being at the scene and picking up the casing that he would get it in the file, but it's your ass for not signing in and for not wearing gloves at the scene."

O'Hara dropped back into silence for a few seconds. "And Pooch's okay with this?"

Ernie dropped his voice. "We both decided that must have been the way it happened. How else would your prints have gotten on that casing?"

Ernie could almost hear O'Hara thinking at the other end. "Tell Pooch I'm sorry. I'll file the report." O'Hara was silent for a moment. "What about Jamison?"

Ernie hadn't really thought about that. It was a bridge he would cross later. "I'll handle Jamison.

O'Hara seemed to be able to process that before asking one more question. "Ernie?"

"Yeah?"

"I'm not going to let anybody take a fall for me."

"St. Claire was a prick. Just file the report."

Ernie hung up the phone. He could feel himself breathing deeply. Now all of them were over the line. It wasn't the first time he had crossed the line, but in the past he had just nudged past it a little. There was no way back from this. He thought about it for a moment. He wasn't sure why O'Hara fired when he did, but he knew one thing. A cop like O'Hara wouldn't have used his backup gun unless he had a reason and O'Hara's reasons for doing things had always been good enough for him. He pushed it to the back of his mind. Maybe O'Hara would tell him and maybe he wouldn't, but Ernie knew one thing—he wasn't going to ask. And if the situation was reversed, he knew O'Hara wouldn't ask him.

Bill O'Hara put his phone down on the desk in his den. The sun had gone down and the natural light in the room was fading with the dusk. He hadn't bothered to turn on the lights; the darkness matched his mood. It was hard for him to accept Ernie's help. He understood the line Ernie was crossing. He also understood that Pooch was doing the same thing. He hadn't asked them to do it but he knew he would do it for them. The difference for him was that he would never ask any man to help him. It just wasn't in him. It was how he saw himself. And now he would never see himself the same way again.

O'Hara wasn't the kind of man who made excuses and he hadn't spent his life accepting excuses. He was responsible for his own behavior. He knew it. All his life he'd been in control of himself. Now, after the last twenty-four hours, he had lost that control. For the first time in his life he felt adrift, cut off from the confidence that had always been his lifeline when others around him were uncertain. As soon as he fired his Walther at St. Claire he realized that his better judgment came a trigger pull too late.

O'Hara rubbed his hand over his face. He hadn't showered or shaved. He hadn't done much of anything—except drink. The Walther was on the coffee table. It wasn't registered and it wasn't traceable. He had thought about it during the long nights he spent seated in his car, waiting for St. Claire to appear at the school, just as he knew St. Claire would. And St. Claire did.

He wasn't sorry about St. Claire. As far as O'Hara was concerned St. Claire was a monster. St. Claire was going to hurt Garrett. He was convinced of that, but he should have yelled at him; he should have waited a moment longer. All he saw was a murderer coming at a victim. He was so intent on making sure that St. Claire never hurt anyone ever again that he didn't wait. But O'Hara was a victim of his own brutal honesty. He knew he didn't wait because he didn't want to wait. O'Hara looked at justification in terms of the result, not the means getting to it.

He hadn't spent the last twenty-four hours feeling sorry for himself. But he was sorry that he left the scene. When he saw Garrett hold St. Claire after he went down, O'Hara instantly knew that the least that would happen to him was that he would lose his badge and his pension, and the worst that would happen was that he would sit in the defendant's chair where he had put so many other men. He admitted it to himself. He had panicked and taken off.

The realization that he had done what he had so often disdained in other men had been difficult to take. The hardest part was the realization that he was more like other men than he had ever admitted to himself.

Most of the last hours were a blur because he had downed more than a fifth of bourbon. He got up and took his glass and the second bottle of liquor to the sink. He watched the last of the brown liquid swirl down the drain. He never thought of himself as a man who needed a crutch. He had spent some of those blurry hours staring at the Walther. As he looked at the gun, the thoughts that crossed his mind were a crutch too. O'Hara straightened up. He would wait it out, but no matter what, he wasn't going to take anyone down with him. It had been his decision alone and he knew it when he pulled the trigger.

After talking to O'Hara, Ernie studied the photographs on his desk that he and Puccinelli found in the manila envelope in Garrett's car. Garrett's face stared back at him. Some looked like high school pictures; one looked like a college yearbook photograph. There was also a picture of St. Claire. Something about that one set Ernie's senses tingling.

He couldn't keep the photographs for long, but he needed to take a closer look. He hadn't been able to put his finger on it when Puccinelli showed him the pictures, but they triggered something at the back of his mind. Ernie leaned back in his chair. He put the photographs back in the packet. He decided to look at the location where the picture used in court had been taken, the one that Garrett testified she had not known St. Claire was taking.

Late in the afternoon Puccinelli picked through the pile of paper on his desk. He was rereading all the reports, trying to find the thread his instincts told him was there. But he was so tired his mind had begun to drift. The ringing phone startled him. It was Faxon in the forensic lab. He sounded agitated, at least more agitated than usual. "Pooch, we need to talk." Faxon gave him a short explanation.

Puccinelli hurried out of the office and headed for the stairway—that was faster than waiting for the elevators. When he came back up he would wait for the elevator and rationalize his walking downstairs as his exercise for the day.

Faxon handed Puccinelli the rough draft of the forensic report. There it was. There were makeable prints on the aerosol can from St. Claire's car—St. Claire's and some unknowns. Faxon waited until he was through reading. "I ran St. Claire's prints first. He handled the can but he wasn't the only one. There are other makeable prints on it and they don't belong to St. Claire. Any thoughts?"

"Not at the moment." Puccinelli decided to keep his thoughts to himself, at least for the time being. Something was coming together in his mind, but it was just gut thinking and he needed to roll it around in his head some more.

"Okay, we'll keep working on it." Faxon nodded. "Right now the criminalist wants to talk to you. I haven't seen him this excited since they found a way to test DNA. He's in his office." Puccinelli asked Faxon to burn a quick copy of the draft report for him. He would pick it up after talking to the criminalist.

Andre Rhychkov was a first-generation Russian American who liked to be called Andy and wore loose-fitting Hawaiian shirts, jeans, and expensive sneakers that were perpetually stained with things nobody wanted to ask about. He had grown up on American cop shows and at an early age had made it his goal to be a crime scene analyst. But he was more than a crime scene ant who combed over carpets and bodies looking for lint and hair. He was one of those guys who worked with computers and DNA. When Puccinelli entered his office, the expression on Andy's face reminded him of a teenage boy who had just gotten a peek at his first *Playboy* foldout.

"So what you got, Andy?"

"Two things for which you'll owe me tickets to the Giants game. I know you have season tickets."

"No tickets unless you got something that will make this case or get me laid."

"Making this case is one thing but getting you laid? I can't deliver the impossible. Anyway, I got the syringe that you took out of St. Claire's coat. It was filled with succinylcholine. We've heard of that before, right? But I got a lot more than that."

Rhychkov picked up a plastic bag with the can in it, smudges of print powder still clinging to it. "What I got, Pooch, is something nobody's seen before. First off, it isn't hairspray."

Puccinelli rolled his tongue around in his mouth. *What was it with all the forensic wonks that made them drag everything out?* He shrugged his shoulders. It was annoying but he was used to it. This was their thing. "What is it?"

"Xenon gas with a few other things mixed in."

"Xenon gas? You mean like the stuff they put in neon lights?"

Rhychkov shook his head. "No, better. I couldn't figure it out at first, but I realized that thing on the top was some kind of mouthpiece. You put it over somebody's face and you push, just like pushing on the valve in a spray-paint can releases the spray. That forces the xenon gas into the person's mouth.

"Most people who aren't expecting something over their face will immediately inhale, pulling the spray into their lungs. That's what this is for. They're using it in Europe for an anesthetic. It leaves no trace. Nothing in the liver. It breaks through the brain barrier and 'poof,' you start to lapse into unconsciousness. There's something else mixed with it that I think is sevaflurane. It's another type of anesthetic. All very fast acting and metabolizes quickly. We might find a trace of sevaflurane in the liver if we knew what we were looking for and if the person was dead almost immediately. But if they stayed alive it would be gone because it metabolizes so fast. It's heavier than air. It will knock you out in a couple of breaths. With a smaller person like a woman, she would be disabled almost immediately."

Puccinelli reached over to weigh the plastic-bag-encased can in his hand. "So how would someone get hold of this shit?"

"That's the hard part." He plopped on the edge of a stool near a microscope. "The sevaflurane is pretty standard. Comes in a bottle and you can get it at any hospital, or an anesthesiologist like St. Claire would probably have it on his shelf. But the xenon is pretty expensive. Doctors in Europe have been experimenting with it. I read all about it. Tricky stuff, but the big thing is it doesn't leave any trace as long as the person is alive for a while to metabolize it.

"So that's how he did it. Then when he was through with his victims, he would use the succinylcholine and it would look just like heart failure. We wouldn't have found the succinylcholine unless we knew exactly what to look for, and even then we might not have caught it."

Puccinelli watched as Andy forced the can against his glove, the hiss of gas audible. "See? Really simple. But what's this the techs said about the prints? There were other prints consistent with somebody else holding the can?"

"I know. I need to go back and talk to Faxon, see what else he can tell me."

Andy shrugged. "Well I understand the prints came from a person with a small hand."

Puccinelli's face froze. He stood up and walked toward the door. "Don't write up the report yet. Hold it. I'll call. I don't want anybody to read it yet. And thanks, Andy. I appreciate it." His mind already was working like a jackhammer. But like a jackhammer, he was starting to break through.

He was at the door when Andy called out, "One more thing. I got some trace DNA off the mouthpiece. I'm guessing saliva from one of the victim's mouths. We're working on it now, but it's going to take a while to match it up if we're able to. I have the DNA profiles on the victims but if the DNA is mixed up because saliva is on it from different people, well . . ." Rhychkov shrugged. "As soon as I have it, you'll get it and I get my tickets."

"Let me know what you find as soon as you get it." Thoughts now crackled across Puccinelli's brain like a lightning bolt. He hesitated for a split-second before pounding on Ernie's name on his phone. Without saying hello, Pooch spoke as soon as Ernie answered. "We need to talk."

When they met outside the medical center, they decided to talk to St. Claire's lab assistant, Donald Wilson, who had testified in the trial. Wilson was sitting in St. Claire's lab when the two investigators walked through the door that still had St. Claire's name on it. Wilson looked up. His face was drawn and gray, either from lack of sleep or the situation with St. Claire, but it was evident that he was emotionally drained. Immediately, Puccinelli sensed that Wilson wasn't going to be a problem. He didn't look like a person who would be confrontational. Wilson lowered his eyes when they flashed their badges, focusing on his desk. The muffled sound of dogs barking could be heard through the walls.

Puccinelli got right to the point, laying the photographs of the aerosol can down on the desk. "Do you have any idea what this is?"

Wilson picked up the top photograph. "Where did this come from?"

"That isn't the question. Do you know what this is?"

"Yes, it's an aerosol canister that has anesthetic gas in it. Dr. St. Claire was experimenting with different types of anesthetic gasses and their application, including using them in field hospitals under primitive conditions as opposed to complex anesthetic applications." Wilson held the photograph, sliding his forefinger back and forth over it as if to rub out the image before gently placing it back on the desk.

"We found this can in Dr. St. Claire's car. Our lab has analyzed it and determined it contains some kind of specialized gas."

Wilson interjected. "Would it be xenon gas or sevaflurane?"

Puccinelli nodded. "That's it."

Wilson slumped heavily in his chair. "And you think he used this on those poor women? To subdue them?"

Ernie said, "And you don't?"

"I don't know. I still can't believe Dr. St. Claire did any of this. I worked with him. All of this work was supposed to help people. I still think you're wrong about him. I don't think he hurt those women. He once told me you thought he had something to do with those murders. He said he didn't."

Ernie softened his voice. It was obvious that Wilson was struggling with the thought that he had worked with someone he had completely misjudged, and maybe even helped. "And do you think differently now? Is there something you've thought about that might help us?"

The lab assistant kept looking down at the desk, his shoulders slumped. "Your people came out during the trial and went over the van. Did they find anything?"

Ernie decided not to mention the hair from two of the victims found in the van. "Is there something you want to say?"

"After I testified I thought about what I'd been asked, about body bags and transport. I said that we keep a log about use of the van and that was true, but I looked and there was nothing in the log with Dr. St. Claire's name. So I had no way of knowing whether the van had been used, and if Dr. St. Claire had taken it out I wouldn't know unless I saw it."

Wilson's face showed he was struggling. Puccinelli prodded him to continue. "And?"

Wilson couldn't make direct eye contact. "There's a log book when a body is picked up, what time it's brought in and who the decedent is, who brought it in and made the pickup. But if nobody signs the log sheet, then we would never know the van had been used."

Wilson continued to stare down at the desk while his voice dropped down to a whisper. "You see? I looked at the logs after I was asked about it at the trial for the times when those young women disappeared."

"So what are you saying?" asked Puccinelli.

"I'm saying that somebody who had access to the keys to the van used it, and they didn't use it to pick up a decedent, and they didn't sign the log. And . . . and . . ." Wilson choked up, turned his eyes away from them, as if he couldn't pull the words out of himself. After he regained his composure, he continued. "The night Ms. Garrett disappeared? I didn't connect it to the van until after I testified."

Puccinelli's voice snapped out, "Connect what to the van?" Wilson shrank back at the menacing tone in Puccinelli's voice.

"When you sign the van back in, you put down the mileage. Usually the mileage is just twenty or thirty miles, but this time when it was signed back in it had over a hundred miles on it."

"So? I don't understand. Get to the point." Puccinelli was out of patience.

"Don't you see? Somebody used the van and didn't log it in but when the next person used it, they put down the mileage when they brought it back and there was mileage that didn't match with the crime scene pickup. The van was used to travel at least sixty or eighty miles, but the mileage wasn't logged out. Somebody used the van when they weren't supposed to and they drove it at least sixty miles."

"But you didn't say anything?"

Wilson's eyes were imploring. "I—I couldn't imagine—I didn't believe," he stammered. "Why does it matter now?"

As far as Puccinelli was concerned, Wilson had withheld evidence, although he imagined Wilson may not have understood the importance of what he knew at the time. Puccinelli's exasperation with the lab assistant was palpable to the point of rudeness. "So is there anything else?"

"Yes." Wilson reached for a bottle of water on his desk. "We keep an inventory of body bags that we use in our work. There were bags missing from our inventory that were unaccounted for."

Ernie interjected, concerned that Pooch's aggressive attitude was going to interfere with Wilson's cooperation. "How many were missing?"

"Four. Four bags."

Now Ernie's anger spiked. "And you knew three woman had been murdered, and then Garrett disappeared too."

It was a statement that seemed to slap Wilson with reality. He shrank even farther into his chair. "Yes, after I was questioned at the trial I realized that the inventory should have shown four more bags. But I didn't know what they'd been used for. I couldn't say they'd been used for those women. I just knew the number was the same."

Wilson's face scrunched up in an almost pitiful expression. He looked back and forth at the two investigators. "I admired Dr. St. Claire. You may think I should've been suspicious, but how could I be? I knew Dr. St. Claire. It just didn't make any sense to me. It still doesn't."

Ernie let the explanation hang in the air and then asked, "Do you know what succinylcholine is?"

"Yes, it's used in application of anesthesia to relax the air passageways. We use it with our animals."

"Is there any reason Dr. St. Claire would have a syringe full of it in his pocket when he was shot?"

"No, it's very dangerous, and if he had it with him it would have been in his medical case."

Wilson stood up. "I can show you the other canister. They were specially made because of the pressure and are a little heavier than a normal aerosol can. The xenon we order from Europe. I can show you the invoices."

The pain on Wilson's face was evident. He hesitated before leading the two detectives through the door into the lab. "I never thought he could do something like this. He was a brilliant man." Wilson straightened up. "He was my friend. He wasn't a murderer."

"Did Dr. St. Claire ever use this aerosol-type anesthetic with people that you are aware of?" Ernie asked.

"That was the next step. He planned on using it eventually in surgery but not yet. Just on animals."

Puccinelli followed Wilson and Ernie through the door into the lab. The barking of the dogs and the acrid smell of animals and urine flooded his senses. Wilson went straight to a locked door to a closet. One aerosol can was on the shelf. Wilson started to reach for it when Ernie grabbed his arm. "We'll take it. Don't worry about it."

When they were finished with Wilson, Pooch and Ernie stood in the parking lot. They had Wilson show them the coroner log for the van. There was a mileage gap between the previous time it was used before the Ventana, Symes, and Johnson murders that didn't match the pickup locations for the next time the van was used. It was obvious that somebody used the van at some point when the other murders took place but didn't log it in.

The aerosol can was in a plastic bag in Puccinelli's hand as he began to evaluate what they had heard. "So the question is why? Why the hell would St. Claire kill those women? Just to find out what would happen with his toy aerosol can? And what about those other prints? Did he do it by himself? Because I can tell that Wilson wouldn't have been any help. He can barely deal with dogs let alone people."

Although nobody was near them, Pooch lowered his voice. "It looks like Jamison was right. St. Claire used the coroner's van with the lights to pick up those women. He used the body bags to put them in when he dumped them. And then the same van was used to pick them up from the crime scene. That way any evidence that was in the van would be explained, because it had been used to pick up the bodies and transport them to the morgue for Gupta to work on. The red light we found in his trunk? Maybe he used that when he stopped Garrett, if you believe her, maybe he used the van." Ernie shrugged.

"Look, I don't think he did it by himself." Pooch blurted out the words. "And I don't think you do either. I'm thinking somebody helped him." He paused. "And I'm thinking that somebody was Garrett."

From Ernie's expression Puccinelli could tell Ernie hadn't bought into it yet.

Ernie's next words reinforced that impression. "But why? And why the whole thing at the house? I think he was just a sick asshole and he did it to find out what would happen. But why would she help him? Why? This isn't the kind of thing women do."

Puccinelli opened the car door. "Sometimes you never know the reason why, but it's usually the simple explanation. And the simple explanation is because he could. We know he was tracking these women. He did it and now we know how he did it. Why he did it is something that, at this point, I don't give a shit about. For all that smooth European doctor act, he was just another asshole with a short circuit."

Ernie shook his head. "But why would she help him, Pooch? Look, maybe St. Claire was practicing on the other three women before he went after Garrett. Did you think of that? Maybe she was the target all along. Look at the way he fabricated an alibi. The others were just trial runs."

Ernie got in the car and Puccinelli slid behind the wheel before answering. "Maybe, but here's what we need to find the answer to. Why would she lie?" His sarcastic tone was evident. "Because she's been lying over and over again. People usually lie for a reason, because they're afraid or they're trying to protect themselves. What are we missing here?"

Ernie expelled a long sigh. "People lie for lots of reasons and sometimes it only makes sense to them. I don't think she helped him."

Puccinelli started the car, shaking his head in disbelief. "You risked your ass trying to save her and you just can't accept that maybe she didn't want to be saved. We both know that most women don't get involved in something violent unless they've hooked up with the wrong guy. I'm always amazed at how much some women will do to please some dirtbag."

"Maybe, but why would Garrett help him with those other women? We've both seen women kill, but usually it was because they're really pissed. For her to help him do something like this—murder three young women—she'd have to be just as crazy as he was."

Puccinelli pulled the car out from the parking lot of the hospital. "I'm telling you our Miss Garrett isn't the snow queen she wants everybody to believe. And by the way, nobody saw crazy when they looked at St. Claire either."

Ernie didn't respond. He was lost in thought. It barely registered with him when he heard Puccinelli call Faxon. "Charlie, you were asking about a name for those prints on that can? Run Elizabeth Garrett."

Chapter 44

It hadn't taken Jamison long to find Bobby Allison. As he studied the information on the flickering computer screen, he mentally kicked himself. He hadn't asked Beth Garrett because he never thought about asking, and he hadn't checked his facts, something that he always tried to do. He didn't need to think about why he hadn't checked. He had allowed what he wanted to believe to obscure his judgment.

The background check hadn't been difficult. Bobby Allison died in a car accident when he was fourteen. The Allisons were neighbors, living several houses down from Beth's family. They would have known each other, but Bobby wasn't ever Beth's boyfriend. She was younger than him by almost ten years. Given the time frames, Beth probably would have been around five when Bobby had been their neighbor. He had been dead for over twenty years.

Beth had a ready explanation during the trial when McGuiness confronted her with the letter, just as she had when Jamison had asked her. And when he asked her mother about Allison, she had said, "No, you must have heard wrong." Jamison turned off the computer. *No, I didn't hear wrong.* What bothered him most was that Beth hadn't really missed a beat. The response had come out of her mouth so easily; in fact, all her answers had come out that way.

There were only a few explanations, Jamison decided, and one of them wasn't one he wanted to think about. The ringing of the phone interrupted his spasm of recrimination. It was Ernie asking him to meet over at Puccinelli's office.

When he entered Puccinelli's office at the sheriff's building, Jamison could tell from their expressions that something was wrong. Pooch spoke first. "Matt, we've run into some"—Pooch seemed to be searching for words—"some issues that we need to discuss with you, so you need to sit down for a minute." He waited until Jamison situated himself in the chair in front of the desk and continued. "First, it looks like you guessed right about the body bags and the coroner van. We saw St. Claire's lab assistant, Wilson, and it's pretty clear that somebody used the van on the nights of the murders and four body bags are missing. It all points to St. Claire using the body bags and the van to move the bodies. So anything we found in the van would be consistent with the van simply being used to pick up murder victims, and any evidence on the floor would be consistent with that."

Jamison interrupted. "Four body bags? So he did intend to use that last one on Elizabeth?" He started shaking his head. "I talked to her mother this morning—"

Pooch shook his head, holding up his hand before he dropped the other shoe. "Just a minute. Look, Matt, there's more. There was a can in St. Claire's car, an aerosol-type can. It had a mouthpiece on it and Andy Rhychkov says it has an anesthetic gas in it. There's some DNA on the mouthpiece that he's testing for but it's going to take a while. It won't surprise me if we find DNA from one or more of the victims on it. According to Andy it would have immobilized any of them almost immediately. We've been over to St. Claire's lab and there's another can like this. Wilson, his lab assistant, says St. Claire was developing it experimentally, for use on a battlefield or for emergency situations away from a hospital."

Jamison immediately leaned forward. "So St. Claire used this aerosol can on the victims and Andy thinks that would have helped him control them?"

Puccinelli hesitated to reply, and Jamison was surprised to see a shaken expression take hold on his face. "Not him, them. I think it helped *them* control each victim. Matt, I think two people were involved." Pooch glanced over at the stone-faced Ernie. "It never really made sense that St. Claire could have done this by himself, although it was possible. St. Claire's prints are on the can, but there are other prints on the can too that are consistent with somebody else gripping it." Pooch said nothing more, and looked over at Ernie to pick up the explanation from there.

"Matt, forensics confirms the prints belong to Elizabeth Garrett."

Shock registered on Jamison's face as he struggled a moment for control of his emotions.

Both Pooch and Ernie watched the younger man confront the reality of the situation. "I'm sorry, Matt." It had been obvious to all of them that when it came to Garrett, Jamison's judgment was clouded.

Silence filled the room. Jamison's face was ashen. Finally he told them about the letter that McGuiness introduced at trial from Bobby Allison and how she had lied about that too.

Puccinelli's voice was as soothing as he could make it. "We didn't see this coming either."

Ernie interrupted before Pooch went any further. "And, Matt, there's something else. We have the issue of who shot St. Claire. It wasn't Garrett or her father. We think—"

Before Ernie could finish, Jamison stood up, holding his palm out to stop the conversation. He measured his words very carefully. "Whoever it was, I don't think we'll ever be able to find out." There was a long, lingering silence before Jamison said with quiet conviction, "It wouldn't be the worst thing if we never find the shooter in this case. I think I could sleep at night."

Puccinelli leaned back in his chair, his eyes narrowing before he gave an almost imperceptible nod of acknowledgment. "What about her? What are we going to do about her?"

Jamison walked to the door. "We talk to her, but it isn't her I'm worried about right now. You guys have the other situation under control?"

Ernie answered cautiously, "Other situation?"

Jamison's face had aged measurably in the last few weeks. The prosecutor's eyes had lost any lingering naïveté. His words came out in a precise, measured tone. "Take care of him." He paused. "He's my friend too."

Nobody said anything. Jamison opened the door before turning. "Get a wired room set up. I don't want to talk to her without a recording."

Chapter 45

Back in his office, Jamison sat, brooding about the case and Elizabeth Garrett. It was difficult to keep his mind focused. Confronted with sharply conflicting pieces of evidence and contradictory explanations, Jamison had convinced himself of what was the truth in order to convince the jury. It was what an effective trial lawyers always did; a jury couldn't be convinced to believe if the lawyer himself didn't believe it. He had chosen to believe, even though logic should have made him question what the truth was. From the very beginning he had dismissed the uneasy sense that she was looking right through him. Now he realized she had been.

He recognized the irony. He had been unable to convince a jury and now had to think that maybe they had seen what he had chosen to ignore, human intuition guiding their decision and trumping all the rhetoric. He had to know the truth.

He could feel regret, but he couldn't change any of it. Where had Garrett been when those women were killed? Maybe she had an explanation for her fingerprints that would make sense. For all he knew, there was a simple explanation. St. Claire may have used it on her and she had grabbed the can. But he needed to hear that explanation, as did Ernie and Puccinelli. There was only one way to get it. They had to ask.

Jamison kept thinking about what kind of case they would have if she was involved. First she was the victim and St. Claire was the stalker. Then she wasn't a victim, but now she was a suspect?

All the evidence he used that pointed in one direction would now have to point in another. If Garrett was involved, and as far as Jamison was concerned that wasn't a solid conclusion yet, then they wouldn't be able to use her testimony to prove what St. Claire did for purposes of MO. Would St. Claire have been a step ahead of them on that one too?

No defense attorney was going to let her testify to prove her own guilt. And then there would be the major stumbling block, the problems created by Detective Longworthy's suddenly finding incriminating evidence *after*

St. Claire's car had been thoroughly searched by experienced forensic technicians. That was the linchpin evidence that directly linked St. Claire to the murders. To prove Garrett guilty, Jamison would have to prove that St. Claire was guilty. Even though he knew he couldn't use the evidence Longworthy said he found, that didn't mean that he wouldn't have to disclose that evidence if he went after Garrett. The fact that police officers may have planted evidence would adversely impact every inference a jury would be asked to draw because it would cast suspicion on every other piece of evidence. And it would take Longworthy down along with the rest of his case. The only way he could prove Garrett was involved, if in fact she was involved, would have to come from her own mouth.

Jamison looked down at his legal pad. He had been trying to diagram it out. All he had drawn was an endless series of circles. He reached for the phone. When he talked to Beth she needed to be on his turf, and he needed to have his head screwed on straight. Jamison knew what St. Claire was. What he didn't know was what she was. Instead of calling Beth Garrett, he dialed another number.

Dr. Levy agreed to meet him at his office at the university where he taught graduate psychology students.

~

Jamison was waiting outside his door when Levy came walking down the hall. All he said to the younger man was, "Matt, let's go inside and talk. I can tell you have a lot on your mind."

Seeing Jamison's agitation, Levy made a reflective comment. "Dr. St. Claire's dead and in a very primitive but effective way justice has been served. Or"—Levy hesitated as he regarded Matt carefully, the right corner of his mouth lifting into an inquisitive expression—"has justice not yet been served?"

As Jamison explained the current situation and the land mines of facts and contradictions confronting him—the fingerprints and the letter—it all came out of his mouth in a torrent. That he felt confusion, anger, and disappointment was evident to the psychologist but it was also evident that no small amount of pain came from reality lapping up against expectations. It was what happened when people saw another person more clearly, as if a veil had been removed, when their emotions no longer obscured their vision.

"So," Levy observed, "I take it Ms. Garrett may not be the victim you thought her to be?" Levy put his fingertips together and brought his hands to the tip of his nose before lowering them and looking across his desk.

"St. Claire was clearly manipulative, but then again, he may not be the only one who was manipulative. People—all of us—have a number of complex motivations for what we do. Frequently, it's difficult to tell what the motivation really is unless the person tells you, and most of the time they won't. It isn't whether she is telling the truth or lying that is the issue for me.

"Matt, in my practice I've seen a range of female behavior and oftentimes it is as inexplicable as it is dark. Some women live out power and sadism through the actions of the men they're involved with. And while the vast majority of women are predisposed biologically to be nurturers, that doesn't mean that females don't have anger or aggression issues. They simply learn to express their anger and aggression differently and often in more indirect ways. You have to realize that while most men and women wince at causing other people pain, there are some who simply enjoy inflicting pain. Whether they do it directly or more obliquely, the real question is why." Levy paused to pour ice water into a glass. "And that is something psychologists struggle with every day.

"Women are not necessarily all that different from men, they just act out differently or by different means. We just don't often see *this* kind of conduct in women, possible involvement in serial murders as opposed to being only emotionally involved with a serial murderer. Do you understand?"

Jamison nodded slowly but there was still confusion on his face. "Why in the world would she be drawn to a man like St. Claire?"

Levy cut in. "And you think human behavior is supposed to make sense? Most human behavior makes no sense if we look at it in a logical fashion. It is perhaps easier if we look at it in terms of motivation rather than logic. Why do people do dangerous things that might hurt them? For the thrill, yes? But logic should tell them that where there is a real risk of being hurt, then the action isn't worth the potential consequence. And yet, people do it anyway, again and again."

Levy sensed that Jamison was still resisting his conjecture. "Let me tell you a story. I had a case where a woman came to me because she was in an abusive relationship. Every Friday night she would sit in her chair in the living room waiting for her husband to come home. And every Friday night he would come home intoxicated. She would wait for him and then meet him at the door and tell him he was a miserable, worthless son of a bitch. He would respond by beating her and then go up to their bedroom and pass out. The next day he would apologize profusely and promise to do better. This happened every Friday night and only on Friday night.

"I asked her what would happen if she just sat in her chair and didn't confront him when he came home. Her answer was that he would then simply go up to their bedroom and wouldn't hurt her. When I asked then why didn't she sit there in her chair instead of confronting him, her answer was that if she did that, then she would be giving him a free pass for coming home drunk. You see, Matt, logic has nothing to do with it.

"The reality is that Ms. Garrett may have been a victim or maybe she wasn't a victim at all. There was a relationship here between her and St. Claire and it's not news to any of us that relationships are very complicated. Men and women play out fantasy sexual submission scenes all the time. It is the difference in a real relationship between a woman who prefers to feel that she is receiving her lover, and a woman who actually wants to have sex but who isn't comfortable with the responsibility. So her relationship always has to involve elements of dominance and, sometimes, danger."

Jamison blurted out, "It's not normal, dammit."

Levy smiled. "What's normal and what's not? The key issue is whether it's consensual. The biological distinction between aggression and sex is very slight.

"Think of it this way. The basis of sexuality in the animal world is not sentimental. Humans have engrafted it with sentimentality. We are not Neanderthals who hit women over the head and have our way with them, and women are not Neanderthals who accept such conduct. But the conduct is a part of our deeply buried genetic behavior. In this respect, for these two individuals, I am talking about a possible pattern of behavior in which the boundaries of sexual conduct are a matter of consent and the behavior is like a play in which both people act out a part to get the pleasure they seek."

Jamison blinked rapidly. "You're saying that Elizabeth and St. Claire may have been acting out an elaborate game? What about the trial? Why would she put him through that? What about the risk? Suppose the jury had believed her, convicted him? What about—"

Levy gently brought the unspoken issue to the surface. "I think what you really mean here is what about you? Isn't that what you're asking? You may have been part of that game or you might actually represent something that Elizabeth Garrett really wants her life to be, to love and be loved by a man like you. You see, Matt, regardless of how this woman presents herself to the rest of the world, inside her head she *knows* what she is, and that the world may not understand what she likes to do—or needs to do."

Jamison stood and began to pace as he listened to Levy.

"She may not be able to understand her own behavior and she may actually want her life to be different. What she wants to be and what she is are not necessarily things she can control."

Jamison shook his head. "Why would she do this? Even if logic has nothing to do with it, if Beth was involved in all of this I need to understand why. I have a professional decision to make as to how to handle her when we talk."

Levy's face took on a pensive expression. "I can only speculate, but there is perhaps a possible explanation. In some people there is what is commonly referred to as a borderline personality disorder. We don't know precisely what causes it. The most recent research indicates that it is the result of events that occur before the age of five and sometimes as late as seven. Not everyone who is molested has this as a consequence, but it's common that women who have this disorder were sexually molested.

"Many of these women have suppressed the memory of the sexual molestation or it occurred in the first three or four years of life and the person may not even remember it. Sometimes it isn't suppressed at all and they are always aware of its presence. What we don't know is why it has such an adverse effect on some people and not others.

"If I had to speculate, I would suspect that this Bobby Allison may have something to do with this. Why would his name come out as a person she would pick so abruptly when confronted with the letter? He was older than her, correct? Based on what you've said, he's not a person you would expect would come to mind unless he's someone who has never *left* her mind.

"My guess is there's something there, probably buried very deeply. She may not even remember what happened or if she does remember, it's unlikely that she has ever told a living soul, including her parents. Even if she doesn't remember the details it's likely that she is aware of a shadow at the back of her mind, and she's frightened of it, even terrified.

"What we do know is that such an event, even though it happened years and years ago, has a very significant capacity to disrupt the way the person is wired. It can lie suppressed for years and then there can be some event, sometimes stressful, that triggers the consequence and you get acting out in all kinds of aberrant and very self-destructive ways . . ."

"What kind of aberrant ways?" Jamison asked. His voice was filled with tension, he knew, but he needed to hear it all.

"Promiscuity, infidelity, detached relationships, inability to maintain secure relationships because of self-worth issues. A predator like Alex St. Claire could easily have sensed such vulnerability. And in a very bizarre way, their individual psychological issues might be symbiotic. He would very easily feed on her vulnerability and she could very easily fall prey to his charisma to fulfill her own sexual needs or whatever subconscious sense that she has of herself. Sometimes, as difficult as it is to understand, people engage in degrading or self-destructive behavior because they feel they are worthless human beings and the behavior is consistent with that."

Levy's tone softened as he tried to help Jamison accommodate the reality of what he was going to do, as well as accept that his failure to see the situation clearly was much more understandable than he had allowed himself to believe.

"Matt, don't be too hard on yourself. If I'm right, then Elizabeth Garrett is a profoundly troubled person. She's manipulative and this will not change, at least not without years of psychotherapy, and even then it may not be successful. It is likely that she controls herself while interacting in the outside world, but make no mistake, in her mind this woman is aware that what she is inside, the combination of her feelings and fears, is very different from what she presents to the world. And the tension of this duality—of keeping what she is inside and how she presents herself to the outside world—creates terrible stress for her."

"And for the rest of the world." Jamison uttered the words without anger, more in weariness.

"Ah, the world? It's likely that no one knows or will know unless there's a triggering event," Levy replied. "What you see is what she wants to be. What she *is* may remain unseen or maybe was seen only by Alex St. Claire."

"And with him gone now . . .? What will happen to her do you think?"

"Well, of course, that may largely depend on you," Levy responded. "If she was a participant with St. Claire or maybe encouraged him, then the vehicle for her to act out her fantasies is now gone also. She won't act without him and unless she finds somebody else, she'll simply go forward.

"But, there's also the possibility, as I suspect you hope, that she had nothing to do with what St. Claire did. She may be innocent as you think of innocence even though she played a part in his dark games. When you talk to her, you'll see it and you'll know what you can prove. That's for you. I'm a psychologist, not a criminal investigator."

Jamison stood. "Thank you, Dr. Levy. And we shall see. However," he added as the two men shook hands, "in court, what you know and what you can prove are not always the same. Sometimes what you know is more important than what you can prove or, perhaps, even want to prove."

Levy nodded thoughtfully, releasing one last thought. "It occurs to me that all of the victims looked alike." Jamison stopped and leaned against the door, waiting for Levy to finish his thought.

"But the one St. Claire didn't kill was Elizabeth Garrett. It's possible the others were simply a substitute for her. He couldn't bring himself to kill her because he may have in his own way felt something for her that he didn't want to lose. By killing the others he could accomplish his fantasy without really hurting her." Levy shrugged. "It is a burden of psychologists. We think too much sometimes and form theories that can only be answered by people who very rarely really tell us the truth." Levy paused. "If they understand the truth at all."

As Jamison walked out of the psychologist's office, he tried to push what he had just heard to the back of his mind. That he hadn't seen Elizabeth Garrett for what she was had been a mistake. But now he had to put that behind him. He had to move on to what lay ahead, where there were perils he was aware of and others he knew were still hidden.

Chapter 46

Ernie picked Beth up at her home. He had decided the simplest explanation was the best and told her earlier when he called they needed to go over more details of the shooting and that Jamison was at the office and it wouldn't take long.

Once they were on their way, Ernie kept the conversation casual on the ride down to the sheriff's office, letting her talk. He didn't want to say anything that might arouse any suspicions about the real reason for the meeting.

Still, he was also angry, at himself for not picking up on what now seemed to have been so clearly in front of them all, and for O'Hara, who was hanging out to dry to protect somebody who, it now seemed, was less deserving of their protection.

And then there was Jamison. Ernie liked him, and he regretted holding back from Jamison the existence of the photographs from Garrett's car. But his instincts and experience told him in the long run it would be better for him to decide when and how to use them. He would apologize to Jamison later.

Jamison was sitting in Puccinelli's office when Ernie arrived with Elizabeth. When this day was over there weren't going to be any winners. He realized that. He had thought carefully about how to approach the questioning. He knew he was taking advantage of the rapport they had built through the trial but shook off any reservations. He needed answers no matter what the consequences. He let his hunter's mind take control.

Every interrogation has a rhythm and you have to keep that rhythm going. You start out slowly, particularly with a woman. He also thought about the ethics of his doing the questioning. He would be exploiting the trust he had built with her, but then again he knew now that he didn't know this woman, not really. The reality was that they had built nothing. Trust had been a one-way street, and it had been all him.

He had considered letting Ernie or Pooch do the questioning but that wouldn't make sense to her, and he needed for her to not be cautious. He had to have a reason to talk to her, one that wouldn't cause her to be defensive. Going over again what happened that night when she left her car by the side of the road at the cemetery would not make sense. He had weighed his options and come to the only decision that would not cause her to wonder why he was asking questions.

That would mean starting with the shooting of St. Claire. That case was open. The three men had discussed it and agreed. He would begin by asking the questions and Pooch and Ernie would interject depending on how the questioning was going.

Jamison concentrated on the subtlety of the process of interrogation, the decision when to read a suspect their Miranda rights. It wasn't whether the person was under suspicion that triggered the ritual reading of their rights, all the legally required cautionary questions people see and hear on television that immediately transform a conversation into an interrogation in the mind of the person talking. Whether Miranda warnings were required depended on whether the person *believed* they were in custody and *thought* they had to answer questions—that and the inherent intimidation of an interrogator jabbing at them with questions and playing with their mind.

But legally, Jamison intended to use the fact that in real life there is nothing wrong with asking a person questions even when they are the focus of suspicion as long as they don't know it, as long as a reasonable person would not think they were in custody.

He had learned long ago from O'Hara and Ernie, as well as from watching other detectives, how to slowly dissect a suspect in interrogation. First you see if they will lie or they will say something incriminating, and then you decide whether to read them their rights. Sometimes you kept the conversation going or you decided to let them walk out the door while you continued to build your case. You let them keep thinking that they were misleading you, instead of realizing you were going to use those lies against them when you were ready.

Jamison had decided that he wasn't going to read Elizabeth her rights unless and until her answers had only one explanation, and he had no choice before he asked the next question, the one that had the barbed point.

It was a slow dance. It took patience and it required the ability to read subtle cues. Sometimes a lie was just as good as an admission, but much depended on whether the person answering the questions was aware of what the interrogator was doing. Letting a suspect walk out the door could be used later to show it wasn't an interrogation and the DA was still investigating. It was like a tightrope walk. Above all, Jamison needed to keep the suspect talking. He didn't want them to stop until they either confessed or lied their way into a corner. It was all about control.

But to have control he needed to truly understand the person in front of him. An experienced interrogator would size up the suspect, watch them, measure them, circle around them, and probe for the weak spot. And then plunge in the knife.

He forced himself to smile as she sat quietly, waiting. When he began, Jamison kept his voice soft and modulated. With women O'Hara always said investigators had to have a conversation and had to avoid making them defensive until getting to the point where the interrogator would make a deep cut. "Beth, we want to go over some of the details of the night St. Claire was shot. We need to clear up some questions. It shouldn't take long, and then we'll get you back home."

"Will you take me back?" He could discern the hint of trust, of friendship, as if that was what they were, friends.

Jamison smiled. "Sure." He paused. "You said you didn't see the person who shot Alex?"

Jamison caught her hesitation and the way her eyes moved away from him before she responded. It was a cue she was thinking. Jamison could now see that she really wasn't trying to remember the events of that night so much as she was trying to decide how to answer.

"He must have been behind me or off to the side because I never saw him. I saw Alex walking toward me, and then when he was maybe fifteen feet away, I heard the shots. They were quick. I don't know how many there were."

"You say 'he.' Did you see the person shooting? How do you know it was a man?"

"When the shots . . . when I heard the shots, I turned my head for an instant. I may have seen a man. But then I looked back at Alex when I heard him cry out and he was falling. After that I didn't look anywhere else. I began to scream. I know that."

It wasn't much, but there was tension building in her demeanor. Still, he wasn't sure. She was being asked to relive what would be a traumatic experience for almost anybody. She was guarded. He could see it.

The time had come to probe deeper. Keeping his voice low and unthreatening he asked, "Beth, do you have any idea who the person was who shot Alex?"

She looked around the room. They could see she was thinking carefully and there was reluctance in her voice when she answered. "Whoever it was, I think they were trying to keep Alex from hurting me. Isn't that enough?"

Jamison's mind was churning furiously. He could see it in her eyes. She knew who shot St. Claire or thought she did. She wasn't willing to say. She must have guessed it wasn't necessarily an answer he wanted to hear anyway. "Did Alex say anything before he was shot?"

"He said, 'Elizabeth.' He always called me Elizabeth. But that was all he said."

"When Alex approached you, Beth, did he have his hands out? Was he threatening in any way?"

"No." She shook her head. "Other than the fact that simply him being there was frightening, he didn't say or do anything. He was just walking toward me when I heard the shots, and then Alex kind of turned, twisted, you know? He stumbled toward me, starting to fall, and I reached out to him. It all happened so fast." Her hands showed the tension in her body but Beth's voice was controlled. "I was frightened, scared to death. I saw a man who still terrified me shot right in front of me."

Jamison was conscious that he was biting down as he clenched his teeth. He forced himself to keep calm. "Of course, we understand you were frightened. Anybody would be." He continued to watch her carefully, waiting for an explanation that might exonerate her or, more honestly, one that would not.

"Did Alex say anything after he was shot? While he was down on the ground. Do you remember?"

Beth's mouth drew into a straight line. Her head leaned back as she looked toward the ceiling. "He said he loved me. That's what he said. I couldn't understand the rest. It was just a few words but he said that."

"And did you say anything to him?"

"Does that really make a difference?" Her tone was questioning and her eyes began to narrow. "Why is that important? Aren't you concerned with who shot him?"

Puccinelli had been watching carefully and observed the tension building. He tried a different approach. "Ms. Garrett, we're concerned with knowing as much as we can about what happened. You never know what might help or what's important. What you said to Dr. St. Claire, is there some reason you don't want to talk to us about that?" Whether Pooch intended it or not, his last question had a bite to it

Her answer came back with its own edge to it. "I just don't think it's important."

Now Ernie added, his voice soft and non-threatening, "We understand. You say lots of things to somebody who's dying. You don't have to mean them, I suppose."

Elizabeth looked at each man waiting for her answer. "I told him what I thought of him. I don't want to think about it."

Jamison could feel the question welling up in him. It was dangerous to shift questions quickly, but an abrupt shift in subject caught people off-balance and what Jamison often got was an unguarded response. His question came out with a sharpness that startled even him. "Beth, who was Bobby Allison, really?"

Perhaps it was her expression. Perhaps it was the sense that he had pulled open a scab, but what came out of her mouth had the anguished sound of a person who had been slapped by someone they trusted. "Bobby Allison? Why would you ask that? He isn't important."

Jamison persisted. "Beth, I need to know about this. I know you didn't write that letter to him that you testified about. So what is he to you?" It was the first time he, in effect, had said she was lying. He expected her to be defensive. The look of betrayal that shadowed Beth's face also told him he had inflicted pain.

"He's someone from a long time ago." Her voice sounded almost child-like before it took on a harsher edge. "Who he was isn't important. What he did doesn't matter now. I've put it behind me. All I can say is that when I saw that letter his name came out."

The truth of Levy's words crystallized in Jamison's mind. He knew he was opening a door that had long been closed out of fear and self-preservation, but he had to ask. "Beth, did Bobby Allison hurt you? Did he touch you when you were little? Is that what happened?"

The air in the room had grown heavy with visible desperation. Elizabeth's eyes darted around the room, silently pleading with the three men to stop. She had kept this door closed from everyone, including herself. She was suddenly forced to relive those dark moments, each detail sharply etched in the recesses of her mind. The answer came out in a whisper. "I was little. It wasn't my fault. I don't want to talk about it. Please don't make me talk about that."

Even hardened investigators could feel compassion. None of the men in the room said a word. They had no stomach for this. Each of them had seen it before in the faces of too many children, too many investigations into depravity and the human wreckage it left behind. And now they were looking at the adult the child had become. What had the taking of innocence made her?

But the question had to be asked. Jamison had to know. "The letter that you testified you wrote to Bobby Allison, you wrote that letter to St. Claire, didn't you? That's why his lawyer had it, isn't it?" Beth stared coldly into Jamison's eyes. Her body began to tense, coiling like a snake. Her gaze moved around the room. Her expression darkened. It was no longer the face of a child.

Her voice was harsh as she fought to regain the control she had cultivated so carefully. "I don't want to talk anymore about this. If that's what you are going to ask about, then I want to go. *I want to go now.*"

Dr. Levy was right, Bobby Allison had taken her innocence from her, and now Jamison saw that he too had taken something from her. Whatever trust she had placed in him was gone.

Ernie knew from long experience that there could come a point during an interrogation when a suspect's body language and tone communicated their real emotions. Particularly they tell you that they feel threatened. It was like watching a man put one foot back and begin to curl his hands when he thought that he might have to defend himself. The edge to his voice and the tension in his body told the observer that the man realized he may not be safe. Every skilled interrogator knew that moment and recognized that he must either pull back or move forward. Whatever he did, he didn't want the suspect to stop talking.

Ernie saw that Jamison needed to pull back, and he also realized that Jamison didn't know how. He had anticipated this might happen. It was the reason he had said nothing about the pictures he found in Elizabeth's car.

Ernie leaned in, sliding his chair to the side so that Elizabeth wouldn't be looking directly at the prosecutor. He needed to shift the inquiry, or they were going to lose her. "Beth, we want you to look at some pictures." He reached behind him on the desk for the manila envelope that had been hidden in the trunk of her car. He kept his eyes on her. Her body stiffened. She was staring at the envelope. He slid the photographs out and handed her a photograph of herself when she was much younger. "Do you recognize this picture of you?"

Ernie watched her carefully, maintaining eye contact. He was trying to read her face. He had read thousands of faces staring back at him while he questioned them. Some he could read, some he could not. In this case perhaps what was more important to Ernie was she didn't ask where he had gotten the photographs. Her eyes were locked on the envelope that contained them.

Jamison said nothing, but he was also caught unaware. Finally Beth answered, "It's me. I was in high school."

Ernie shuffled through the photographs, making a point of keeping the manila envelope directly in plain view, and pulled out a photo of St. Claire standing beside a car.

"Do you recognize this picture?"

She glanced at it and then raised her eyes, looking directly at Ernie. "It's a picture of Alex."

"And he's standing next to a car, correct?"

"Yes."

"Is that your car?"

Elizabeth fought to regain control of herself and her answers. "What are you getting at? I don't understand. That's my car but I don't know anything about it. He could have taken that anytime." She looked back at Jamison, but he kept his eyes on Ernie, avoiding her attempt to have him deflect the questions.

Ernie turned to the desk, opened a folder, and took out the photograph that had been introduced in court by St. Claire's attorney. "Do you remember this photograph?" He laid down the slightly blurred photograph of Beth turning away from her car, her hair swirling out behind her.

"That's the picture that Alex's attorney showed me during the trial. I said I didn't know it was being taken." She turned again toward Jamison, her hand reaching out to touch his arm, as though she was trying to establish some level of contact with him. As her hand touched him, a hint of perfume wafted up. "You remember, Matt. You said it had been taken from a distance." Elizabeth kept her eyes directly on Jamison, waiting. Jamison looked down at her hand and paused. Ernie could see the heat rising in Jamison's face. Elizabeth moved her hand away when Jamison didn't respond.

Ernie put the two photographs next to each another. It had taken him some time to put it all together. "I want you to look at the background in these two photographs. Do you notice the building in the background of the photo of Alex St. Claire next to your car?"

Elizabeth's face seemed to lose all its softness. "It's the same building that's in the picture Alex took of me and used in court. Is that your point?"

Ernie placed the two photographs on the desk. His voice stayed low but had an insistent tone to it. "My point is that somebody took this photograph of Dr. St. Claire standing by your car *at the same place* that was in the photograph of you that was used in court *and* the same time. Your car. Do you have any idea who?" He held up the photograph from the trial that St. Claire's lawyer had offered into evidence and placed it right next to the photograph from the manila envelope that had been hidden in her car that showed St. Claire posing next to her car.

Ernie's voice hardened as he shoved the photograph in front of Elizabeth that St. Claire's lawyer had used in court. "You gave this photograph to Alex St. Claire, didn't you? Isn't that the reason that St. Claire's lawyer had possession of it? And you kept possession of the other one, the one with Alex St. Claire standing next to your car, didn't you?"

Elizabeth moved her gaze past each of the men, before turning back to Ernie. Her voice didn't conceal the defiance. "I told you before I didn't know he was taking pictures." She paused for only a second, looking at Jamison before turning away. "Maybe Alex had a picture taken of him standing there so he could make it look like he was supposed to be there, just like he did with the *Queen Mary* tickets and baby clothes that he lied about at the trial. Where did you get those pictures?"

Ernie held the manila envelope in his hand, staring at Elizabeth. "Ms. Garrett, we found this envelope in your car, hidden in the wheel well of the trunk. You have no idea how it got there? Do you have any idea how this picture of Alex St. Claire got in this envelope kept in your car, a picture that was taken at the same time as the one used in court?"

Before he could say anything more, Elizabeth lashed out. "My car? You searched my car and found that? After everything else Alex did, you're asking me how that got in my car?"

Ernie didn't answer. He picked up the photograph in front of Elizabeth that was used in court. He held his hand on it for a moment, watching her as she watched him turn it one way and then the other. "You gave this photograph of you to Alex St. Claire, didn't you? And you weren't telling the truth when you testified you had never seen it before, were you?" Ernie's voice was low and calm, almost therapeutic.

Elizabeth was silent. She watched as Ernie slid it back in the manila envelope. Ernie could see it in her eyes. She didn't have an answer. She was off-balance. Nor would she be able to focus on what she was being asked without thinking of what had been found in her car.

The rhythm of the questioning had changed. Elizabeth's voice had taken on a tone they hadn't heard from her before. Maybe it was just defensive and she was offended. Maybe she was trying to sound offended, but it was also unnaturally shrill. But there was a pivotal moment here and he couldn't wait. Puccinelli reached forward. "Ms. Garrett, do you know what this is?" He held up a plastic bag with the aerosol can inside it. "Have you ever seen this before?"

She reached for the bag and Puccinelli pulled it back. "May I see it?"

Puccinelli shook his head. He held it just out of her reach, the canister glinting dully through the plastic bag.

They watched intently as Elizabeth stared at the aerosol can. "I've never seen that before. I don't know what it is." Her face was impassive, having no expression, but more importantly to the men watching, she showed no curiosity. She didn't ask what it was or why he was showing it to her.

Setting the container down on his desk just out of Elizabeth's reach, Puccinelli focused on her reaction as he said quietly, "We think it was used to subdue the three women we know St. Claire murdered. It has an anesthetic gas in it. The cup on the top was forced against the face of the victims and they inhaled the gas."

Elizabeth stiffened in her chair, staring straight at Puccinelli. "And you think Alex did that? Murdered those women? Why would he do that?"

There was a split-second of hesitation. "You think he killed those women and then came after me?"

Measuring her body language, Puccinelli softened his tone. "Yes, we think he did that to those women. We're waiting for DNA results from the plastic mouthpiece, but that's what we think." Then he leaned forward, his face within a foot of Elizabeth's. "Did he use something like this on you?"

"No, not that I remember." Her voice didn't hold the indignation that they would expect of a person who saw what was used to disable them.

Puccinelli's words plunged straight at her. "Then do you have any idea how your fingerprints got on this can?"

"My fingerprints? Are you saying my fingerprints are on that?"

Ernie's voice caused her to turn away from Puccinelli. "Your fingerprints are on that can. You held it and so did Alex St. Claire." Ernie allowed a gap of silence as he observed Elizabeth's face, especially her eyes. She would either be defensive and confused or she was going to go on the offensive. Either way it would reveal something.

The tone of her voice and her body language answered the question. "Matt, why am I here? Do you think I had something to do with this? Is that what he's asking? Do you think I helped Alex hurt those women? Look what he did to me. Why would I do that?"

~

Jamison had been carefully observing the back-and-forth between the detectives and Elizabeth. It was clear she wasn't afraid. She was going on the offensive. "He kidnapped me. He came back after me just like he did before." Her voice was raised but it was an assertion. She wasn't pleading. "You heard it. He planned it. He made up an alibi." She looked over at Jamison. "Do you think I'm lying?

Puccinelli cut in, repeating the question more forcefully. "Ms. Garrett, how did your fingerprints get on this can?"

Elizabeth met the question with silence.

Jamison knew it had already gone on too long. They needed to either read her her rights or end it. "Beth, you said you don't know what happened after St. Claire stopped you that night by the cemetery. He came to the car. He had a knife. Then you remember waking up in a dark room. Is that right?"

"I'm not lying."

Jamison was grateful when Ernie quietly interrupted. "I never said you were lying, Beth. I pulled you out of that bedroom, remember? We're just trying to understand what happened. Could Dr. St. Claire have used this aerosol can on you? Do you have any memory of that?"

They were giving her an out, but they could sense the time wasn't right, and he knew that they were dangerously close to an illegal interrogation if they hadn't *already* crossed the line. They knew that if they read Garrett her rights, the discussion was going to end.

Elizabeth seemed to relax slightly. She was thinking, trying to choose the answer that would make them stop. Her eyes fixed for a few seconds on each man in the room. Her words came out in a measured cadence, precisely enunciated. "I don't remember him using anything like that. If he did, maybe I grabbed it and that's how my fingerprints got on the can." She looked at Jamison. "I don't know how they got on that can and I don't know where those pictures came from either."

Jamison would realize later that was the moment he saw behind her eyes. It was like seeing the eyes of a cat staring at him in the darkness.

She turned to level her gaze on Ernie. Her tone was measured. "You want to know about when Alex was shot? When Alex came toward me I didn't know what he was going to do. I heard the shots. I saw the man with the gun running toward us." Elizabeth paused before her next statement but she said it with deliberation so that there could be no misunderstanding. "It was dark, but for a second I thought I knew who it was, but I'm not *absolutely sure*." She let the words "absolutely sure" linger for a second before continuing. "Do you want me to . . ." She hesitated, watching them carefully and then letting out the last word. "Guess? Do you want me to guess? He fired so quickly—before Alex—I don't think Alex did anything. Alex called my name and was walking toward me."

There was no mistaking the implication as she uttered her next words. "Maybe the man just *wanted* to kill Alex. If that's what he wanted, then he did everyone a favor—especially me." She let her words hang in the air before repeating herself. "Maybe he just *wanted* to kill Alex." Her last words fell heavily on the silence in the room. She followed each of them with her gaze and finished, settling her focus on Jamison.

Jamison felt himself swallowing and sucking in air. She knew who shot St. Claire, and she knew they didn't want to hear the answer.

He inhaled and then let his breath out slowly. "No, Beth, we don't want you to guess. I think that's enough. Maybe we'll never know what happened. Ernie will take you home. I think that's best."

At that moment, Jamison couldn't gauge what he saw in Elizabeth Garrett's eyes. Maybe it was a hint of triumph. Maybe it was a hint of resignation. It was his decision to end the interrogation.

Jamison stood up and extended his hand. He could see it in her eyes; the defiance was gone. "Good-bye, Beth." There was nothing more he had to say.

Ernie followed her out the door and Jamison returned to the chair. Whatever she had done, she was a victim too. That didn't justify her conduct but maybe it explained it. He couldn't prove what really happened between her and St. Claire, and most of all, Jamison knew that he didn't really want to even if he could. Sometimes the truth was so layered by what a person wanted it to be that they would never know what it really was.

Jamison reached over for the manila envelope. He slipped open the flap and found the photographs of Dr. Alex St. Claire standing in front of her car with the background that Ernie had seen.

The cold realization that in court she had held the photograph of her in her hand and adamantly insisted she had never seen it before settled on Jamison. She had lied in court when she said she didn't know that picture was being taken and he had defended her. Jamison ruefully recalled that he had even brought in a photographic expert to testify that her version was possible. One more explanation that so easily slipped off her tongue. That she could answer so quickly, without apparent guile, that was what made her words so believable.

When Ernie had pulled out the photographs, Jamison was surprised and then momentarily angry that Ernie hadn't shared them with him first. But then he had realized that Ernie understood the photographs would make Jamison too angry to use them like the razor slash they could be in an interrogation. It was experience and cold judgment by Ernie. Ernie would apologize later for holding out, but there was nothing to apologize for. Ernie had been right and Jamison knew it.

Jamison was still staring at the photograph when the phone in Puccinelli's office rang. When Pooch put down the phone he explained. "Matt, that was Andy Rhychkov down in the lab. They got the DNA results off the mouthpiece. Andy says it had DNA from Symes and from Ventana. He also said the mouthpiece has other DNA on it but he can't identify it, at least not yet." Pooch's face showed fatigue seeping from every pore. "Andy says it's consistent with the victims having this mouthpiece shoved up against their mouths."

Jamison fingered the photographs and let Puccinelli's words sink in. His eyes were fixed on the smiling face of Alex St. Claire, the same smug expression that St. Claire had when he walked out of court a free man. Jamison pulled open the flap of the manila envelope and placed the photographs back inside. Closing the flap on the images of Garrett, everything that had been clouding his own vision fell away, and his mind was suddenly piercingly clear. He knew who he cared about. Jamison made his decision.

O'Hara had said it to him time and time again, laughing every time somebody said a trial was a search for the truth: What was a lie and what was the truth? The truth was only what could be proven and it wasn't a lie unless it could be disproved, and all the rest was for lawyers to confuse the issue.

The manila envelope sitting on the desk and the plastic bag with the metal canister appeared to Jamison as remains of the day, the final remnants of ruined lives. O'Hara's words kept ringing in his ears. "If you can't prove it's true and if you can't prove it's a lie, then you got nothing, and sometimes nothing is the best you can do."

Jamison stood up and spoke to Pooch. "Close the file."

"What about her?"

Jamison waited for a moment before answering. O'Hara was right. Sometimes a prosecutor had nothing and it was the best he could do. "Close the file. Call O'Hara. Tell him I said he was right. Sometimes the truth is better left lost in the dark."

Jamison walked toward the closed door, placing his hand on the doorknob. "And tell him one other thing. Tell him we have no idea who killed Alex St. Claire, but whoever it was did the world a favor."

Chapter 47

After the questioning of Elizabeth, Jamison returned to his office, slamming his body into his chair. He needed Garrett to prove that St. Claire was a murderer, and he needed to prove St. Claire was a murderer to have any basis of proving Garrett was anything other than a victim. He didn't have St. Claire and he didn't have Garrett. Besides that, he knew serving up O'Hara was the price that would have to be paid for going after Garrett, and that price he was not willing to pay.

Jamison stared out the window, his reflection staring back at him. As he thought about the consequences to Elizabeth Garrett of things done years before, he pondered whether people create the life they live or did their life create them? Perhaps for some people, the path they take is not a matter of choice. Did Elizabeth Garrett make actual choices or simply react to what she already was when St. Claire seized upon the flaws he saw in her?

As he watched Elizabeth during the interrogation, he had thought to himself that she didn't have to choose St. Claire. She could have found somebody else. Now as he reconsidered it, he realized that perhaps St. Claire was the *only* choice she had. His reflection in the glass gave him no answer.

His mind began to touch upon the tangled web that had ensnared him, pulling him into the dark recesses of the lives of Elizabeth Garrett and Alex St. Claire. He had argued for the guilt of Alex St. Claire because he believed Elizabeth and because Alex St. Claire was a murderer. But whatever Alex St. Claire was, it had become clear that most of what he had said about Elizabeth was true.

Now drawn back from the heat of the trial, Jamison recognized that he had rationalized Garrett's explanations because he could not accept that a murderer might be telling the truth. The twisting lies of Garrett and St. Claire were like a choking vine that strangles a tree until it becomes one with the bark and wood. Where the lies and reality began and ended was indistinguishable even in retrospect.

Who had really told the truth about what happened that night by the cemetery? Alex St. Claire said it was all a game between the two of them. And it was—even the trial. That St. Claire and Elizabeth Garrett had moved across the chessboard of this case like a king and queen left Jamison with the realization that St. Claire had looked upon him as merely a pawn in a private game.

It made no sense. There were still unanswered questions. When they found Garrett in St. Claire's farmhouse, they had found no evidence related to the other victims. There was nothing either at St. Claire's house in the city. There were just enough bits and pieces to the puzzle to tell him that St. Claire did everything and enough empty spaces to not make it clear at all. The lack of answers ground on Jamison.

That night, as he lay in bed, he knew himself well enough to know that sleep would not come to him until those answers came. He was right. He could not stop his mind from churning through the facts and contradictions. It was a sleepless six hours, but by morning he saw the vague outline of a missing piece.

Jamison rolled out of his sweat-dampened bed and grabbed the phone. Already at his desk, Puccinelli answered on the first ring. "Pooch, was there anything else in St. Claire's car besides the aerosol can and the light? Anything at all?"

"There was the plastic bag with the bills in it that we removed from St. Claire's console," replied Puccinelli. "I have it right here. Let's see. Just some tax stuff it looks like, and some utility bills and the car registration. Nothing that I thought was important. Wait—I don't know if this means anything, but I'm reading the envelopes for the bills, and the bills went to a post office box instead of St. Claire's address. They're all addressed to something called the St. Claire Trust, care of Alex St. Claire, trustee, same trust that owned the car."

Jamison felt his heart skip a beat. "I'll be right over."

Puccinelli was waiting for him when he walked into the detective's office. He held up the bag with the bills. "Okay, St. Claire paid taxes like everybody else. So?"

Jamison took the bills and began opening them. He wasn't worried about anybody's privacy at this point. St. Claire was dead. The bills were all the same. Each of them was either a tax bill or a utility bill for an address nobody knew about. Jamison had pushed his trusts and estates class from law school to the back of his mind. It wasn't something he used as a prosecutor. But he understood what the bills meant.

The reality of it struck him with the force of a hammer blow. There was *another* house that St. Claire had access to, and because it was owned by a trust it never showed up in the doctor's name. Jamison shoved the bills in front of Pooch. "Do you know where this address is?"

Puccinelli laughed. "I've been doing this a long time. People dump bodies all over this county, so there aren't many corners I haven't been to." He examined the address. "Yeah, it's in the foothills about thirty or forty minutes away."

Jamison was already moving to the office door. "Call Ernie and tell him to meet us at this address." His decision not to call O'Hara was deliberate. He knew this time O'Hara needed to stay away and let others do what needed to be done.

Jamison and Puccinelli were parked in the gravel driveway of the house listed in the St. Claire Trust. The house was vacant. The windows were shuttered. What was immediately apparent was the isolation. There were no other houses in sight.

It wasn't the house that interested Jamison at the moment, but the barn. They looked around back and found a small compact car, which Pooch ran and determined was a rental. The car had dust on it. Jamison knew when they checked that it would come back rented to St. Claire. The doors to the barn were locked. He turned to Pooch. "Break it," he said firmly.

Puccinelli's expression was unsure. "Do we need a warrant?"

"St. Claire's dead. What we need are answers. Call for whatever you have to and break it."

By the time Pooch got a deputy whose area included the vicinity of the house to come over with a bolt cutter, Ernie had arrived. The deputy snapped the lock and slid back the door. As soon as the fluorescent lights came on so did the answers. To the side of the large room was a steel table, just like the one that Dr. Gupta used, just like the one they found at the farmhouse, just like the one Elizabeth described.

"Call forensics. Get them up here."

It was Ernie who found the loose board covering a space in the wall. After photographs were taken, he removed the box hidden inside. Jamison and Pooch peered over his shoulder when he opened the box. It held what must have been St. Claire's childhood treasures, a shiny rock, a picture of a boy holding a fish next to an older man, a bird feather—the gleanings of a young life.

There was also a computer memory stick in a clear plastic bag. They would have to wait to find out what was on it. They picked up the laptop sitting on a nearby table. Jamison wouldn't allow anybody to open it. He knew it was encrypted. St. Claire had gone to far too much trouble to make the mistake of leaving either his laptop or a portable memory stick easily accessible.

~

It was maddening; they were on the edge of unearthing something that could fill in the unanswered questions that had been eluding them for weeks. While they waited several days for a computer technician to break into St. Claire's laptop, forensics tested traces of DNA found on the steel autopsy table in the barn.

The DNA matched that of Ventana, Johnson, and Symes, which explained why they had found nothing before at either the farmhouse where they found Beth Garrett tied to the bed or at St. Claire's house in the city.

St. Claire hadn't taken Ventana, Johnson, or Symes to either of those locations. He had brought them to the barn that nobody knew anything about. They also found trace DNA that they couldn't identify. It came from a woman, but it wasn't Elizabeth Garrett.

It took the forensic computer analyst two more days to break the password on the laptop and the encryption on the memory stick. As soon as Pooch called to let them know the computer could be opened, Jamison was back at the sheriff's department. Ernie was with him.

The men stood watching as the computer analyst shoved the memory stick into the laptop, entered a password, and clicked on the icon for the encrypted thumb drive. It revealed an inventory list with women's names and dates. Their eyes passed down the list of names, slowly, one by one. They saw the names of Ventana, Johnson, and Symes, but they weren't first. There were more names ahead of them on the list. Names that they didn't recognize.

Jamison reached down and moved his finger across the touchpad, tapping on the first name.

Photographs of a bound woman unfolded like the petals of a flower. The young woman's face was etched with terror. And then as Jamison tapped, one by one, the photographs chronicled her last images of the world until her eyes were closed. There was no doubt that what they saw with the final photograph was her last moment.

Jamison scrolled through the gallery of names, pausing at each one, opening it with the reticence of someone who didn't want to see beyond the closed door of a darkened room. With each name, photographs showed a young woman either tied to a bed or otherwise bound in various poses, her final moments meticulously chronicled and preserved.

Slowly Jamison touched Ventana's name and they watched as her face revealed the shock of realization of what she knew was to come. Jamison relived in his mind what he had seen on that isolated road where her body was found, and he could only hope that what she thought was to come was not as frightening as what did come to pass.

As Jamison opened the images of Johnson and Symes, he looked at the dates inscribed next to their names. The photographs, like Ventana's, were taken on the last day of their lives.

But one name remained—Elizabeth Garrett. Jamison hesitated and then moved the curser across the digital inventory, touching her name. The first image unfolded of the back of an unclothed woman, her hands bound to the headboard of a bed, her face turned away from the camera. Each image revealed more of her body as frame by frame she turned toward the camera, her hair shielding her face.

Before Jamison opened the last image, Ernie pointed to the date next to the gallery of photographs of Garrett. It was the day that St. Claire testified she had called him at the hospital, the first day Elizabeth testified that she had seen Alex St. Claire in ten years, the day that she testified filled her with dread and led to St. Claire's pulling her from her car on the dark road that bordered the cemetery.

Each man stared at the final photograph in silence, recoiling at the flickering image. Elizabeth's arms stretched away from her body as the bindings pulled her hands above her head, the long brown hair no longer concealing her face. Her eyes were open as she looked straight into the camera. She was smiling.

The women's names on St. Claire's memory stick did not take long to identify. A search put each woman on the list in places where St. Claire had been in the past. Some dated back to the years he spent in England. All the affected agencies had been notified, including Interpol. All except one on the list had been murdered. Elizabeth Garrett was the final name.

Where the photographs of Garrett were taken was made clear after Jamison directed another search of St. Claire's home in the city. St. Claire had testified they went there the day he saw her at the mall. She had denied it under oath. The photograph placed her in his bedroom. It was clear from her smile that was a place she wanted to be.

St. Claire's shuttered house in the hills also didn't give up its secrets easily. Searching it on the day they found the hidden computer, the dust shrouded rooms revealed nothing. But after the second search of St. Claire's home in the city, investigators went back and began tearing it apart board by board. While Jamison watched, Ernie and Pooch pulled musty clothing from long untouched drawers and bureaus. Pooch found an antique wardrobe with an almost invisible notch on the bottom. A hiding place crafted by an artisan from long past held a secret from the present, a meticulously maintained scrapbook. It was filled with memories of Elizabeth Garrett, photographs of when she and St. Claire were young, graduation announcements, the brittle paper evidences of life.

And at the end of the scrapbook there was a single page of a letter, only the first page. When Jamison looked at it, he knew where the rest of the letter was. It was still in evidence. This was the first page of the letter that Elizabeth Garrett had said was written to Bobby Allison. The letter she had under oath so convincingly denied she had sent to Alex St. Claire, as he had testified.

After the search, Jamison sat quietly in his office, the smiling face of Elizabeth Garrett frozen on St. Claire's computer all too vivid in his mind. He held the single page of the letter loosely in his hands. The words "Dear Alex" were written in Garrett's now familiar handwriting. The letter, the photograph, the lies—all pieces of the shattered case that had consumed him as he tried to prove St. Claire's guilt—coalesced like the colored glass of a kaleidoscope into an image of fractured lives.

The relationship between Alex St. Claire and Elizabeth was a web of deceit. But to what end?

He stared out the window as the lights of the city began to flicker on. St. Claire had never given his lawyer the front page of the letter or the photograph of Elizabeth in his bed. If McGuiness *had* been given them, he would have used them like a razor to cut Elizabeth to ribbons. Jamison's case would have irreparably fallen apart. The only reason it hadn't was because Alex St. Claire kept them to himself. Over and over Jamison asked himself, *Why*?

And then the reality of it struck him. As Elizabeth held St. Claire the night he was shot, she had said that Alex would never hurt her because he loved her. Maybe that was the only true thing she said. Maybe that was the only explanation that made any sense in a case that made no sense.

Jamison's reflection in the window confronted him with the eyes of a man who had subtly changed in the last months. In that moment, he finally came to terms with a reality of life, with the realities of the lives of all the faceless people hiding behind those lit windows flickering in the distance. Each human being wants to be loved for what they are but very few people actually reveal it and expect or get acceptance. They are afraid to reveal their true selves because they are afraid of rejection.

They present an image from which their hidden self rarely emerges. We reveal our true selves only to the most trusted, and the greatest gift we can receive in return is acceptance of what we are. Alex St. Claire knew what he was. Perhaps Elizabeth Garrett was the only other person in the world who knew what he was, and accepted it and him.

Maybe in his own way St. Claire really loved her, and sparing her that courtroom humiliation at the hands of McGuiness was his recognition that she was the only person who really knew him, and still loved him anyway. Jamison recognized the irony. Perhaps St. Claire was the only person who really knew what Elizabeth Garrett was, and in turn accepted her. In the swirl of emotion and contradiction that was this case, perhaps St. Claire not giving McGuiness the weapons to destroy Elizabeth Garrett was an act of love.

Jamison slipped on his suit coat and thought to himself that everyone in this case had made choices that carried consequences. St. Claire was dead. Elizabeth would be alone, left, as Dr. Levy would have said, to wander the dark recesses of her mind. He had made choices too, about Bill O'Hara. He didn't know if others would make the same decisions but he could live with the consequences of his. He understood now that justice was neither black nor white. He would have to learn to live part of his life in the grays.

He gave one last glance at the view of the city from his window, lights glowing from offices and homes that Jamison knew contained people concealing dark thoughts that should never see the light of day. People who looked just like everyone else.

Chapter 48

Almost a week had passed since they had looked at the final image of the Elizabeth Garrett photographs. Ernie and Pooch knew it was now time for them to close their personal file. Puccinelli pulled his coat tighter around him. The early morning air carried a chill enhanced by the water slapping against the side of his fishing boat. He hadn't been out on the lake for a long time, too long. The fishing boat, the lake water, the time away from what he did every day was something he savored. San Luis Reservoir, at the edge of the Central Valley, held back its choppy waters tightly against almost barren hills. The wind blew relentlessly.

Puccinelli looked at the other three men who sat in the boat. Bill O'Hara's dark complexion was looking a little greenish. O'Hara had told them he didn't like boats, but he understood he had to come. So had Ernie and T. J. Longworthy. Pooch, Ernie, and T. J. kept their eyes on O'Hara as he reached into his pocket. The dull blue glint of a Walther PPK flashed in the morning light.

O'Hara dropped the magazine out of the butt of the Walther and thumbed the bullets out one by one into the cold water, watching the slight splash as each brass casing twisted down out of sight. Puccinelli did a silent count as the bullets flipped out of the magazine. Two short of a full magazine, but Pooch knew O'Hara always carried one more in the pipe. O'Hara then racked the slide on the Walther and the last bullet flipped out into the lake. Three short of a full load. O'Hara stripped the weapon, separating the Walther into its parts. The barrel made a splash as he threw it out into the lake. Ernie snorted with derision. "You throw like a girl."

O'Hara extended his middle finger of his left hand and then tossed the rest of the Walther out into the lake. They watched the spreading ripples where the last of the gun entered the water. No further words were exchanged.

Puccinelli moved the throttle forward enough to get the boat underway. "I think that's enough fishing for today." The rest of the trip to shore was in silence. Each man seemed lost in his own thoughts. However Pooch suspected they all shared one thought. They were now all in.

The next day, Jamison walked into O'Hara's office. He had talked to him on the phone, but this was the first time they had seen each other since St. Claire had been shot. He sat down heavily on a chair in front of O'Hara's desk. O'Hara asked, "You got something for me?" He smiled. O'Hara didn't bring up why he had been away, and Jamison didn't ask.

Jamison held a sheaf of papers in his hand. "I need some investigation done and I don't want it to go to the bottom of the pile."

O'Hara's lips parted slightly as his mouth curled into a smile. "You aren't ever going to go to the bottom of the pile, Boss."

O'Hara leaned back in his chair and crossed his legs. The glint of a chrome-plated Walther PPK showed in the ankle holster wrapped around his leg. When Jamison caught a glimpse of it, he knew the display was intentional. He got it. O'Hara in his own cryptic way was giving him permission to ask and Jamison played along. "That a new Walther? You lose the other one? It looks like a pimp gun."

"Yeah, the other one got lost. I was doing some fishing and it fell overboard. Damndest thing. That gun was never registered anyway. I picked it up off the street a long time ago." He watched Jamison's expression to see if there was any reaction. There wasn't. As Jamison stood and started for the door, O'Hara made a parting comment. "They wouldn't call it a throwaway gun if you were worried about losing it."

Jamison got up and stood in the doorway for a moment before heading back to his office. "Good to have you back, Bill."

O'Hara's face betrayed a flicker of emotion. "Good to be back." Both men waited a moment for the other one to fill the gap of silence. But neither of them said another word.

About the Author

James A. Ardaiz is a former prosecutor, judge, and Presiding Justice of the California Fifth District Court of Appeal. From 1974 to 1980, Ardaiz was a prosecutor for the Fresno County District Attorney's office. In 1980 Ardaiz was elected to the Fresno Municipal Court, where he served as assistant presiding judge and presiding judge. Ardaiz was appointed to the California Fifth District Court of Appeal in 1988 and was named the court's Presiding Justice in 1994. Ardaiz retired from the bench in 2011 and remains active in the legal profession.

Ardaiz's first book was *Hands Through Stone*, a first-hand nonfiction account of his work on the investigation and prosecution of murderer Clarence Ray Allen, the last man executed by the State of California.

Also by James A. Ardaiz

The true story of the hunt for a cold-blooded killer

"A frightening story with all the tension and color of a first-class mystery novel." —*Crime Magazine*

$24.95 Hardcover

Hands Through Stone

How Clarence Ray Allen Masterminded Murder from Behind Folsom's Prison Walls

by James A. Ardaiz

Even hardened detectives were shaken by what they found at Fran's Market in rural Fresno that night in 1980. Three young people lay in their own blood on the market's concrete floor, executed by a merciless killer, while a fourth victim barely held on to life. Then a grim investigation became even grimmer when the evidence led to the man who ordered the killings — a convicted murderer already behind the walls of Folsom Prison.

Hands Through Stone reveals the true story behind the Fran's Market murders and their psychopathic mastermind, Clarence Ray Allen, the last man executed in California.

Written by James Ardaiz, one of the first investigators on the scene and the prosecutor who built the case against Allen, ***Hands Through Stone*** gives the reader an insider's view of the tortuous, multi-year investigation that brought Allen to justice. Ardaiz takes the reader step-by-step through every gritty, down-and-dirty piece of police work that painstakingly built the case against Allen, giving readers an unparalleled feel for what it's really like to work a professional murder investigation.

A true crime story that reads like an intricate mystery novel, ***Hands Through Stone*** dramatizes chilling scenes of murder, dogged investigation, and a gallery of quirky real-life characters no novelist could invent: cops, witnesses, victims, villains, and, above all, the enigmatic evil that was Clarence Ray Allen.

"Goes inside the room at Fran's Market and gives not only the events on the infamous night but the feelings of the horror of the seasoned investigators. A must-read for readers and writers of mystery books." —*The Poison Pen*

Available from bookstores, online bookstores, and QuillDriverBooks.com, or by calling toll-free 1-800-345-4447.

True Crime Cops and Murderers

$14.95
Paperback

400 Things Cops Know

Street-Smart Lessons from a Veteran Patrolman

by Adam Plantinga

Written by a veteran police sergeant, ***400 Things Cops Know*** takes you into a cop's life of danger, frustration, occasional triumph, and plenty of grindingly hard work. In a laconic, no-nonsense, dryly humorous style, Plantinga tells what he's learned from 13 years as a patrolman, from the everyday to the exotic. Sometimes heartbreaking, sometimes hilarious, this is an eye-opening revelation of life on the beat.

$18.95
Hardcover

Apprehensions & Convictions

Adventures of a 50-Year-Old Rookie Cop

by Mark Johnson

At age 50, Mark Johnson wanted a career change. What he got as a new life of danger, violence, and stark moral choices. ***Apprehensions & Convictions*** is Johnson's explosive memoir of how he became the oldest rookie in the Mobile, Alabama, Police Department. In a crisp first-person narrative that is by turns action-packed and contemplative, Johnson writes frankly of the experiences, challenges, disillusionments and dangers that transformed him from an executive to a cop.

$14.95
Paperback

California's Deadliest Women

Dangerous Dames and Murderous Moms

by David Kulczyk

A masterpiece of pure trashy tabloid fun, ***California's Deadliest Women*** is the definitive guide to the murderesses of the Golden State, a horrifying compendium of women driven to kill by jealousy, greed, desperation, or their own inner demons. From Brynn Hartman, who killed her husband, comedian Phil Hartman, to chemist Larissa Schuster, who dissolved her husband in acid, these 28 killers show the fairer sex can be as deadly as any man.

Available from bookstores, online bookstores, and QuillDriverBooks.com, or by calling toll-free 1-800-345-4447.

CPSIA information can be obtained
at www.ICGtesting.com
Printed in the USA
FSOW03n1056091017